THE SILVER
TONGUED
ROGUE

THE DRAGON GATE SERIES
VOLUME III

RANDY ELLEFSON

Evermore Press
GAITHERSBURG, MARYLAND

Evermore Press, LLC
Gaithersburg, Maryland
www.evermorepress.org

Publisher's Note: This book includes fictional passages. All
names, characters, locations, and incidents are products of
the author's imagination, or have been used fictitiously.
Any semblance to actual persons living or dead, locales, or
events is coincidental and not intended by the author.

The Silver-Tongued Rogue / Randy Ellefson. -- 1st ed.
ISBN 978-1-946995-57-5 (paperback)
ISBN 978-1-946995-58-2 (hardcover)

Join my newsletter to get a free eBook, a chance to join my ARC Team, see bonuses, get early looks at covers, and more: http://www.fiction.randyellefson.com/newsletter

CONTENTS

ACKNOWLEDGEMENTS

Thanks to Daniela Zorilla, Annika Powers, & Erica Thajeb

Maps by Randy Ellefson

Cover design by Miblart

This page intentionally left blank.

CHAPTER ONE

THE LAST
ONE STANDING

As he woke to a roaring vortex of flashing lights and wind, Eric Foster thought for a moment that he was dreaming. He had been asleep on the floor of Jack's apartment, but now he stood on something invisible, feeling wide-awake and invigorated. Had he gotten a full night's sleep, or had the spell summoning him done that? The T-shirt, shorts, and underwear he was wearing disappeared for a few moments. He didn't bother to cover himself as he stood nude before the others, his short black hair rustled by the air. Then his expected black leather armor and boots appeared, snug and supple, a short sword on one hip. He had hidden knives throughout his clothing, lockpicking tools were in one pocket, and a black rope was coiled about his waist like a belt.

Across from him stood Anna Sumner. The summoning spell had braided her blonde hair behind her ears, and the gold Corethian Amulet hung around her neck. Those and her white priest's robe with its golden trim would have made her seem elegant were she not still standing with one forearm desperately covering her breasts, the other hand over her crotch. Now dressed, she relaxed her posture and saw him smirking. She flashed a rueful smile and seemed to sigh. It was so loud that even if she screamed, he'd hear nothing.

To one side stood Ryan LaRue in golden plate mail, a matching helmet tucked under one arm, a giant sword on one hip, and a gold lance in one hand as its butt rested on the invisible platform beneath them. As a big, tall man, he always looked huge in the gear, and he seemed far more comfortable with his role now as a knight than when they had started all of this. He flashed a resigned smile and ran a hand through his blond hair, likely mentally preparing himself to be their spokesman on arrival.

Across from Ryan stood Matt Sorenson, a black wizard's robe hiding his thinness. His wavy brown hair rustled in the air, one hand tightly gripping a staff, the crystal atop it dark because he wasn't using it. Eric caught his eye and arched an eyebrow, which Matt saw, nodding before his eyes drifted away and his lips began moving. They had previously discussed the possibility of him erecting a protective shield once they arrived, if they seemed to be in immediate danger. For the first time, Eric realized that he and Matt could communicate during this with sign language, which Matt knew because his mother was deaf, and had taught a curious Eric.

Suddenly the vortex ended, and Eric blinked in the bright sunlight, the sun high in a cloudless sky. His dark eyes darted past the expected stone pillars of the circular Quest Ring surrounding them, the glowing blue runes on the stones already fading. Outside the ring on one side stood most of the people who had brought them to whatever planet they were now on instead of Earth. Many wore armor of various kinds, but no weapons were drawn. A few more warriors casually stood to either side and behind. He noted two wizards—one behind them and another, who seemed like the one who had cast the summoning spell, before him.

Eric began to relax, noting the ocean all around them below. They stood atop one of the higher, grass-covered hills on a large island. The warm air smelled of spring, wildflowers blooming nearby. A small mountain range loomed nearby and blocked the view beyond, but on either side of it could be seen an expanse of sea. A port city with tall, wooden ships in the harbor lay miles away below them, with towers and a castle above it all. A winding path led down from their position to a clearing among the trees, where a dozen dragons sat patiently so that Eric knew they were steeds. Since horses could have easily been used to get them to the city, he surmised that they would be flying to a different continent. It lay in the distance in another direction, the shoreline visible from here. Behind it were taller, snow-capped peaks that pierced the clouds forming around them.

Beside one of the wizards stood a striking woman in black plate mail etched in blue, a sword at her waist. She wore it all well, seeming calm, assured, and unimpressed. Her close-cropped, jet-black hair hardly moved in the gusty winds, blue eyes dancing from one arrival to the next, a look of growing interest and menace surfacing in them. It seemed clear that she had expected something and hadn't gotten it—and Eric had a bad feeling he knew precisely what it was.

"Greetings!" Ryan boomed in the voice Eric had first heard him use while playing a knight at the Maryland Renaissance Festival. "We are the Ellorian Champions and are glad to—"

"No, you are not!" snapped the warrior woman, eyes cold. She yanked her sword from its sheath and the other warriors nearby did the same, the sound of metal ringing. She came closer and into the Quest Ring as everyone else stayed just outside it. Eric swore but didn't draw his sword.

Ryan faltered. "Uh, why do you think—"

"You think I wouldn't recognize my own *brother*?" she snarled, eyes turning to Matt.

Anna gasped.

What? thought Eric, startled. *Oh shit.* Ryan's uncertain eyes met his.

They had been impersonating the Ellorian Champions for two months, but not because they wanted to. It just seemed safer than admitting to being four people mistakenly summoned for quests they weren't qualified for, didn't want, and yet had to complete before being sent home. That someone summoning them would realize the truth was bound to happen eventually, but a relative being present had never occurred to him. Matt was impersonating the wizard Soliander, whose robes he wore, Soliander's famous staff in one hand. And apparently this woman was Soliander's sister.

"Listen," he began, holding up placating hands, "we can explain, if you just—"

"Where is Soliander?" the woman asked, turning toward Matt. She extended the sword toward his neck, though she came no closer. Eric wondered if she knew about the spell on the staff—the one that made any blow aimed at Matt strike the attacker instead.

"Taryn!" Matt said, sounding surprised. He didn't look afraid. "You're Taryn, his older sister."

She arched an eyebrow. "How do you know that?"

"Uh, long story. I have his memories in my head and—"

"What? How is that possible? What did you do to—" A look of menace appeared. "Seize them!" Taryn swung a fist at Matt's hand and knocked the staff to the stones. Then she slugged his jaw. He fell into an unmoving heap. Guardsmen closed in with swords raised.

"Wait!" Eric yelled, heart pounding. "We are no threat to you." He put one hand on Ryan's sword arm to stop him from drawing the steel. Magic incantations behind him made him look back. A wizard pointed at Ryan, who slumped to the stones with a clatter.

"Eric!" cried a panicked Anna, backing away, one hand on the golden amulet at her neck. She began crouching as if to surrender, but the butt of a spear struck her head from behind and she fell forward to Taryn's feet.

In sudden fury, Eric swung around and clobbered the guard who had done it, a spray of blood and teeth erupting. Another guard closed in, and Eric kicked out to stun the wrist holding a spear. A second kick and the man doubled over before an elbow to the back levelled him. He sensed Taryn closing in from behind and turned, one hand on his sword hilt, but her sword point was at his neck and he stopped moving.

"Yield," she commanded, blue eyes cold. They stared at each other. Eric removed his hand from his sword. Footsteps came from behind and several hands pulled his arms back painfully, a rope wrapped around his wrists. Someone took his sword, then patted him down for knives. He silently counted as they did so. Only he and the Silver-Tongued Rogue Andier, the man he impersonated and whose armor he wore, knew where every last one of the blades was, and his captors couldn't find them all.

"You didn't have to do that," Eric said, glaring at Taryn and indicating his unconscious friends.

"Maybe I just *wanted* to."

"What are you going to do with us?"

She walked away without answering as the guards forced him down on the Quest Ring's stone floor, where his friends' bodies lay unmoving around him. Despite the adventures they had already experienced, he'd never seen them laid out helpless like this—and so quickly! Maybe they had just gotten lucky before now. But the truth was that Taryn had surprised them with the sudden attack. He nodded to himself. She was wily, respectable. Neither was it surprising if she was really the sister of Soliander, the Majestic Magus, a man known for his intelligence. What would a sibling rivalry have been like?

He watched Taryn approach a tall, well-built man in a black and silver tunic, a ceremonial dagger at one hip and black trousers tucked into matching boots. He carried himself like a noble and had short black hair and dark eyes. Were they siblings? Soliander did have a younger brother, too. Eric regretted that he and the others knew so little about the real Champions, as their ignorance might be a serious liability right now.

As Taryn stopped beside the man, he said, "I will reluctantly concede that you handled that expertly."

"Nothing pleases me more than your praise, Lord Dari, especially when it's so sincere." Taryn glanced back to meet Eric's gaze.

A brief frown appeared on Dari's face. "The more time I spend with you, the more I understand why my old habit of snide remarks was not viewed favorably, as much as I enjoyed making them."

She favored him with a smirk. "Are you flirting with me?"

"Is it working?"

Definitely not brother and sister, thought Eric.

She lifted her blade and fingered the edge, adopting a philosophical tone. "Some consider it a bad omen when they unsheathe a sword and don't draw blood with it. Perhaps this is a problem you are willing to solve for me."

Unconcerned by the implication that she was going to cut him, Dari replied, "Some would consider that a threat to a Prince of Andor."

Taryn put her weapon away as Eric continued listening. "Pity. I thought you might be honored to have your blood on my blade."

"What now?" Prince Dari asked, nodding at Eric, who had stopped listening for a moment on hearing the word "Andor."

He knew the name. Ryan, lying beside him, was pretending to be Lord Korrin, a Prince of Andor. If Dari was also a Prince of Andor, he was a relative, maybe even Korrin's younger brother. While Eric didn't know what the real Champions looked like, he knew that he and his friends bore enough resemblance to fool those who hadn't met them. Dari had black hair and dark eyes, but Ryan, and therefore Korrin, had blond hair and blue eyes. He pursed his lips, wishing he knew what Korrin looked like so he could judge whether Dari seemed that closely related.

Regardless, that at least two relatives of the Ellorian Champions had tried to summon them was no coincidence. Were the rest of the families involved? Were they here? They were going to want answers and would be understandably hostile if they thought the impersonators were somehow responsible for the real Champions being missing for three years now. Eric and the others had taken their place by accident and played along, trying to figure out how to be heroes and somehow break the cycle of unwanted quests for which they were now summoned.

He perked up. Almost no one knew that the real Champions hadn't been voluntarily doing the quests. They were magically summoned into a Quest Ring that bound them to do it before they could return home. And now that was the fate of Eric and his friends. Did the Champions' families know? If so, they were almost certainly sympathetic—and that sympathy might extend to Eric and the others if he could convince them they were victims, too, not perpetrators. Maybe they would help despite Taryn's attack just now. He understood her doing that. Precautionary, at the least. The real Champions were formidable. Eric and his friends had succeeded at several quests, and caused

word to spread that the Ellorian Champions had supposedly returned. Others could assume they were fearsome. He
admired Taryn's quick thinking.

She broke his thoughts on saying to Dari, "Every last
person here must be sworn to secrecy. They already were,
that we were attempting the summoning, but it is even
more important that no one knows what has happened. See
to it that your men obey."

So she wasn't in charge? This surprised Eric. She certainly acted like she was.

Dari asked, "General precaution or is there more?"

She shook her head. "We need to bring them back to
Andor and interrogate them to find out what has happened."

We're on Elloria, Eric thought, not surprised.

"Why wait?"

"Not here. I don't want more secrets spilled and
spreading."

"Fair enough, but let's send the unconscious ones and
the guards down to the dragons to get ready for the flight.
We can ask that one a few questions."

Taryn ordered some to remove Korrin's golden armor
from Ryan, the Corethian Amulet from Anna's neck, and to
wrap Soliander's staff in a cloak. Eric nodded to himself.
The items were famous across worlds. Seeing them together left little doubt as to their supposed identities. They
were to be brought to Andor as four bound prisoners of no
importance. He stifled any outward display of emotion as
the order was carried out, the sight of his unmoving
friends being disturbed upsetting him. At least he was
awake to witness their treatment, and he vowed to do
nothing to inspire their captors to render him unconscious,
too. Only Matt stirred, a moan escaping him as men lifted
him and the others, carrying them down the path and

away. Finally, only Taryn and Dari stood on the hilltop, inside the Quest Ring, looking down at Eric as he sat.

"You may rise, or do you need help?" Taryn smirked at Eric, who sat cross-legged, arms behind his back. He rose smoothly anyway, years of martial arts mastery making this no challenge. She seemed somewhat impressed, which told him she admired skill.

Eric said, "Taryn of Aranor, I assume? And Prince Dari of Andor."

"And you are not Andier of Roir," she replied, unfazed by his realizations. She was a hard one to impress. "Who are you?"

Time to at least appear cooperative. "Eric of Maryland. I doubt you've heard of it."

"Planet?"

"Earth. Are you Korrin's brother?" Eric asked Dari, who cocked an eyebrow.

"How did—" The prince stopped himself, but Eric had his answer. "We're asking the questions."

Taryn asked, "Do you, like your wizard friend, somehow have memories of the Champions?"

Eric wasn't sure how much to tell them, especially if they weren't going to share intel themselves, but the answer to her question should have been obvious and he wondered if condescension would make her slip. "If I did, I would have recognized both of you and wouldn't have asked that, now would I?"

The briefest of frowns touched her lips and he knew she had pride in her intelligence. They silently regarded each other. "The names of your friends, and who is who."

"We're all from Maryland. Matt is the one you punched in the face for not being your brother. Ryan is Korrin. That leaves Anna as Eriana."

"How did you come to be here instead of the Champions?"

Eric admitted, "We don't know."

Dari snorted. "You are clearly pretending to *be* them."

Eric frowned at him on purpose, hoping that showing the same contempt for him that Taryn did might help form a bond with her. "That doesn't mean we know how we've been substituted."

Taryn eyed him shrewdly for several seconds. "Where were you when the substitution first took place?"

Eric realized she knew this wasn't the first time. The Champions had supposedly done several quests after being missing for years, with word of each quest spreading rapidly. Their families had undoubtedly heard. She had figured out that the real Champions did not complete the recent quests and wasn't bothering to ask him to confirm it.

He replied, "Earth. A place called Stonehenge. It's a monument. Looks like a Quest Ring, though we didn't know that at the time. There are no Quest Rings on Earth."

"Then why were you at this Stonehenge?"

"Vacation. It's a famous landmark. It suddenly lit up and brought us to another world, where we first learned about all of this."

"To Honyn," she surmised.

"I assume you've heard of the quest and its outcome."

She nodded. "And the others. That is how we knew they had returned after being missing, or so we thought. Why pretend to be them instead of confess?"

He shrugged. "It seemed safer. Better we wonder who people expect us to be, than everyone else wonder who we are."

She eyed him quietly again. "You must have known someone would realize the truth eventually."

"Yes. But we didn't anticipate the Champions' families summoning us. We hoped to have more answers first so we could better deal with the fallout. Why did you try to summon them?"

Dari appeared ready to tell him not to ask questions again, but Taryn put a restraining hand on his arm, calculating eyes on Eric. "What did they usually do after a quest?"

He considered, realizing she wanted to see if he could figure it out. "Go home. But they haven't because it isn't them."

"You are returned to Earth afterwards."

"Yes. So you have been wondering why, after they were missing for three years and then resumed quests, they have not come home. You want answers. And now that we're here, you want more of them. Well, so do we."

"Then I assume you'll cooperate." Taryn indicated that he should walk toward the path leading to the dragons. "Oh, before I forget," she began, following him, "you've been summoned for a quest to recover a stolen blue dragon egg and return it to the Kingdom of Novell, where we stand." Eric frowned and she laughed. "Yes, I know we must tell you the quest within an hour of your arrival or you are not bound to do it and can send yourselves home."

She didn't elaborate, and Eric knew why. Now he and his friends had no choice but to cooperate with an interrogation—because all Taryn and Dari had to do, to imprison them on Elloria forever, was never tell them how to achieve this quest. Trying to escape was pointless. That she had outmaneuvered him explained the spark of humor in her eyes. She was fearsome.

They descended the dirt path as he looked around, wondering why this place had been chosen for a Quest Ring. The rings were sometimes in a central location in a castle—but given that one was likely to be used only once, if ever, that was a waste of space. He had chatted with a few of their previous summoners and learned that the rings were like tourist attractions (not that that expression had been used). They were seen as a status symbol and conversation starter, nobles from one land expressing admiration and thinly disguised jealousy that they didn't have one. Not everyone could. It had taken Soliander and then his apprentice Everon many months to create them in various places. No one really knew how many existed except Everon.

The now familiar sight of dragons caught his attention. Having ridden a few, battled another, and even seen an undead dragon hadn't muted his awe. Most of the dragons present were red, a few gleamed silver in the sun, and one was black except for a gold streak on its chest and head. All but the latter wore a saddle and reins. Each dragon was large enough to swallow him whole. All but the black one ignored him; that one watched as he approached, a familiar intelligence and cunning in its enormous golden eyes. He wondered what sort of breath weapon it had—fire, lightning, ice?—while also hoping he didn't learn the hard way.

He had already noticed that the guards wore two different insignias on their armor. Most had a blue dragon head facing forward on the white sail of a ship. He surmised that this meant Kingdom Novell. Only a handful of warriors wore the symbol matching Prince Dari's—two gold daggers pointing downward to form a V, on a red background. Taryn wore no symbol that he saw, which made him wonder whether she worked in the official capacity of her kingdom Aranor. As he waited, guards began loading his unconscious friends onto one dragon or another, strapping them in place. Prince Dari walked away and climbed onto the larger silver one, seldom taking his eyes off Eric for long. From behind him, Taryn removed his bindings and, to his surprise, returned his sword, though she kept the knives.

"I'll be clear this time," she began, holding his gaze. "If you run, you'll get an arrow in the back. If you attack, one of the wizards will stun you. If you try to jump off your dragon into the ocean, you'll find the dragon's magic is holding you on. The dragons will not obey you. If you upset me, I'll get the information I want the hard way."

Eric appreciated both subtlety and directness when used at the right time. Sensing this might sound like he was flirting and wanting to avoid that, he said, "Only a fool would upset you."

"Most men are fools."

"I am not."

"I know. Mount the remaining red."

Eric approached the dragon, who lowered his wing for him to climb. Not until seating himself in the saddle did he notice Taryn climbing the black dragon's wing. Somehow, it didn't surprise him that this was her steed, nor that she didn't use a saddle. He had gone without a saddle once before out of necessity but still preferred the seat, mostly for its emotional and psychological comfort. He needed to get over that, he now knew, because it would toughen him up like her... but what happened if the dragon fell unconscious and couldn't keep him on anymore? He smirked. He would crash into the ground and die anyway, so maybe it didn't matter.

Prince Dari's silver dragon was the first to lift off. They circled above, clearly waiting for the others, but it wasn't until Taryn rose into the sky that anyone else did so, too. Eric permitted himself a grin, certain that Dari held little authority. If needed, maybe he could drive a wedge between the prince and anyone else. He didn't want to make enemies of anyone, but if Dari was already that, then weakening him in any way he could was wise.

Eric watched as the island and its Quest Ring, the way home, disappeared behind them. That wasn't the only way back, as another such ring could do it, but this was likely the closest one to Andor. He surmised that the kingdom didn't need one. After all, Korrin was from there. If a quest was needed, all the king had to do was ask his son to do it, not summon him and the others. He assumed the island kingdom was an ally of Andor, which was both a city and a kingdom. Getting back to the Quest Ring would be harder with both of them as enemies. He had to convince them of their innocence but sensed that Taryn, at least, was amenable to that. He would find out soon enough if the rest of the families were more like her or Dari, who seemed to have assumed the worst. Now more than ever, Eric might have to live up to the reputation of Andier, the Silver-Tongued Rogue, and talk their way into an alliance.

Without one, they were never going home.

CHAPTER TWO

THE INTERROGATION

Ryan heard the familiar, low voices of his friends as he awoke. He didn't feel like he had been sleeping. He lay on his back. A two-story ceiling of limestone was overhead, a lantern hanging from a chain to one side. To his immediate right stood a wall. Turning his head, he saw Eric, Anna, and Matt sitting on a low bench that was part of the room's opposite wall

Sitting up, he swung his feet to the stone floor. His armor was gone, leaving only the white cloth gambeson underneath. This buttoned down the front. It had long sleeves, and a collar, and overhung his waist to mid-thigh. Somehow, it was always clean at the start of a quest, as if was just washed, or new and unstained by sweat or the chainmail to which his plates were attached.

"Hey," said Anna, coming to his side. "How do you feel?"

"Where are we?" Ryan asked, noting that the room was empty, a lone wooden door leading out.

"We'll get to that," she said. "They said you'd wake up in a few minutes and left."

"I feel fine. Who are you talking about?"

Eric answered, "The wizard who knocked you out. He reversed the spell or something and left. I only have a few minutes to bring all of you up to speed before we have to answer a lot of questions. We don't need to get a story straight, because I think we're going to need to be honest. I'm pretty sure they don't mean us any harm."

"Speak for yourself," said Matt, frowning.

Ryan noticed that Matt wore a new silver headband and didn't have a black eye. "What's on your head?"

"Something to prevent me from casting spells."

That didn't bode well, but he wasn't the only one capable of the supernatural. At first, Anna had only healed people by calling on the gods to channel their power through her, but their group had later learned that she could also do offensive spells.

"What about you?" Ryan asked.

Anna shook her head. "They took the amulet, so I'm back to having a hard time reaching the gods here. I could do it if I knew their names, but I don't."

Only now did Ryan notice that she wasn't wearing the usual white robe of Eriana, but a simple golden dress. Matt's black robe was gone, too, a red one replacing it. A tunic and leggings had replaced Eric's leather armor. He nodded at them.

"Did you put those on yourselves?" he asked.

"Yeah," said Eric. "They know we aren't the Champions and don't want anyone else to know that, so they have disguised us as regular people. They confiscated any distinctive clothes or items."

"You think we can get them back?"

"If we handle this right, yeah."

Then Eric told them all that he knew, had surmised, or had been told—including that both Anna and Matt had been healed so that neither had a head wound. They had been here an hour in a palace in the city of Andor. It lay on a plain along the western coast of the continent Veskyn. Further west across the Madura Ocean stood Onder Isle, where the Quest Ring lay inside the Kingdom of Novell.

This quest was supposedly an easy one—it had only been conceived to make the Quest Ring summon them, since that wouldn't happen without a valid quest. For once, they would not be sent into considerable danger.

Map of Kingdom Novell

"And yet there may be plenty of danger from the families," Ryan observed.

Eric admitted, "There could be. We don't know who will be there or their attitude, so we need to pay attention. Read the room and the people in it. Are they hostile or disbelieving? Be honest but don't volunteer too much. No speeches or monologues about anything. Make them ask us questions. I think we have a real opportunity here."

"How so?" Anna asked.

"They know more about the people we're impersonating than anyone. If they agree to help us, think about how valuable they could be."

"There is a lot we don't know," Matt admitted.

"They may agree to help us," continued Eric, "if they understand that we did nothing to hurt the real Champions, and we're innocent victims doing what we can in this. We know the real champs weren't voluntarily doing this.

That means their families probably know, too, even though other people don't. The families could realize that we need their help. We may even be their best chance of getting back Eriana, at least, since we know exactly where she is."

Ryan appreciated Eric's ability to think through these issues. And he was right, as always. The priestess Eriana, the Light Bringer, was back on Earth helping them set up a home base with the few people who knew the truth about what was going on and why they kept disappearing from Earth. This was a card they had to play, being able to trade information about Eriana for help. But they had to be careful. Volunteering that would go down better than only coughing up the info for something in return. But it would relieve their hosts to learn that one of the Champions still lived. That she was helping them strongly suggested their hosts do the same. The problem was proving it.

A knock on the door ended further talk before a guard shoved it open and gestured for them to follow. From habit of being their apparent leader, Ryan went first, striding down a long, narrow hall and past its doors. Soon, they entered a tall oval room, bright with sunlight from tall windows, tapestries of battle scenes flying from the walls. Ryan stepped through between an area of raised benches, most of them empty. More lay along the far wall. In the room's center awaited four high-backed chairs with red and gold cushions, all facing his right, where two empty thrones stood. Other, less ornate chairs sat on either side of the twin thrones, Ryan's impression being that the other seats were temporary. Were these for the family members of the Ellorian Champions?

He flushed a bit, feeling guilty for pretending to be Lord Korrin. For the first time, no one on a quest looked at him and believed he was the dragon-slaying knight. He was just an imposter with no stature. A prisoner. The change was almost comic. It was time to be Ryan LaRue, a rich kid who hadn't done much with his life because he'd been atoning for accidentally paralyzing his younger brother in a childhood accident. It wasn't until these quests had started that he'd finally accepted that Daniel didn't really need him. He felt it important to show their hosts that he and the others had done well on their quests, that they weren't some sort of embarrassment to the reputation of the true Champions.

A middle-aged man in a fine tunic of gold and red, and whom Ryan took to be the Court Marshal, banged the steal-shod butt of a wooden staff on the parquet floor. The din reverberated around the hall, and the chatter quieted.

"We shall introduce the families and friends of the Champions, should any be present. Andier of Roir, as expected, has none in attendance."

That's interesting, thought Ryan. They had learned little about Andier, and all of them suspected that this was by design—not because no one would tell them, but because Andier kept everyone from knowing anything to tell them. But that was conjecture. Maybe this quest was a chance to learn more about all of them.

"Solun of Coreth, brother to the Lady Eriana of Coreth."

Ryan's eyebrows rose. They had all met Eriana on Earth and learned much about the quests, but only now did he realize how little he knew of her personally—including that she had a brother. An attractive, blond-haired and brown-eyed young man entered from one side, his left hand missing at the wrist. He wore a plain tunic with no symbol on it, suggesting that he was not nobility.

"Her Highness, Princess Alia of Coreth." In strode a regal woman in her forties, a purple gown flowing behind her as she moved to sit beside Solun.

"Commander of the Dark Blades, Taryn of Aranor, sister to Soliander of Aranor."

Ryan hadn't seen Taryn since she initiated the attack on them. Now she strode in wearing black gambeson and trousers like his, her black boots sounding as commanding as she looked. One hand gripped the hilt of a black dagger at her waist. He didn't want to cross swords with her. She walked an air of authority and yet somehow still seemed feminine.

"Prince Dari and Princess Cariss of Andor, brother and sister to Lord Korrin, Prince of Andor and Heir-Apparent to the throne."

That surprised Ryan. They hadn't known that Korrin was heir to the throne. The prince and princess took seats to either side of where their parents would sit, Dari frowning, his sister curiously looking at Ryan and his friends without malice. She was pretty, long blonde hair braided, her blue eyes bright.

"His Majesty, King Sarov of Andor, and Her Royal Highness, Queen Lina, father and mother to Lord Korrin."

Ryan felt curious to meet the only parents of a champion who were present. It begged the question of where the other parents were. Such thoughts ceased when a tall, big-boned man entered, gray eyes sorrowful as if something weighed on him, though his bearing was erect and proud. He appeared to have once been a physically powerful man and retained some vigor into his fifties. Beneath a simple crown of gold, with inset rubies, his long blond hair was streaked with gray. He wore a tastefully embroidered gold tunic and red leggings that gave the impression he wasn't overly impressed with himself while still making a good showing of his status.

Beside him, one hand linked with his arm, walked the queen. She was slender and regal in a gown of light gray, the color somber as if she were caught between hope and mourning. With rich parents, Ryan could at least relate to the idea that an heir was missing; to his parents, he fit that description even now. It might give him a way to bond with Korrin's parents. A crown lay atop the queen's golden hair. Her blue eyes were alert and kind.

Once the king and queen were seated, Prince Dari rose and strode forward—still dressed in his fine tunic, polished black shoes having replaced his boots. He took a position halfway between the thrones and the four Earth friends, on whom he turned his back to address the court. Nearly twenty in all, some present hadn't been introduced and sat on either side of the room.

"Lords and ladies," he began, "our first matter is the most important. What is revealed here today cannot leave this room under any circumstances. To do so could jeopardize the reputations and lives of the Ellorian Champions. They remain missing despite our attempt to summon them on Onder Isle earlier today. The spell did work, but in place of those we love and admire, these four arrived."

This caused a murmur, but neither the king nor queen seemed surprised. King Sarov asked in a booming tenor, "They arrived via the summoning spell? You are certain it was no other way?"

"Yes, father. The stones of the Quest Ring lit as expected and faded after. And in talking with them, we know that they have somehow been substituted for the Champions. They are the ones who have completed each of the recent quests."

A groan followed this revelation, and the queen asked, "Does this mean there is no sign of them?"

"We do not yet know. We only discussed the situation briefly with one of them, and thought it prudent to have this interrogation with all interested parties present."

"I can answer your question, Your Highness," Ryan said, "if I may." The queen's eyebrows rose, but then she nodded. He stood up slowly to show that he was no threat. "We have seen both Eriana and Soliander, but have not seen or heard any word of Korrin or Andier. Two of them live, at least." Another murmur spread through the room. "We have been impersonating the real Ellorian Champions, but I can assure you that we want no part of doing so and have only done it to save our own lives. Just as the Champions were summoned and bound to a quest against their will, so are we. We believed that admitting our real identities would make it more likely that we would be killed. I am grateful to hear Prince Dari caution everyone to keep this secret until we can all determine how best to proceed."

He paused for a moment and chanced a look at Eric, who nodded in approval. Ryan turned back to the nobles. "We are all from a planet called Earth, and a country called the United States—in a state, or what you might call a province, called Maryland. My name is Ryan LaRue. I have pretended to be your son, the knight Korrin. The woman with me is Anna, in the role of the priestess Lady Eriana, of course. The slender man is Matt, and he has acted as the wizard Soliander, while the shorter man is Eric, in the role of Andier, the rogue."

Taryn rose and came closer. "You have seen my brother. Where?"

"On the planet Honyn. He attacked Matt in Castle Darlonon while we were there to close the Dragon Gate. We had no opportunity to discuss anything with him. I'm afraid we don't know much more, or what he is doing and why. Or where he is now."

"Why did he attack Matt?"

"We aren't sure, but as you noticed when we arrived here, the summoning spell changes us into their clothes and gives us their items. From what Matt told us, there are now two copies of Soliander's staff, because Soliander had one during the attack and so did Matt. He may just have been trying to retrieve it, though our impression was that the encounter surprised him and he did not expect to see Matt at all... not to mention with his possessions, or copies of them."

Taryn turned a cold eye on Matt. "Did you harm my brother?"

The wizard looked a little wide-eyed at first, then assumed a relaxed confidence that surprised Ryan, especially since Taryn had slugged him the last time they met. "It was self-defense. He had cast the *Mind Trust* spell on me and was, well, going through my memories. I had to get away."

Taryn shook her head. "The spell is forbidden. Soli would not have done that."

"He did, and my impression was that it wasn't the first time he used it on someone."

"No."

A bit snidely, Matt said, "I'm sorry if it bothers you to hear, but he has done worse. He is the only one who could have opened the Dragon Gate on Honyn, and he is the one who did. You know of that quest and that I am not lying about this. He put the lives of everyone on that planet at risk just to lure someone into a trap."

"What trap?" Dari asked.

Matt replied, "Someone had stolen a scroll, which he had written, from the rulers of Honyn. The scroll reveals the location of soclarin ore, a precious metal Soliander uses for fashioning powerful items, which includes the keystones in the Quest Rings. Soliander didn't know who had stolen the scroll and wanted to find out. He suspected it was Everon, the man who had trapped the Champions in the unwanted cycle of quests. He would be able to get revenge on Everon if true, and if Everon sprung the trap, but it was someone else who did so. The Dragon Gate kept the dragons banished from Honyn to the only planet where soclarin ore could be found. Letting the dragons loose to destroy Honyn was a risk Soliander was willing to take in his desire for revenge on Everon. Many people died for that, and *we* nearly died. It would have been worse if we could not close the gate and complete the quest, because he left it open. You understand? He left it open and we're the only reason it's closed and the dragon horde has not obliterated Honyn." He paused and looked at Taryn. "I don't know who your brother used to be, but he isn't doing things that heroes do anymore."

Taryn stood silently glaring at him. "What were you trying to hide from him that you needed to attack him?"

Now it was Matt's turn to glare. "Have you ever had that spell cast on you? No? Maybe I'll learn it and cast it on you, then go through every private memory of yours."

"Matt," cautioned Eric.

"I can laugh at every mistake you've made. Every embarrassing moment. Remember things you've told no one."

"Matt!"

"I can learn everything and make you feel my amusement about it all."

"Matt!"

He finally stopped, nostrils flaring, eyes bright with energy. No one said anything for a moment before he quietly added, "Don't stand there disapproving of me for putting a stop to it. Your brother deserved me setting him on fire. If I cast that spell on you, you would split me down the middle and enjoy it."

Ryan looked at Taryn and saw a troubled gaze that had softened, if only a little. Matt had made an impression on her, at least. The sincerity may have held value.

Taryn observed, "You claimed to have Soliander's memories." This caused a stir.

"Only some of them," said Matt.

"How? How did this happen?"

"I had a copy of his staff when he immobilized me, then cast the spell. He had somehow made my staff unable to function, but I could control his and made fire erupt from it. His pain ended the spell chaotically instead of in a controlled way. Something about this caused a transfer of his scattered memories into me."

"He was injured?" Taryn asked Ryan had the impression that this answer might be dangerous.

Matt shrugged as if not worried. "I didn't stay to find out, but he later attacked Lorian, so he lived."

"Lorian?" Prince Dari asked. "I know that name. An elf of Arundell."

"Yes," said Ryan, trying to wrest the conversation away from Matt, in case the wizard started giving attitude again. Enough of that. He wondered what was going on with him. "Lorian has been a great friend to us. He is the one who told us what we knew, until recently, about the Champions. Without his help, we would never have survived."

"And what *do* you know?" Dari asked, turning to him.

"Wait," said Taryn, looking at Matt. "What memories of my brother do you have? Do you know where he has been these past three years?"

Matt shook his head. "The problem is that whatever memories of his I have are scattered. I can't recall anything on purpose. For example, when you summoned us, I didn't recognize you—not until you said something about me impersonating your brother. Then I recognized you from Soliander's memories. When you were kids, I know that he used to call you—"

"Stop," she said, looking flustered.

Ryan glanced at Eric, who seemed to smile slightly. Matt had unnerved her. But he was playing with fire—Taryn didn't seem to be the sort who tolerated being screwed with. Not by a long shot.

Dari began, "We could use the same spell on him to learn what—"

Taryn snapped, "It is forbidden."

After a long silence, Ryan said, "We are happy to tell you what we know. Such a spell is not needed. We are hoping you can help us, just as we may be able to help you."

Dari frowned. "And what could you possibly help us with?"

"We know where Eriana is." Amid the stir that followed, Ryan added, "She is on Earth and contacted us in the last week. She is safe and in good spirits. She very much wants to come home, but there are no wizards on Earth powerful enough to send her. But you may have wizards who can get to Earth and bring her back."

Nodding at Matt, Dari asked, "What about him? He has bested Soliander. Surely he has the power to do it."

Ryan shook his head. "That was luck. He is not that strong yet." He saw Matt shoot him an irritated look. "This is complicated, but on Earth, magic hasn't worked in a long time. There are no wizards. Matt hasn't even been able to practice what he's learned when we go back. He can't take a spellbook with him. Or Soliander's staff. None of us can take anything."

"That makes little sense," said Dari. "You're lying."

"No. Something has happened to change how everything works, and we think we know what, but it's a long story. We pieced it together with help from Eriana."

He explained how someone on Earth had summoned the Champions from Elloria to Earth's past, a thousand years ago. Magic was about to stop working. Their quest was to prevent that. But Soliander saw an opportunity. Knowing they were somehow magically bound to the Quest Rings and unable to refuse being summoned, he tried to let the magic on Earth die and send them all back at the same time. This would free them from the summonings. But disaster struck. Only Soliander appeared to have returned home. Eriana remained trapped on Earth and was thrown forward in time to twenty years ago. There was still no sign of Korrin or Andier.

"She has aged twenty years?" someone asked. It took a moment for Ryan to realize it had been Eriana's brother, Solun.

"She has lived twenty years on Earth, so the aging is natural. We can let her tell you the details of the life she has lived, but I will say that until we met with her and told her only a few years had passed, she thought that a thousand years had gone by. And that all of you were dead. She was understandably emotional to discover that this was not the case."

"If I may speak, Your Majesty?" asked Princess Ali of Coreth. The king nodded and she continued. "You may be unaware, but Lady Eriana once saved the king and several others in my family, being granted land and title for the honor. She is a dear friend of the crown. We are grateful to hear that she lives. We pledge our full support to any efforts to return her home and will aid you as needed."

Ryan tried to not let on how relieved he felt. "We would be grateful for any help."

"You say magic did not work there... or does not?" asked Dari, frowning at him. "Which is it? You can't seem to get your story worked out."

"It didn't work until we unknowingly returned a magic pendant to a place called Stonehenge. It wasn't designed as a Quest Ring, but the person who summoned the Champions to the past turned it into one. When we returned the pendant, not knowing its true nature, magic was unleashed once again. It appears to be slowly awakening."

"But no one knows how to use it?" Taryn asked. "What of the elves?"

"There are none, and no dwarves or other creatures, like dragons. The spell that stopped magic also banished them."

That caused a murmur. Ryan knew that what he thought of as fantasy creatures had been on every world they had visited so far, though he and the others had only seen a handful each time. It no longer surprised him, now that he knew the truth, but seeing an elf or ogre still took getting used to. And their return to Earth was only likely to accelerate. How was the world going to react to that? Not well.

Dari asked, "So we know the wizard has limited skill, and yet you have survived several quests. What of the rest of you? Are you a real knight?"

"No," Ryan admitted. He was going to say more when the prince interrupted.

"So, you know nothing of honor."

Ryan deadpanned, "You're the ones who summoned us without our permission, then attacked us."

After a moment, Taryn laughed, then looked at a red-faced Dari. "Well, assuming you're telling the truth, we can certainly help train any of you. What of the others? Can you heal people?" she asked of Anna.

"I have learned to. Eriana just taught me how to use her amulet, as well."

"You were doing it without it before?" Taryn seemed impressed.

"Yes. It is now easier to reach gods I do not know. That is what the amulet is for."

Taryn turned to Eric. "And you? You fight well enough with hands and feet. What of the sword?"

"Still learning."

Dari snorted and addressed the room. "Here we are, worried about the Champions' reputations being ruined if people know these are imposters. But it seems apparent that we should tell everyone before these buffoons destroy their reputation by continuing to pretend—and embarrassing them, and us, with whatever disastrous quest they ruin next!"

Matt bristled. "If I could substitute you for us, I still wouldn't. You'd probably only do half as well as your brother." He stopped, then added, "You seem half the man."

"Matt!" Anna whispered, aghast.

Dari turned crimson and whirled toward the wizard, drawing the dagger at his waist. But Taryn cut in front of him with a look of cold menace that stopped him.

"You would protect them?" he snapped.

"The wizard is the key to finding my brother," she began, "and you won't touch him until I say."

"Enough!" said the king, sounding weary. "Dari, put that thing away and sit down. Has anyone examined the items they arrived with?" He gestured to one front corner of the room. There stood a table on which lay Soliander's staff, Eriana's amulet, Korrin's lance, and Andier's many knives. Behind it were armor stands—one bearing Korrin's full suit and sword, another with Andier's leather and sword, and the remaining two with Soliander's and Eriana's robes draped over them.

Taryn walked over and hefted her brother's staff. "Yes, Your Majesty. Each has been examined by those most familiar with them. They appear to be authentic."

His tone calmer, Dari asked, "How do we know they didn't just *steal* them?"

Taryn snorted. "No one is getting the staff from my brother unless he's dead. Your Majesty, we have no reason to think these aren't real. But I do think we need to confirm the imposters' story."

"Agreed," he said. "We will privately discuss how to do so."

"There is another matter," Dari said, before pointing at Ryan. "This one is impersonating royalty in our kingdom.

That is a crime punishable by death. Surely we will not overlook it?"

Ryan quickly scanned those present to judge their reaction, which seemed contemplative but not enthusiastic. Then Eric spoke.

"Technically, we were pretending in Kingdom Novell, not in Andor, and that is outside your jurisdiction. There has been no crime of that sort committed here."

To his surprise, Taryn laughed, a reaction shared less strongly by others. Ryan flashed a smile at Eric, hoping that there wasn't the equivalent of an international agreement to honor the laws of another country if they were similar, like the United Nations on Earth.

"The prisoner has a sound argument," began the king, amused, "if only on a technicality. Still, we cannot overlook the impersonations, however well-intentioned or self-preserving they may have been. Until we decide how next to proceed, they will remain under guard as special guests. Confine them to the royal guest suites. They are to be treated well in the meantime."

This last part seemed directed at his son, who looked at Ryan with an expression he wasn't sure how to read. Maybe Eric had seen it. He was better at that sort of thing. It almost seemed like Dari was angry with him, or resentful. Even jealous? Maybe it didn't matter, but Eric was always keen to know exactly what someone felt, because it could matter if things came to a head. Better to be prepared than not. But Dari was just one of many here, and he seemed to have less stature. How much trouble could he cause? He almost laughed at the sentiment, knowing underestimation when he thought it. He would monitor Korrin's brother and see if he could befriend him, if only to keep closer tabs on Dari. But he would have to be sincere, not because he thought Dari was wily, but because Ryan was not. He could approach it as just trying to understand Korrin better. But then maybe he should ask the princess. What was her name? Cariss? Yes, she seemed excited and more receptive. He'd get more out of Korrin's sister, he was sure. But then maybe each could tell him different things.

As they were escorted from the room, he cast a look back at the table with the real Champions' possessions. He didn't quite feel naked without the armor, because he'd gone without it before when safe in a castle prior to a quest, but they were literally defenseless. Of all the reasons to feel vulnerable away from Earth, this was one he hadn't seen coming.

CHAPTER THREE

MANDRELLAN

Princess Cariss loved a delightful surprise. The one she left behind her as she strode from the great hall had certainly been unforeseen. Four imposters pretending to be the Champions... her brother Korrin still missing! The story nearly burst from her lips with every step on the parquet floors, and yet she could tell no one. A secret of this magnitude wouldn't last. She knew at least one person she simply had to tell. The wizard Mandrellan could be trusted. He had saved her life once and proven his good counsel countless times since. Her parents might even now be contemplating informing him. The thought added urgency to her steps. She had to be the first, for if she couldn't tell Mandrellan, no one else offered an ear.

He had kept secrets before. Only a few people knew that the Champions—the real ones—hadn't been voluntarily questing. The families had all agreed to keep that secret closely held for the same reasons they didn't want this new revelation spreading. The truth would harm the Champions' reputations, inspire people to stop summoning them, and thereby deprive countless worlds of hope. She had always admired the Champions' willingness to sacrifice themselves in this way. Admitting that they didn't want to do it was the obvious way to stop it all, and yet they had kept quiet. The toll of the unwanted quests had been apparent to those closest to them—though Korrin tried to pretend, even to them, that he had no issue with it. Soliander had been the most vocal and angry. Eriana tried to soothe him, Andier watched with those appraising eyes, and Korrin stifled his disapproval of Soliander's fury. Cariss had witnessed one of these exchanges, and something about it told her that it hadn't been the first.

Her older brother had always been noble to a fault. Long before the quests or her learning that they had ceased to be voluntary, she had admired Korrin even as her younger brother Dari resented him. Her sympathy for Dari's ego had been limited. She hadn't appreciated his lack of remorse when Korrin went missing. Dari had seemed almost happy about it, and had once claimed prematurely that he should be named heir-apparent to the throne in Korrin's ongoing absence. Sometimes he tried to downplay all those snide remarks he'd previously made, not only about Korrin, but also about the other Champions, whom he had refused to refer to that way. Any similar words like "heroes" also made him frown. And until the Champions disappeared, he had reacted that way to anyone people admired, finding amusement in those who died while trying to help others.

Dari didn't reveal such sentiments anymore, of course. He hadn't been dumb enough to outwardly gloat that his famed brother had vanished, but she knew he didn't miss Korrin. Not once had he expressed concern, so she wasn't sure what to make of his performance in the great hall just now. Had it been a show? And for whom? Likely their parents. He had seemed more confident and somehow invigorated by Korrin's absence, as if the sun could never shine on him until Korrin was gone. And once word had reached them the Champions had resumed their quests, the cloud that once hung over Dari had reappeared in his brown eyes.

Korrin was a threat to him, she now understood. A threat to his claim to the throne, surely, but that had never been real anyway. Then again, that wouldn't stop a man from fancying it his, she knew. Korrin had personally cut down one such pretender on a quest. But surely it wouldn't come to that here in Andor! No, Korrin was a threat to the esteem in which everyone held Dari, or even the attention he received. Part of her didn't blame Dari for thinking this way, but she thought he needed to grow up.

She sighed as she rounded another corner, nodding absentmindedly to others passing by. That they had told no one of the attempt at summoning her brother and the others was just as well now that it had resulted in this surprise. Dari had insisted on being at the Quest Ring, ostensibly to welcome Korrin back and represent the family, but she had wondered if that was all. Taryn was more than capable of overseeing the whole affair. Cariss wished she could have been present see Dari's reaction when the four imposters had appeared. Had he been thrilled? Relieved? Disappointed and surprised? She would never know. One thing was certain—he was genuinely curious where Korrin was now that two of the four had been seen alive, and perhaps equally fascinated to know that his brother was free of that cycle of unwanted quests. He had once laughed about the involuntary part, saying it was ironic punishment for Korrin's pride, that he could save so many people. What did he think now?

As she arrived at her suite of rooms, the door stood open, and a guard advised her that he had let Mandrellan into her sitting room beyond the antechamber. Her heart lifted. The wizard could once again offer her helpful counsel. He was quite astute, and knew that a gathering of nobles had taken place without him being invited this time. He had probably assumed she had news, but he would never guess what it was.

Thoughts of Dari had dampened her excitement, but now she tried to relax. She pulled a long pin from her blonde hair to let it fall past her slender waist, which a lavender belt held her flowing, green dress against. She loosened it slightly and kicked off her shoes to walk barefoot on the cool stones here, as was her habit since childhood.

She swept into the room to find Mandrellan already standing, arms folded so that each hand clasped the other forearm inside the sleeves of his plain blue robe. Dark, penetrating brown eyes smiled warmly at her. Cariss had always found his gaze mesmerizing. His black stubble beard framed his jaw from below, matching the short hair atop his head. His eyes stood out from the pale face, their deep brown making even a smile seem intense. He was only a few years older than her in his late twenties, but his command of situations suggested he was much older and wiser, that mind of his seeing things hers seldom did. She hadn't known another person from the planet Artimon and could never tell what, if anything, about him was the influence of home or just him.

"Are you alone, my lady?" Mandrellan asked, his voice smooth and strong.

For an answer, she turned back to the guard. "You may close the doors." She turned to the wizard and smiled, noticing as she neared him that he seemed relieved. "I have the most interesting news, but you must promise to tell no one of it."

"Of course." He bowed. "Your trust is as sacred to me as your life."

Cariss moved to sit on a velvet divan, gesturing for him to join her. "This time, it is especially important that no one knows what I am going to tell you."

That playful smile she so often admired appeared. "You have my full attention."

She casually remarked, "My family just tried to summon the Champions." Cariss watched in anticipation of his reaction, which she had imagined countless times over the past week as plans unfolded, but the expression of alarm wasn't what she had expected. It vanished almost as quickly as it came, a look of quiet urgency replacing it. Maybe it hadn't been fear after all. But then she realized the reason it might have been and gushed, "I'm sorry for not telling you sooner! My family made me swear to secrecy! I still trust you. You must believe me."

His eyes widened, and he gripped one hand with his, smiling. "Of course, my dear. I did not doubt this for a moment. You merely startled me. I trust the summoning was not successful?"

She smiled anew. "Oh, it worked."

Mandrellan's gaze intensified, and his eyes darted to the door and back to hers. "You must not joke with me about something so important."

Cariss laughed. "You are taking this much too seriously! I can see this matters as much to you as to myself."

"Yes. I have offered my counsel and aid in finding them many times precisely because I want to see you happy that Lord Korrin is safe and home. Given this, I am disappointed that I was not among those chosen to assist."

"I am so sorry, Mandrellan." The last thing she wanted was for the bond between them to suffer. "I lobbied on your behalf but—"

"You should have tried harder." He rose and turned away from her, stepping toward the exit.

She felt a stab of pain at his rebuke and, for a moment, was at a loss for a response. Would she lose her trusted advisor over this? He had literally turned his back... "It's not my fault. I—"

"I fear you do not trust me at all, even after all that I have done for you." He took more steps to leave.

Cariss rose and quickly caught up with him. "Please don't leave, Mandrellan! I could not bear it. I need you here. Please tell me what I can do to make it right."

He stopped and turned to her, frowning, his eyes hurt. "I don't see what you can do. It is clear I am not to be told what is happening. My counsel cannot be of use to you in my ignorance."

That gave her an idea and she took one of his hands with both of hers. "I came to tell you what happened!"

"You did not even know I was here."

"Yes, but I was going to come find you if you weren't here. I knew you would be here because you hear so much, even that which is not meant for your ears. You would hear of a gathering of nobles and wait for me to find out why. And you did! I know you trust me to tell you what happened, or you would not be here even now!"

"And yet you are teasing me instead of being forthcoming."

Again, she wasn't sure how to respond. "Well, I, I only wanted to have some fun revealing the extraordinary news. Please forgive me. I'm just a silly girl. You say so yourself all the time. Please. I will tell you everything."

He sighed in apparent resignation. Then he smiled and relief consumed her. "Well, perhaps if this silly girl can stop being silly long enough, I may still be able to counsel her."

"Yes!" She tugged him back toward the divan, nearly dancing with excitement. "Come, come. I will tell you everything." His smile broadened, and she lost any sense of hesitancy. He could have every last secret she had. "What do you want to know first?"

"Where is Lord Korrin now? And the others?"

"We still don't know. He didn't show up. Neither did the others." He shot her a penetrating look that made her tremble. "Four imposters appeared! It's the most amazing

THE SILVER-TONGUED ROGUE | 47

thing! My brother and the others are still missing. I'm *happy* about this, but these four friends from a place called Earth are the ones who have done these recent quests. And when we summoned the real Champions, these four appeared instead."

Brow furrowed and eyes dark, the wizard asked, "How can there be substitutes? It's not possible."

"No, I wouldn't have thought so."

"It's not."

She smiled. "How can you be so sure? It's almost like you know how the Quest Rings really work." When he looked startled, she laughed. "I'm only teasing."

"Yes, of course. I have read about them. That is all. I have no firsthand knowledge. But the spell could not..." He trailed off.

"Replace them? Yes, I know, and yet it has happened. How could this be?" She wasn't really expecting an answer. He didn't know how the spells worked any more than anyone else—except that awful wizard Everon, who had trapped her brother and the others in the cycle of quests. But it appeared that cycle had come to an end.

The wizard rose and began pacing. "You are certain that it is not them, but do these imposters know the whereabouts of Korrin and the others?"

"Nothing about Andier or Korrin, I'm sad to say. But they met Eriana on Earth."

His eyes bored into hers so intently that for a moment she felt afraid. "They are sure? How can we know they speak the truth?"

She rose and put one hand on his arm to calm him. "If you had been there, the details they gave, they could not have been lying. The story is fantastic, beyond anything but the true story of the Champions. Eriana has helped them. You know what this means? The quest cycle is broken, and at least two of them live!"

Mandrellan's eyes sparkled with intensity as he looked away, thinking. "The cycle... Yes, it must be... And others have taken their place. Eriana is free to..." Suddenly his eyes swung to hers and he gripped both of her arms forcibly. "You said two? The other is Soliander?"

"Ow, Mandrellan. Please!"

He frowned before he suddenly let go and retreated. "I beg your forgiveness, my lady. I am overexcited."

Cariss crossed her arms, feeling flustered. "Alright," she said, hearing herself sounding pouty about it, so she collected herself. "Well, anyhow, the news on Soliander is quite disturbing."

Mandrellan arched an eyebrow. "How so?"

"It seems that he attacked these four imposters on Honyn, where he opened the Dragon Gate as some sort of trap."

The wizard pulled back. "A trap for whom?"

"Someone on that world. He had stolen a scroll that detailed the whereabouts of soclarin ore. Soliander didn't want anyone to have that. You remember that the keystone inside each Quest Ring is made from it, and so are many of Soliander's most powerful items, like Korrin's sword."

"Yes. I recall. Where is this scroll now?"

"Back with the rulers of Honyn."

Mandrellan looked away, clearly thinking. "And if the scroll is stolen, what happens? Or what happened then?"

"Apparently, with the scroll stolen, Soliander assumed its possessor might want to go through the Dragon Gate to the world where the ore is and get it. So he opened the gate to lure him there and killed him! We think he had hoped it would be Everon, but it was not. I should like to kill that wizard myself, if I ever meet him."

The wizard nodded, eyes alight. "Perhaps you will get the chance. I admire your devotion. One could assume that stealing the scroll again might cause the same result, Soliander trying to trap the perpetrator. That would make it easy to know where Soliander would arrive to catch that person, assuming anyone knows what we just discussed."

"Only those in the throne room just now, and these imposters, or perhaps a few on Honyn. Are you thinking that if someone stole the scroll on purpose, we could meet Soliander when he arrives?"

He smiled. "Something like that, yes."

"You are clever! I should suggest that to my father."

"No, no. Please don't. I think there is too much going on now that is unknown. It is an opportunity we can discuss with him later."

Her excitement turned to disappointment, but she trusted his judgement. "Sure. We may have another way to find Soliander. The wizard, the one pretending to be Soliander, said that he has some of Soliander's memories. Those might include his location." Cariss saw Mandrellan's eyes grow intense again, then dart to the door and back.

"How? What does he know? Where is he now?"

She related Matt's story about how the mind reading spell had given him some of Soliander's memories, but the thoughts were scattered and he couldn't recall anything on purpose. She included how he recognized Taryn despite never having met her. "The imposters are under guard for now until we can confirm some of their story."

Mandrellan rose to his feet and grabbed his staff. "And Taryn? Where is she?"

Cariss shrugged. "Still in the great hall. They were making some arrangements. Where are you going?"

He had taken several steps toward the door, but now stopped and turned back. "You must trust me. I have an idea of my own that I dare not share with you now. The secrets you have entrusted to me, I will keep. I ask only that you do me the same courtesy and tell no one that we have spoken of these matters, even after they say the truth can be known."

That confused her. Why would he want that? But she still felt the need to smooth over their relationship and agreed, watching in dismay and concern as he left. The talk had not gone the way she'd anticipated. Something about it still bothered her, but when dwelling on such things, he was the one she normally spoke to. Well, lately anyway. They had met several months after the Champions disappeared, and since then, he had come and gone for weeks at a time, often updating her on inquiries he had made about their whereabouts. It was as if he were scouring the worlds himself for some sign of them. This filled her with gratitude, that he was such a great friend he would do this when he had no other reason beyond wanting the heroes found, on principle. Maybe that was the reason for his hasty departure.

It had been months since she'd seen him, but when word first spread of the Ellorian Champions doing the Honyn quest for the Dragon Gate, their first quest since going missing, he had arrived within days to ask for details. Now that she thought about it, he had seemed similarly intense and concerned, then confused like the rest of them that Korrin had not come home following the quest. He hadn't left since then, vowing to remain close by to assist if needed. Where he went when not here was no secret; his home and own affairs on Artimon beckoned. She wondered if that was where he was going now, as he sometimes did not tell her before disappearing again. She would ask the guards at the World Gate to tell her if he left. There had been enough worrisome surprises lately.

It wasn't until her thoughts drifted to these imposters and how little she knew of them that she realized the same was true of Mandrellan, despite all the time they had spent together.

CHAPTER FOUR

OIL AND LILAC

For the umpteenth time, Matt fingered the thing on his head that stopped him from accessing magic. He suspected magic was keeping it there and badly wanted to know how to take it off. Or put it on, for that matter. Being off Earth normally excited him because he could do magic, because otherwise he was the same old Matt Sorenson— weak and uninteresting. With the power of magic available on quests, that had all changed, even when he was back home, because he achieved things on quests that made him feel powerful, invigorated, and just awesome. It was like he finally had some sort of purpose. And he knew he enjoyed these quests more than his friends.

Instead of being sent back to the room they were in before, they had walked through the high halls of a palace; he had expected a castle. Tall windows provided a view of manicured gardens with sculptures and fountains below their position on the second floor. They were on a hill overlooking the port in the distance. Tall wooden ships lay at anchor in the harbor, their sails furled, except on the two that were sailing away. Such a sight often filled him with wonder that they got to visit places like this. And he so often wished they could do more than immediately set off on a quest. Might it not be wonderful to learn about one of these kingdoms in a way that didn't involve monsters, dragon hordes, or some other threat to all life?

Their escort of a dozen King's Guards, all in golden uniforms, had led them past curious onlookers. They no longer looked important except for their treatment. Whispers were bound to start. This was something they really needed to discuss with the families—how best to handle revealing the truth to those who didn't know, whenever that happened.

After several minutes of walking through gilded halls, past ornate paintings, and mostly human gawkers, they were shown into the large Blue Suite, which had two bedrooms and a sitting area between them. Windows provided views in several directions, inspiring Matt to gaze out to snow-capped mountains in the distance. Now he wanted a map.

Breaking his thoughts from behind him, Anna asked, "How do we think that went?"

Matt turned back and watched while Eric inspected the room, as if searching for surprises.

"I thought it went pretty well," began Ryan as he sniffed at a decanter or of what appeared to be orange juice, "but then I was doing the talking. How do you guys think I handled it?"

"Better than Matt," remarked Eric, who looked at the wizard, "but I think you got lucky with the reaction you received."

"Thanks," Matt said dryly.

Anna took a proffered OJ from Ryan and sat down on a couch. "Let's not wait for their decision on what happens next. What do we want out of our next talk with them?"

"The quest," Eric started at once. "We'll still need to get details on that. There's some small chance we can escape and do it and go home, so let's at least find out what we have to do."

"Yeah," said Matt, "but it's gonna be a lot harder if I can't get this damn thing off my head. I doubt anyone's going to tell us, but we need to figure out how to remove it. For all I know, I might not even be able to use the Quest Ring to send us home!"

Anna frowned. "I hadn't thought of that, but I think all of us can do it. We would need Soliander's staff. If they don't let us go or cooperate, we could be in trouble here."

"Well," began Eric, sitting down near Anna, "I think we need to figure out who seems like a soft target for getting information out of. I mean, Dari isn't likely to tell us anything unless we trick him into it. He's got an ego and some sort of chip on his shoulder. I'm probably the best to trick something out of him, but Ryan, since you're pretending to be his brother, he's probably more interested in you."

Ryan agreed. "Yeah. I'll see what I can do. Maybe challenge his pride in some way."

"Right," said Eric, "but first you'll have to see if that's what's driving him."

Matt smirked. "He's transparent. Maybe I'd have better luck goading him."

"I'd really like to talk to Eriana's brother," began Anna, "and that princess from Coreth. If I update on her in more detail, they could be allies."

Eric nodded. "I want to talk to Taryn. I'm not sure the rest of you can handle her. No offense. She's just very clever. Talking to her is like playing chess."

Matt said, "She's like the female version of you."

Eric laughed. "Exactly. Another big factor here, one we'll need their cooperation for, is to see Korrin's Home Ring. I'm dying to know what one looks like."

An image of one appeared in Matt's head, not for the first time, from Soliander's memories. "I could draw one, but yeah, let's see his. Part of me is wondering if it still functions, or if there's any sign of something being wrong.

In fact, it would be good to compare his to the others'. What if Eriana's and Soliander's are fine, and we know they're alive, but Andier's and Korrin's are damaged? It could suggest something."

"Interesting," said Eric. "Let's ask about the Home Rings. If they agree to help us, I'd also like to know if they can send people or things to Earth."

"Yes, like spellbooks," Matt suggested, "and any materials I need to cast spells. With magic starting to work on Earth, I really need to be able to practice."

"What would be even better is training," said Ryan. "Magic, sword fighting, archery. We can only do archery at home, but the modern bows we have are too different. We haven't had any training since the first quest. They mentioned it back there, too."

Eric said, "You know, that brings up another point. Taryn told me the quest we're summoned for is an easy one and not urgent. What if they agree to cooperate and help us? We could stay here indefinitely and get trained up before doing the quest and going home. There's nothing urgent back there."

Matt was about to express his enthusiasm when a knock on the door preceded the arrival of Taryn, who strode in with several of the King's Guard a step behind and to each side. She flicked an indifferent glance at the others but came straight toward him and stopped within arm's reach. She smelled slightly of oil and lilac.

"Matt, I'd like you to come with me."

"Why?"

"There are things you may know about my brother's whereabouts, or at least his activities, and I would like to learn what they are."

He couldn't blame her, but he wanted something, too. "Maybe if you remove this thing from my head, I'll answer your questions."

Taryn pursed her lips. "I understand your reluctance. I was hoping this wouldn't be viewed as a trade, but as potential allies helping each other. But if you have questions about my brother, or anything else, I would be happy to answer them."

He arched an eyebrow. "Why would you?"

"The way I see it, if you are in the situation you say you are and you need our help, we'll be allies. If not, you'll be imprisoned here a long time and unable to pass along what I tell you to anyone. In either case, there is no reason not to give you some information."

Matt held her gaze for a moment. "I can't argue with that."

His glance at Eric received a nod of approval and he followed Taryn from the room. While several guards stood outside, none accompanied them on their walk. She apparently didn't consider him a threat without magic. He frowned on thinking that this was true. As if reading his thoughts, she interrupted them.

"I wanted to apologize for striking you at the Quest Ring. You were potentially very dangerous, and I had to act quickly."

Matt looked at her wryly. "I still am."

Taryn smiled. "Not with that Crown of Voids on your head."

"When are you going to remove it?"

"Once we confirm enough of your story to believe you."

He shook his head. "You already believe me."

She nodded. "I do, yes, but it is the king's decision." She looked up at the Crown as they walked, for he was taller than her. "You are not the first wizard I have put this on."

Images flashed in Matt's head, of a young and terrified Soliander, waking from a nightmare of undead climbing up through the floors of their home to consume both of them.

He was about to lash out with magic to stop a threat that wasn't there when Taryn slid the device onto his head. Then she pinned him to the crude cot, talking gently to calm him. As with Matt's own memories, he didn't feel them so much as recall the images and random phrases, but he did sense the gratitude and admiration Soliander felt for his older sister. He loved her.

Matt stayed silent until she led him into an unguarded suite that he realized was her quarters. Several swords lay on a table, a pointed shield leaning against a chair. The dark blue décor suited her boldness. This was not a woman who would live somewhere pink. She went over to a bar in this sitting room while he glanced into the bedroom, seeing the sheets thrown back and rumpled. Tidying up wasn't her thing either. He wondered if a maid service had been told to stay out because she didn't like things too neat. Watching her shapely backside and thinking about the bed made him wonder what sort of man would attract her attention—and survive it. Probably Eric, but certainly not himself! Still, she was sexy.

"Let's forget about your brother for a minute," he began, as she began pouring red wine into silver steel goblets with dragons carved on them. Somehow that seemed more appropriate for her than glass. "You're obviously just visiting."

"I live where I am," she said, coming toward him with the drinks. He took the one she offered and watched her sit on the edge of the couch. He remained standing, sipping the bitter drink. It tasted like Merlot. He failed not to make a face. She smirked and asked, "Should I get you milk instead?"

He returned the expression and asked, "Do you have any?"

She laughed. "Good. I like some banter. It's a warrior thing."

"I think you liked it before you became one."

"We understand each other already."

"And what do you think you understand about me?"

"That you're in over your head. That you're a nice guy. That your life has been upended and you should be rattled, desperate for help, needy and scared. And yet you're not. You stand at your full height instead of cowering. You show defiance. You're quick-witted and aware of nuances that some people twice your age cannot grasp when they're explained to them. You challenged Dari in front of the king. You defeated the dragon horde of Honyn. You even beat the Lords of Fear. There is steel in you. And power. You are strong, more so than even you may realize. To be honest, you remind me of my brother."

That startled him out of wondering if she was flirting with him. "Right now, I'm more curious about *you*."

She swallowed a mouthful of wine. "I have a place in Aranor. But you could've guessed that. Don't see it much."

"I was about to ask if you don't stray far from home, but you do."

"I go where my blade is needed and I like the work. I may not be the hero my brother is, but I don't let the evil shits of this world destroy the lives of their betters."

"Good." Matt could admire that, as someone long bullied growing up. "What's this about you being Commander of the Dark Blades?"

Taryn lounged on the couch. "We're a thousand strong, mostly warriors. Those who need us can hire us. There are places that are too small to have their own knighthood or army. They can hire mine. Sometimes we briefly add to one that already exists. We're often the ones with the most dangerous or important job, like protecting a royal family. We're the most elite."

Matt noticed that she said this with pride but not brag-gadocio. She seemed comfortable with who she was, au-thority exuding from her. "You're its leader."

Taryn nodded. "From the start. It was my idea."

A formidable woman. And out of his league. No won-der she didn't feel threatened. "All humans? Any women besides you?"

"Mostly men, but we have elves and dwarves among us."

"So then you must act nobly or no elves, at least, would be with you."

"Did you doubt that?"

"Not really. Are your Dark Blades here?"

"Only a few. I've been here often since the Champions supposedly returned. It was my idea to summon them when they weren't returning after quests. It seems I am responsible for you being pulled away from your world this time."

He felt glad for the information. "You could not have known."

Her eyes narrowed. "You said you are not a wizard on Earth, but I cannot tell what it is you do. I seldom meet a man I cannot understand."

He smirked. "Do you like a mystery? Spoiling it by tell-ing you might have you lose interest in me."

She looked him directly in the eye. "Nothing is going to make me lose interest in you."

Matt flushed a little and tried not to show it. She was too alert to, well, everything, and he knew what Eric meant about how talking with her was like playing chess. He would lose. He returned her direct look, not bothering to hide his attraction; she could think what she liked of it. Pursuing her wasn't something he felt would work any-way—for any number of reasons, including her being out of his league, him being awful at flirting, and there being far more important things on his mind. If she wanted him by some miracle, she knew how to find him and likely exactly what to do with him. And he felt certain she would take what she desired if that came to pass. It wasn't like Matt was going to say no. The thought brought some humor to his eyes and, to his surprise, she seemed to flush a little.

"I am not a wizard on Earth," he admitted. "Life is very different there." He paused, not sure how to explain something like computers. Saying he was a software developer wasn't going to make any sense. He spent a while trying to describe modern life, using objects like a wagon to say how they had become machines called cars—and that these didn't need horses, but something dug up from the earth to run. His description of gasoline, as poor as it was, had her wondering if it was a magic potion, and he struggled not to overexplain anything. He avoided mentioning airplanes in case they sounded too unplausible. He didn't want her to think he was lying. Through it all, Taryn was fascinated. He'd never had someone hang on his every word like this. At times she seemed to doubt him anyway, but he always had an answer to her questions, and those led to more so that he spoke in depth about Earth.

Finally, she said, "Well, you are either the most fantastic liar I've ever known, or you speak the truth."

By now, he had taken a place near her on the couch. She got off the arm of it to sit beside him, turning so that one calf was on it as she faced him. Sensing her conclusion, he asked, "Which do you think?"

"You're no liar. So, I was right that you were not a wizard before this began. You work with these devices, computers you called them. I am all the more impressed that you have succeeded on your quests."

"I learn quickly. Lorian trained me on the first quest. He knew we were imposters and helped us." Matt briefly recounted their experience with the elf Lorian, who had known the real Champions and learned the truth about him and the others and their situation. "I've done okay since then, but I really need more training. There is no time on a quest, and none between quests. There is no one to teach me on Earth and I do not have access to anything I would need."

She leaned forward, scrutinizing him before nodding. "I will see to it that something is done about this."

"I would be very grateful for that."

"I am impressed that you have survived this long."

He confessed, "I am able to control your brother's staff very well. I rely on it to draw power, to control it, and even to help me decide what magic to do. I may not be able to cast a fireball spell, but I can summon fire from the staff."

She appeared to think for a moment before patting his leg and rising for the decanter, refilling both goblets before sitting again. "Well, I certainly want to know more about you, but I really brought you here to see what you know about my brother. You have concerned me."

"I'm afraid that anything else I tell you will only worsen your concerns."

"Tell me."

He wasn't sure where to begin, but said, "He had a dark elf working for him on Honyn. The elf was spying on us and we caught him. Soliander killed him through a communication orb so that the elf couldn't talk to us." He saw that all of this took her aback.

"You are certain?"

"Yes. He also killed the wizard who had stolen the scroll, the one that revealed the location of soclarin ore. It was a trap. I assume actions these are out of character for him?"

Eyes troubled, she nodded. "Do you have any sense of what would make him do these things?"

"He is searching for Everon. That much I know."

"Aren't we all," she muttered, frowning. "You know who he is?"

"Yes. Eriana told us and I began to remember from Soliander's memories. He was Soliander's apprentice. He is the one who trapped the Champions in the cycle of unwanted quests, which were originally voluntary. My sense is that Soliander wants revenge. He also believes that Andier, Korrin, and Eriana are dead, and that Everon is ultimately responsible."

"That would explain it," she said. "He was never very forgiving. And he has a volcanic temper. But to kill others who get in his way is not like him."

Matt asked, "What can you tell me about him? I'm not sure if it would help, and he's your brother, so I understand not wanting to, uh, betray his confidence to me. He sees us as enemies, I think. Well, I'm not really sure what he sees us as, but given that he attacked us..."

She waved him off. "No, it's okay. I don't know what would help you."

There was something he'd been wanting to know for two months. "How would he view the four of us impersonating the Champions?"

"Good question. He would understand that you are trapped, too, like they were. He should be sympathetic, not upset with you. Honestly, he was the most upset about the whole thing. I know he felt responsible for it because Everon was his apprentice and betrayed him, and did this to them. I don't understand why he would attack the four of you or be after you in any way."

"Maybe he just wants information?"

"Yes, that could be it. He is keen on knowing as much as he can. He may be wondering what you know of him.

Oh. I know a reason. He knows you have a copy of his staff now, and he'd be wanting that back." She chuckled.

Matt watched her, unsure what to make of that. "Was that an understatement? Is that why you laughed?"

"Yes. I'm sorry, Matt. But I'm afraid you are a big target for him."

"Great. That's just what I need."

"Maybe I should stay with you, to protect you."

Matt smirked. "I got away from him the first time."

She shook her head. "You won't a second. Trust me. You caught him by surprise. He'll be prepared for you next time. If he catches sight of you..."

"You think you would be able to stop him? Reason with him?"

She nodded. "Yes. He would never harm me and has always listened to me."

He sensed that that was true from the memories, but still asked, "You are certain? My sense is that he has changed."

"It's a chance I would be willing to take. If he has committed himself to evil, he knows that I more than anyone else would come after him. I would spank him senseless."

A memory of her spanking her younger brother's bare red butt as a boy popped into his head. His eyes widened. Then he laughed. Nothing took the intimidation out of Soliander like that memory.

Seeming amazed and amused, Taryn asked, "Did you just remember a spanking I gave him?" Matt nodded. "What other memories of me do you have in there?"

He shrugged as, a montage of her and Soliander as children drifted through his mind. The one that stood out was of Soli walking in on a nude, teenage Taryn, who didn't bother to cover herself before she made him leave. Matt blushed furiously, eyes darting to her breasts and away. She arched an eyebrow, then smiled.

"Well, now you're making me curious," she teased.

"Let's change the subject. Do you have any idea why he wouldn't come home?"

Taryn pursed her lips. "I really don't. I haven't had a chance to think about it. It could be guilt if he thinks the others were dead. Maybe he doesn't want to answer questions; he was never interested in explaining himself much. He likely didn't want to face the families. Some of it is trying to get revenge on Everon, I'm sure. Keeping everyone from knowing he's back makes that easier. Everon may come out of hiding if he thinks Soliander is dead. There could be a lot of reasons."

Matt nodded. "Yeah, it makes sense."

"Can you tell why he hasn't come home?"

"No. I have memories, but not the thoughts that led to them. While I can sometimes see what happened, I can't understand why unless the reason is part of the memory. I also can't tell the order of memories. It makes it harder to make sense of them."

"Maybe it's not as useful as I was thinking."

"Yeah. But it has its moments." He pictured her nude again without meaning to and flushed.

She smirked knowingly. "I always wondered if Soli remembered that. Now I know."

He began to laugh. She was way too astute, but he liked it. Trying to change the subject, he asked, "Since Soliander went missing, have you tried to go to his home?"

"Yes. Couldn't get in." She eyed him curiously. "Can you tell why?"

Knowing that this was a test, he thought for a moment. "I'm not remembering anything, if that's what you're asking. But I assume he has magical protections there." As he said it, something occurred to him. "I have the staff. It got me past spells of his before on Honyn. I think... yes, it can get me by some of them. I remember them now."

She leaned forward. "You're certain?"

"Yes. I would remember more if we were there. Seeing things can trigger a memory."

She appeared to consider that. "Then maybe we should go. But I'm not sure what point there is, since we know he isn't there. I had wanted to go before to find some sign of him."

"There might still be things to see, though he isn't there anymore. He doesn't live there. We want to see all the Home Rings to see if there's anything different about them now, but we would need... well, no, the memories just came back. I can remember what they looked like before they disappeared."

"You wanted someone who already knew what they had looked like before. You think they have changed?"

He shrugged. "We don't know. We're just trying to figure out where Korrin and Andier might be, if they need help, or if they would be able to help us. We have some idea what happened with the quest on Earth to break them out of the cycle."

She rose to refill her goblet. "Tell me about that. You only touched on it before." Bringing the decanter, she filled their cups.

Matt saw no reason not to tell her, so he explained about the quest that brought the Ellorian Champions to Earth. The part they had left out before was Morgana's threat to all life—and that the only way Merlin could stop her was to stop magic from working, which was why he cast the spell to drain magic from Earth and into the fae world. The last of the magic lay in a pendant that, if returned to Stonehenge, would undo his spell. Magic would return.

Morgana had a vision of the Champions. She modified Stonehenge to act like a Quest Ring and summoned them to her time frame, a thousand years ago. Their quest was to undo Merlin's spell before it finished draining the magic, by returning the pendant to Stonehenge, but they refused once they learned the danger she posed. When Soliander realized that they could break free of the quest cycle by letting Merlin's spell finish, they decided to let it happen but use the last of Earth's magic to send themselves home at the last moment. The resulting explosion sent him back as expected, but there had been no sign of Korrin or Andier—and Eriana did not arrive in the present in Coreth, but twenty years ago on Earth.

In the thousand years since, the pendant somehow made its way to Anna—who unwittingly brought it to Stonehenge with Matt, Ryan, and Eric while on vacation in Europe—and Merlin's spell was undone. Moments later, a wizard on Honyn tried to summon the Ellorian Champions, and somehow they appeared in the Champions' place. They'd been stuck in the same unwanted cycle of quests ever since.

"That sounds too extraordinary to be invented," Taryn admitted.

Matt nodded. "We only know these things from Eriana. That reminds me. I have a favor to ask."

"Name it."

"Anna would like to talk to Eriana's brother and the princess from Coreth, to tell them more about the life Eriana has lived on Earth these past two decades."

"I'll arrange it."

"Thank you."

She watched him. "I appreciate your honesty. I can tell that you are telling me the truth. There are those who say honest people are weaker because they can be known and therefore manipulated. There is a wisdom to this—but honesty is still a quality I admire and respect. You would do well to learn more duplicity, as much as I hate to suggest that. It will just help you protect yourself. But in lieu of that, you have my sword at your disposal, should you need it. I am confident that you will soon be free here in Andor and I will have the pleasure of removing that device from your head."

Matt held her gaze and lifted his goblet as if to toast, feeling a little tipsy. "To those having the strength to do what's right."

Taryn smiled and raised hers. "To those having the strength to do what's right."

Then they drank.

CHAPTER FIVE

NEW FRIENDS,
OLD FRIENDS

When Matt returned later that afternoon, he filled in Anna, Eric, and Ryan, who thought he'd done a good job with Taryn. Ryan had removed his gambeson in favor of a gold tunic and tights they had brought him. Before long, they were served dinner in their suite, which they weren't allowed to leave for the rest of the day. It was just as well. Since the quests began, they'd become used to having too much excitement at once—but it was still fatiguing. They talked over their situation for a bit,

First came a frank talk about whether Anna could trust one of the boys in bed with her. She was the one to casually raise the subject, for while two of the guys could fit into the other bed, one would need to sleep on the floor unless he joined her. She didn't want someone getting sore or a poor night's rest. She trusted them all they all decided to act like adults. She chose for Matt to join her without explanation.

In the morning, Taryn made good on her promise to get Anna an audience with Eriana's brother and the Princess of Coreth, whom Anna told everything she knew about the priestess. The hardest part was explaining that Eriana had lived for twenty years on Earth because the quest had taken her a thousand years into the past, and when Soliander broke the quest, she was hurled almost to the right timeline, just two decades short. Anna told them that Eriana hadn't known about the time issue. She'd thought the quest to Earth was in the present, that it had hurled her forward nearly a thousand years, and that therefore everyone she knew was dead. Her brother and princess took this hard, empathizing with Eriana's apparent loss and how relieved she must have been to learn the truth from the new Champions. From this reaction, Anna knew that they were good people, and they were grateful to her for giving Eriana this peace of mind. She came away from the meeting certain they had become allies.

She returned to their suites to find Matt burying his nose in a spellbook. Taryn had tried to get Soliander's for him but been denied, so she'd obtained another one. The others were reading scrolls or other books about the world. Ryan was learning about the kingdoms of the Champions—Andor, Roir, and Aranor—and Novell, the one with the Quest Ring. His studies included histories and heraldry. Eric was looking into street-smart information like the cost of goods, which organizations were respected or feared, and local customs.

Shortly after lunch in their rooms, Ryan sent word to Prince Dari that he would like to meet. He provided a reason at Eric's suggestion. The true motive was to learn more about Dari's bad attitude toward them and whether it could be mitigated, but that wasn't the kind of thing he could admit. One story they discussed—claiming to want help in understanding Korrin's role. That would allow them to bring honor to the family by behaving as expected. But they wondered if this would backfire. Afterall, it meant continuing to impersonate Korrin instead of admitting the truth, and Dari already seemed angry about the ruse.

"Maybe I should just challenge him to a duel," Ryan joked in frustration. "*That* he would accept."

Eric laughed. "He might. But seriously, saying you want to apologize won't work. I'm not sure insulting his ego in some way would either. Maybe you could ask his opinion on what would happen when, not if, we admit to not being the Champions—and how we can minimize the problems this causes for his family. I think we need to seem like friends who want to help, not like a threat. He views us as enemies now, I'm sure."

They all agreed and sent a messenger, who returned so quickly with a refusal that they felt the strength of Dari's scorn. Undeterred, they asked Korrin's sister, Princess Cariss, the same question and received an equally quick invitation for Ryan to join her in her rooms, with two of the King's Guard present at all times. She brimmed with curiosity while greeting him, and accepted his suggestion to walk around the palace as they spoke. This gave him the chance to know more about their location, and possibly into life in Andor.

At first, he had little opportunity to ask anything because her questions came so quickly. Like Matt, he steered clear of subjects that might invite disbelief—but he told her about being from a wealthy family like her, hoping to of creating a bond. He sensed that Cariss was kindhearted and sympathetic, so he even confessed to the once deeply-held secret that he had accidentally paralyzed his younger brother Daniel in childhood.

"And healers could do *nothing*?" she asked, seeming wounded by the idea. He'd already noticed that she wore her heart on her sleeve. That he liked her apparent innocence made it easy to connect with her. Her presence was as warming as the morning sun streaming in through floor-to-ceiling windows in the galleries where they walked. Outside, he saw the bustling city streets and badly wanted to go there for a stroll instead of here, but it would have to wait. And likely never happen. One of these days they would get to do a quest that involved spending time in a big settlement, instead of in the wilderness fighting monsters or worse.

"Nothing to make him walk again. He is bound to a wheelchair," Ryan added, explaining what that meant.

"I can see why you devote yourself to him. This speaks very well of you. I would do the same, giving up my life to make amends. Well, more to ease the suffering I had caused."

"Are you close with your brothers?" Ryan asked, fishing for details of family dynamics. They rounded a corner and ascended wide steps toward a room full of portraits.

"Yes, both of them. They are not close with each other, however. Dari has always resented Korrin, and it is easy to see why. Everyone admires Korrin, who became a knight like our father, exceeding him in every way. Dari refused even to train as a knight because he rightly knew he wouldn't match Korrin's prowess."

"Korrin is older?" They had stopped at a painting of the family, which he only knew from recognizing everyone except the man he impersonated. They did look alike, except that Korrin's portrait bore a confidence Ryan had never felt. Now he at least knew what the man looked like. He would get the others here before long to see him. A world without photographs made it hard to know who anyone was unless you met them personally. Maybe there was a portrait of the Champions around here somewhere. He hadn't personally seen Soliander, so only Matt knew what he looked like. And no one had any idea about Andier. They could bump into him and not know it.

"Yes," Cariss answered. "I am second. Dari is third. He is so sensitive to comparisons that I cannot even call him my little brother without vexing him. I am not surprised that he refused to see you, much to his shame. That is the trouble with him. He acts in ways others cannot admire, then resents their disapproval—and so he continues to act that way out of spite, or resentment."

Ryan had heard of such cyclical behavior. "A feedback loop. That's what we call it on Earth. I wanted to ask you something. Your brother seems very upset with us, and I understand that we have been impersonating Korrin and the others and that this could upset everyone, but I felt like there was more there. By contrast, Soliander's sister has been open to the idea that we are not simply villains."

Princess Cariss nodded. She described how Dari had been overshadowed by their brother, then freed of that with Korrin's disappearance, and finally felt apprehensive about his return. But she said she didn't know how to interpret his reaction to Ryan and the others.

"I don't think he is disappointed that Korrin didn't appear," she admitted. "I suspect he's not sure how to react to you. You have, through no fault of yours, introduced uncertainty to all of us—but his fortunes, or what he believes to be his fortunes, are more affected."

"In what way? Does he feel that Korrin's return would be bad for him?" By now they had moved toward a balcony they stepped onto for a view of the port.

"I am certain he does. He felt invisible before. Then he didn't, until today. Even the idea of Korrin returning has sent him into turmoil. He is not sure what to wish for, I think."

Ryan observed, "So then maybe he would be interested in helping us understand Korrin's whereabouts? At the least, it would remove his uncertainty."

She beamed at him and laid a hand on his arm. "Yes!"

"The best way for him to do that is to help us understand what might've happened to Korrin."

"How could he do that?"

"We know Soliander purposely didn't come home. Er-iana was trapped. Is there any reason to believe Korrin would not have come home if he could?"

"No. None at all. He would be here. Of that I am certain."

"I am hoping to see his Home Ring in case that gives us any ideas. We understand that the return spell was bound to the Home Rings and that something clearly went wrong."

She perked up. "Yes! You must see it. Something has happened to it, and we have long feared what that could mean."

Princess Cariss took his hand and led him back toward Korrin's suite, not far from hers, as the guards followed. Her touch was gentle, her hands smooth, and they reinforced the impression that she was quite the opposite of Taryn. He wondered if she had ever set foot outside the palace at all, not to mention by herself. She seemed to live in a protected environment—not on account of the guards, who were there because of him, but because she seemed oddly unworldly. Was her life all courtly gossip and unimportant issues? It didn't matter much, but he kept thinking the real world would eat her alive. Rather than finding that contemptible, he thought that she was charming in a naïve sort of way. He felt a little protective of her and wondered if that was how her brothers saw her. Were they overly protective? Was that the reason for her seemingly untarnished innocence?

They soon arrived at a pair of double doors bearing the carving of a knight on horseback charging a dragon. A lone guard stood there and let them into a large suite.

"Is the room always guarded?" Ryan asked, unsurprised that their escort continued to follow them. Only now did he realize they were protecting the princess from him more than preventing him from going anywhere. He frowned and wondered what he needed to do to convince them he wasn't the sort to attack a woman.

Princess Cariss answered, "Yes, on account of the Home Ring. Sometimes people are curious. You might think that anyone admitted to the royal palace would be on their best behavior, but the number of boors among the aristocracy is rather high. Even without a drink in them, some take a fancy to seeing Korrin himself, or his armor, or the ring."

"It was guarded before he disappeared."

"Yes. Come. Let me show you."

She explained that they had turned an adjacent room into Korrin's Quest Room, where he kept armor, weapons, and other items he might need for a quest. And, of course, his Home Ring was in there. She led him to the wide doors and pushed them open. Beyond lay a knight's armory—rows of lances and spears on one wall, various swords, maces, hammers, flails, and other weapons hanging from another. On armor racks stood several suits of armor, seemingly one of every kind: plate armor, plate mail, chain mail, leather armor, studded armor, and more. A wall of shields hung behind them. Bows, arrows, and accessories filled cases around the room, and in the center stood the Home Ring.

The circle spanned eight feet in diameter and bore similar rune carvings to each Quest Ring Ryan had seen, magic words presumably lighting when used. He wondered whether they glowed blue like Quest Rings or another color. While parquet formed the palace floor here, they had fashioned the ring of white marble with gold markings. A matching wall two feet high surrounded it and had to be stepped over to get inside. Altogether, the circle seemed simple enough in construction. What caught his eye was the long, jagged crack across the floor of it and up the wall, then around from the inside, over the top, and partway around the outside. Marble dust was visible on the floor outside the ring, and black scorch marks followed the crack. A chunk of stone had broken off and fallen inside the circle.

"I assume it wasn't always damaged like this."

She shook her head. "At first, when Korrin disappeared as he always did, we thought nothing unusual of it, but sometime later the guard out front heard a cracking sound and came inside to find this."

"It hasn't been touched since?"

"No. This was our first sign that something was wrong. Before long, when he still didn't return, we asked Princess Alia about Eriana and learned she hadn't been seen in Coreth either. Inquiries were made about Andier and Soliander, though they were more difficult to learn about. But it soon became apparent they were also gone. We have left Korrin's Home Ring untouched. What do you think it means?"

"I don't know. We were hoping to see each of the Home Rings and compare them. Maybe that will suggest something."

"Like what?"

Ryan pursed his lips. He didn't want to admit the logical conclusion—that if Korrin's and Andier's Home Rings were damaged and they were missing, and if Soliander's and Eriana's were intact and they lived, that might imply something he didn't want to say.

"We honestly don't know. Do you know the condition of the others?"

"Not Soliander's. No one can reach his. But Eriana's is damaged as well, split in two I believe. Andier's is blackened as if burnt, but not cracked. That's just one more reason we've been concerned these past years—but we've also wondered whether they were unable to return home because of the damage. We had hoped that this was the explanation, but it seemed unlikely."

"Why?"

"Soliander is powerful enough to send all of them home even without using the Quest Rings. We had wondered if he was hurt or killed. Now we know it is not true. I wish I understood why he has not returned."

"So do we." Ryan walked around the Home Ring to see it from all angles. "I have wondered what these things looks like."

She arched her eyebrows. "You don't have... Oh, I hadn't thought of that." Something seemed to occur to her. "How do you get home? The Quest Ring returns you, but to where?"

"To wherever we were before being summoned."

"Oh. That makes sense. I think." She did seem to be mulling that over, and he waited quietly. "But what if you were on a quest just completed, and another quest summoned you? You would be sent back to the last quest, would you not? You could be sent somewhere unfavorable."

He hadn't thought of that. "We don't know. We haven't had two quests back-to-back, but we *have* been sent back in circumstances that were a problem."

She frowned. "How so?"

He took a deep breath and explained about how they'd been stranded at Stonehenge after the first quest, as three weeks had passed and their transportation had been taken in the meantime. When she seemed sympathetic, he decided to tell her what happened to Anna—being returned in the middle of a highway and being struck by a car and paralyzed—all while skipping over details about what a car really was. With no healers available, Anna had remained in that condition until the next summoning spell healed her. Princess Cariss got the point anyway and was horrified, tears in her blue eyes.

"Will this happen when you leave *here*?" she asked, taking his hand in both of hers.

Feeling a pang at her distress, he shook his head. "No. No, we were asleep in a friend's home. We will be safe this time."

Barely relieved, she asked, "But what of the next time?"

He shrugged. "It could happen again. It's one reason we'd really like to know how to create our own Home Rings, as long as we're substituted for the real Champions."

She dropped his hand to take both his cheeks in hers. "You poor man! All of you! I will speak to my father about this." Then suddenly she gave him a hug that he couldn't have returned even if he thought that was wise, both his arms pinned to his sides by hers.

"Step away from her!" a voice shouted.

Ryan turned to see a glaring Prince Dari striding toward him with several more guards behind, hands on their sword hilts. He frowned and didn't move as Cariss pulled back and turned to her brother.

"Hands weren't *on* her," remarked Ryan, irritated. He didn't like this guy. Besides, he had another source of information and help. Who needed this assclown?

"Dari!" protested Cariss. "Do not speak this way to our guest."

Ignoring that, the prince scowled at Ryan. "You do not have the king's permission to be in this room, or anywhere but confined to your quarters."

"The princess invited me. Perhaps if you had not turned down my invitation to talk, you would not be so quick to find fault."

Dari frowned. But before he could speak, his sister put both hands on his chest and loudly announced, "You are embarrassing me with your boorish behavior. Step out of these rooms at once, and take your guards with you. We were having a fine time getting acquainted until you decided to play the hero."

Ouch, thought Ryan in amusement, wondering what she was talking about. Maybe she was made of sterner stuff than he had realized. Dari looked startled, then embarrassed, and finally angry. He turned a hate-filled gaze on Ryan, who wasn't sure how to react. Part of him wanted to goad the guy, but he also suspected that wouldn't be wise. He silently stood his ground.

"You've shown him enough," the prince said. "Until we verify his story—and even after that—they are not to be treated as guests, but prisoners. Rectify this at once." Without waiting for a rebuttal, he turned and left.

Princess Cariss waited until the footsteps faded away, then turned to Ryan. She pursed her lips. "I'm afraid you have made an enemy of him, though I agreed with your response in its entirety." She smiled. "We will worry about him later. Don't concern yourself. I will talk directly with our parents to make sure he doesn't lie about what happened here today. He is known to be subjective and is unlikely to be believed if his details differ from mine."

Ryan bowed his head. "Thank you. I sincerely appreciate that. I regret what just happened and wish there was some way to be friends with him."

She smirked. "Sadly, he is not known for having friends. I suspect you can see why." Ryan decided not to reply, and she added, "Would you be so kind as to join me for dinner? I would love to learn more about you and your friends. In fact, they are invited as well. I will make some arrangements."

Ryan smiled at her. "Yes, we would love that."

She beamed at him again. "Wonderful! I look forward to it." She turned to the guards. "Please escort him back and inquire as to whether they need anything. I expect their needs to be met as if they were my own."

The guards nodded and turned to go but paused at the door to wait for Ryan. He bowed to Princess Cariss from the waist, wearing a big grin. "My lady."

"Sir Ryan," she replied, smiling fondly.

He walked away feeling lighter on his feet. She was certainly pleasant company, but the important part was that he felt certain they had at least one friend in the court. Seeing Korrin's Home Ring had also resolved a mystery, and he suddenly realized how much he disliked the ignorance that came with their situation. Information reassured him like never before. His only worry now was that the certainty that he, if not the rest of them, had an enemy in Prince Dari.

But at least Dari's enmity wouldn't come as a surprise.

<hr />

Not for the first time, Anna wondered how things were going back on Earth. Their friend Jack was supposed to be working with Eriana, Ryan's brother, and Ryan's family lawyer to find and purchase an estate for them to stay in. The media and authorities were always trying to track them down, compromising their privacy. But they needed somewhere to live—and seldom, if ever, leave –so that they no longer had to worry about being returned to a highway like she had been. The real Champions had Home Rings that they were sent back to after a quest, but she and the boys did not. Staying at the estate all the time, they would never be traveling when summoned. It would be a kind of prison, but better safe than dead. It would also allow them to practice swordsmanship, archery, or even magic when Matt could tap into Earth's awakening energies.

She wondered what could free them from their current predicament. No one, including the lovely Princess Cariss, could tell them what was happening. People seemed eager to verify their story, but there was no word on how that was being done. She knew that word spread of each quest, so it seemed plausible that inquiries had been made on each of the three worlds they had visited before. But how long did this take? Whose word would their hosts accept as proof that they were innocent victims and not perpetrators who had done something to the real Ellorian Champions?

And then, just after lunch, the answer strode right into their suite. An elf with long, blond hair soundlessly appeared, his brown leather embossed with forest designs. A bearded dwarf tromped beside him in boots, clanking with each step as his armor and a hammer at his waist made a racket. Behind them waited Taryn, Princess Cariss, and the King's Guard.

Anna jumped to her feet as her friends rose. "Lorian! Rognir!"

"Aye, lass!" said the dwarf, his voice gruff but friendly. "It's good to see you still in one piece!"

The elf Lorian smiled and looked ready to bow in greeting, but Anna ran to him and gave him a big hug, noticing he still smelled like the wilderness. She disengaged to see Rognir approach Ryan and look up at the big guy.

"You didn't come to hug my knees, did you?" Ryan asked with a grin, resuming an old joke about the difference in their heights.

The dwarf bellowed, "A quick blow to the back of those wobbly knees and you'd be down where I can give you a proper greeting!"

Anna noticed that both Eric and Matt were grinning, too. If there was anyone they trusted when away from Earth, it was these two, who had shepherded them along their first quest to the Dragon Gate and taught them so much that their gratitude could never be properly expressed. And now here they were, saving them again, which became apparent with their next words.

Lorian began, "The King of Andor sent word to my king that you were here. Of course, only a few of us on Honyn know you are not the Ellorian Champions. We were asked for an account of your identities, your character, and the story you had told us. Rognir happened to be visiting, so instead of simply replying, the king sent us. We have just finished meeting with King Sarov and a few others and have shared what we know."

Taryn interrupted, "We also received messages—not about your identities, but about your handling of quests—from the other worlds you have helped. You are heroes regardless of your situation, even in spite of it."

A beaming Princess Cariss came forward. "On behalf of our families, please accept our apologies for your confinement. You are no longer to be under guard and have the free run of the palace grounds as our honored guests. We also recognize that you have not pretended to be the Ellorian Champions out of malice. You are innocent victims of the villain Everon as much as they were, maybe even more so. To this end, we are united in our desire to help you in any way we can."

An audible sigh of relief filled the room, and a celebratory mood took hold. They soon decided to spend several days on Elloria. They had no pressing business back on Earth, and this was the safest they had felt since the whole questing business began. Within an hour, each was given their own rooms for additional privacy. They were adjacent to each other and in a less-used wing of the palace. Lorian and Rognir received nearby quarters, and they cleared out a hall to use as a weapons training area and meeting room, far enough away from others not to be overheard.

Lorian and Rognir intended to stay until the Earth friends returned home, mostly to lend a hand with training. The dwarf was a priest and spent time chatting with Anna, giving her more ideas about how gods could help her when channeling power through her. She had learned on a recent quest that she could not only heal people, but also hurt and even destroy the undead. Being a weapon wasn't something she really wanted—but if it turned the tide of battle in their favor, so be it. It seemed like a long time ago that she didn't believe in gods, the atheist in her quieting as proof of divinity mounted. Her new occupation was humbling but inspiring and she still felt great curiosity about interacting with the god of Earth, whom she had finally reached right before this quest. She still had more work to do there, she knew. Eriana would help once they were reunited.

Lorian once again assisted Matt with magic training. Since no one now thought Matt was Soliander, the Majestic Magus and one of the most powerful wizards anywhere, this could be more openly pursued. Taryn was able to retrieve her brother's spellbooks and staff for him, but as a matter of secrecy, everyone agreed not to publicly use anything belonging to the real Champions. They were to admit only to their real names and origin. This meant Matt could not use Soliander's recognizable staff, nor could Ryan or Eric wear Korrin's or Andier's armor or weapons. Taryn took it upon herself to secure new items, and, for the first time, Ryan and Eric felt they had their own equipment.

That reminded that that they couldn't bring anything back to Earth with them. No one understood why this was, but it may have had something to do with not having Home Rings, and their substitution being some sort of seemingly permanent accident. So they started talking about someone traveling to Earth, which held multiple advantages. Spellbooks and needed materials could be brought for Matt. Training could take place at home. Help could also be there if Soliander or anyone else showed up to cause trouble—in fact, Taryn even suggested that her force of Dark Blades make the journey and guard this new estate. Of course, they weren't aware that men and women with guns were needed, not swords. But that raised the subject that several of them—Taryn, Lorian, and Rognir—were deeply curious about Earth and wanted to visit. But first, someone had to know how to find Earth to travel there.

"There is a spell," said Lorian, as they gathered in their new meeting space—just the four Earth friends, elf, and dwarf. "It can be used to locate worlds, but we need something from them, usually."

"Like what?" Anna asked, worried that this doomed their chances. "We can't bring anything with us on a quest, any more than we can take something back."

The elf smiled. "A drop of blood from one of you could do it."

Matt frowned. "That makes sense."

Anna remembered how squeamish Matt was about blood. The same had been needed for the magic affinity test Lorian had conducted on him back on Honyn.

The elf said, "We should first try to locate the world that way. If it works, we can try to connect a magic portal to the world. We could then travel there without the locator spell."

Eric pursed his lips. "I certainly trust you, Lorian, to come to Earth. But I do wonder about setting a precedent by opening the planet to visitors from other worlds. Would others be able to locate Earth once that happened?"

"There are other spells that would allow one to locate a planet. It is just difficult to do so without something from that planet. Someone may have already located Earth."

Matt said, "Earth was locked for a thousand years so that magic wouldn't work, but that ended when we took the Champions' place. We know that Soliander might have an interest in finding us, and he knows we're from Earth. I hadn't considered an inability to find the planet, but what if he got our DNA from something on the Honyn quest?"

"DNA?" Rognir asked, puffing on a pipe, the sweet-smelling smoke pleasant. No one seemed to know about secondhand smoke or the dangers of smoking at all.

Anna began, "Each of us has DNA in our hair, blood, and more. It can be used to identify someone because DNA is unique to each person. If Soliander had blood or hair from one of us, he could theoretically locate Earth and go there."

The elf nodded. "I think we need to try ourselves. It is all the more reason to have friends there, ones who understand your situation. I would like to research the spell and gather what we need. It shouldn't take long."

In agreement, the others watched him and Rognir go. Left alone, they discussed Eric's point. Did they have the right to bring people from other planets to Earth? What if Lorian brought a pathogen that infected people and caused widespread sickness? In fact, why hadn't they caused such sickness on the worlds they visited? But Matt had the answer from Soliander's memories. All spells that traversed worlds inoculated those using them. It was like getting a flu shot so that, even if you carried the virus, you weren't contagious. Skilled healers had helped to invent or modify world-crossing spells, and even spells for magical travel between any two points on the same planet. There had been mayhem before that.

All the same, they agreed to limit the number of people visiting Earth. Rognir could pass for a short person, but Lorian would have to hide his ears. Neither were going to fit in at first, and they would likely gawk at everything for a time. This resulted in some tension-breaking jokes about elves in space, or both of them getting addicted to afternoon soap operas. Or coffee. But the seriousness returned when the elf did.

"I have everything we need," he said, laying a spellbook on a table, then flipping it to a spread, where elven script flowed across two pages. Pictures of worlds spinning, solar systems, and shooting comets lay among the words. The elf had once cast a permanent spell on all of them to let them read, write, and speak various common languages—so Matt and Anna, the only two who looked, were able to read the words. These were in either elvish or Nu'Eiro, the language of magic.

The spell indicated that it would only show the planet in its solar system, meaning it only proved a planet could be found. Since Matt was still squeamish about blood, Eric offered his finger, giving a drop of blood to the small mirror Lorian lay on the table. Then the elf cast the spell.

In the air before them, a kaleidoscope of galaxies flashed by while the spell searched for its target. Spiral, elliptical, and irregular, they spun in different colors like a computer animation from NASA. Finally, the familiar-looking Milky Way galaxy appeared as the searching slowed to focus on one of the swirling bands—into which it dove before soaring past the outer solar system, passing recognizable planets like Neptune, Saturn, and Jupiter. Soon, the spell stopped zooming as a blue planet rotated slowly before them.

"That's Earth!" Matt said, looking fascinated.

"You are sure?" Lorian asked.

"Of course. I'd recognize it anywhere. I don't suppose we can zoom in?"

Lorian arched an eyebrow and Anna explained, "He means getting a closer look."

"No. This is only for locating the world among the planets."

She asked, "What does it take to arrive in a particular spot, if you're casting yourself there?"

"Visualizing it is the best way. If you know what a place looks like, it is easy enough to arrive there."

Matt said, "Good. That's something we can do."

"Yes, but I cannot."

Matt asked, "Well, is there a way to give you memories without, you know, using that *Mind Trust* spell on me?"

The elf nodded. "There are spells that will allow you to show someone your memories."

Ryan asked, "Is this a current view of Earth?"

"Yes. Why?"

"I was just curious. We have devices back home that can store images, and I just wondered if the spell would work in a similar way, with an old image, but probably not."

Eric asked, "Now that we've located it this way, is it also possible to communicate with someone there? Every time we leave, no one knows where we went or what's going on. We don't have Home Rings, and if we could talk to someone there, we could tell them exactly when we would be arriving so they could be there to help. Maybe Matt could learn such a spell."

"That's brilliant," said Anna. Eric always had the best ideas and thought farthest ahead.

Lorian said, "It is possible to magically communicate across worlds. Is there anyone you would like to contact? We could arrange it."

"Jack."

Matt asked, "What is needed to contact a particular person?"

The elf said, "Without a communication orb, it is helpful to have something of theirs, but not necessary if you are certain where they will be."

Matt sighed. "We know where he lives but can't be sure when he'd be there. That would matter, I assume?" The elf nodded.

"Not true," said Eric. "We know we were asleep when summoned, though we don't know what time that was. Still, we can figure out the time of day there based on the time of day here."

They agreed to try reaching Jack. But first, Matt would learn the spell and try it the next morning when they knew Jack would be in the apartment asleep. Anna looked it over with Matt and saw that the only materials needed were those easy to find in a city or town, like glass to aid seeing to another world, water to aid a connection, and a bit of someone's blood to locate the planet. The rest would depend on his visualization and concentration. He spent some time picturing Jack's apartment in as much detail as he remembered, but since he had seldom been in the bedroom, Anna drew some pictures. She had been sleeping there the night of their summoning and had a fresher memory.

With this settled—and now that they felt the palace was safe—they went their separate ways until meeting back in their wing just before dinner. Anna asked Rognir for more time to study together and he agreed. Ryan sought out Princess Cariss, who introduced him to some knights. They believed him to be an aspiring one, so they agreed to teach him about not only weapons and armor, but chivalry and expectations. Matt worked with Lorian on magic. No one had any ideas for the Silver-Tongued Rogue, so Eric found himself alone and decided to see about getting into trouble.

CHAPTER SIX

PRINCES AND TROLLS

The trick to no one knowing what you were intending was to act like you were intending something else altogether. A bit of misdirection could do wonders. To that end, Eric strolled the palace halls and inquired about everywhere other than where he intended to go, as if he was just familiarizing himself with palace life. There was some truth to this, as his curiosity coupled nicely with a sense that such knowledge might benefit him and his friends. And so he learned where the kitchens and dining halls were, and whether jails were here (they weren't). He found out where the guests' quarters were and which parts of the palace were used and how often. Galleries of artwork were scattered throughout the palace, with servants answering questions about the people in each and their importance. He saw a portrait of the Ellorian Champions, and now knew what his counterpart looked like. They could have been brothers. Statues of one hero or another helped him learn about important figures from Andor's past. He noticed that one of the largest statues was one of the Dragon Slayer, Lord Korrin. What did his brother, Prince Dari, think of this? There was no statue of *him*.

Most people in the palace were human, but he now encountered several elves, dwarves, and even halflings in his wanderings. The latter seemed the friendliest and provided a wealth of information on recent happenings, from trade issues to gossip... including the rumor that the families of the Ellorian Champions had gathered for an unknown reason. Many people were chattering about it, and the consensus was that they were trying to understand why the heroes weren't returning home. Some people believed there had been a falling-out of some kind. Others thought the Champions were too busy with quests. One rumor even suggested that Eriana had married Korrin. Or Andier. Or Soliander. And started a family. That this didn't explain anything didn't seem to matter to anyone.

After two hours of walking around, Eric finally stepped from inside the palace onto the grounds. He had been told not to leave, but he didn't consider this a departure, as the U-shaped building enclosed this garden. Here he found a few lords and ladies but more servants than anyone, as they tended the grounds. The four-story building cast much of the garden into shadow, a few small towers extending higher into the sky from the golden roof.

He sat on a bench and observed those in attendance occasionally glancing up behind him at the path to his destination. It wouldn't be a difficult climb. The challenge was timing it so that no one shot him in the back with an arrow, but he saw no archers. Still, a private word with the person he sought would last longer if no guards appeared. It was time to make an impression on someone, an impression designed to create doubts as to whether screwing with him or his friends was wise.

His bench provided cover behind some of the taller manicured hedges and, by after he'd sat there for some time, it appeared that others nearby had largely forgotten him. They were also moving away on their business, whether that was gardening or exchanging gossip. The time had come, so he turned around, rose, and strode to the wall.

Clearly, the architect hadn't considered how easy it was to climb the exterior by placing various decorative stonework designs for Eric's use. Skirting the windows, it took less than thirty seconds to climb onto the fourth-floor balcony. He cast a quick glance at the garden below and felt satisfied that no one there had noticed, though someone looking through one of the many windows might have. With little to do about that, he cautiously stepped inside Prince Dari's rooms.

No one was there. This didn't surprise him—and it gave him a chance to look around, though there wasn't much to see except some maps spread on a table. He had long wondered about this planet, Elloria, since they were pretending to be people from here. The Kingdom of Andor lay on the western coast and seemed to be mostly grasslands except to the forested north, where a town called Elfton hinted at the origin of the elves he'd seen in town. Due east were several mountain ranges—the Hills of Andor, the Towering Peaks, and farther east, the Peaks of Aranor, beyond which lay the Kingdom of Aranor, on the eastern coast. Even on the map, the deserts there made it seem harsh, just like Soliander, the most famous person from Aranor.

South of the mountains lay the town of Coreth, Eriana's home. Only now did Eric fully realize that it wasn't a kingdom in its own right, just another place inside the Kingdom of Roir, whose capital lay farther south. This meant Andier and Eriana were from the same sovereign power. Knowing this would prevent him from making a mistake in conversation. He needed to hit the books again, having focused on the kingdoms of Andor and Roir so far.

He studied the map and then decided to fold up it up and take it. He likely could've gotten a copy, but stealing something trivial from the prince amused him. It would anger Dari without being important enough to throw him into prison. Besides, they were honored guests. While they

weren't invulnerable to getting in trouble, such petty irrita-
tions warranted nothing, and Dari complaining would only
make him seem more unreasonable and subjective. That
was part of Eric's plan—to reduce the esteem in which the
prince was held so that if he had planned to cause trouble
for them, he wouldn't be taken seriously. But what he really wanted was to goad the prince into being an ally. And
from what he'd seen and heard of the man, goading was
what it would take.

Map of the Kingdoms Andor, Roir, and Aranor

He moved about the suite, seeing a desk full of letters.
Some were scented in perfume and written in flowing
script. He scanned a few, seeing that most were from fawning admirers, but a few were less flattering, even rebuffing
him. Among the authors was a princess of Novell, the island kingdom they had arrived on. He wondered what sort
of arranged marriages took place here or if they even mattered for Dari. Maybe such things were on hold until Korrin's fate was known. With Korrin alive, his wife would
become queen, but with him dead, Dari's wife would be.
Other letters were from other lords, whether princes,
dukes, or lesser ranks. Some were nearly as fawning, oth-

ers bawdy, and several quite formal in tone. They revealed Dari's habits—card games, hunting, and the opera.

The rest of the suite held little interest—there were only a few swords that appeared ceremonial and showed no signs of wear on the hilts. Only one differed in that regard, but not by much. A closet full of shoes, tunics, hose, and even a few robes made him wonder which occasions called for what attire. He didn't see a suit of armor anywhere but suspected one existed and must have been elsewhere. A brief check for hidden doors or compartments yielded nothing. Dari seemed the sort to sneak around, especially in light of those letters. How many bastards had he fathered?

After half an hour, Eric grabbed a book on trade that appeared to be well-used and settled in at the map table with a decanter of wine. He poured a glass from it, not because he intended to drink, but to put on a show of making himself comfortable. To that end, he also put his feet up on the arm of another chair and did his best to look overly familiar. Nearly an hour passed before the doors to the suite opened, heeled footsteps sounded on the stone floor. Eric hefted the wine glass to his lips and tried to act like he was being interrupted as the steps neared and Prince Dari appeared, a smirk disappearing at the sight of him.

"How did you get in here?" the prince demanded, eyes darting around the room as if looking for trouble.

Eric gestured to the window. "No guards on the balcony. You might want to fix that. It appears anyone can get to you at any time, and you'd be defenseless."

The prince frowned and came closer so that only a few steps separated them. "I'm hardly defenseless. You're the one without a weapon." He put one hand on the dagger at his waist, an embroidered tunic of blue and white above his white hose and black shoes.

Eric slid one of the prince's own daggers out from under one of the maps. "You shouldn't leave weapons lying around, either. I took the liberty of rescuing this from the floor."

Dari frowned. "I should have the guards throw you off the balcony."

"If you were man enough, you'd do it yourself. But let's stop flirting with each other and get down to business. I surmised you wouldn't agree to meet with me, so I took matters into my own hands."

Not disputing that, the prince asked, "What do you want?"

Eric decided to get to the point. Chitchatting with the prince wasn't going to get him anywhere. "I want to know if we can count on your help while we're here on Andor, or when we return to Earth."

The prince snorted. "You've managed to get this far without it."

"Yes, you aren't necessary. You might even be useless. But what concerns me is that you might be a problem—yet another thing we must overcome to succeed at a quest, to escape from this cycle of them, or even to find your brother and Andier."

Dari's eyes had registered increasing outrage. "Watch your words, imposter."

"Is that the issue? You don't like us impersonating them?"

"Of course not. It is a crime, regardless of how you escaped punishment for it. It is also wrong."

Eric didn't disagree, but wasn't going to admit it. He and the others had discussed admitting they weren't the Champions on every quest more than once, and always arrived at the same conclusion—that it was safer to pretend they were such formidable people as a way to ward off additional trouble. It didn't always work. "Do you think it wiser to admit the truth? Most who know agree that we are safer with the ruse."

"I couldn't care less if you are safe or not."

"A charming sentiment. So I am right that you do not have our best interests at heart."

"My only interest is in the whereabouts of Korrin. You would—"

Eric purposely interrupted him. "Then our interests are shared. Your best way of finding him is to help us. No one thinks *you* have the ability to locate him."

Dari frowned. "You have no idea what I am capable of."

"Enlighten me." He had long been good at seeing through an empty boast, and when the prince looked startled and changed the subject, he smirked to show he knew it.

The prince asked, "What is it that you think you can do to locate Korrin? Eriana found *you*, as did Soliander."

"And you'll notice they both sought us, not you. Your brother would do the same. We are of greater interest to him than you, for obvious reasons." He purposely tried to imply that this was personal. Dari glowered, and Eric got the impression he'd struck a nerve.

"Nothing is more important to my brother than family—especially not *you*. He likely doesn't even know you exist."

"Maybe he's forgotten that *you* exist." Eric sipped some wine and made a face as if it wasn't good enough. That wasn't hard, given that he was more of a beer drinker.

Dari's face turned purple, and he snapped, "I am a Prince of Andor! Next in line to the throne!"

Eric had wondered about whether his older sister, Princess Cariss, was next in line, but one thing he'd learned was that such things changed with every kingdom. He said, "You're not next in line as long as Korrin lives. Is that the problem? Does he stand in your way, even while missing?"

Dari glowered. "You dare say such things?"

"Only with the confirmation of his death do you become heir-apparent, is that right? As long as he's missing, you don't know. If he's dead, you face one future you can prepare for. If he shows up, you can go back to living whatever life you had before his disappearance called your future into question. I would think you, of all people, would want to help us learn what has happened to him. What is Korrin's fate? What is yours? And yet you claim not to care what comes next. Explain that to me."

"I owe you *nothing.*"

"You don't. But you owe yourself some certainty. Aren't you tired of wondering? We can do everything without you. And maybe that's what you want—to stay comfortable here in your fine hose and tunic, drinking wine, dancing with ladies, playing cards, and watching the opera, while we go off into danger. And sooner or later, we'll hand you the answer to the question of your fate if we find Korrin. That's kind of weak, though, isn't it? To let us do it? How good a leader would you be as king if you can't be proactive and rise to a challenge? With that attitude, all of Andor must be praying for Korrin to be found safe. They'll still have a strong leader in him when your father is gone."

Eric decided to stop there, thinking he'd overdone it. But it had to be said. The prince's face had turned various colors, from white to red and back again.

"Listen to me," Dari began quietly, full of suppressed menace, one hand on his dagger, "do not ever call into question my desire to find my brother again. You dare spread rumors like this, and I will personally cut you in half."

More politely, Eric lied, "This is what people are already wondering. I only came to tell you so that you can prove them wrong. You can lose their faith, or you can renew it with a show of interest in finding your brother."

Dari sneered triumphantly. "No one knows who you supposedly are, so they won't care if I help you or not."

"They'll eventually know. We'll be famous once the truth gets out. And they'll find out you did nothing to help us, or even that you stood in our way. Whether Korrin is alive or not, your honor, integrity, and devotion to family will be questioned. Is that what you want?"

The prince's eyes hardened and he pursed his lips. Eric felt certain he had successfully cornered the man and it was time to go. He slowly rose, mindful of the prince's white knuckles on the dagger as he skirted him toward the door, where he stopped and looked back. The prince hadn't turned.

"I know what it is not to want this," he began, trying to sound like he commiserated. Part of him actually did— and he had long ago learned to sincerely embrace sentiments like this to get the reaction he wanted from his listeners. "I would rather stay home and live my life, but my choice has been taken from me. Yours has not. I know you can be a great asset to everyone, most of all yourself. I believe this is in you, even if no one else does. This may be the opportunity you have been waiting for—to show everyone you are a match for Korrin in bravery, honor, integrity, and more. You will face the consequences of your decision about helping us either way. The smarter play is to take command of your reputation and future rather than letting it command you. Should we need your help, I look forward to seeing you step up and do so as if it was your idea and not mine. Our little secret."

He opened the paneled doors and stepped out between two guards, who looked surprised to see him emerge instead of the prince. He nodded at them and was several steps away when the muffled sound of glass shattering came through the door amid cursing. He surmised that the decanter now lay in ruins. It was unfortunate. The wine wasn't half bad.

———— •··• ————

The next morning, Matt sat leafing through one of Soliander's two spellbooks, the one with gold lettering on its black leather surface. He had skimmed through the entire book more than once so that he knew most of what was in it, just not how to cast them. Practice was the only way to memorize them all—unless there was a spell for that, but he hadn't seen one. He seldom had time to study on the quests and could never bring the books back to Earth. The others liked to tease him that he was just being a geek, burying his nose in this book or the other all the time, but they all knew he needed to do it.

A messenger soon arrived to tell them that the Champions' siblings had invited them to breakfast, and that afterwards they would complete at least part of the quest. The dinner Princess Cariss had intended to arrange the night before hadn't happened. They escorted the four friends to a nearby private dining room used only by the royal family and their more personal guests. Soliander's sister Taryn, Eriana's brother Solun, and Korrin's brother and sister, Dari and Cariss, were the only ones present. Prince Dari glowered and his smiling sister excused his surliness, saying she had forced him to be there as a princely duty.

Dari frowned. "There are many duties of our station, dear sister, but this is not one of them."

Matt cleared his throat. "Don't take this the wrong way, but if you'd rather not join us, I see no reason you need to. With respect to Princess Cariss."

"He'll be fine," she replied, and Matt got the impression that she was forcing a smile out of awkwardness about her brother's behavior. "I almost wish Mandrellan were here to cast some sort of spell to improve your manners."

"Mandrellan?" Anna asked. "Who is he?"

"Her pet wizard," replied the prince. He recounted how Mandrellan had saved her life once, before snidely remarking, "Everyone is a hero around here."

Matt sensed that they were going to continue bickering and decided to change the subject. He looked to Taryn as he asked, "So we're only doing part of the quest today?"

Taryn nodded. "Yes. We will retrieve the dragon egg that is currently east of here and bring it to Andor for safe-keeping. When you are ready to return home, we will go to the Novell Kingdom, where the Quest Ring stands, to complete the quest—giving them back the egg. You can then go home from there."

Matt had wanted to try contacting Jack now with the spell, but it would have to wait. It wasn't urgent anyway. "What happened before summoning us for this quest?"

"This is not to leave this room," Taryn began, "for reasons that will become obvious. The blue dragons of Novell are sacred to that kingdom. Dragons don't lay eggs that often, but as a group there are always some every year. The dragons allow the people of Novell to know about new eggs due to the celebrations this causes, so word always spreads. Well, someone stole one of the eggs and they want it back."

"Do we know who?"

Taryn smiled. "Yeah. It was us." She let them absorb that before continuing. "We had to think of a quest in order to summon the Champions, but we didn't really have one, so we invented one."

Eric frowned. "How does that work? It has to be a valid quest."

"There is a way to fool the Quest Rings, and this isn't something you should go around telling people."

Matt nodded. The last thing they wanted was someone summoning them for quests they couldn't even achieve. From what they knew, each Quest Ring had an oracle-like property that determined whether a quest could be done and was worth their time. A quest to open a can of peanut butter would not be deemed important enough for the Ellorian Champions. A quest to create world peace was too vague and unlikely to be successful. It had to be realistic but challenging, and to that end, those using the Quest Ring to summon them had to try resolving the situation themselves at least twice. Those attempts had to be mentioned when casting the spell that activated a Quest Ring.

"How does it work," Eric asked, "when a wizard stands at the Quest Ring and casts the summoning spell? I know you must answer some questions, but who is asking them? I know it's the Quest Ring, but is it just a voice, or is there an illusion of some kind?"

Taryn replied, "The wizard casts the spell, which awakens the oracle in the keystone. The oracle appears as an illusion of a man that looks like my brother. It asks a set of questions that must be answered. They include not only what the quest is, but also what has already been done to resolve the situation. The oracle evaluates the replies—and it can sense whether people are lying, or have bad intentions, and even whether the account they have given is true. It's quite a good oracle."

Matt noticed that she seemed proud of her brother's work inventing it. "How were you able to fool it?"

"Careful planning by King Sarov. What I'm about to tell you was his idea. He hired someone to steal the dragon egg and take it somewhere, while spreading misinformation about its location. The people of Novell tried to retrieve it but failed. So did the dragons. King Sarov then asked me and some of my men to do it, but we were unable to as well. I didn't know it then, but while I was tracking it, King Sarov knew my plan and told those who had the egg how to evade me. Until I returned, I also didn't know that he had invited Eriana's brother and Princess Alia of Coreth here."

Eric observed, "He was orchestrating something."

"Yes. He had told Kingdom Novell of my attempt, and this led Novell to suggest that we use the Quest Ring in their lands to summon the Ellorian Champions. It seemed to be their idea but, once again, King Sarov had instigated it. This meant that none of us who were present to summon you had any idea what was really going on and so we could fool the oracle into agreeing to summon you."

"Clever," remarked Matt.

"And troubling," said Eric. "I hope no others think of such a ploy."

Taryn said, "We have a better understanding of how everything works."

"So now you know where the dragon egg is," said Anna.

"Yes. It's a few hours away on dragonback, in the mountains to the east. We can be there by noon, get it from those who have been ordered to hand it over, and return."

"An easy quest," observed Ryan. "I'm almost disappointed, but not really."

"Who is coming along?"

Taryn replied, "Just the four of you, me, and three of my men."

"When do we leave?"

"The dragons will be saddled as we speak."

Talk turned to their destination, which lay with the borders of the Kingdom of Andor. The dragon egg was being held in a small village in the foothills of the Hills of Andor, which were technically mountains. The king had sent word to expect Taryn and others soon. They expected a peaceful handover.

Matt noticed that Eriana's brother Solun, who was younger than her, seldom said much, though he often looked at Anna as if he wanted to talk to her. She noticed his gaze and finally engaged him in conversation—more about his sisters more than himself, by his preference. They had known little about Eriana's life before the quests except the hints Lorian had dropped months earlier—that her rough childhood led to a spiritual awakening of tremendous power. Solun was light on details, but he said all three of them were kidnapped as children and used for slave labor. Matt got the impression that sexual abuse was involved but felt uncomfortable asking.

After years of this, Solun said, he and Eriana tried to escape, with their youngest sister Diara. But Diara was afraid of punishment and resisted. Solun sacrificed himself by fighting their pursuers so that Eriana could escape alone and return for help. His captors cut off his hand for it. Years passed before Eriana, now a powerful priestess, found Solun with help from knights. But Diara and Solun had been separated and it took longer to find and free her.

"Were the people who did this to you ever punished?" Anna asked.

Solun looked away and down, then nodded. "Yes. Soliander found them years later, after Eriana told him about it."

Matt cocked an eyebrow, wondering what the powerful wizard might have done. This time, no memories popped into his head. He was no stranger to bullying, though he'd experienced nothing of this magnitude. "What did he do to them?"

Solun glanced at him, and then smiled in satisfaction. "He never told anyone."

Matt's eyes narrowed and he tried to look encouraging. "But he told you, didn't he?"

A twinkle lit Solun's eyes. "Yes. I wanted to know. Eriana didn't. Diara did, but he wouldn't tell her. Only me."

Matt couldn't help wondering why that was. Did Solun look up to the wizard? Did they have a bond? "What was it?"

Solun pursed his smiling lips. "Just don't hurt anyone Soliander is loyal to."

Anna asked in concern, "Are they still alive?"

Solun paused. "In a manner of speaking."

Matt watched him closely, seeing a young man who enjoyed the vengeance Soliander had taken on his tormentors. What did that say about Solun? He wasn't forgiving, certainly. Could Matt blame him? Not really, not without more details. The missing hand had to be a permanent reminder of trauma, making it harder to leave behind. Had Soliander earned Solun's loyalty? It seemed like it. He glanced at Taryn, who watched Solun with an unreadable expression.

He asked Solun, "Do you think Soliander is still loyal to his old friends?"

"Absolutely. Nothing could ever change that." He paused and shook his head in admiration. "You should've seen his face when he told me what he did to them. You'd think they had hurt him instead of us."

Note to self, thought Matt. *Don't piss off Soliander.*

Eric observed, "It sounds like there is precedent for him doing, uh, wicked things."

Taryn spoke up. "My brother has always hated those who hurt others. He is a good man, which is why he's so offended by awful behavior. He is very idealistic and, in a way, unrealistic about what people are really like."

"You seem pragmatic," Eric observed.

She nodded. "I am, as are you. But Soli wants the world to be different from how it really is. He struggles to accept that it is not. I'm certain that drove him into the quests, the desire to make wrongs right again. I think it's partly why he's so infuriated by Everon betraying him. It wasn't just the physical problem of unwanted quests, but the philosophical betrayal. For all the good he had done, he was punished. I spoke with him about it a number of times, and I've never seen him so angry."

Matt could understand that, and almost wished he could just talk to Soliander without fear of being attacked by him. Taryn's words had raised a question. "We haven't actually done anything to hurt him, so this is all making me wonder whether we really need to be concerned about him coming after us."

Taryn sighed. "He has no reason to, except for information. I don't think he would actually hurt you."

Ryan smirked. "Tell that to Lorian. Soliander cast a lightning bolt at him."

Taryn smiled. "He doesn't miss unless it's on purpose."

"Really?" Anna asked in surprise. "That would be encouraging."

"And nice to know." Matt laughed. He imagined throwing his hands up in surrender if something similar happened to him. He felt like their next meeting with Soliander was destined to be violent. Maybe he should worry less. He shook his head. The guy was too intimidating. Matt doubted he would ever stop being afraid of him.

They got ready after breakfast, bearing the weapons of the Ellorian Champions, but earing different clothes so that they wouldn't be recognized. Anna hid Eriana's Corethien Amulet under a cloak. Matt wore a tunic and trousers. He brought Soliander's spellbooks and the staff, wrapped in a blanket so they wouldn't be identified. Ryan left behind his lance, since they weren't expecting to fight dragons. He wore the silver plate mail loaned to him, and sheathed Korrin's sword in a different scabbard. Eric had done the same with Andier's short sword—but his new brown leather didn't have nearly as many places to hide throwing knives, forcing him to leave half of them behind. Still, they didn't expect to need them.

At the palace stables, they met Taryn and stowed their gear on horses. Mounting quickly, they trotted behind her on cobblestones that led into the streets of Andor. Matt smelled the chilly spring air, the horses they rode upon, the sea at the docks, and a mixture of baking bread and the acrid stenches of medieval sanitation. He was now accustomed to horseback riding. The gait of the black gelding beneath him felt natural, his hands absently controlling the reins. The clacking of hooves mixed with the sound of a hammer rhythmically hitting metal on an anvil. It echoed between buildings, wagon wheels rumbled nearby, and the voices of men, women, and a baby crying were all heard. It still seemed quiet compared to Earth cities.

While the palace lay at Andor's heart, the castle stood on a hill at the north end. Rainwater stained the light limestone, and pennants flew from its towers. The streets narrowed, their pace slowing. Matt read off the red and gold street signs nailed to houses of light stone and dark wood—Fountain Road, Blade Street, Wicker Way, and Castle Road. Elves, dwarves, and halflings in simple clothing mixed with the mostly-human population, but the market square just outside the castle walls was mostly empty when they arrived. Stalls of familiar-looking fish, fruits, meats, and breads stood on the loose straw strewn over the dirt to either side of the road.

Three of Taryn's Dark Blade warriors awaited them at the open castle gates. One was a business-like elf, more muscular than slender, black plate mail over his light skin. Matt saw dragons in the courtyard—one black, one red, and two silver. Their size never failed to intimidate. They were taller than a two-story building and wider than a dump truck, with heads bigger than a car. Their huge mouths and teeth drew Matt's eyes before their massive, taloned feet. Their tails could knock someone over with ease. Wings blotted out the sky when extended. That Matt and his friends had killed two on the Dragon Gate quest still amazed him. He knew dragons differed across worlds and even on the same one, but most dragons on Elloria could shapeshift and do magic. Two people would ride each.

"You're with me," Taryn said to Matt, to his surprise. He followed her to the black dragon, the biggest of all, and avoided taking Taryn's proffered hand to steady him. Gingerly trying not to hurt the huge beast made it more difficult. Once he started walking like it was just another thing to step on—the thought making him chuckle—he found it easier. He soon sat behind Taryn, hesitantly following her instruction to put one arm around her. She somehow seemed soft despite the black chainmail. Unlike the other dragons, this one had no saddle. Matt held onto his staff, which lay across his lap. A glance revealed Ryan and Anna together, and Eric with the elf on the red dragon. The remaining dragon carried the other two Dark Blades warriors.

They took to the sky, leathery wings snapping at the cool morning air. The sun streamed across the mountains in the distance, casting beams of gold into the valleys. He saw frost on the shadowed hillsides to the north and east and south, the blue of the ocean becoming very dark just a hundred yards from shore. He'd watched just enough nature shows to know that this meant the continental shelf dropped away quickly to deep water.

Andor was a large city of red-roofed homes, most of them two to three stories high. Towers throughout the city soared into the crisp air. Some had high bridges between, which swung in the gusty sea breeze. You would have to be crazy to walk on those spans, and yet he saw a few people doing so, clinging to the railings. He spied the streets they had ridden on before gazing out over the port where ships came and went, smaller fishing boats heading out.

As the dragon gained altitude, they flew away from the ocean and into the blinding sun. Matt wished he had sunglasses. He settled for gazing down at the cobblestone roads, which gave way to dirt farther from Andor. They followed the river northeast, nearing a lake that sparkled with reflected sunlight, the sprawling, unwalled town of Godsted on its southeastern shore.

From the map, he knew that the Hills of Andor, a low mountain range, were due east. Beyond them rose the Towering Peaks. Somewhere to his right, to the south, lay the Kingdom of Roir, Andier's home, and Eriana's hometown, Coreth.

An hour after passing Godsted, the dragons descended west of the mountains. Aside from a dirt road, Matt saw no sign of a village. The ground rushed up and their black dragon thrust out its wings to slow them. They touched down gracefully, dust and loose grass kicking up.

As the other dragons landed beside them, Matt and his friends looked around warily. He only relaxed on seeing Taryn and her men calm. He got down to the ground, where he unwrapped Soliander's staff and shoved the wrapping into his spellbook bag.

"Where's the village?" he asked.

Taryn pointed toward the foothills. "Allowyn is that way. They have a lot of livestock that the dragons would terrify, so they'll stay here. It's a half-hour walk. Bring anything you think you'll need."

She indicated that it was safe out this way because all danger lay on the other side of the village, deeper into the mountains. The mountain trolls around here had scared away everything else, but they knew better than to attack Allowyn because of the response from Andor. The result was a veritable truce, though skirmishes happened when villagers went too close to the troll caves. Taryn intended to spend a little time here and told the dragons to be back in two hours if they decided to leave.

They began the hike up a slight incline, a mix of deciduous trees and evergreens dotting the light forest. The dragons disappeared behind them as the way turned frequently around boulders and hills no wagon could get over. Grooves and gullies in the path from wagon tracks gave way to a cobblestone road in disrepair, random stones missing and sometimes a hole big enough to trap a wagon. A stone pillar had the town's name carved on it, and Matt spied an old, dilapidated low stone wall in the trees.

"Taryn," said the Dark Blade elf, holding up one hand. Everyone stopped, listened, and looked around. Matt didn't hear anything, but Taryn and Eric both pulled out their swords. The elf unslung a bow from his back and the other two Dark Blade warriors did the same.

Ryan put his hand on his hilt. "What is it?"

"Something's wrong," said Taryn, eyes up the trail. The elf took the lead, Taryn and Eric moving behind warily. Ryan, Matt, and Anna were in the middle as the two remaining Dark Blade warriors brought up the rear. They took another two dozen steps before Matt heard faint voices in the distance, in the direction of Allowyn. The voices were shouting, but the tone didn't sound panicked.

They broke into a jog, stopping from time to time to listen, but something about Taryn's demeanor suggested her wariness was dropping. At last, they finally rounded a curve in the road to see the village's oak walls and wide doors, which were open but guarded. Three men and a woman in chainmail turned at the sight of them, hands going to sword hilts and a crossbow until Taryn held up one hand and put away her sword. The others followed suit and approached the guards, who mostly relaxed.

"Ho there," said one. "What business have you here?"

"Taryn of Aranor, Commander of the Dark Blades. King Sarov sent word I would be coming."

They lowered their weapons. "He did. Too bad you didn't arrive sooner."

The group reached the gate and peered past. They didn't see much happening but heard a commotion further in. Outside the walls to one side, Matt saw numerous pens of cows, pigs, and what he thought were elk. They were restless, sometimes moving as a pack to one side of a fence and back again as a man there sought to calm them.

"What happened?" Taryn asked, scowling.

"Trolls. At the far gate. We fought them off, but not before they did a lot of damage. Killed a few people. They attacked the men King Sarov had here and made off with some case they had. It was almost like they were looking for it."

"Shit!" Taryn jogged onto the main street through town, the rest of them following behind. The buildings were one or two stories high and close together, with wooden beams for walls and thatched roofs. Except on the main road, straw-covered dirt was all that lay underfoot, a few puddles from rainstorms still drying out.

"Do we care about this case?" Eric asked, loping along beside her.

She snorted. "Yeah, unless it was empty. The dragon egg was in it."

"God da—" Eric stopped himself.

The village wasn't large and they soon passed into the market square, which looked like a triage center, people in bloody clothes here and there. Matt saw a middle-aged man crouch beside another wounded man and put one hand on his forehead, lips moving as if praying. But nothing happened to the groaning man and the apparent priest apologized. Anna saw this and went to help. By silent agreement, Matt and the others waited nearby as Taryn got the attention of a guard and had a tense conversation Matt didn't overhear. When he next looked at the man Anna was helping, he was sitting calmly and not moaning in pain.

"So glad you're here," said the priest wearily, rising as Anna did. "I'm afraid my strength is spent."

"Sure," she replied. "Who else can I help?"

"This way." He led Anna around the wounded and Taryn returned.

"We're going to need to go after them," she said.

"Who?" Ryan asked. "The trolls?"

"Yes, and the king's men. One of them was killed here. So were a few guards. The king's men took off in pursuit of the trolls and we need to follow, and quickly."

"What about the dragons?" Matt asked. "Should we go back to get their help?"

"No time. I'll send a guard to tell them. Maybe they will reach us in time. It depends on whether they stayed there or not."

"What's the rush?" Matt asked. Taking four dragons into a fight seemed quite comforting, though he didn't know how bad these trolls were.

"Trolls think dragon eggs are a delicacy and aphrodisiac. That egg isn't going to last long."

Eric and Matt exchanged a look. If they didn't return the intact egg to Novell, they were trapped on Elloria. "Right. Then let's move. Anna!"

The priestess finished healing a man and joined them and got filled in as they walked. They soon reached the western gate, which the trolls had demolished along with several nearby buildings. Matt was used to seeing dead bodies covered by sheets from on TV and in movies, but here they either lay where they had fallen or had been dragged into a row. He counted seven altogether. Three trolls lay unmoving—one at the gate, one farther inside in the ruins of a building it had crashed into as it fell, and another outside the walls with arrows in its back. They were twice as tall as Matt, with gray, mottled skin covered in sparse, black, coarse hair. Their arms seemed disproportionately long, their heads bulbous and hideous, with two tusks jutting up from fat lower lip. They wore ill-fitting shirts, vests, and trousers, all stained, ripped, and not big enough. Their bare feet were filthier than the rest of them, and Matt could smell one from ten paces.

"This is what we have to pursue?" he asked, wrinkling his nose. "How smart are they?"

"Not very," answered the elf with them. "They will be easy to track. The guards said they left two hours ago, though. They likely have entered their caves by now."

"Great," muttered Eric. "This isn't going to be so easy after all."

"Well," Taryn began to Ryan, "you said you were almost disappointed not to have a real quest. It looks like you've got one.".

CHAPTER SEVEN

THE DRAGON EGG

Ryan adjusted his armor as they looked over at the entrance to the troll cave. This plate mail wasn't as nice, or quiet, as Korrin's, and he now realized he had become spoiled. It didn't fit as well, either, with some of it chafing enough to distract him despite the sight before him. He and the others stood behind trees and a boulder, the worn dirt path to the caves to one side. The large footprints were unmistakable and had been easy to follow. The trolls had done little to hide their trail. He wondered whether that was down to stupidity, confidence, or acceptance that tracking them wouldn't be hard regardless of what they did.

Three trolls stood outside the entrance, tossing rocks at pieces of wood floating down a stream of rushing water, which emerged from the mountain to the right. The wood looked like it had been part of a crate or barrel, suggesting that someone was destroying these inside the mountain. Ryan remembered hearing that the trolls had stolen a few items along with the dragon egg case. It seemed they were smashing them open inside, taking the contents, and throwing the destroyed containers in the river. The trolls outside had made a game of hitting the pieces with stones, sometimes groaning or laughing deeply at each other's performance.

The black cave beckoned behind them. It was set into a mountain face of dark stone that looked like it had once seen a landslide. Piles of rock had been moved aside and the cliff face was mostly smooth except for cracks. The path split, one fork entering the cave, the other fork continuing left into the trees and foothills surrounding them.

The dragon egg was almost certainly inside the cave network. So were any men from the village. They had found no bodies, just blood and a few pieces of torn armor or broken arrows. The evidence suggested that the men had caught up with the trolls and been defeated, then carried, dead or alive, into the troll cave. This had potentially become a rescue mission for both them and the egg, though Ryan knew where his priorities lay. When asked, Taryn admitted that trolls were not above eating people. No one knew how many men had pursued the dozen trolls, so they decided to rescue who they saw but not search the caves or they'd never make it out.

"So what do we do?" Ryan asked. "Maybe Matt can cast a spell. Don't trolls turn to stone in sunlight? I'm surprised they attacked the village during the day."

The elf responded, "That may explain the morning raid. The sun's rays were not upon the village or the path there."

Ryan looked up and then back the way they'd come. The sun was getting higher, the shadows in which they stood likely gone in an hour, and those trolls were going inside to escape it. But they didn't have an hour to wait.

As if reading his mind, Eric asked, "Can we lure them into the sun?

"Doubt it," said Taryn. "They aren't smart, but not that stupid either. Luring them down the other path might work because it'll stay in shade a lot longer. But then what? Fighting them will make noise that brings others from inside."

Anna said, "I was able to make weeds come out of the ground and pull down undead. But I'm not sure if it would work. The god I contacted then was offended by the undead existing and agreed to help."

"Are there any gods who care about dragons?" Eric asked.

"Yes!" said Taryn. "Anna, if you can reach the goddess Drakonon, there's a good chance of her intervening."

"Okay. I will try, but it might take a bit." She placed a hand on the amulet, which would help her connect with the gods of this world, especially now that she had a name.

Ryan turned to Matt, who appeared to be thinking. "Got anything? Something quiet, so we don't cause attention? Put them to sleep? Open a pit that swallows them and then closes?"

"There's always fire from the staff, but it would make them scream."

"Sudden death is better," said the elf, surprising Ryan. Elves revered life like he did. But he had to admit that a quick death was probably best if they could not be subdued.

He said, "I'd prefer a way to immobilize and silence them for however long this takes."

They soon agreed on a plan to set in motion. Ryan and Eric walked onto the path and into full view of the trolls, acting as though they were caught up in conversation and didn't realize what lay ahead until too late. The three trolls looked at them in surprise that turned to amusement. One troll could easily handle two men. They began approaching and Ryan and Eric turned away, sprinting along the path parallel to the mountain and into the trees, the mountain's shadow on them. Ryan didn't have to look back to know that the trolls were following at an awkward run, their heavy footsteps making loud thuds, tree branches cracking.

Ahead, the dirt path twisted and turned around trees and hills, the foliage thin enough to see through. Mat didn't think they'd get trapped or caught.

After several minutes of this, he and Eric saw behind the trolls, where the elf and Taryn flanked Matt, who ran between them. Now seemed far enough, and they turned to face their pursuers.

Ryan held up two weaponless hands as if for mercy. "Please. We don't want any trouble."

"Trouble?" one troll asked in a deep, raspy voice, leering. Or maybe it was trying to smile. Ryan couldn't tell. "We have fun now."

Ryan risked a glance past them and saw Matt standing still and concentrating. "This fun wouldn't involve eating us, would it?"

"Yes!"

Eric asked, "Did your friends carry a dragon egg into the cave? That sounds like it would taste better than us."

"Yes!" one bellowed, scowling. "No sharing! Only for the king."

"How many trolls inside get to eat dragon egg?"

"Good question," said Ryan. Eric was always wily. "Is it a hundred? A thousand?" Could the trolls even count that high? They looked confused, especially when a cloud of green gas appeared around their heads. Their eyes bulged as they grabbed at their throats, coughing as they struggled to breathe. Ryan backed up, sensing that the brutes were going to collapse—which they did moments later, the ground shaking with the thuds. Everyone waited a minute in case they moved again. Beyond Matt, Taryn, and the elf, Ryan saw Anna and the other two warriors, who joined them.

"No one should find their bodies any time soon," said Taryn, heading back.

They pulled out swords and reached the dark cave entrance, which was ten feet wide and twice as tall. They listened carefully before entering. Only dim torches lit the way. Stepping around loose or jutting rocks required constant vigilance. The last thing Ryan wanted was to fall with a loud, echoing clatter. The cave floor rose around a few corners before ending in a larger cave. Ahead of them lay a gorge twenty feet across and forty feet down to the stream Ryan had seen. A drawbridge of thick tree trunks lashed together spanned the distance but was raised, and the mechanism to lower it was on the far side, where a troll sat napping. Beyond it, a tunnel awaited.

Ryan turned to Eric. "Think you can get over there somehow? You're the rock climbing, parkour guy. We should knock the troll into the water so no one finds it."

Eric examined the rough, jagged walls while the elf prepared his bow and Matt got a spell ready as backups. Eric found a viable path and descended toward a stone outcropping that extended over the water. Then he unwound the rope from around his waist, making a wide loop. Across the water, at the top of the other side, was a stalagmite. It took three tries, but he got the loop around it, tightened the slack, and wrapped the rope around one arm. Then he gently swung over the river to strike the far side feet first, but he had rotated slightly, his side striking the wall, too. This made an audible sound and he bounced out a few feet. The troll stirred but didn't awake as Eric reached the wall again, steadying himself. He got a secure position and nodded up at them with a grimace. Using the rope, he climbed to the top, peeked over the edge at the nearby troll, and clambered up.

Ryan let out a breath. "Now what? It seems unsportsmanlike to kill a sleeping troll."

Matt replied, "You should've thought of that before. Better than a woken troll killing Eric."

"I guess I can't argue with that."

As they watched, Eric slowly drew his sword and approached the troll. He hesitated, then examined its rickety chair next to the drop-off. He seemed to be considering how to knock the troll down the gorge instead of killing it. He began doing sign language to Matt, whose mother was deaf. At Eric's request long ago, Matt had taught him the skill, which sometimes came in handy. Ryan and Anna were supposed to be learning it but hadn't gotten far.

"Eric wants us to be ready in case this doesn't work," said Matt.

Taryn frowned. "It's just a troll. He should kill it and be done with it."

Matt shrugged and didn't relay that to Eric, who had found a loose rock he could easily swing. He practiced a few times before finally slamming it into the front chair leg, the one closest to the gorge. It cracked but didn't snap until a second blow hit just as the troll stirred awake groggily. The chair wobbled. Eric ran away from the edge, turned, and charged the troll, who was struggling not to fall as the chair began to collapse in the desired direction. Eric jumped and kicked forward with both feet, striking the troll in the waist. It lunged for him even as it began to go over the edge, one giant hand catching his foot. Anna gasped, but then a bowstring snap split the air and an arrow pierced the troll's forearm so that it let go. With a cry of surprise and anger, it tumbled over the side with the chair, striking the wall once before plunging into the stream with a loud splash.

Ryan wondered how deep the water was and got his answer when an unconscious troll floated to the top, blood on its head, one arm twisted at an odd angle. But the stream was deep enough to carry it away. He thought it might have been dead anyway, but he saw it move just before it disappeared around a bend.

With a look of relief, Eric grabbed the winch and began lowering the six-foot-wide drawbridge, which squeaked uncomfortably and struck the other side with a hard thud. Everyone held still, listening for footsteps or voices, but they heard nothing. Then they crossed the bridge and joined Eric. Only one troll could cross this bridge at a time, but two careful humans—or those fleeing for their lives—might do it together.

"Just kill it next time," said Taryn to Eric. "There are likely hundreds in this place, so being nice could mean your death. And maybe mine."

Eric sighed. "Fair enough."

Ryan had always been the one who didn't want to hurt anyone or take a life, after accidentally paralyzing his brother. It had taken their entire first quest and several brushes with death or serious injury to snap him out of it. Eric had always been the one with the almost ruthless attitude. Had something changed? Or had it been killing a sleeping troll that gave him pause?

They crept farther into the cave and the next tunnel, going only twenty steps before they reached a crossing route in a widened area. This time they heard a commotion of loud voices—perhaps cheering?—in the distance straight ahead. With no sounds right or left, they continued on to a similar but larger intersection, with the noises once again louder before them. To the right and left were stairs. This time Ryan wanted to check one side out—so he and one warrior went to the left, while Eric and another went right. All returned within a minute.

"What did you find?" Eric asked.

Ryan replied, "Just a bathing pool with that stream running past it to a little waterfall. No one there. You?"

"Dining area, kind of big, mostly empty. Four trolls, stuffing their faces. There were other tunnels. I wonder if the egg is in a kitchen in that direction."

Taryn was looking the way they had been going, deeper into the mountain. "My gut tells me the commotion we're hearing has something to do with the egg, and the men who were captured. We may find both there."

"And a lot of trolls," said Ryan.

Taryn looked at Matt. "You're sure you don't know spells that can hide us in some way?"

Matt made a face. "I know a fog spell, but it won't make sense in here. I assume they would get suspicious."

She nodded. "Yeah, but if it's thick enough it could help us anyway. Maybe get it ready? And anything we can use to slow them down, get them disorganized and confused."

Matt nodded and got out a spellbook, flipping through it.

Eric suggested, "What if you cast the fog spell and the poison gas one? The gas can only kill a few, I'm guessing, but the fog spell you did once before spread really far. What if they think the fog is what killed some of them? They would try to stay away from it, not realizing it wouldn't hurt them. It could cause a panic."

Taryn said what Ryan was thinking. "That's genius. But also dangerous. Panicking trolls could crush us in a stampede."

"And they might destroy the egg by accident," observed Anna.

"And I can't cast two spells at once," said Matt.

Eric nodded. "Right, but when you cast the fog spell before, you got it started and then gave the vial to someone else. They kept blowing over the top of it to spread the fog. Do it first, give it to someone else, and then do the gas spell."

Matt said, "Yeah that could work, but we still need to know where the egg is first, and it would be better to make the panicking trolls go away from it."

"Drakonon, the dragon goddess I've reached, might be able to help me spread the spell," said Anna.

Eric said, "Time for me to sneak up there and see what I see. All agreed?"

They exchanged looks without dissent. Taryn accompanied him into the tunnel, which soon turned so they were out of sight. Ryan felt nervous. All it would take was for one troll to see them, but maybe they were distracted by whatever celebration was going on. Quiet footsteps announced Eric and Taryn's return sooner than he expected.

"What did you see?" he asked.

"A big cave," said Eric, "with at least a hundred trolls. Most have their backs to us, facing the troll king. He's on a platform with a few others. They've got several men from the village tied up or hanging from a pole. Some looked dead already. Others were being beaten, and the trolls were cheering. Four trolls ripped apart one guy as we watched."

Ryan swore, feeling sick at the thought. "The egg? Did you see it? We have to get the hell out of here before they catch us."

"No way they catch us," Matt said, and Ryan saw his knuckles white around the staff, his face uncharacteristically cold, eyes hard. "I'll fry them all if they try."

"We did see the egg," said Taryn. "It's on the platform with the king. It's still in its case, which is open. If the case was closed, we could risk the fog and poison gas idea."

Eric said, "Yeah, but did you see the other tunnels? Two of them were near him. I'm wondering if that dining area we saw has a tunnel that connects to one. We could get up there and do the spell near the front. The panic would go in the other direction, away from the egg and toward where we are right now."

"Yeah," said Ryan, "but how do we get the hell out of here after we have it?"

"The water," Eric answered. "If they panic and run down this way, we could follow, then make it to that pool you saw. I think if we jump in there, it will carry us all the way out. We might have to fight our way to the pool some, and Matt could do some other spells, or get fire out of that staff. I think we can make it."

"First I need a vial of water from that pool to do the fog spell," said Matt, searching for it in his possessions. "I have the vial. Just need to fill it."

"I'll do it," said Eric. "I want to see the pool and the waterfall."

Matt gave him the vial and together, Eric and Ryan went to check it out. The pool cave had filthy discarded clothes in various places, many wet. Giant goblets and empty plates lay haphazardly about. The remnants of food, most of it still on a bone, were also here. One thing was certain—the trolls were slobs. A barrel had been smashed, and Ryan had the impression that this was the source of some of the wood he'd seen floating in the stream outside. The pool seemed natural, and to one side of it all lay the rushing stream and then a waterfall. Having a surer step, Eric went closer, peering down to assess the likelihood of being hurt when going over it.

"I think we'd be okay."

"You *think*?"

Eric smiled and put away his sword. "I'm more worried about you sinking in that armor."

Ryan hadn't thought of that. "Yeah, some of us might need a buddy to help us stay afloat. It doesn't look that deep."

"We'll figure it out."

Eric filled and stoppered the vial before they rejoined the others. Then they crept toward the dining area Ryan had seen earlier. It was fifty feet wide and had several tunnels leading away. The trolls only seemed to have one construction style—logs or branches lashed together with vines or rope. Each of the tables and benches were made this way, with abandoned plates and goblets suggesting that something had interrupted the trolls. Maybe they had been called to the celebration, which could be heard from two different tunnels. No pattern existed for the placement of furniture. Of the trolls Ryan had seen here before, only two were left, their backs turned as they loudly talked of their resentment that the king and his favorites would get to eat the dragon egg.

"What do we do?" Ryan whispered.

Taryn looked at the elf, who got another arrow ready. So did her other two Dark Blade warriors. Eric pulled a couple of throwing knives from beneath his clothes.

To Ryan, Taryn said, "Let's try to sneak up behind them. If they hear us, we move aside and the arrows fly. Then we close in. Quickly."

Ryan nodded and they stepped from the tunnel into the room. Korrin's armor would have been quieter, but the trolls were making enough noise not to hear them. The real danger was that one would turn its head and see an approaching threat from the corner of its eye. He couldn't tell if the haphazard layout helped or hindered their attempt to stay directly behind their target. They had to move left around one table, and which put them too close to the peripheral vision of one troll—so they went right around the next, but had the same problem with the other. Ryan glanced back and saw that the archers had entered the room and moved to one side a bit for a clearer shot around him and Taryn. Eric had crouched below the top of tables and was using them as cover to get nearer from another side. Another fifteen feet to go.

Suddenly one of the trolls turned its head too much and caught sight of Ryan, its eyes widening. They grew wider still at the sound of bowstrings. Two arrows struck its head, another thudded into its throat. It reached up with one arm as if to pull at them, but Eric's knife hit it in the neck and it fell forward onto the table.

The other troll was already turning to rise, but Ryan and Taryn were on it before it could do anything but raise its arms defensively. Sword blows sliced into it several times before first Taryn and then Ryan plunged their swords into its chest. It opened its mouth, blood spewing out, and Ryan thought it would yell to draw attention. Taryn was faster than he was, yanking her blade out and slicing across its throat to kill it. The troll fell back on the bench and then rolled to the floor, knocking the table aside with a clatter. She stabbed the other one to be certain and everyone regrouped at the bodies, listening intently.

"Nice work," said Eric, getting his knife back and wiping it on the dead troll's shirt. "I can hear the celebration through this other tunnel, so let's check it out."

The group quickly surveyed the other tunnels to make sure no one would come up behind them. It appeared that either the egg, or more likely the torturing of the prisoners, had practically cleared out the place. Eric and Taryn set off in the lead again. They followed the tunnel a short way around several turns. This revealed one fork they didn't take before a last turn just yards from where it ended, the voices very loud.

Ryan got his first look at their destination, but he mostly saw a natural pillar eight feet wide standing two steps into the cavern. The few trolls he could see were facing to his right, but he barely saw any at all due to the obstruction, which hid them from view as well. Not until they stepped out would they be seen. He wanted to get past Taryn and Eric to see better but sensed they wouldn't let him out of caution. Both were carefully peering out for longer than Ryan wanted. What if someone saw the bodies they'd left behind?

He heard a deep voice speaking a language he didn't understand. Lorian had once cast a spell on them so they could understand elven, dwarven, magic, and a few other languages, but troll hadn't been one of them. The tone was celebratory, boasting, and cajoling, sometimes causing laughter, a jeer, or a cheer. Then a human shout and a scream of pain split the air. A roar of approval followed.

Finally, Taryn and Eric came back.

"Get ready," said Eric to everyone. He fingered two of his throwing knives. "Matt, time to start that fog spell."

"What's the layout?" asked Ryan.

"We're near the front, but not all the way. When we do the spells, most of the trolls will go left toward where we were before."

"And the rest?"

"Probably toward the egg to the right, where the Troll King and the prisoners are. I think we might have to fight our way to it. Anna, see if you can help spread the fog back toward the tunnel we were in before, even down it. We want the trolls to stay away from the room with the water-fall, or we'll be fighting our way to that, too. If the fog is thick enough, maybe we can sneak through it."

"I'm not sure about this plan," Anna admitted, looking nervous, "but I think I can do that."

With the risk of being caught rising by the minute, Matt held the vial of cold water to his mouth and whispered the magic words.

"Obscure all sound and light,
A haze that blinds like night."

Then he blew across the top of it. Fog began to form and pour over his hand to the floor. He gestured outward with the other arm, and it began to flow toward the trolls. Ryan took the vial from him and continued blowing over it and gesturing—this time upward to create a wall of fog, rather than a creeping carpet. He didn't anyone to see them when they looked over at it. A glance at Anna showed her concentrating, one hand on the golden amulet around her neck. How would he know when and if she succeeded in gaining godly help? But it soon became clear, for the fog thickened at once and began to push away from them at the speed of a foot a second.

"Matt," said Eric, who had stepped into the fog, "Do the poison spell when I give the cue. Come up here."

Ryan could no longer see what was happening beyond the tunnel exit, because his friends blocked the way. But even they were barely visible through the fog despite being five feet from him. This might actually work.

A muted commotion sounded from the trolls, but it sounded like surprise, not fear. Ryan didn't hear Matt cast the poison gas spell, but he could tell when it happened. The voices turned concerned. Then bellows began, so many that even with the fog dampening the sound, the panic impossible to miss. A rumble of many footsteps lasted only a few seconds before shouting replaced it. A bellow sounded from some distance behind them, and Ryan turned in alarm.

"The bodies," said the elf.

"Right. I think we're about to have company," replied Matt. It seemed like Anna was capably handling the fog spell in one direction—so Ryan turned around and blew across the vial, sending fog back toward the dining area, gesturing wildly to speed it up. At the least, any approaching trolls wouldn't immediately see them.

Taryn said, "Let's move."

Ryan wondered what to do with the vial. Then one of the Dark Blade warriors took it and jogged back into the tunnel, returning without it moments later.

The fog toward the dragon egg was so thick that Ryan took Anna's hand and led her forward, coming up behind Taryn and Eric. They were moving past the pillar with Matt, to the right. In that direction, the fog was thinner and revealed a handful of trolls. One wore a big, fur-lined cloak and carried a jeweled mace—the Troll King. He saw them and hollered, pointing.

"Down!" shouted the elf behind him. Everyone ducked—until arrows whistled overhead and Taryn yelled to attack. Chaos erupted.

Eric threw two knives before yanking his sword out as Ryan passed him. Taryn had taken the first troll. As a fist swung at her, she stepped back and cut into it with her sword. Ryan went past her for the Troll King, who swung a mace prematurely. It whooshed by. There would be no blocking that, and a blow would incapacitate him. He stabbed the king in the thigh and yanked the sword back out. Then a roar of heat over his head made him duck, a spout of flames from Matt's staff catching the king's cloak and setting it on fire. The flames otherwise missed him on their way to the trolls beyond him. They screamed, the smell of burning flesh making Ryan gag. The king yanked at the burning cloak as Ryan sliced across his leg again. Suddenly the elf was next to him, the Troll King's mace swinging at them. They stepped back and it missed. Then the Troll King yelled something.

The elf cursed. "He's telling them the fog isn't deadly or we wouldn't be in it."

"Shit," Ryan said, not sure the others heard that. "Guys, we're getting company!"

He heard a sickening crunch behind him. And then a body land hard in the fog, flung by contact with something.

He risked a glance and saw Eric and Taryn still fighting. It must have been one of the Dark Blades. A human voice he didn't recognize screamed in pain from within the fog before suddenly being cut off. The footsteps and voices were getting nearer. But Matt turned to face them and spoke a word.

"Kunia!"

The sound of bodies falling made Ryan wonder what Matt had done.

The king nearly hit Ryan but missed. He stood on wobbly legs covered in bloody gashes. Beyond him, the fog had cleared from the burning trolls, who had fallen dead. The captured men were spread on three racks, grievous wounds on their naked bodies. One man had his head caved in. Another had been torn in half. The remaining one had a mangled arm and wasn't moving. Beneath them on the platform were two other crumpled bodies.

The Troll King lunged and hit Ryan in the chest with the mace, knocking him to his back, his chest in agony, his breathing painful. But the motion made the king lose balance and stumble on his weak legs. He was going to land right on top of Ryan, crushing him.

"Kunia!" Matt yelled, thrusting with one hand, and the Troll King's body flew five feet away to land with a thud. The elf was instantly on him, stabbing him through the chest and neck until his body stopped moving.

"Ryan!" said Anna, appearing above him as he lay on his back. She laid both hands on him. "Please, heal this man so we may save this dragon egg."

A soft glow spread over her hands and suddenly Ryan could breathe. He rose as Taryn finished off the other troll, who had been down on one knee. Eric was already moving onto the platform with everyone else following. The sounds of cautious footsteps grew louder in the fog, which had begun to thin, hulking shapes lurking and nearing.

"Where's the egg?" Ryan asked, not turning his back on the fog to look.

"Got it," said Eric. Ryan heard a case closing and buckles snapping.

"Can you heal him?" Taryn asked, voice strained. Ryan didn't turn to see who she meant.

"You're hurt," answered Anna.

"I'll live. He's nearly dead. Are you strong enough?"

"Let me try."

Ryan backed up with Matt, glancing over to see Anna healing the remaining hostage, whose wounds closed quite a bit, though he still didn't look good. "How do we get out of here now?" he asked.

Matt looked at the tunnel. "Back the way we came. Quickly. It's the only way."

He was right. Ryan helped Anna, who seemed fatigued, as Taryn and the elf quickly cut down the prisoner and dragged him along. Eric and the remaining Dark Blade warrior held the black dragon egg case between them. The box was two feet long and a foot wide, eighteen inches high, but one person could handle it if needed. Ryan frowned. No one was able to fight, because their hands were full.

They entered the tunnel, where the fog from the discarded vial was only two feet high. To his surprise, the trolls from the dining weren't here. Hadn't they heard all the commotion? But maybe they had gone the other way to see what the panic was about. He and Matt were in the lead and went past the fork in the tunnel, around two corners. The trolls were coming and saw them, shouting. Even if Matt burned them, getting over the corpses would be difficult. They weren't making it to that stream again, so they took the only option—the other fork.

The group hurried into the other tunnel, ascending, the climb steeper and more arduous but only a minute long. They reached another cave, where two female trolls in tattered clothes were chatting—one topless, with misshapen breasts that he wished he'd never seen. Their features were more delicate than those of the males, but they were still hideous. Ryan tried to look menacing but saw from their startled, wary faces that they weren't going to try anything. There were two ways out of this tunnel. The sound of trolls getting nearer below added urgency.

"We need to find the stream if we can," said Eric.

Matt shook his head. "It might've worked before, but there's a good chance there's no way into it now."

Taryn eyed the female trolls and observed, "We have two hostages if we want."

Ryan turned to the elf. "You speak troll. Ask them how to get out of here or we kill them." The elf cocked an eyebrow but did it, got an answer that was obviously defiant from its tone, and turned back, frowning.

"It's that one," Ryan said, pointing at a tunnel. "She glanced at it when you asked."

"Good enough," said Eric, and he made the other guy carry the chest so he could take the lead.

This tunnel opened into a large cavern, where light shone in from an opening far above them. Hundreds of trolls were here. Some stood around a fire roasting an animal. Others sat on a giant rock drinking and laughing. Children who were as tall as Ryan ran around after each other. More tunnels branched off in different directions, with no way to tell which led outside. The group stood frozen, shouts behind meaning they were trapped. A troll in the cavern shrieked at them and scores came at a run, most brandishing weapons.

Eric pointed to one side, where the cavern wall jutted out twenty feet and would protect them from some directions. They took up position and put down the dragon egg case and wounded prisoner, Anna staying near him and the archers getting bows ready.

"Fire at will," said Taryn, and the archers let fly at a target the elf called out. Better for them all to hit the same one and possibly kill it than just to wound three of them.

"What do we do?" Ryan asked. There were too many.

"My shield," said Matt, and he gripped the staff with both hands. Moments later, a white light shone from the crystal atop his staff. A translucent barrier with a soft white glow to it cascaded down around them with a radius of twenty feet.

Taryn observed, "That'll buy us some time."

A running troll threw a rock that bounced off the barrier and Matt winced. "Not much. Remember, every blow weakens me. Time to say a prayer."

"That gives me an idea," said Anna, and Ryan turned to see her touching the Corethian Amulet around her neck and closing her eyes. He exchanged a look with Eric, wondering if his friend had any ideas, but saw only an uncommon look of worry in place of calculating intelligence. They were going to die in this troll cave. And judging by what had been done to the prisoners, it was going to be horrific.

Was it okay to kill themselves to avoid it? The God of Earth forbade it. Would Ryan even get to heaven from this planet? Did it matter where he died? He hadn't thought of that before. Watching the hostile trolls reaching the barrier and beginning to swing at it, he questioned the mercy of killing each of his friends rather than letting them be tortured and killed. He had gotten past his fear of hurting anyone, but this was "next level" moral agony.

The trolls from the tunnel they'd exited arrived, looking furious. One bellowed at the others, pointing fingers and clearly announcing something. Ryan looked at the elf for translation, but the archer was busy aiming an arrow he let fly, striking the speaker in the head and killing him. Then he turned to the others.

"He was telling them we killed the king, but I stopped him.".

CHAPTER EIGHT

A LADY OF FEAR

Eric looked around in desperation and saw movement by the ceiling opening. Something big was outside. It had two wings that flapped once before being pulled close. It plunged toward the hole and passed through. The wings snapped outward, and Eric recognized a descending black dragon. A red dragon came through, then a silver and another red. The trolls scattered for the tunnels, trampling each other. One of the red dragons sprayed a spout of fire at them but missed. Taryn's black dragon landed and morphed into a tall man with dark skin and blue eyes, clad in black leather. The others remained in dragon form as he strode over to them. The trolls continued running.

"How'd you find us?" Taryn asked, as Matt dropped the shield.

"I told them," said Anna, dropping her hand from the amulet. "Well, I told the goddess where we were. I asked her to guide them here."

"I could kiss you right now," Ryan said, laughing. "You just saved all of us. I'm surprised we didn't take more damage."

"I healed myself once with the Trinity Ring," revealed Eric, putting his sword away and grabbing the egg case. "Let's get out of here. I see you aren't wearing saddles."

The dragon nodded. "We did not have time to retrieve them, but our magic can hold you on until then."

"Then let's go," said Eric.

Everyone mounted up. The black dragon, still in human form, lifted the wounded, naked prisoner with ease and laid him atop one of the other dragons before climbing down. Eric was no stranger to male nudity but felt relieved when the remaining Dark Blade warrior, rather than himself, had to sit with the guy. With a jump, one by one, each dragon lifted off and flew straight up with powerful thrusts. Eric's dragon used the cavern ceiling to grab onto and pull itself through the opening, which was small enough to make flying out more difficult than dropping down and in.

Then they were up in the sky, cloudiness having overtaken the sun. This wasn't Eric's first time Eric on a dragon without a saddle, and he once again found that his legs were held firmly in place by the dragon's magic. A glance at the others showed that they looked worried. He laughed a little, letting the tension fade. They had narrowly escaped alive. He tried to ignore the likelihood of their luck or ingenuity running out eventually. But he felt that they were getting better at this.

Hours later—after retrieving the saddles—the group landed in Andor, changed clothes, and ate a late lunch. This was the safest Eric had felt on a quest. It was almost too bad that they had to go home soon, probably the next day, with no chance to practice the skills they needed. He hadn't done badly with his sword this time, but then he hadn't been facing someone with a similar weapon, just two giant fists. He'd only needed to dodge those, then thrust into the troll's thighs and calves. The Dark Blade warrior who was flung back into the fog and killed could have easily been himself. His martial arts skills had once again helped him to survive a sword fight.

They had secured the dragon egg in a vault under the king's protection. Eric and his friends had looked at it. It was hard, leathery, and uniformly oblong, unlike bird eggs back home. A slight blue hue to it was the only indication of the color of the dragon inside. No one was certain how old it was, but it was not expected to hatch. That was almost too bad. They'd never seen a baby dragon.

The others seemed more fatigued than he, and they retired to their rooms one by one, leaving him alone with Taryn. He liked Soliander's sister for her pragmatic attitude, command, and take-no-shit demeanor. She handled herself well and was a welcome addition to any mission, not that they would have another with her. He knew Matt was attracted to her and tried to put in a good word for his buddy, who needed to get laid. Then again, so did Eric. Their situation made dating impossible, though being a conquering hero who got the girl was still a possibility. But while Taryn had his attention, he wasn't one to fool around with a girl who a friend of his might have been interested in. This was true even if Matt had less than a day to make a move, which he wasn't good at doing, partly from lack of trying. But Eric felt there was a decent chance of seeing Taryn again, just like Lorian. With that in mind, Eric cut short the drinking he was doing with her because he got the impression that she was getting frisky.

As Eric reached his wing of the palace, he stepped past the two guards at the double doors and went in. He looked forward to some time to unwind alone. On every quest, they were almost always together. Even when separate, they spent time with other people, never truly being alone. He didn't mind, really. With the danger so often around them, being alone meant more danger. For once, he felt at peace with their setting. He reached his rooms and pushed open the double doors, shoving them closed without looking around.

Someone grabbed him from behind and put a knife to his throat, so close to his jugular that he didn't dare move. A sweet perfume seemed familiar and told him it was a woman, the body that pressed into his back soft despite what felt like leather up against him. Whoever it was didn't stand as tall as him.

A sultry alto voice said, "It's nice to see you again, Andier of Roir."

He tried not to react to the name, since no one here thought that was his identity. Did this person know his real name, too? The voice sounded familiar. "Who are you?"

"I'm sad you don't remember. We fought so passionately together, and then sweetly held hands as we walked."

Ignoring the sarcasm, he thought hard, realizing that the only person he'd held hands with anytime in the past few months was... *Oh shit.* "Kori of Nysuun."

Mockingly, she said, "You *do* remember me!"

This was bad. She was a ruthless assassin who had ably fought him by hand and foot, which reminded him of something. "I remember that you had one less hand the last time I saw you with the other Lords of Fear. You seem to have grown it back."

"Aeron was nice enough to heal me. I'm sure Eriana would do the same for you. Now, enough chatter. I want you to move toward the bed and face me. You know what I put on my blades, so you need to cooperate."

"A fighter of your skill doesn't need poison."

"And the best part is that I know you mean it." She nudged him and he moved to where she indicated, halfway between her and the bed, three strides separating them. When he turned to face her, he saw her in the familiar black leather, sensual and yet poised for violence. The last time he'd seen her, she'd sported red hair, but now it was golden blonde with a streak of red, like the colors of Andor. And her hand had indeed grown back. All he could think was that the other lords might be here capturing his friends.

"Are your friends with you?"

"Do you see them?"

"Don't be coy."

"Will you relax if I tell you no?"

He paused. "Yes."

She smirked, her dimples making her lovelier. "You're a poor liar. Your friends are safer than you."

"Very reassuring."

She looked at him almost fondly. "I enjoyed our little fight on Rovell, except it was too brief."

Did she really come here for banter? He wondered whether she was stalling while something else happened to his friends. He knew better than to try something with her. They would have to be on their own for now.

Eric asked, "Why are you here? What do you want?"

"Information. But first I need to make sure you won't try to hurt me." She smiled.

"You're the one with a poison knife in your hand."

"And you usually have knives all over you. And you're fast with them. You may not be wearing the leather, but I assume you're still armed. So take off your clothes."

Eric cocked an eyebrow. "This isn't a ploy to get me nude?"

A mischievous twinkle appeared in her eyes. "I didn't say that. Now strip before I cut your clothes from you. Don't be modest. You don't seem the type."

Eric sighed and began removing his shoes, then tunic, and then undershirt. He met her gaze and she nodded, so he stripped off his leggings to stand nude.

"Satisfied?" he asked with a smirk.

She eyed him. "Very. It's nice to see a nude man who is still well-armed."

"Maybe you should undress as well. That way I won't have to worry about your knives or anything else you have. We can be equals, like when we last fought."

She smiled mischievously. "Interesting idea. I heard another one—that you and your friends are not the real Ellorian Champions. Perhaps that explains your poor swordplay."

Great. So much for keeping that a secret. Who else knows? "I don't suppose we can trouble you not to tell anyone."

She put away the dagger and unbuttoned her leather top. "Maybe if you tell me what I want to know, I'll keep your secrets."

"And what do you want to know?"

Kori opened her top to expose her torso, dropped the leather behind her, and then started on her pants. Eric felt himself stirring and didn't bother to hide it. It had been a while, regretfully. He wasn't sure having sex with this assassin was a good idea, but stripping her of poisoned knives couldn't hurt. Her boots came off, and then she slipped out of the pants to stand as bare as him. She quietly padded across the floor to him, stopping within inches, eyes playful. He saw that his body wasn't the only one reacting to this.

Kori said, "Now we can have a proper interrogation."

Voice husky, he replied, "I'm kind of not in the mood to answer questions."

"Good, because I'm not in the mood to ask them."

She took both his hands in hers and slowly lifted them to her breasts, then reached down for his manhood, biting her lip. He leaned forward as if to kiss her, then hesitated, still unsure about this. Were her lips poisoned for a kiss of death? Slowly, she put her hands on his chest and shoved him backward onto the bed, then gently climbed on top of him to straddle his waist. He touched her breast and felt her shudder. Her lips went to his neck. He finally decided this was the best way he was likely to die on one of these quests and let himself do what he wanted...

Several hours and trysts later, he leaned on one elbow as she lay beside him on her back, arms above her head. He traced a scar on her side, getting a better look at the dragon tattoo she bore.

Eric asked, "So, did you come all this way for this?"

She held his gaze. "Yes." He flushed but didn't look away. "I don't have to tell you it was worth it."

"No, you don't," he admitted, leaning down to kiss her shoulder. "What now? Was this part of torturing me for information?"

"No. It was part of enjoying you."

The suspicious part of him wondered if she was flattering him to make him think she liked him, but he didn't really think so. Their lovemaking had been especially surprising in one particular way—the constant staring into each other's eyes, even when passion brought them to their most unguarded moments. Either she was a good actress—and he had no doubt she was—or some sort of honest connection had been formed. She did like him, was even fond of him, and had smiled shyly more than once, her body flushing. And for that reason he flushed, too, at her words. Now the question was what, if anything, had changed between them. Where did they go from here? But to get that answer, he wanted to know where she came from before now.

"Tell me about yourself," he suggested, lying close. "Where did you learn to fight?"

She stretched luxuriously. "I'll tell you one thing for each thing you tell me."

"I asked you first."

"Okay. Eric." She smiled at his visible surprise that she knew his real name—but then maybe he should have ex-

138 | RANDY ELLEFSON

pected it, given that everyone here used it. "The Blackened Brotherhood taught me to fight. Hands, feet, knives, the sword."

He wondered what that organization did, but instead asked, "Did they teach you to poison, too?"

"Yes. Now, where did you learn to fight?"

The answer wasn't as interesting as hers. "There are schools that teach different kinds of fighting with hands and feet. Nothing fancy, and nothing about knives and swords."

"You seem like a beginner with a sword, but your knife throwing, where did you learn it?"

"Where I grew up, we have something called a Renaissance Festival, where people put on a show of skills with contests like knife throwing. My talent was noticed when I attended, so someone invited me to be a performer and helped me improve."

"You did not learn it to kill."

"No, but you did?"

"Killing was the goal." She said this matter-of-factly.

"Anyone in particular?" He hoped for a good reason and that she wasn't just interested in murdering people for amusement.

"Yes, everyone who destroyed my life. They murdered the woman I loved." She looked him in the eye. "And now they're all dead."

He watched her, sensing that she had told the truth. Her bisexuality came with no hint of embarrassment like it might have back home, and he accepted it without judgment. Showing no disapproval, he remarked, "That is fierce justice and loyalty."

She ran her hand through his hair. "I am loyal to those who deserve it. Maybe one day that will include you. Are you loyal to your friends, Anna, Matt, and Ryan?"

"Very. How do you know our names?" She could have heard them from the conversations here at the palace, but he hadn't seen her here and wanted to be sure.

"My master has spies in many places, including now on Earth. A fascinating world, from what I've heard. I am eager to visit and learn more."

He tried not to react to this. How did her master get to Earth? And who was he? The man had clearly been of evil intent before, and the last thing he wanted was the Lords of Fear showing up back home. "Maybe I can tell you what you need to know and spare you a trip."

She pressed against him. "You don't want the pleasure of me in your own bed?"

He smirked. "I didn't say that. Who was this woman you loved? Why was she murdered?"

She pursed her lips. "Love between women, or between men, is forbidden in Nysuun—even for a princess like her."

"And were you a princess?" He really needed to study how kingdoms and titles worked to understand who had what sort of power in the places they visited. A crash course was in order once they got home.

"I was a countess. We were young, and never touched each other, but our love was plain, and they condemned us to death. On two pyres facing each other, so we could watch the other die, they tied us naked and standing. Then they lit the fires."

"But you escaped."

She nodded. "A boy who loved me was among those who tied my bonds. He had purposely done so poorly so that they were loose, and I escaped through the flames. A guard nearly stopped me before the boy struck him and I got away. But they threw him onto the pyre in my place and he died for my freedom."

Eric watched her carefully and saw the look of someone remembering, her eyes not on him. Such barbarism
rarely happened in the United States, and was never sanc-
tioned by the state; even the death sentence was carried
out humanely. It was the sort of evil story heard about
third-world countries. He noticed she seemed angry about
the boy's death. That spoke well of her.

"How did you go from fugitive countess to assassin
through this brotherhood?"

"I stole what I could to survive and made my way to
my family's estate. They gave me what they could. They
were good people, and would not punish me for my love,
but others were not so kind. I fled as the king's guards
were arriving. I learned later that a stable boy told the
guards of my family's aid to me. They burned our home to
the ground with my family inside, as a warning to others
about my forbidden love and about aiding enemies of the
king, who had burned his own teenage daughter to death."

Eric had felt her body stiffen and move restlessly with
anger and turmoil, as if she could not lay still while revealing what he again sensed was the truth. "Why are you willing to tell me these things?"

She looked him in the eye again. "My history is no secret, and I would rather you hear it from me. And because
you asked."

Was it really that simple? She seemed more complicated than that. But then maybe she just missed a human connection. Or everyone was too afraid to talk to her. She was
certainly intimidating, but there was a vulnerability to her
that made her exciting. He wondered how lonely her life
was now, serving some master who sent her and the other
Lords of Fear to destroy people. Did no one show interest
in her like he was doing? Or were they only men she didn't
consider worthy for whatever reason? A foolish guard. A
court dandy. A man who couldn't keep up with her mind

THE SILVER-TONGUED ROGUE | 141

or physical skills like he could. Had he truly attracted her attention? But maybe he was kidding himself and she was just using him as a means to some end he didn't know. He had to admit, he liked her. And only a fool wouldn't respect her.

"You found this brotherhood, or they found you?"

"Both. They learned that I was looking for them and who I was. They claimed they also wanted the King of Nysuun killed for their own reasons, and didn't much care who else I eliminated. Like all in their service, I had to be magically bound—so that I could not leave them—before they would accept and train me. I foolishly let them bind me, having lost everything already. I was willing to lose my freedom for the chance at vengeance."

Thinking that was savage and desperate, he asked, "How long before you got it?"

"Years. Years of training, years of denials, years of lying. They never wanted the king killed. I learned that they had tricked others into the brotherhood with false promises, those who had nothing left but hate. We were powerless due to the binding."

"And yet you escaped this, too. How?"

She smiled without humor. "The one I work for now. He found me and revealed that he could undo the spell binding me to the brotherhood. He asked only that I sometimes work for him, but promised that I would otherwise be free."

"And so you had your revenge at last."

"Yes, and on the brotherhood, too. I killed them first—all but the others bound like me, and who my master also freed. I then returned to Nysuun and killed that stable boy who betrayed my family, and the guard who threw the boy who loved me on the fire, and finally my king and all his evil brood."

He watched her quietly, noting the spark of excitement that had appeared while she talked of revenge. She was fierce, passionate, and deadly. And he admired her.

"What does your master have you do?"

She shrugged and ran a finger down his cheek. "That I cannot tell, but it is only the evil who have something to fear."

He doubted that but stayed silent about it. "So you have a life without love and friends now?"

"A woman in my position makes few connections that matter. You interested me, especially after I learned you were only pretending to be Andier, and so I came. I will enjoy what's left of my humanity in these brief moments, between all the things I must do." She caressed his cheek with what seemed like genuine fondness.

"You seem to have plenty of humanity left."

"Maybe. But what good is it? For forming connections? All those who love me die."

Is that what she really thought? "It doesn't have to be that way. You can live a less dangerous life."

"Perhaps I prefer not to create the opportunity again. I lost years of my life to love and hate and almost lost it all."

"Aren't you still losing years of your life to it, in service to some wizard?"

"I do not serve him out of love or hate."

"Loyalty?"

She considered. "Yes."

"And now you have no life at all but in service to another."

"I did not say that. I come when he calls. I am otherwise free to do as I please. Now, enough about me, Eric of Gaithersburg."

He stiffened again. They had not told anyone on Andor the city where they lived, only the state. And her master was on Earth. Were people back home in danger? They needed to attempt contacting Jack now. He tried to still the alarm she had awoken.

She pushed him onto his back and climbed atop him, playfully pinning his arms above his head with hers and kissing him. "I know who is out here," she said, touching his cheek, "but I want to know who is in here." She placed her hand on his heart, and then his temple. "Who are you?" She sat up and pulled his hands atop her thighs, her hands over them.

He took a deep breath. "I appreciate how forthcoming you've been."

"But you're not going to do the same?"

"I have concerns that you and your, uh, friends, and your master, are a real threat to me and mine."

"I already know you are Eric Foster of Gaithersburg. And Anna Sumner, Matt Sorenson, and Ryan LaRue all live there. Or nearby. There is nothing you can say about where you live that we don't already know."

There was no question that they were all moving the minute they got back. Concern for their families had him wondering what to say to get them to leave town and never return. It was something to think about later.

When he said nothing, she said, "I'm sorry if that bothers you. I did not mean it to. We are not trying to kill you. It's true that my master isn't exactly pleased with what you did to the Orb of Dominion, but it's better anyway."

He cocked an eyebrow. "You don't care that we broke it?"

"Oh, I care. I am not a fan of enslavement. My master has his reasons, which he did not share, but that just makes it harder to agree with him. The orbs are evil for what they can do. Part of me is glad that you broke one and that I was still able to fulfill my oath to do what he wants."

He decided not to admit that it could be put back together and that only he, Matt, and the dragon Jolian knew where the pieces of the slave orb were. The wizard Kori worked for had the master orb, which allowed him to perpetually control anyone who looked into the slave orb, until the sphere broke and released everyone's minds. "And your friends? Lord Voth wants Matt dead. I think Garian does, too."

"Yes, both of them would be happy to kill Matt—or worse—for the injuries he caused. They have no sense of humor."

He smiled, then began to laugh. Matt had burned the undead knight Lord Voth to a crisp, melting away whatever flesh was still on him so that only a skeleton remained. He turned serious. "Do the others know where we live?"

"No. My master doesn't tell them as much as me. In this case, it is because he knows they want revenge—and my master has ordered us not to harm you. But angry men do dumb things."

He smirked. "*Now* you tell me you are ordered not to harm me. What does he want with us?"

"He seeks the real Champions. I don't know why, so don't ask me, but he knows you aren't them. I'm assuming he knows what they look like and was surprised at the sight of you in Ortham through the orbs."

"You didn't know before then?"

"I did not."

"Do the other lords know, too?"

"I don't believe so." Kori shifted atop him. "Now, I've answered more of your questions. Time to answer mine. How did you come to replace the Ellorian Champions?"

He wasn't sure what to admit and who wanted to know this—her, her master, or both, which seemed likely. Maybe if they found out, they would leave them alone. "We don't know. It wasn't on purpose. We don't have a choice."

Kori's eyebrows rose. "What do you mean? You do not choose to come on quests? Or you did not choose to replace them?"

"Both. One day we were summoned to another world and welcomed as them. We had no idea what was going on, or who they were. We don't know how it happened and there's nothing we can do about it. We get summoned without warning and we have to finish the quest or we can never return to our world. We've been pretending to be the Champions because everyone thinks we are. Except here, of course."

Kori gazed at him intently—judging, he knew—and long moments passed before she spoke. "Did they do this to you? Make you take their place?"

He shook his head. "It seems to be an accident of some kind. And our impression is that things don't work quite like they did for them."

"What do you mean? Give me an example."

He wondered what to say that wouldn't cause a problem. "We can't take anything back with us. The real Champions could, but not us."

She looked intrigued. "So if you tried to take the Orb of Dominion to Earth, you wouldn't have had it anymore when you arrived."

"Right." From the thoughtful expression she wore, he could tell she believed him.

"What happens to the item? Does it stay where you were before you returned to Earth?"

"We don't know. We've never been back to a world that summoned us to ask if anything was left behind when we disappeared. For all we know, the item comes with us but..." He shrugged, not sure what would make sense to her. "Maybe it's stuck between worlds or something."

"That would be one way of hiding something so no one could get it."

He hadn't thought of that. "Including us. So don't give me a gift you might value, or you'll never see it again after I go home."

She smiled and scrutinized him again, pursing her lips. "You are trapped as I once was. And yet you don't seem angry."

He nodded slowly, considering how he felt about all of this. He seldom had time to think about it. "I think our circumstances are not at all similar aside from that, so maybe that's why. Mine is an accident, not someone trying to kill me because of who I love. I understand why you wanted revenge. Are you still angry?"

She sighed. "No."

And yet there was something. "Bitter?"

She looked down. "Empty."

Eric squeezed her thighs with both hands. He had the impression she was lonely and far more vulnerable than he would have guessed, though that could just make her more dangerous. "Do you trust anyone?"

"No," she said at once.

"Not even the other Lords of Fear?" Was the necromancer, Aeron, summoning undead in the palace even now? Was the wizard Garian after Soliander's items or Matt? The undead knight Lord Voth could be after Matt right now, too.

Kori frowned. "Especially not them. They have a bond."

"How so?"

"Aeron freed Voth, with my master's help. And Aeron and Garian enjoy the dark side of wizardry together. And they are all boys, of course."

"And their master favors you."

Her startled gaze suggested she hadn't thought of that. Rather than deny it, she squeezed his hands and sighed. "I would like to see you freed one day. Until then, you have my sympathies."

"And after?"

"Maybe I'll come visit for a tryst." She shook her hips and he felt himself stirring again.

Holding her gaze, he said, "You won't leave again if you do."

To his surprise, she blushed but didn't look away, showing a boldness he found sexy. "I knew there was something about you I had to investigate. You haven't disappointed."

"Your master didn't send you?"

"I didn't say that." She leaned over, giving him a long, deep kiss before pulling away and climbing off. He suddenly felt cold and sat up as she slid off the bed, sighing on the way to get her clothes. "Unfortunately, I must be going. But I do have a few last questions."

"Am I going to see you again?"

She slipped her pants on. "Maybe. What about the Champions? Do you know where they are? Soliander is the most important."

"We don't know where he is, but we think he attacked us on our first quest." He didn't see any reason not to admit they didn't know much about the real Champions. He reluctantly got up and walked to the foot of the bed beside his pile of clothes.

She cocked an eyebrow. "So he *is* alive. Why did he attack you?"

"We don't know. It happened fast and then he left. Wasn't feeling chatty."

"He wasn't known for conversation. What about Andier?"

"No sign of him."

"Korrin?"

"Same."

She finished dressing silently—and somehow looked sexier in the outfit now that he'd seen her without it. She turned and headed for the exit, pulling a knife into one hand. Kori looked at him and smiled, then tossed him the weapon, which he let hit the floor just in case the blade nicked him. "I know you can't take it with you, but something to remember me by."

He leaned over and picked it up. "I couldn't possibly need something for a reminder."

She appraised him. "You are a worthy replacement for the Silver-Tongued Rogue."

He noticed that she hadn't asked about one of the Champions. "You haven't asked about Eriana. I assume you heard that she's with us on Earth."

She paused at the door, eyeing him one last time. "Well, she was, yes—but when you return to Jack Riley's apartment, you won't find her there."

The comment startled him. No one had mentioned Jack to anyone, not even to their hosts. "Why is that?"

"My master took her."

CHAPTER NINE

OTHER WORLDS

Having finished using it to commune with more gods on Elloria, Anna once again wrapped Eriana's Corethian Amulet in a soft cloth. She was in the guarded meeting hall where the boys also practiced combat. They could only use the Champions' items here or in a closed room.

Everyone but Eric had now emerged from a brief rest. Earlier, she and Rognir had talked about how to contact aloof gods, or those who didn't agree with her personal outlook. He knew less than Eriana, whom Anna vowed to speak with once back to Earth.

She turned away from the Amulet's cabinet to see Matt still at a table. His nosed was buried in two different spellbooks as he sat beside Lorian, who was looking through one of Soliander's. Matt still memorized as much as he was able to. All of them had memorized a few spells for him, too, writing them down on Earth. They also needed to do more to gather materials back home, but it had been less of a priority with magic only starting to awaken. Hopefully, Matt would be able to cast something at home soon.

She went to sit near them and watched Ryan swing a hammer at Rognir's direction. The dwarf was more of an expert at this than the elf. Ryan had already finished swordsmanship practice with Lorian earlier. He was getting better. The training he had for playing a knight at the

Renaissance Festival helped, but those mock battles didn't compare to the real fights against warriors with years of training and experience. Sometimes it was a wonder the four of them were still alive. Since swords were less useful against undead, Ryan was learning some basics with the hammer, mace, and flail. He was athletic and seemed to make good progress, though she saw that he looked frustrated. He was pushing himself all the time with good reason, but maybe he needed to cut himself some slack.

They had filled in both Lorian and Rognir on the details they had learned about the Champions and Eriana—including that Soliander's apprentice, Everon, had betrayed them and made the quests involuntary. And that Eriana was on Earth and doing fine. Both the elf and the dwarf could be trusted to keep secrets. They had proven their loyalty and friendship.

She'd been wondering where Eric was, but now he strode into the room, adjusting his tunic as if putting it back on. His hair looked mussed, and he seemed either agitated or excited. Anna wasn't sure which until Eric called Ryan over to the table as he paced beside it.

"What's wrong?" she asked, sitting up straighter.

"We have a problem," he announced under his breath, coming close enough that Anna caught the scent of perfume. She leaned closer and inhaled, then pulled back, asking a question she felt certain she knew the answer to.

"Why do you smell like a woman?"

He flushed and that confirmed it. "You don't want to know."

A sweaty Ryan reached the table with a non-sweaty Rognir and poured himself a goblet of water. "What's up?" he asked, breathing hard.

Eric said, "Listen! Kori of Nysuun, one of the Lords of Fear, is here."

Anna's eyes widened. "What? Wait a minute. Is *that* who you just had sex with?"

He looked at her in annoyance. "Is that really the part you want to hear about?"

"Yes," said an enthusiastic Matt. "Well, mostly. Was, uh, the Garian guy there? Not in the mood to fight him again. Or Lord Voth."

"She said none of the others are here—but that's not something to just believe."

"Did you really have sex with her?" Ryan asked, with less judgement than Anna. When Eric looked unsure how to answer, he joked, "Asking for a friend."

"Enough kidding," said Anna, thinking they weren't taking this seriously. "What happened?"

Eric sighed. "She came to get information about me. Us. She knows we aren't the Champions, what our real names are, and what city we live in on Earth. So does the wizard she works for—and he's looking for not only us but the Champions."

Amid the looks of alarm, Matt asked, "I don't suppose she admitted who he is?"

"No. But there's something more important. She said the guy kidnapped Eriana from Jack's apartment after we came here."

Suddenly they were all talking at once until Anna finally quieted them. "We need to contact Jack now. Matt, are you ready to do that spell?"

He nodded. "Yes. But let's work this through first. Why would Kori just tell us that? Seems odd."

Eric shook his head. "I don't know."

"You didn't ask?"

"She left right after."

Anna frowned at him. "Why didn't you go after her? You should have captured her." *And not had sex with her,* she irritably thought.

152 | RANDY ELLEFSON

He opened his mouth, then shut it.

"What?"

He pursed his lips. "I wasn't wearing anything."

Anna huffed in irritation. "Well, with the way you never cover yourself, running around the palace buck naked after Kori shouldn't have deterred you."

Rognir gave a short laugh and slapped Eric's back.

"Do you think it's a trap?" Ryan asked, refilling his goblet. "Maybe she wants us to try rescuing Eriana."

Eric admitted, "Yeah, it could be. But we don't know who she works for, so I don't see how we could even attempt to get to Eriana. We have no idea where she could be. It doesn't seem like a trap to me."

Lorian asked, "Why else would she admit it? What were you talking about before she said it?"

Eric gave them a brief recap and added, "I think she was just telling me the truth. It didn't seem planned."

"Maybe she's wilier than you think," suggested Anna, frustrated. Why Eric was doing having sex with one of their enemies, who'd once tried to kill them, was beyond her. He'd always been the smart one, but here he was acting like the dumbest. She was trying hard not to scold him; she wasn't the sort to do it normally, but these were unusual times. Their lives depended on good judgment, and his had been the best before now. Maybe that was why she suddenly felt so threatened and vulnerable. She counted on him. How was she supposed to trust him after this?

Ryan said, "I think we need to gather as much info on them as we can. We heard that there are rumors about who they work for. That could give us an idea where Eriana is."

Eric appeared to be thinking hard as he said, "The other question is who could possibly know about Eriana being on Earth, or about Jack's apartment, well enough to do this—

or even get there from another world? The only people who knew about that are in this room."

Matt shook his head, face serious. "Only one person comes to mind—Soliander. He could've learned about Jack from the spell he did on me. We didn't know about Eriana then, but we thought he might come after us. What if he did—and he found out he could look for us in Jack's apartment—and then he found Eriana there?"

Ryan looked puzzled. "But that would mean that... oh shit. The Lords of Fear work for Soliander."

There were groans of realization. Then Eric observed, "That would mean Soliander has the master Orb of Dominion. His voice was the one we heard through it in Ortham."

Matt's eyes were wide, but Ryan spoke first. "Do you remember when Garian reached for Matt's copy of Soliander's staff, and the voice snapped at him not to touch it?"

"It's him," said Matt, eyes far away. "I remember now. I can see all these images. I remember him talking with Kori when she was still with that brotherhood, and after he freed her from it. I see Aranor, the throne room, and Lord Voth as the king encased in ice until Aeron and Soliander freed him. Voth is King of Aranor, but his allegiance is to Soliander, who is really in charge of the kingdom. I can see Soliander teaching Garian wizardry. Garian is his apprentice. They are all afraid of him but respect him and are loyal."

Lorian swore in elven, startling Anna. "We must keep this a secret, but we need to tell those who must know."

Rognir said, "We should prove it first. The lad's memories may not be enough to convince anyone outside this room."

Ryan looked at Matt in annoyance. "I wish you would remember stuff sooner."

"I can't, man. It's just like when someone reminds you of something and you go, 'Oh shit! I remember!' There's

154 | RANDY ELLEFSON

nothing I can do. But I can see it. Now that I have these memories, I can think about them to uncover more."

Anna said, "So if Soliander is the guy controlling the Lords of Fear, that might be why he wanted us captured instead of killed. He wanted information from us."

"Right," said Eric, "and Kori admitted that the Lords of Fear didn't know we weren't the real Champions at the time. They acted like they didn't know—and Kori claimed that she's the only one of the four who knows now. Also, she doesn't seem to know her master is Soliander, from the way she talked about it. She said they're looking for Soliander, too."

Lorian observed, "That might be useful, knowing something about her master that she does not."

Anna asked, "Why is Kori the only one of the four Lords of Fear who knows?"

Eric replied, "She appears to be Soliander's favorite."

Matt nodded, then blushed. "Yes. He cares about her, but he's not in love with her. They are having sex." After a moment, he asked Eric ruefully, "Did you get a good look at the tattoo?"

Eric's eyes widened, and then he looked embarrassed.

Ryan smirked at him, "Soooo, you're sharing a lover with Soliander."

"Let's change the subject."

"Okay. We'll talk about that later."

"No, we won't."

Anna felt slightly amused despite the situation—but like many women, she refused to show anything but disapproval. "If we hadn't defeated the Lords, he would've enslaved our minds and been able to learn everything he wanted... if the slave Orb of Dominion had actually worked on us."

"Why did it not?" Lorian asked.

Matt said, "I had cast the *Mind Shield* spell to prevent it. Then we captured the slave orb, chased the lords through the gate to another world, and destroyed the orb. We hid the pieces so it can't reform itself."

Anna said, "I think we need to talk to our hosts immediately."

Eric shook his head. "Let's confirm it first, then figure out what to say. We don't want then to overreact."

"Agreed."

"We need to think about the timing of our spell to contact Jack," said Matt, flipping through the spellbook before him. "We don't know exactly what time it was on Earth when we were summoned to Elloria, but it seemed like maybe 9 AM here. Does anyone recall the last hour they saw a clock?"

They thought for a moment and Ryan said, "Before midnight."

The others nodded.

"Okay," Eric began, "so a nine-hour difference, I think. We forgot to ask how many minutes and hours there are in a day here, but it seems pretty close to Earth. And now it's around 6 PM here, I think, so that means it would be around 3 PM on Earth. I'm not sure how likely it is that Jack would be home."

"He doesn't have a job anymore," said Ryan, "since I'm now paying him to work for us full-time, so he might be."

Eric said, "Right, but it's the middle of the day and he will not be sitting around waiting for us. He's probably doing things out of his apartment."

"Is it worth a shot?" Anna asked. "How hard is the spell, Matt? Lorian?"

The elf considered. "It is not difficult to cast, but it does take significant energy from the user. If we try now and fail, Matt may not be recovered in a few hours to try again. I could do it instead, however."

"I think it's worth a try," said Matt. "Give me a few minutes of quiet and we'll do it and see what happens."

The others agreed and moved away to talk amongst themselves. Anna bit her lip, wanting to say something to Eric, but he saw her frown and looked chagrined, an uncommon sight. Maybe she didn't need to say anything at all. He likely knew what she was thinking. Had Kori seduced him in some way? Was that a goal? Had Eric been compromised? That was almost more suspicious than her deciding to reveal her master had Eriana. There had to be some ploy going on here. Anna normally wasn't suspicious, but these were uncommon times.

Matt indicated that he was ready and they stayed back as he cast the spell, Lorian looking on. The wizard reluctantly nicked himself with a knife to get a drop of blood, which he squeezed onto a small piece of glass. He then dropped it into a goblet of water, speaking magic words they all understood.

"Hear my words across the stars,
Our minds are one, near or far."

A shimmering curtain of air hung before them, about the size of a large TV but square. Jack's apartment could easily be identified from the vantage point of the front door. The couch stood to one side, an end table next to it, another in front, and a TV hung on the wall across the room. Horizontal beams of sunlight slanted through the blinds across the tan carpet, suggesting that it was late afternoon. They couldn't see a clock or any sign of movement. An open laptop sat on one table, but the screen was dark and a pad and pencil lay beside it. There didn't seem to be anyone there, even after Eric yelled Jack's name a few times.

"He would be able to hear us, I assume?"

"As if you were standing there," confirmed Lorian.

"He could see us, too?"

"Yes."

Eric yelled a few more times before Anna asked, "Can we make this view move at all?"

The elf cocked an eyebrow. "You mean as if we stood there and turned our head, or walked further into the room? No. Interesting concept, however."

"How long can the spell last?" Ryan asked.

Lorian shrugged. "It depends on the strength of the caster. This sort of spell can be draining, given the distances involved. I would suggest we stop after a few minutes and try again later, or else we run the risk of being too fatigued to do it again."

Anna sighed, disappointed. But he was right. They gave it another five minutes before ending the spell. They would try again in the morning here, when it was night there. They would use Jack's bedroom next time. Despite not seeing Jack, she felt encouraged that Matt had succeeded with this spell. He was getting stronger, more confident and more controlled. Now, anytime they were on a quest, they could still communicate with people back home. It took a moment for that to sink in, the others sharing her growing enthusiasm and discussing how they might benefit, such as contacting Lorian when they needed him. They remembered his estate from their visit, so they briefly discussed a room Matt could always use as a place to contact someone. Lorian pledged to always have a servant within hearing range of it. For the first time, Anna felt like they were getting more control over their situation.

That night, they resolved to stay together until bedtime, which would be early so they could wake in time to reach Jack in the morning. They decided to tell their hosts what they had learned regardless of how that went, agreeing to let Eric decide what to reveal. Anna was no longer so trusting of his judgment. He hadn't lied to them, at least, telling them straightaway—well, after he finished having sex with her—about Kori. The revelation that Soliander controlled the lords, and had even created them as a team, raised concerns about Kori's motives. Maybe this was a trap after all. It hadn't taken them long to realize he was her master.

But this raised an important question—did Soliander know that Matt had some of his memories? Because that was how they had figured out Soliander controlled the lords. If he didn't know Matt had his memories, it was less likely this was a trap. If he did, it was almost certainly a trap to get them to rescue Eriana. Regardless, they would assume the worst. Anna sighed, tired of the uncertainty.

In the morning, the four Earth friends, elf, and dwarf once again convened in the meeting room, the doors closed. After consulting with Lorian, Matt said he felt ready to do the spell again—and did so. This time, the window across galaxies showed blackness, but the glow of a white digital clock read 2 AM and cast soft light over Jack's bedroom. Under the sheets lay a lone figure, one bare leg sticking out.

"Hopefully, he's not naked," said Ryan, breaking the suspense.

Matt said, "Yeah, there should be a kind of etiquette to this. It's like a Peeping Tom spell."

Anna frowned. "Just what the world needs."

"Jack!" yelled Eric. But the figure in bed didn't move. He yelled again and it gave a groan of displeasure. "Come on, Jack. Wake up. It's Eric and the others. You aren't dreaming. We need your help."

Clearly groggy, the familiar but hard-to-see figure of Jack sat up and looked around, the sheets falling to his bare waist. His head whipped in their direction. "What the hell?"

"Hey," said Eric, "try not to freak out. Matt learned a new spell so we can talk to you from where we are."

"Damn. Wow. Okay. Um, shit, what time is it?"

Eric said, "Sorry, but because of the way the spell works, we had to do this when we were pretty sure you'd be there. We can see you, so don't get up if you're not decent."

The shirtless Jack pulled the sheets around his waist more. "Yeah. Yeah, I can see you guys, too. You look like you're at RenFest or something. No armor and all?"

"We don't have time to explain right now."

"Sure, but who is that with you? Is that a dwarf?"

"Yeah, and the elf, Lorian. Listen—"

"Wait. Are you guys back on Honyn?"

"No. Look, I know you have questions—but the spell only lasts so long, and it makes Matt weaker."

"Yeah, sorry. What do you need?"

"Is Eriana still there? Not at the apartment, but—"

Jack sat up more, then flipped a light on the nightstand, his lean torso and facial features more defined. His short brown hair was sticking up. "No, man. You're not gonna believe this. Soliander showed up here and took her." This prompted several groans of resignation, and Jack cocked his head. "Did you guys already know that?"

Anna said, "Sort of. One of the Lords of Fear, Kori, told us—but she didn't say who'd done it, and she can't be trusted anyway. That's actually why we're contacting you. What exactly happened?"

Jack answered, "They talked for like five minutes before he grabbed her, muttered some magic word, and they both vanished. It was definitely him."

"Shit," said Ryan. "We thought he might show up."

"When was this?" Eric asked.

"The morning after you were gone."

"We would've been there if it wasn't for this quest," said Ryan.

"Are you okay?" Anna asked.

"Oh yeah, I'm fine. He didn't know I was here or listening until the end, and he clearly didn't care as he left with her."

Anna asked, "Did Soliander know she was there?"

"No. He was looking for you guys. I can't figure out how he knew to come here. Freaked me out a little. Haven't seen any sign of him since. They were both surprised to see each other. She hugged him. He saw that she'd aged twenty years and learned why. He felt bad about it. Guys, he feels guilty about the betrayal by Everon, his apprentice, the guy you said trapped all four of them in the cycle of quests."

"Yeah," Matt said. "Everon altered the summoning spell inside the Quest Ring keystones, which he made without Soliander being aware of it. That's what made the quests involuntary and binding. He also created a ton of Quest Rings on a lot of planets. We don't even know how many."

"To be fair," started Eric, "I don't blame Soliander for wanting revenge."

"There's something else," said Jack. "When he was here, he admitted to living under a new name—Zoran the Devastator. Does that mean anything to you guys?"

Lorian breathed sharply through his nose. He stood up and began pacing. "No. No, this can't be. How can he be Zoran? The things that man has done." He closed his eyes, shaking his head.

"What is it?" Anna asked.

"It makes sense. Awful sense."

Rognir puffed at his pipe. "It does explain a few things. I think we will have to talk about this after we're done with Jack here, but if this is true, then we all have reason to fear Soliander. He is wicked."

Eric said, "Okay, let's table that. But Lorian, do you know where Zoran lives? What planet? Continent? City maybe? Where might he have taken Eriana?"

The elf started to answer, but Anna noticed Matt's eyes widen despite his gaze being far away. She motioned for Lorian to be quiet and they all watched Matt in silence. Finally, he turned to them and smiled, a gleam in his eye.

"I know where he would take her. Oh, and he's got her sister, Diara, imprisoned there."

Eric's eyes narrowed. "Didn't she betray Eriana with Everon somehow?"

Matt nodded. "Yes. She helped Everon trap them in the quest cycle by getting hair and other stuff from each of them for Everon to use in the altered spells. Soliander kidnapped Diara for information about Everon. And bait. Everon is thought to love her." He grunted. "Huh, they have three children."

Anna arched an eyebrow. "Are the children with Soliander, too?"

"No."

Anna asked, "Why do you think he took her? Jack, did he say anything? Did she go with him or did he actually force her?"

"Oh, he forced her," said Jack. "She was struggling. He apologized but said he couldn't leave her behind again, not after years of trying to find her. Also, guys, I really got the impression that they were in love with each other. That reminds me. He said he thought he had killed her and the others. So I think he's been a pretty angry guy, guilt-ridden, and ruthless."

Matt was nodding, eyes faraway as if remembering. "Yes. All true. He doesn't have much to live for, in his view. Or he didn't. I wonder how the discovery that she is alive will change him."

"Couldn't have changed him much," said Ryan, "since he kidnapped her."

"Shit," said Eric. "Eriana was supposed to be handling the funding of the estate, too. Minor problem, but we have to do something about this."

Anna touched his arm. "Like what? What are we going to do?"

Eric looked at her. "Rescue Eriana."

CHAPTER TEN

BRIARDALE

Second-guessing himself wasn't one of Jack's habits, but life wasn't normal anymore. He was in over his head. Knowing his friends were in far deeper tempered any desire to complain—but figuring out how to buy an estate for them wasn't going well. With Eriana gone, there was no one else to do it. He couldn't even get a real estate agent to show him one. The first time he'd walked into an agent's office, the man had laughed and asked how he would afford it. He still flushed at the memory. The guy had been a dick to scorn a customer, but he'd known Jack didn't have the means to buy it, so it wasn't like doing so would cost him a client.

Except it would.

After Soliander kidnapped Eriana in front of him, Jack got a hotel room, afraid the wizard would show up again or kill him from a distance. Was that even possible? Everything he supposedly knew about wizardry came from games, books, and movies. He'd been back to his apartment since the incident and had finally became comfortable enough to spend the night. And wouldn't you know, a magic window had opened up while he was sleeping—the exact sort of scenario he'd been most afraid of. Eric had at least been smart enough to immediately say who it was, or Jack might've shit himself and run naked out the door. The thought made him laugh. Maybe he needed to start wearing clothes in bed. These days, you never knew what the hell was going to happen. Better not to get caught with your pants down—or off.

Ryan's brother Daniel had not been pleased about the real estate agent's attitude because he would've gotten the same treatment despite being rich. This was partly due to being in their twenties and trying to buy a multimillion dollar estate. They were the same age and didn't dress that different. Jack was relatively normal, with his close-cropped brown hair and penchant for khakis and a polo shirt when doing formal stuff, like the job he'd quit as a Starbucks manager to work full-time trying to arrange life on Earth for Eric, Ryan, Matt, and Anna now. The pay was good. Officially, he worked for Ryan, but he really worked for all of them, even Daniel, who had tattoos on his arm, long black hair, and a penchant for t-shirts of heavy metal bands. Being in a wheelchair hadn't curbed his life much.

They grabbed Quincy, the LaRue family attorney—or one of them—to help. He was a big, distinguished-looking black man in his 30s and got them appointments at several estates. Jack drove Daniel's wheelchair-equipped van to each location.

They had decided to leave Susan out of everything. She was the live-in nurse Daniel's parents kept on staff for him, even though he didn't need it, and the time to insist that the end was approaching. She was already asking too many questions after being with Daniel when he found the stash of arrows, armor, swords, and more at the family guest house, where Ryan and Eric had been setting up a practice space. And, like the rest of the planet, Susan knew they kept disappearing. She didn't need to know Daniel was now shopping for an estate. They kept dropping her somewhere to shop for him, or for herself, saying they were having some guy time without her. She knew they did not really need her and was actually pretty cool, so she didn't question it much.

Now Jack and Daniel wandered around an estate north of Darnestown, the last major suburb of Gaithersburg, before rural areas took over. The estates here were used for farming or horse boarding—or just for rich people wanting land. Aside from the 3,000-foot-tall Sugarloaf Mountain in the distance, the land was long rolling hills or mostly flat. Wide swaths of open land alternated with patches of trees and the occasional forest. White fencing and a wall of evergreen shrubs lined many estates to prevent people seeing more than a large house far back from the winding Route 28. All the estates had a long driveway through wide lawns. Some had stonework around a steel entrance gate. Most had a guest house, a barn of some kind, and a pond. The trick was finding one where his friends could live together but also take a break from each other.

Then there was security. If the authorities found the property, they would need a justification to enter. But it already seemed like they were trying to manufacture an excuse to interrogate the Stonehenge Four, so keeping the place hidden was preferred. And ignorance was the only way to stop Soliander or someone similar showing up. He could bypass any defenses. Then there were the media. The threat of lawsuits would keep them out, but news trucks out front would reveal the group's location to the curious. White picket fencing wouldn't keep anyone out. Guard dogs, armed guards, and better fencing were all under consideration. But any personnel would realize supernatural forces were at work if Matt practiced wizardry outside.

From the news, Jack knew that some people with newly acquired magic abilities wanted to reach Matt for training. How would he handle such a person showing up? Who knew what they could do to him or anyone else in their

166 | RANDY ELLEFSON

way? He wished Eriana had brought her stash of magic items from Florida before Soliander kidnapped her. One or more might protect Jack and the estate, which he felt responsible for. He had kept an eye out for a property that seemed easier to secure and felt that he was now walking on the best option.

"What do you think?" he asked Daniel, eyes still on the big, forested hill behind the property and to one side of it. The underbrush was thick, and getting through it would deter most trespassers. On the other side of it was the Potomac River. It was unlikely that anyone curious about them would trespass from that direction.

"This is the one," said Daniel, sitting beside him in the motorized wheelchair. "We can put fencing up back there, inside the trees so it's barbed wire and no one sees it from here. I'd like to get my drone from the van and fly it around to check it out."

Jack agreed, having helped with that on one other property. "We'll need cameras everywhere else. Some should be in obvious places, like the front gate, to deter people, but too many visible ones would make people think there's something to hide."

"Right. Didn't Eriana say something about having a private detective? Maybe he's good at that."

"Don't know how to reach him. Maybe we should ask about security firms. You mentioned drones and now I'm worried about someone flying one onto the property. The bigger issue is moving forward on this."

"I think it's time to tell my parents what's going on. That video you have of Soliander taking her from your place will convince them I'm not fucking with them."

Jack didn't really know them, but had a feeling he was about to. He looked over his shoulder at the real estate agent, who was hovering twenty yards away to give them space. "What do we tell her?"

Daniel started in her direction across the asphalt driveway. "I have a few questions first."

Jack followed him, admiring the place, which was called Briardale. An older, two-story guest house with three bedrooms stood across the pavement from the much bigger, two-story house with six bedrooms and a full basement. This newer building was twenty-five years old, with a big kitchen, sunroom, and covered porch running around it. Owned by horse breeders, the state-of-the-art stables had enough room for twenty horses. An apartment over the separate barn could house a barn manager, or one of them. The barn had an indoor ring they could also use for weapons practice. There were two more outdoor rings and a plenty of open ground. Even if they bought it this week, they'd still have a tremendous amount of work left to get it ready. Daniel could help buy things, but Jack would be setting it all up.

They reached the smiling real estate agent, who wore the hopeful expression of salespeople. Her tan business suit, long bob, and elegant glasses made her seem professional and trustworthy. She took them seriously thanks to the paperwork Quincy had done to prove that Daniel, or at least his parents, had the funds to buy such a place in cash.

Stopping in front of her, Daniel said, "I know this place has been on the market for two years, so I assume they want to sell fast."

She nodded. "Yes. It is priced to sell."

"But why hasn't it sold?"

"It's not unusual for big estates to take longer. Only so many people can afford one or have the need or desire. It will pass any new inspection, if that's your concern."

"Sort of. We're not concerned about having any issues fixed, just about delays moving in."

"Well, I can tell you they are very reasonable, so if there's anything you'd like, please let me know. But I will

168 | RANDY ELLEFSON

say they've had everything repaired or upgraded already, so there shouldn't be anything of real concern."

Daniel nodded and indicated they were done. They made the 25-minute drive back to Potomac, where mansions lined River Road and the side streets. Some of the lots weren't more expensive than Briardale, but they had gorgeous houses and hardly any land. Briardale had the land and more ordinary housing, except the newer house's size.

The media presence had died down in the last couple of days, another advantage of vanishing from Earth without being caught on camera. But Jack sighed in frustration as he slowly drove the van past the few news trucks still loitering, two police cars keeping everyone at bay. He'd heard that a similar presence existed outside the homes of Matt's and Anna's parents; Matt lived with his folks, but Anna had a condo that was always being watched. Hopefully Daniel could convince his parents to buy the estate and all of this would be behind them.

━━━ ● · ● ━━━

It was time to tell his parents the truth, but Daniel wasn't looking forward to it. How do you explain that your brother is being teleported to other planets as a knight who must go on fantastical quests? Weeks earlier, they would have assumed he was joking. That was his personality. But he felt all too sober about it. And the tension with his parents had to end. They knew something was going on with Ryan and the other three. The whole world knew about the Stonehenge Four. After that first disappearance, Ryan managed to dodge a lot of questions, but the subsequent vanishing acts had left their parents wondering.

And they sensed that Ryan had confided in Daniel, who could tell they knew it even before they demanded he tell them what was going on. With Ryan often missing—even if he was still on Earth—the arguments with their parents had become Daniel's problem. He didn't mind covering for his older brother. They had been through a lot together, and now Ryan was the one who needed his help instead of the other way around. It seemed like a different lifetime from when Ryan was always doting on him to make up for having accidentally paralyzed him as kids. Daniel had resented all of that well-meaning attention.

But now that was in the past. Ryan needed him. And one problem Daniel could solve for him was their parents. He had been over this in his head many times, just how to convince them he wasn't kidding with the story he was about to tell. They had seen Matt disappear on live TV. They had seen footage of Anna vanishing from behind the wheel of her car, the three friends still inside in a terrible accident that paralyzed one, maimed another, and killed the third. They knew that Anna had reappeared in the middle of the street, a car's dashcam having caught the scene right before another vehicle struck her. She had been paralyzed for days in the hospital before disappearing again. And some time later, security footage had shown her walking out of the hospital on her own two legs with an unknown woman in her forties—Eriana. The media had broadcasted it all, because the Stonehenge Four were famous and highly sought after for interviews and interrogations—by the police, FBI, CIA, and God knew who else.

Quincy was now handling legal matters for all of them, himself, and even Jack, who was helping to keep their lives and secrets safe on Earth. Daniel's wealthy parents knew about the attorney's involvement because the money to pay him ultimately came from their accounts. At Ryan's insistence, Quincy was handling the legal problems Anna's accidents had caused for her. That meant Anna's parents knowing Ryan was paying for it. And since Anna's parents lived next door to Matt's parents, they *also* knew. The time to tell all of them the truth was now. And Daniel's parents deserved to be first.

He reluctantly used the joystick to guide his wheelchair out of his bedroom at the LaRue family estate in Potomac, Maryland. The main house wasn't big enough to get lost in, but still qualified as a mansion. Using it as a home base wasn't a good option because everyone already knew that Ryan, at least, lived here. Security problems already abounded. The media were omnipresent. Curious trouble-makers sometimes scaled the walls. They had hired a new security firm. They had installed more cameras. The police were out front all the time. Leaving meant being followed. And Daniel's parents didn't really know why, just that their oldest son and three friends were vanishing as if by magic, legal troubles were mounting, and secrets were being kept from them.

Daniel sighed as he rolled into the kitchen, where his parents were talking over drinks before dinner. The granite counter tops and stainless-steel appliances were as pristine as ever thanks to the maids. His mother sat at the island, blonde hair around her shoulders, blue eyes clouded until she saw him. Then they turned disappointed and disapproving, a look he had become accustomed to lately and wanted to end. She wore a white blouse and matching, tight skirt to just above her knees, and looked no less lovely at 50 than she ever had.

His father held a bottle of red wine in one slender hand, a gold watch at his wrist, button-up shirt neat and tucked into khakis, a black belt around his waist. Clean-shaven with salt-and-pepper hair, he always looked distinguished and respectable—his blue eyes strong, clear, and direct. That intimidated some people, but had never bothered Daniel before now. The steel in them was a new look that had replaced the kindness he usually showed his children.

They had argued about all of this just this morning, so Daniel didn't bother working his way up to it. "Are you ready to hear the truth?"

His father met his gaze, unimpressed with the suggestion. "We've been ready. Are you?"

Daniel pursed his lips. "I'm sorry for not telling you sooner. None of us thought you would believe us."

"Who's us?" his mother asked before sighing. "You and Ryan? Or the others?"

Daniel decided to start slow and not list everyone who knew at first. That would just piss them off, that they were the last to know. "Me and Ryan, Anna, Matt, and Eric. I don't really have their permission to tell you, but they do trust me to handle things while they're gone, and I'm making the call on this."

She asked, "Why are you telling us now?"

"We need your help. You may want another glass of that wine."

Instead of pouring one, his father took a stool. "Out with it."

Daniel took a deep breath. "I don't want to rehash things, but you know they've been disappearing, whether anyone sees it happen or not."

"Have you?" his father asked.

"No. Not in person."

Looking pained at his own question, his father asked, "Is this wizardry or something? Things are happening all over the world. Some are doing magic by accident, and killing people. Others are doing healing without meaning to, then trying on purpose."

Daniel knew of his father's disdain for fantasy books, movies, and games. Magic happening for real had to irritate him. "I know, and yes, it is magic. They just aren't causing it. They have no choice."

His mother grabbed the wine bottle, her expression equally unimpressed so that he knew she didn't believe him yet. She asked, "What does that mean, they have no choice?"

This was the part they would struggle with, and he had thought long and hard about how not to sound outlandish. Not at first. "They're being magically summoned somewhere. It is different each time, a different place. They have to do something before they can be sent back, and what they have to do also changes each time."

Scowling, his father asked, "Summoned to where? Who is doing this? And how?"

"What do they have to do?" his mother asked, and Daniel wondered if they were peppering him with questions to see if he actually had answers. They were going to be surprised if they thought they could catch him unprepared.

"Slow down. It's never the same twice, except that they disappear without warning and they can't stop it from happening. They always go together, even though they're often apart when they are summoned. And when it's over and they can go home, they go right back to where they were when they're summoned."

His father's calculating eyes were on him. "That's why Anna reappeared on the highway."

"Right. And it's a problem."

His father snorted. "Yeah. How are they supposed to go anywhere when this can happen?"

"That's one of the reasons we need your help. They need to stay in one place while they're on Earth, so that when they're sent back here, they arrive somewhere safe and not on a highway."

His mother fingered her wine glass. "Did you say 'on Earth'?"

Daniel hesitated, not having realized he'd admitted it. Then he wondered whether his accidental revelation and the "oops" expression he wore might convince them he wasn't kidding. "Yes. I know that may be hard to believe—"

"Yeah," his father interrupted, "I was starting to take you seriously."

"Dad, look, I *am* being serious."

"So there are aliens summoning them?" his father snidely asked. "Why don't they come in a spaceship and get them?" His mother laughed and Daniel sighed.

"They're usually humans, for one, and so far they've always been from worlds less sophisticated than ours."

His father asked, "Well, if that's true, then how would people from another planet know who they are to summon them? Multiple other planets? You're going to need a good explanation for that one. And why them?"

"I have a good answer for that. Just hear me out. I swear this will all make sense and explain everything that is happening in the world. Ryan and the others are the cause of it all."

That seemed to get their attention from the way his parents exchanged a look, his father pouring both of them a glass and settling in.

"No bullshit, Daniel. I'm serious."

"So am I."

And so Daniel explained who the Ellorian Champions were, and that someone had once summoned them to Earth's past for another quest.

His father asked. "Time travel now? Who summoned them?"

Daniel didn't want to admit it, but his father's frown told him the omission might cost him. "Look, now you accept that magic is real because you've seen it, on camera anyway. Supernatural healing is also being reported. Well, lots of things we thought were myths are real, but they disappeared or stopped working a thousand years ago. The Ellorian Champions and their quest are why."

"Who summoned them?" his father repeated.

"Morgana. And yes, I mean the one you are thinking of. She was real. So was Merlin." He paused, gauging their reaction. No one said anything. His father just stared at him. Finally, he spoke.

"Go on."

"It's a long story, but Morgana was doing bad things with magic. Merlin wanted to stop her. The only way he could was to drain the magic from Earth back into the faerie world, so he cast a spell to do that. It took time to complete, and before it did, Morgana summoned the Ellorians to stop it. But they talked with Merlin and learned it had to be done, so they refused the quest."

Smirking as if she'd caught him, his mother said, "I thought they had to do it to go home."

"Yeah, and that's the issue. They were magically bound to do the quests against their will. But if they were still here when the magic stopped working, it might free them from the unwanted quests. But it would trap them here. It worked. Sort of. Magic stopped working here. All the faerie creatures were pulled into the faerie world. That world and Earth had been separated ever since—until Ryan, Anna, Matt and Eric went to Stonehenge."

This time his father looked intrigued, no doubt because he already accepted that Ryan had been missing from Stonehenge for three weeks. "Why? Is Stonehenge one of these Quest Rings?"

"Sort of. Not really. Morgana turned it into a makeshift one. It's really a portal between the faerie world and Earth. It's the most powerful doorway. From what they told me, Merlin had a failsafe for the spell, which could be undone if a pendant he created was brought back to Stonehenge. We still don't know how it happened, but that pendant somehow ended up with Anna. You've seen it before. She's been wearing it since I've known her."

He stopped again, sensing from their expressions that they were now invested, things clicking into place for them. Stonehenge was the key to making them believe him. He saw that now.

His father asked, "So they went to Stonehenge on vacation and brought this pendant there without knowing it would, what, unleash magic? This is why magic is working? And healing?"

"Yes. They had no idea what the pendant was at the time."

His mother's brow was furrowed. "Is this how Anna went from paralyzed to walking again? You said those Quest Rings heal them."

"Yeah. The summoning spell does it. So does the one sending them back. It took her right out of the bed at the hospital and healed her before she and the others arrived for their quest."

"Wait," his father said intently. "Are they on... they're on a quest right now? Is that why he's not around?"

"Yes."

"A quest to do what?"

"We won't know until they get back and tell us." Daniel knew the answer this time but wasn't going to say it. The trip to Elloria was too complicated to explain.

His mother asked again, "Us?"

Daniel nodded sheepishly. "Me, Jack, and Quincy. We're the only ones who know."

"*Quincy* knows about this?" his mother asked.

"Yeah. Look, Jack already knew because they told him after they returned from Stonehenge. Then they disappeared right in front of him at Anna's apartment Long story. He's been helping them."

"Helping them how?"

"Just trying to cover for them, or look after their things while they're gone. Look, he's literally working for them now. Jack quit his job at Starbucks and is full-time trying to take care of any problems for them here while they're gone. Quincy and I are, too."

His father continued scowling, but Daniel noticed his parents had stopped being snide. "How did Quincy get involved?"

"When Anna reappeared in the highway and was hit by the car, they'd known it might happen. Ryan raced off to get there, but it was too late. A car had already struck her. He was upset and pushed through the police barriers, and they arrested him."

"I remember."

"Quincy got him out, of course—and Ryan and the others, and Jack, decided to tell me and Quincy the truth. I had found the stash of weapons at the quest house here. Susan was with me."

His father put up both palms toward him. "Wait. Wait. Does Susan know?"

"No."

"What stash of weapons?" he asked.

Daniel sighed. "We're getting ahead of ourselves. Listen, when they get summoned, they have to go on quests just like the Ellorian Champions—but they don't have the skills, so they've been trying to practice while they're back on Earth. They bought a bunch of swords, longbows, and other shit. Ryan had them at the guest house and was unloading them from his car when they were summoned. I was playing with my drone later and saw his car there, so Susan and I went to check it out and found of the stuff in there. That's how I started to learn what was going on."

His father said, "So wait, why are they doing these quests instead of the Ellorians?"

"That's the interesting part. We don't really know how it happened, but they've been substituted for them. You asked why people from other worlds would know who they are and summon them. The answer is that they don't. People think they're summoning the Ellorian Champions and they're actually showing up, but it's Ryan, Anna, Matt, and Eric. They've been playing along because they think the reputation of the real Champions prevents people from realizing how vulnerable they are."

His mother asked, "Doesn't anyone realize they aren't these Champions?"

Daniel knew the elf Lorian had but didn't admit it. "No. Few inhabitants of places that summoned them ever saw the real Champions, and Ryan and the others bear enough resemblance in hair color, size, and all of that. Remember, these worlds don't have cameras, so it's not like you can compare photos to them and realize it isn't them."

She said, "Yeah, but the clothes give them away, don't they? The style would be all wrong."

"The summoning spell changes their clothes. Ryan arrives in golden armor and is expected to be the knight Korrin. Matt is the wizard Soliander. Eric is the rogue Andier. And Anna is the priestess Eriana."

His father chuckled. "I bet Anna loves that."

Daniel pursed his lips and admitted, "Yeah, she was really against it, but seeing healing and magic working got through to her and she believed it the more she saw it. From what I understand, she's healed people with the power of a god on these other worlds." He stopped and let them process that. It seemed like every answer had the ability to make them believe him or grow skeptical again, an ebb and flow of taking him seriously.

"So if they're on a quest right now," his mother observed, "they're in danger?"

"Probably." He explained how the elf Lorian had trained Matt in some wizardry, and helped Ryan and Eric with swordsmanship. A dwarf had helped Anna get over her atheism, at least a little. Then he added, "Yes, they are always in danger while they're gone. They've done pretty well despite not being the real Champions."

His father asked, "Well, what about these Ellorians? Where are they?"

Daniel took a deep breath. "That's another interesting bit, and leads up to why we need you now. The Ellorians have been missing for years. But we've found out about two of them. We don't know where Korrin or Andier are, but Ryan and the others ran into Soliander on the first quest. He attacked them."

"Wait," his father interrupted, scowling. "I thought he was a good guy."

"He was. We don't know what happened to him yet, but he's a threat, and one we need to worry about. And this time by 'we' I mean all of us in this room, too, which is one of the reasons I'm telling you all of this. Soliander knows about all of us—where we live. He has been here."

"To our house?" his mother asked, looking around nervously.

"To Earth. He's been to Jack's apartment, looking for Ryan and the others. We don't understand how he knew to look there. It's possible that he'd come here to our house at some point, or even to the Sorenson's house, or Anna's parents', and found out about Jack and tried going there. Remember how after Anna's accident, the one that put her in the hospital, Ryan wasn't here? None of them were at home. They were all hiding in a hotel, hiding from the police and the media. But also hiding from Soliander. He must have found out about Jack somehow and tracked him to the apartment."

His father asked, "Is Jack okay?"

"Yeah, he's fine. Soliander didn't realize he was there."

"Why is he after them?"

"We don't really know—but Matt has a copy of his staff, and he likely wants that back. And it seems like he's searching for the other Champions and hasn't found them. Or, well, he hadn't. Listen, we also know where Eriana is. Or we did. She has been on Earth for the last twenty years." He explained how, when Merlin's spell was completed, an explosion hurled Soliander back to the right world and time... but it trapped Eriana on Earth and threw her *almost* back to the present. She had been living under an assumed name in Florida, married to a banker, and collecting supposed magic items in case they ever worked and were needed.

He concluded, "When Eriana saw the broadcast of Ryan and the others being found near Stonehenge, she recognized the pendant Anna wore and knew they had caused magic to start working again. She sought them out and arrived in Maryland not long ago. She introduced herself and befriended them. She told us a lot of history and has promised to help. And this is where I'm going with all of this. Days ago, she was at Jack's apartment with him. Ryan and the others had been there overnight but were missing in the morning and we assumed someone had summoned them again. While Jack was in the kitchen, Soliander knocked on the door. Eriana opened it and they were face-to-face for the first time in a long time, both shocked to see each other. She let him in, and Jack overheard and recorded their conversation on the security camera he has inside."

Daniel picked up his phone and started the video and audio that Jack had shared with him. It showed the wizard and priestess reuniting, and her expressing concerns about his behavior. The video ended with Soliander grabbing her wrist and speaking a word as Jack ran into the room. He dove for them, but the pair vanished. Both of Daniel's parents reacted out loud with shock and amazement.

His father ran a hand over one cheek. "My God, you really aren't kidding about all of this."

"No."

He asked, "What's to stop this Soliander from doing this to anyone else?"

"Honestly, nothing. It's one reason why you need to know what's happening. So do Matt and Anna's parents. We could all be targets. Maybe Eriana can talk some sense into Soliander, but I don't know. I mean, he just kidnapped her. Anyway, we need to make certain things happen here while Ryan and the others are gone."

"Like what?" his mother asked.

This was it. The big ask. But he now knew they were on board. That video had been the final key. "They need a home base set up, one no one knows about. Not the media, not the authorities, and not someone like Soliander. We were going to buy an estate up near Darnestown. Eriana was going to pay for it, since she's wealthy and she feels some responsibility for all this. But now she's gone. You guys have the money and, well, I'll just say it—you need to buy the estate Daniel and I agreed on, and do it in such a way that it's hard to track who actually owns it. Quincy was working on something for that, like a shell corporation or some shit. I don't know how that really works."

His father waved that off. "I do. Okay, listen, this is a lot to digest. But we get it. That video... Well, if that wasn't convincing, nothing is. I can see now why you didn't tell us sooner."

His mother suddenly grew tearful and came over to him, throwing her arms around him. "I'm sorry we've been hard on you lately. This is a lot. I don't know how you guys are managing it."

"It's okay, Mom," Daniel said, as she pulled away. "You know, you guys have doted on me most of my life. It's Ryan's turn. He's the one who needs you. Magic is starting to work again, and healing, and somehow he and the others are the focal point of the whole thing."

His father nodded slowly, eyes calculating, his jaw clenching with resolve. "Call a meeting tomorrow morning with Quincy. Get Jack here. We'll get this going and then bring in Anna's and Matt's parents." He walked over to a cabinet, opening it to reveal a steel safe, which he unlocked before pulling out a handgun.

"It's time for us to get serious."

CHAPTER ELEVEN

THE PRISONERS

Eriana wasn't sure how long she had been asleep. That was the side-effect of magically induced slumber; it could last minutes to years, though only skilled wizards could do the latter. The one who'd done it to her was among the most skilled to ever live. But she suspected it couldn't have been more than a day, if that. There was no reason for more, unless Soliander needed to think. To figure out what to do with her. She had no doubt he had acted impulsively when kidnapping her, that he'd had no plan. It almost didn't surprise her that, at the very moment they'd arrived wherever they were, Soliander had put her to sleep.

Eriana felt alert, refreshed, and unharmed as she leaned up on one elbow. She was on a soft bed with a plush mattress. Her eyes quickly scanned the room for company, finding no one. Then she examined it more carefully as she tossed the thick blanket off herself and sat up. She still wore a t-shirt, jeans, and short socks from Earth, but her shoes were gone. Beside the bed on a table stood a pitcher of water and a tray of what she presumed was food under a steel cover. It smelled like ham and seasoned potatoes and she sighed. He had prepared, or made someone else prepare, one of her favorite foods. Should she be that pleased he remembered after all this time? Then she realized it had only been a few years for him, not the two decades she'd experienced. Her other thought was unusually suspicious for her, that it was a bribe or peace offering, its sincerity in doubt.

Her stomach rumbled... and she didn't think for one second that Soli would poison her. She had always trusted him with her life and still did, despite knowing he had changed. That was what she most needed to know—who he had become. He had refused to tell her what he'd really been up to these past few years while apparently living under an assumed name. She had no way to compel the truth from him.

But she knew that he had hardened himself, partly from the thought he had inadvertently killed her. Now he knew better. It seemed obvious that a crack in that hard shell must have formed from his discovery that she still lived. She almost wasn't concerned that he'd kidnapped and imprisoned her—not really. He'd said it himself that, having found her after all this time, he couldn't very well just leave her behind on Earth. And so instead of kidnapping Matt, Anna, Ryan, and Eric, he'd kidnapped her.

That made her wonder—was the room designed for one or more of them? Looking around, she doubted it. The accommodations were pleasant, if seemingly not much used. An elegant dresser stood along one wall. A swivel mirror sat upon a stand. A marble bathtub peeked out from behind a foldable privacy screen. There were no paintings on the walls, just lanterns, a crystal chandelier on the ceiling, and windows on each wall. She rose to peer out of one, discovering that she was in a tower.

Snow-capped mountains loomed just outside the window, and she knew they were on the other three sides without having to look. Soliander had always been dramatic, something of a romantic. She had so often caught him staring off at a mountain range as if he was curious what wonders lay within. He found the deep shadows, the surprises around every corner, and the ruggedness appealing. She preferred being able to see danger from a long way off, like she could on a grassy plain.

From one of the windows, she saw more of the castle her tower was a part of. The dark structure seemed unguarded, and below her lay a parapet. Nearby, stairs led down to the rocky ground, a trail winding away among the peaks to who-knows-where.

"Too bad my hair isn't longer," she quipped, thinking of Rapunzel. She spied her shoes casually discarded on the stone floor but left them there. With little else to do, she helped herself to the food and waited for her old friend to appear.

An hour passed before she heard footsteps approaching on the stone floors. Somehow, after all this time, she still recognized Soliander's footfall. He padded quietly like a cat, the leather soles of his boots scraping the stairs just enough for her to hear as she sat still. In bare feet, he could sneak up on anyone. A key clicked in the lock of a dark wooden door, the black metal handle turning. Then the door slid open to reveal Soliander in a black tunic and trousers, tucked into matching boots. He had never explained his preference for the color. She had long ago thought it accentuated a goodness in him that he seemed to want no one to notice, though she knew better. Now, the somber color made her wonder whether it had been a harbinger of the darkness that consumed him.

Soliander entered alone, the heavy door swinging shut. His wavy brown hair hadn't changed, though it had grown longer past his shoulders. But his eyes looked different. She had seen many things in them before. Guilt. Turmoil. Anger. Intelligence. Those were all present, but what struck her was what was missing. Kindness. Humor. Warmth. Nobility. And their absence made his intelligence seem cunning, cruel, remorseless. He was frightening. He'd always had enough power to worry any rational person, but his finer qualities meant only the wicked had something to fear. Now she wondered if everyone did.

Except her.

"First, I must apologize," he said.

Eriana frowned, trying to ignore the rush of pleasure she felt on hearing his voice again. "Do you expect me to take it seriously?"

He looked startled, then seemed to accept that. "No, but I will say it anyway."

"Good." Showing remorse was a good sign, but she hid her relief.

"I meant what I said before bringing you here. I could not leave you again after thinking you dead for three years and suddenly finding you alive, albeit aged twenty years. A long conversation in that place was not the best option."

"And this was?" she interrupted.

Ignoring that, he said, "You wouldn't come. I felt I had no choice but to bring you anyway."

"You could have respected my choice." Something about his demeanor made her remark, "I get the impression you no longer respect what others want for themselves."

He shrugged. "When did anyone respect what I wanted for myself?"

Knowing he meant being summoned against his will, she said, "That doesn't make this right." When he didn't respond, she asked, "What did you gain by putting me to sleep?"

He sighed. "Time to think. I will take you back to Earth, or to Elloria, if you prefer that to being with me. I would like your help first."

Eriana relaxed a bit. He sounded reasonable, at least. "What I *want* is to go to Coreth to see my family. I *need* to go to Earth to help Anna and the others. I also want to stay with you to learn what you know about what has happened, and what you have been doing. But the need outweighs the wants and is urgent."

"Then we both want information from each other. The sooner we exchange it, the sooner you can meet your needs."

She leaned against the bed to make this less confrontational than standing squared off with him. Genuinely curious, she asked, "What help do you need?"

"I need to know who these imposters are and how they came to be impersonating us. What have you learned that you can tell me?"

She certainly had that information to barter with, and there was another advantage to telling him the truth. Hoping to extract a promise, she asked, "If I tell you, will you avoid using that *Mind Trust* spell on them?"

He appeared to consider this, but without much regret on his face. "I can't promise anything, but I trust you, even if you do not trust me. I am not judging you for that. I would not trust me either."

"Very reassuring."

"You know that my reason for seeking them was to learn how they were substituted and whether they knew anything about you, Korrin, and Andier. Tell me what they have told you and I won't need to hear it from them. That would mean not capturing them, which you seem to oppose."

She watched him for a moment, thinking that he had always been both logical and practical. And so she related what she knew, focusing on details that she thought posed no danger. Unfortunately, he fixated on one issue for which no one had an answer. When Merlin cast the spell on Earth to drain magic into the fae world, stripping it from the Earth, he created the magical pendant that, when returned to Stonehenge, would undo the spell and allow magic to return. The fairy creatures—elves, dwarves, dragons and more—would also return.

"No one knows the history of this pendant?" he asked again. "It survives for a thousand years and somehow makes it into the hands of a girl who goes to Stonehenge on holiday."

"I know. I am an expert in antiquities there, and I can tell you no one has ever seen it. I have been looking for it for two decades, and there's no mention of it in any books."

"If I can get my hands on it, I can cast a spell to retrace where it has been. I've traced something for more than a few years, but a thousand?" He then asked, "You have been studying this?"

Eriana nodded. She related how she had married a wealthy man with the means to acquire every potentially magical item—and so she had been collecting them, even though none of them worked. She was partly just searching for the pendant, but she also wanted them in case magic ever started working again, though she had eventually given up hope and only continued out of habit, curiosity, and wishful thinking.

Soliander asked no questions as she spoke for several minutes, and his first question almost didn't surprise her, mostly because his face had tightened as if under strain.

"You have a husband?"

She nodded. "He is a good man who treats me well. That is all you need to know." The last thing she needed was a jealous Soliander imagining any details about her husband or personal life.

He held her gaze, and then changed the subject back to the imposters. "I know their names and more from the spell I did on Matt, but you have talked with them. What do you think of them?"

"They are good people, Soli. And they are not a threat to you, or me. They are victims of this just like we were, only it's worse. They aren't qualified. You don't need to go after them."

"I need the copy of my staff back from Matt."

Eriana shook her head. "No, he needs it. They would be dead already without it."

"What is that to me?"

"You never used that to be so callous," she observed, hoping he wasn't now either and was just being rude. "Everyone thinks they are us. Do you want everyone thinking we are dead when they get killed, because you took the staff?"

"I already thought everyone was dead. People accepted that we were missing or presumed dead. What does it matter if they get confirmation this time?"

"Because it's a lie, one that I won't go along with. And we all have families. That would be a cruel thing to do to them. Look how you felt when you thought *I* was dead."

The way he pursed his lips told her he didn't have a counter for that. "Maybe I'll keep you here after all, and then no one will know."

"Some people already know. This secret isn't going to last. More people will try to summon them, and succeed, and it's just a matter of time before people who knew us see them instead. Besides, are you really going to keep me a prisoner for the rest of my life? You may have changed, but Everon trapped us together for years in the quest cycle. You aren't going to trap me any longer than necessary."

"I've changed."

Eriana knew he was bluffing. "Not in that way. You said it yourself, that everything you've done since breaking free was to ensure you weren't a prisoner again. You will not imprison one of us for your own freedom, especially when setting me free would not harm your freedom in the least."

"You seem awfully certain of that. Is that why you're so calm about this?"

"Who said I was calm? I'm furious that you took me away. I am needed back there. Urgently."

He frowned. "For what? They have done well on their quests."

She shook her head. "They all need training—and I'm the only one on that planet who can help the girl, Anna." She wasn't going to mention buying the estate for them as a new hideout. Soli knew where to find them now. She wouldn't help him understand that they were going somewhere he wouldn't know about. But she had another point.

"Magic has begun to awaken there. That means healing, too. I've lived there for two decades, Soli. They aren't ready for it. People are already freaking out about the Stonehenge Four, as they're known, disappearing on camera like they have. And random people with magic talent can suddenly make things happen. Those people are scared, and people fear them. And then the healers are just gaining their powers, which sounds good, but that world is more desperate for faith and hope than any we ever visited. I don't know how much technology you saw, but it's going to get ugly there soon."

"What does any of that have to do with me? Or you?"

"I can help people. I'm not sure how, but I'm the only skilled person who knows that world."

"Maybe so, but it will presumably be a while before the planet falls apart."

He was right that the Earth itself didn't need her help just yet, but the four friends did. "The new Champions need me back on Earth. The missing Home Rings are a huge problem because of what happens when they return. I am one of the few who can help, partly because only I can heal them if they get as badly injured as before when they go back. They could have returned already. They could be hurt even now."

He sighed. "Yes, I know. I am not completely unsympathetic."

Then maybe some good part of him remained. After hesitating, she added, "You could really help them. Give them the spell to create the Home Rings, at least. Some soclarin ore. Or even create the rings for them. Give them a chance to live their lives when they aren't on some damn quest they don't want. They're just trying to survive, Soli, and they are a lot more like kids than we were. They are in over their heads. This is not their fault—and the last thing they need is not to be able to safely return home, or to be a prisoner there for fear of leaving and being summoned and sent back into the middle of a highway. And they certainly don't need you attacking them."

He said nothing for a minute. She watched his troubled eyes, feeling some relief at the concern they revealed. He was still in there—her Soli, not this cold, calculating man who he wore like a bad suit. Except it somehow seemed to fit him, as if giving in to all the anger he'd felt for so long suited him in an awful way. Was he misdirecting it at everyone? Because going after Everon was one thing. Attacking Anna and the others was going too far and she felt renewed hope that he saw that, however much he might have changed. And his next words comforted her.

"You're making me feel guilty."

"Good. If you won't create the Home Rings for them, then you can at least tell them how to do it for themselves. Or tell me."

He shook his head. "They can't create them."

"Why not?"

"They need soclarin ore to create the keystones for the rings, but they don't have any. And no, I'm not giving them some. Besides, the only place to create the keystones is my old home, because the forge there is enchanted for it, and I'm not letting them in there."

Memories of his home saddened her, for she had spent considerable time there and it was one of the many things lost. She had known at once that they weren't there now, from the construction if not the atmosphere. "Why? What are you hiding there?"

He pursed his lips. "Bad memories."

She eyed him. "Funny. I only had good ones." Then she realized what he meant. "But you mean it's where Everon betrayed you, making the keystones for all the Quest Rings he created without telling you. Us."

"I never should have taught him. I didn't know who he really was. If only I'd been using the *Mind Trust* spell on people back then, none of this would have happened."

"You knew better then."

He shook his head. "I was a fool then. You can't tell me that not doing it was the right thing when someone did the wrong thing to us as a result and we have suffered ever since, our lives destroyed. And for what? To protect the privacy of someone who was there to deceive and then betray me?"

Eriana sighed. "So what now? You become ruthless?"

"Absolutely."

"For what it's worth, I understand what you're saying. I just don't like what you're doing."

Looking grim, he asked, "Have you ever wondered how many other people we've angered on our quests? For every kingdom we save, we destroy the plans and sometimes lives of the so-called villains we defeat. And they have families, people like Everon, who can come for revenge. We may have more enemies than anyone."

"Yes, I have wondered. Is that the reason why you live under another name now?"

"No."

He wasn't one to live in fear, she knew. And now that he was ruthless, anyone would have to be a fool to go after the Majestic Magus, Soliander of Aranor. He was revered and respected—and dreaded by those up to no good. But was he also now feared by those living good lives? Maybe he still cared enough about his reputation to do everything under another name. What would their families think of him now?

Eriana began, "I have been away from my family for two decades. I want to see them, Soli. What do you know about them?"

He seemed relieved by the change of subject. "Your brother is managing your estate and doing well. You needn't worry about him. I have kept watch from afar."

Startled, she smiled at him, relief flooding her. "You are still a good man. I knew it. *Thank you*, Soli. That means so much to me, I hardly know how to tell you."

He poorly hid a blush as he waved this off. "You would've done the same, except Taryn needs no help."

"How is she?" Eriana asked, curious about the no-nonsense warrior she had always liked. She knew Soliander loved and respected her even if he'd never say so. "You haven't seen her?"

"I keep tabs on her as well. She is fine. Commander of a force of men, of course. You know her. No one tells her what to do—it's the other way around."

"She doesn't know you're alive?"

"No."

"Why? You know she adores you."

He shrugged and then smirked halfheartedly. "Maybe I don't want to break her heart."

Eriana sighed, suspecting she wouldn't get anything about that out of him any time soon. But she wanted to ask about her own sister, a subject likely to upset him. But she had to know. "And my sister? What of Diara?"

His expression turned distant. "You don't want to know."

Eriana shook her head. "Is she still with Everon?"

The thought didn't pain her. Not anymore. Without Diara's cooperation, Everon's could not have betrayed them. It was she who had secured a piece of hair or something else with DNA—though only people from Earth thought of it that way—from her, Korrin, Andier, and Soli. Using these, Everon altered the summoning spells he imbued the keystones with, and this was what had made the quests involuntary.

"She still loves him, if that's what you're asking."

"Soli!" she said, tired of him dodging questions.

He looked startled, then frowned. "She is not with him, no. I have separated them for some time."

When he didn't elaborate, she asked, "How can you be sure? You haven't found him. You have found her?"

He held her gaze for a long time. "Yes. I know where she is." He didn't elaborate and she hardened her expression, knowing he was withholding the answer. She wasn't going to ask again, settling for glaring. He looked uncomfortable and she felt suspicious.

"What did you do with her?"

He went to the window and looked toward one of the other towers. "She is here," he admitted.

That was the one answer she hadn't expected. But maybe she should not have been surprised. Vengeance had been such a frequent desire of his. That he would turn that on her sister wasn't unexpected, even if she might find out. Had he truly given up hope that Eriana was alive? Because learning what he'd done to Diara might've ended any chance of her forgiving him for whatever awful behavior he'd engaged in during the last three years. Her sister's condition would therefore tell her more than just Diara's fate.

"What have you done to her?"

"She is fine. I would not hurt her, on account of you."

A good answer. "Why not?"

He shrugged. "You would not approve, whether you still lived or not."

"I want to see her." She joined him at the window and followed his gaze. "Is that where you keep her?"

"I'm not sure it's a good idea for you to see her."

"Why not? You said she was fine."

He nodded. "Physically, yes. But she is ever more in the grip of Everon. Your sister is lost, Eriana. No good that can come from you interacting with her."

"I would see this for myself."

Soliander shook his head. "This is a decision I am making for you."

She gripped his arm and turned him toward her. "No. You don't get to do that. Do you understand me? You will not disrespect me that way. Ever."

He frowned. "Eriana. You must trust me. There is no good that can come from this."

Anger welled up in her, but she hid it well. The man she admired was still in there, but enough of this new guy remained to warp his judgement about what was appropriate. Maybe he needed a reminder that wielding power over others without their permission was exactly what had gotten them into this mess. She put one hand on his heart and spoke a word. From the sudden alarm on his face, he recognized it. But then his eyes rolled back, and he slumped to the floor, audibly snoring.

"You're not the only one with power, old friend."

Eriana leaned down over the wizard and examined his face. The coldness, anger, and contempt had gone and left him more like she remembered—noble, goodhearted, and sensitive. He had never let his power or strength go to his head, but that seemed long over. She felt confident the man she had loved was still in there—she just had to get him out. She sighed in resignation, unsure where to go from here But she finally straightened, walked to the pitcher of water, and returned, dumping it over his head.

He sputtered and came awake with a look of shock, surprise, and outrage. But he quickly recognized the situation and looked up at her smirking face. He relaxed despite his muted glare.

"Was that really necessary?"

Her humorless smile broadened. "No."

Soliander rose, shook the arms of his soaked tunic, then spoke a few words and became instantly dry. He eyed her for several seconds, as if trying to downplay being caught off guard. "Why didn't you leave?"

"For starters, I need your help to get back to Earth or even Elloria. But I already told you. I want to know what you have been doing, so are you going to tell me or not?"

"I haven't decided."

That was better than a no. "Why don't you start with immediately after I last saw you on Earth. Surely you didn't go evil immediately, and you can tell me what you experienced."

With the way he pursed his lips, she knew she had cornered him. He confirmed it by gesturing for her to sit—but he remained standing, slowly pacing as they talked. He let out a deep breath and she feared he would stall, so she took control of the conversation.

"Did you arrive on Elloria?"

"Yes, a few miles from home, in the mountains. I was injured."

"But you used your Trinity Ring?" she asked. With his help, she had designed them for exactly that sort of scenario—when either Andier, Korrin, or Soli, who all had one, were hurt and she wasn't there to heal them. Just as the Quest Rings restored them to health on summoning them or sending them home, they replenished the three healing spells of different strengths in each ring's gemstones.

Soliander shook his head. "No. The stones in it were shattered."

That surprised her, but maybe it shouldn't have. She only remembered a little about the moment he'd attempted to send them back with magic just as magic stopped working on Earth. His look of alarm had told her something was wrong, but she saw nothing like an explosion—just a flash of blinding light at Stonehenge before she found herself standing in a New Zealand field, instead of at home in Coreth.

"What injuries did you have?"

"Broken leg and a few ribs. A concussion."

Frowning in concern, she asked, "How did you get home?"

"I crawled." He seemed a little indignant about that. Changing the subject, he asked, "Were you injured after the spell?"

"No. Nothing. I'm sorry that happened to you. I am curious now, and concerned, what might have happened to the others."

He nodded. "Now you know why I thought you were all dead and I'd killed you, especially when you remained missing. I searched for your bodies." He looked pained, and she knew that must have been awful. No wonder he was angry. She wondered whether survivor's guilt was part of what had driven him since.

She ventured, "You were closer to the spell, since you were casting it. That may have had something to do with your injuries."

"Possibly. It doesn't matter."

"So you made it back, got healed with a potion I assume... and then what?"

"I cast myself to Coreth and your Home Ring. It was damaged and there was no sign of you. I asked around. Your brother hadn't seen you. I went to Korrin's ring, and Andier's. Both were damaged, and only then did I check mine. Neither of them had been seen and that remained true in the weeks after."

"You saw my brother?" Eriana asked in surprise. Then something occurred to her. "Wait. Everyone thinks we all went missing and never returned. How is it that you..." She trailed off, a suspicion forming.

He flashed a rueful smile. "Yes, I made everyone who had seen me forget they had done so."

She stared for a moment. "Why?"

"Lots of reasons. I didn't want people asking what had happened, wanting explanations I couldn't give them. I didn't want people giving up hope on all of you, like I soon did. And I didn't want people asking why I was the only survivor, as if I had done something to all of you. I felt like I had. But having anyone else look at me like I had was too much. Some of them already did, like Korrin's brother, so I used a spell and wiped his memory of my return. He was the first. Then came the others."

Eriana watched him closely, seeing grief, shame, and other signs that the good man she had known was still in there. "What then? You assumed a new identity, moved here?"

He flashed a smile. "Something like that. It's a longer story."

"I have time."

"I do not."

"Is something more important than me?"

He looked startled, smiled, then sighed. "No, but I am important and there are things I must do. Not everything can be delegated."

"Who is Zoran the Devastator?" she asked. "You referred to yourself that way back on Earth. If you're going to walk out of this room to go devastate someone or something, I'd just as soon you stay here and talk to me."

"Why? So you can talk me out of it?"

"Something like that."

"Some people deserve to be devastated."

"Like you?" she asked, hoping to get him to recognize that his upset of the past three years could lift. "Are you a little less devastated to know I'm alive and well?"

He looked at her and slowly smiled like the man he used to be. The expression transformed his face entirely. "I am more thrilled than I know how to tell you."

"Well, why don't you think about how to express it and come back later. I would like to hear it. For my part, I am far beyond thrilled to see you again, Soli. It has been three years for you, twenty for me. Based on the math, I should be more upset about the time apart than you, but I am not. Maybe it's time to start letting it go."

He pursed his lips. "You were always the best of us." They stood in silence for several moments before he went to the door, opened it, and turned back. "I need to decide what to do after what you've told me. It might be a while, as I have matters to attend to. I'm sorry for all of this. It is not what I would have wanted, if I'd foreseen finding you. I will return you to wherever you want, and soon. In the meantime, you will come to no harm here. You must know that."

Meeting his eye without humor, she admitted, "I don't know what to trust about you. But even if you let me go now, I would not leave. I want to know what you have been doing, Soli. Don't come back in here until you're prepared to tell me."

He sighed again. Then he left.

———— •··• ————

When the door next opened that night, Eriana half-expected Soliander despite not recognizing the footsteps as his. Instead, a dark elf entered, his skin and hair black, red eyes unfriendly. It had been a long time since she'd seen one. No dwarves, dragons, or anything else for twenty years on Earth, and the first non-human she sees is a sinister dark elf. She had nearly forgotten their existence—and the haughtiness in their expressions and body language. This one seemed deferential, and even bowed his head slightly. Soliander must have intimidated him, and the reality of the unsavory dark elves working for him did nothing to put her at ease about his activities.

"What do you want?" she asked, remembering that bluntness worked best.

"I am Darron, my lady," he answered smoothly, waiting by the open door. His eyes lingered on her clothing a moment, but he didn't seem intrigued by her Earth clothes. She wondered if he had been there. "I am to escort you to another guest."

She cocked an eyebrow. There could only be one other guest she cared about. "My sister?"

"Yes."

Eriana rose at once and donned her shoes, gesturing for the dark elf to proceed. She had considered what to say to Diara since Soliander had left hours earlier, but she really wasn't sure where to begin. The tension between them had dominated their relationship, but she held out hope that it was gone. It had been twenty years for her. Being negative wasn't her focus. But it had only been three years since her disappearance for Diara, who always seemed to dwell on negative thoughts. Had anything changed since then? Had she come to her senses and regretted what she had done? Or had she gotten worse, as Soli suggested? Eriana was well aware that the one wound she could never heal was the hate in her sister's heart. Had time done anything to soften it?

She eyed the slender dark elf before her, a torch in his hand, as they descended stone steps that curled along the inside wall of the tower. She had spent half her life in castles, towers, and homes without much convenience—the other half spent in the luxury of modern plumbing, toilet paper, soap and shampoo, and convenient ways of dealing with feminine problems. Smooth cars with air conditioning, radio, and comfortable seats had replaced bumpy wagons on hard wood with nothing but the elements around her. She had become used to glancing at a clock instead of the sun or night sky for the time. And information came at the touch of a finger, whereas now she didn't even know what planet she was on, not to mention what was going on in the world. For the first time, she realized that going back to her old life might be something she just couldn't do. And she felt renewed appreciation for how the replacement Champions were coping.

She and Darron passed several landings they passed before arriving at what she assumed to be one of the main levels of the castle. She confirmed this as they walked down several halls, peeking into doorways to sense that they were on an upper floor. She saw few other people, and wasn't surprised because Soliander had never been one for much company. Those people she did see were either humans or more dark elves.

They soon ascended another tower, once again climbing in winding circles. She knew from experience that imprisoning someone in a tower had advantages—there was only one way down, unless jumping to your death counted as a second. The keep seemed well-kept given how few people she'd seen, but then Soli wasn't above using magic for even mundane tasks. She wondered what the dark elf did for the wizard.

"How is it that a dark elf works for... Zoran?" No sense in revealing Soliander's true identity without understanding the consequences.

"The master offers unparalleled opportunities."

"For what? Power?"

"Yes. Everything else follows."

"And yet you seem afraid of him."

"He is demanding. And he does not tolerate failure."

"What does he do to those who fail?"

The elf cast a haunted look at her. "Something you don't want to experience. I had done it to others before he did it to me."

"Well, you survived, so it couldn't have been that bad."

Darron shook his head. "I did not."

"Then how... ? You..." She wasn't sure she wanted to finish the sentence. It was too ghastly.

"It is as you surmise. He turned me to a pile of hot ash, but the necromancer Aeron restored me at his behest. I have been given a second chance to please the master and in this I will not fail."

Eriana followed in aghast silence. This matter-of-fact story of murder and rebirth at Soliander's hands was her first true hint of the crimes he had committed. She didn't want to hear any more right now, feeling fatigued after a long day that was probably going to get worse.

Unused to the climbing, she felt her legs protesting as they reached a wooden door some hundred steps up. Dim light shone under it, but no sounds came from the other side—even as Darron unlocked it with a dark key and thrust it open without knocking. He gestured for her to enter.

"I will await you at the bottom." He turned and descended, soft steps fading with the disappearing torchlight.

The room before Eriana was similar in size and furnishings to the one she had just left, two dim lanterns casting light on the cold stone floor and the bed against the far wall. The only sign of life was a lump there under the sheets and comforter. It didn't stir, and she wondered if her sister had been told she was coming. She hoped for ignorance. Diara's initial reaction could tell her much for its honesty.

She stepped into the room and swung the door closed behind her with a mild bang that caused no movement. For a moment, she considered how best to continue before walking to the foot of the bed, grabbing a firm handful, and yanking down the comforter all at once. As expected, the figure, which had been laying on one side, lurched upright. Long, disheveled brown hair hid much of her angry face, though several thick scars were still visible through the strands. But the hair couldn't hide her furious brown eyes.

"Stop your games, dark—" She stopped. Her eyes widened, then rapidly scanned Eriana up and down, narrowing in suspicion, and finally glaring anew.

"It's nice to see you, Diara," Eriana said, relieved and concerned at once.

At the sound of her voice, her sister recoiled as if struck. Then called out to the room. "Is this another trick, Soliander? Darron? You got the voice right but she's as old as my dead mother, you fools."

Eriana absorbed that for a moment, wondering what the wizard had been doing to her, before saying, "It's not a trick. It's really me, Diara—and yes, I am twenty years older than when I disappeared with the others."

Diara snorted. "I don't believe that for a second. If it's really you, prove it."

Eriana knew no illusion could do what she was about to do. "Come closer."

Her sister smirked and crawled across the bed, closer than they had been in years even before the Earth quest. The strain of their relationship had kept them apart long before Diara's betrayal, and in fact had led to it. But Eriana gripped Diara's jaw from below, thumb on one side, fingers curling around the other, just like their mother used to do to them. This near, she could smell sweat and see that her sister hadn't washed in some time, although there was a tub in one corner. Was she refusing to use it or had Soli lied about taking care of her? She'd learn soon enough.

She spoke a few words and a soft glow spread over Diara, her hair straightening as if freshly washed, dirt vanishing from her face and fingernails. A healthier color was restored to her face, now clearly visible. Only now could Eriana see that she had gained weight, her face and breasts fuller, neck thicker, and hips tugging at the waist of a sleeping gown that had seen better days. Eriana recognized the sight of a woman who had given birth at least once. It startled her. Diara kneeled back on her heels and regarded her as if trying to make sense of her.

"That grip," she began almost fondly, "mother used to do that." Then something seemed to occur to her and she sneered. "You could have gotten that memory from the spell you did on me."

"The spell?" Eriana stopped herself and clenched her fists. "He cast the *Mind Trust* spell on you? Damn it, Soli." Then she realized it was obvious. Of course, he would have done that. Diara could know where Everon was. He wouldn't have left this up to an interrogation.

"Don't you ever get tired of these games?" Diara asked. "What's the point? You already know everything."

Eriana wondered that, too. Was Soli trying to break her? "I guess the first thing I need to do is get you to accept that it's really me."

Diara laughed. "Can't wait to see how—"

Eriana spoke again and felt her sister's eyes lock onto hers, Diara's sight in a magical grip that let her see the truth of what was before her so that it couldn't be denied. It was a spell used to bring brief sanity to the insane, peace to the delirious, or clarity to the deceived. After a few seconds, it ended. Her sister blinked a few times as if clearing her eyes from a bright light. And now would come the expression that told Eriana where they stood.

But Eriana couldn't read it. Diara's eyes held too many questions—too much surprise. No hatred, at least—but no happiness. A kind of neutrality lay there, disguised by lack of understanding.

"I have been on another world for twenty years," she explained, "because a spell took me back in time. And I was trapped there until Soliander found me and brought me here, yesterday, I believe."

Her sister arched an eyebrow, the first sign of old contempt returning. "You *believe*?"

Eriana pursed her lips. "He put me to sleep. I did not yet ask for how long."

Diara's eyes narrowed. "Why would he do that? He adores you." She sneered. "You mean to tell me you are enemies now? How wonderful!"

Sighing, Eriana said, "We are not anything. We have lived different lives and hardly know each other."

"You're like an old hag now. He wouldn't want you anyway. Who would? You can't even have children!"

Eriana's heart clenched at the confirmation that her sister was just as hateful as ever. "But you did. How many nieces and nephews do I have?"

Briefly startled, Diara responded, "It won't matter. You will never meet them."

"Where are they? Surely Everon isn't raising them while running for his life from Soliander?" She hadn't meant to goad her, but it slipped out.

Diara glared. "You know a lot about running, don't you? You ran from Jorad so fast you forgot to bring me and Solun with you, and look what that bastard did to us. Maybe I should be happy just to have scars on my face instead of a hand chopped off. Our brother didn't deserve that for trying to help you escape. You did. You're the one Jorad should have chopped a piece from, but you got away clean."

Eriana had heard some of this before, but that last part was too much. She snapped, "Really? You think him stabbing me in the stomach so I wouldn't have his bastard child was getting away clean? Never being able to have kids because of that?"

"Oh, but you have kids, remember? You baby me and Solun like you think you're our dead mom. And look at you now! You even *look* like her!"

"That's enough, Diara."

"It'll never be enough! No amount of pain and suffering is too much for you."

"Is that why you betrayed me to Everon?"

"Yes! You deserved it. Jorad just wanted you. Beautiful, lovely Eriana. He kidnapped all of us just to get *you*. And then you betrayed us by running away without us. And then you had the nerve to come back a healer, of all things, to save us! A renowned priestess! The Lady Hope, they call you. If only they knew, knew how you crushed the hope out of your dear brother and sister to save yourself. They all think you're so noble, going around saving everyone, everywhere on your damn quests. It makes me sick. Just looking at you makes me want to vomit. So yes. Yes, I made sure you could never say no again. Forced you to have to save everyone whether or not you wanted to. You can never run away again. You'll never escape being a hero now, dear sister! I hope you choke to death on your false heroism!"

Eriana flushed at the awful, vengeful logic, which struck home precisely because it made sense. But that just gave rise to her own upset.

"You are the betrayer in this family, Diara. And I haven't seen you since you stabbed me in the back to tell you how *sickening* it is. We were Jorad's prisoners *together*. You more than *anyone* should know just how horrific it is to be a prisoner, and you imprisoned me again. How dare you? Who do you think you are to do that to me? *I'm* the one who *freed* all of us from it. Not you. You didn't do a thing to help us escape. Your brother and I tried to get you out of there *with* us. If you hadn't been such a fool when we were running, we might all have made it. Instead, he sacrificed his hand for you just so I could get away and come back to get you both, and you're nothing but resentful about what we gave up. I forgave you for your cowardice that night because you were eleven years old."

"Well, you *should* have! Don't act like your *forgiveness* was so noble. I was a child!"

Fury tore through Eriana. "So was I! And you're still a child now. You might have the body of a woman, but that's the only part of you that's grown up. I'm sorry I didn't save you sooner, Diara. I got men killed trying to help me find you. I had to leave the priesthood to come get you. I gave up everything to rescue you. I didn't want or expect a thank you, but I sure as hell didn't expect you to repay me by *imprisoning me all over again!*"

"Well, you should have. It just shows how big a fool you are not to see it coming. And now I'm a prisoner again!" She jabbed an accusing finger at Eriana. "And it's all your fault!"

"How is this my fault? You know what? I don't want to hear it. Just shut up."

"What's the matter? Afraid of an argument you can't win?"

With an angry thrust of her hand, Eriana spoke a word and Diara collapsed on the bed, unconscious. Eriana was shaking, years of wondering about the logic behind this betrayal having an answer more terrible than any she could have anticipated. She knew Diara had hated her. It wasn't like she'd tried to hide it. But this was a stab in the heart like she had never known. Tears filled her eyes as she strode from the room. They had dried by the time she swept past Darron at the bottom and climbed to her own "prison," where she slammed the door shut and stalked back and forth.

However much this logic of Diara's was her own, she was certain Everon had contributed to it. For the first time, Eriana thought she might not stop Soliander from killing Everon if she found herself there when he tried.

CHAPTER TWELVE

THE SONS OF THE MAGI

Luna Rose Williams stared at the smoking screen of her laptop in shocked disbelief, then at her hands. The energy had come from her fingertips. She was certain, though there was no evidence—no scorch marks or anything. No, that was just the computer—a small fire still crackling in the cracked screen. It was already unplugged, and she knew the battery hadn't exploded. She had seen the fiery darts fly into the laptop.

Andy was going to be upset, even though the computer wasn't his. She needed a good story. She hadn't expected to be the first person they knew who'd cast a spell, however accidentally.

She got up and started pacing around her London flat, bare feet nearly soundless on the hardwood floor. The kettle began whistling that her hot water was ready, but she needed something stronger than tea now. She just turned it off before grabbing red wine from the rack beside the stainless-steel fridge. Andy would help her decide whether to tell the others. She wasn't sure she wanted the attention. Bloody hell, she was so scared right now and didn't even want to tell her boyfriend.

The front doorhandle rattled and she poured herself a big glass, noticing that her hand shook. What if it happened again? She didn't even know what caused it, so how could she prevent it?

Wearing just his running shoes, socks, and grey jogging shorts, Andy Rion opened the door. His sinewy torso gleamed with sweat, his chest not heaving even though he'd probably run here up four flights of stairs like usual. He met her gaze, his face immediately falling, dark eyes going to her shaking hand. He always noticed everything. Always.

"What happened?" he said, his accent a familiar but odd mix of British and American English.

Luna gulped her wine and was about to answer when he sniffed the air and turned toward the laptop, his face registering surprise that swiftly passed. He was always so quick to mask his expressions, but she still thought, maybe wrongly, that she was the only person for whom he dropped his guard.

"I, uh, the battery, I think it did something."

He arched an eyebrow, and she knew he didn't believe her. The man was impossible to lie to, but she actually liked that he could see right through her. Just not right now. He was kind enough to let the fibs go without comment and did so now.

He came over and leaned up to kiss her, since she was two inches taller than his five-and-a-half feet. She cupped his smooth cheek, then ran a hand through his black hair. It was a couple of inches long and perpetually disheveled. She'd made a game to try messing it up so that it looked bad, but it never worked. It somehow symbolized his perpetually unfazed demeanor, down-to-earth attitude, and internal strength. Maybe it was the black belts he held in multiple disciplines, but he always came across as being able to handle anything thrown at him.

Except maybe some fiery darts she hadn't meant to throw.

"Well," he began, pouring himself a glass of wine, "as long as the hard drive is fine, we can get stuff off it. I'll try in a bit."

"Can I borrow yours?"

He smirked and walked over to it. "Not sure I should let you."

When he placed it on the counter, she opened it and he typed in a passcode. With the screen unlocked, she saw what she thought of as a camera gallery. A dozen video feeds were running, but most were off. Some cameras—especially the one at Stonehenge—were only on at night, and were carefully hidden.

"What if you're wrong," she began, "and some faeries come through during the day?"

"We'll find out about it on the news when they scare the shit out of everyone. It's only the remote doorways between worlds where I think they might show up in daytime, but I still think the first fae to arrive will be from the Unseelie Court."

She sipped more wine. The Unseelie Court preferred nighttime shenanigans, but something worse than that was probably coming. A decapitated dwarf had already been found, minus the head, near Stonehenge but not been identified. Andy suspected it hadn't been one of Earth's little people, but an actual dwarf from Elfhame, the land of fae.

"I hope you're wrong," she said. "They're going to be angry that humans made magic, and them, disappear from Earth for a thousand years. Even the good fae from the Seelie Court might be furious."

"I suspect a war is coming. Speaking of, Oliver wants a meeting tonight. Something about a big announcement."

Luna chuckled. "I like how a war coming reminded you of Oliver."

"Knew you would. I'm hitting the shower." Andy began walking away, as silent as ever even with his shoes on. He could've been a cat burglar.

"Maybe I'll join you." Luna pulled the tie from her long brown hair and tried to relax. The last person she felt like dealing with tonight was Oliver, their fearless Grand Master. He'd been calling more frequent meetings of the Sons of the Magi ever since the Stonehenge Four appeared on the world's stage. But this was the third time in a week even though they only used to meet once a month. She couldn't blame him. After a thousand years of the society waiting for magic to return, it had actually happened. Part of her had never really believed any of it. If anything, Andy had always been more serious about it, even though she was the one who'd introduced him to the Sons of the Magi and got him accepted.

The stash of supposed magic items he'd acquired had gotten him in more than Luna being second in command. Luna had seen him at multiple auctions where they had sometimes competed for the same item and before meeting. While her parents were wealthy and gave her the means to pursue her hobby, Andy had always been coy about where he got the money, as some items went for over a million. Between that, his quiet footsteps, and his jokingly evasive remarks about an innocent past, she sometimes wondered if he really was some sort of jewel thief. But then he'd likely just steal the magic items, wouldn't he? Why purchase them? Maybe he was a computer criminal. He certainly knew more about computers than anyone else she'd known, and she sometimes wondered if he knew how to hack.

Then there was the way he could scale a wall, or jump over things, skills he said parkour had given him. She didn't doubt it, having seen him in action. For a man in his thirties, he was in superb physical condition. He even seemed to know his way around swords, knives, and other medieval weapons in a way that suggested he'd used them for real, but he always shrugged off her questioning looks. One of these days he'd tell her more about his life, especially if they were going to spend the rest of theirs together, as often seemed the case. The story about him making his own way since he was a boy in America before moving to Britain seemed plausible, but sometimes that made her wonder if he was just a good liar.

Despite all of that, she trusted him and didn't wonder anymore why he'd stayed with her all these years. For all his evasiveness about his past, he was remarkably direct with her about what he thought and felt about her. No one had ever said the things he did, not to mention looking her in the eyes like she was the only person who existed. She bit her lip and decided to join him in the shower. A little fooling around was just the thing to take her mind off the rest of the day.

Hours later, the couple entered an old, three-story library in Knightsbridge, the posh west side of London, the noisy streets silenced when the doors closed behind them. A few patrons were spread out among the ancient books in which the Gilded Library specialized, but none looked up. The redheaded librarian, one of their society's members, smiled as they walked along the front wall's bookcases to one end. A quick look around and a nod from the librarian, and Luna briefly pulled *The Necronomicon*, *Tobin's Spirit Guide*, and *The Occido Lumen* to trigger the secret door in the corner to swivel open. She and Andy stepped inside, and it closed behind them. Dimly lit stairs curled downward, past the first basement level to the second, hidden one, reachable only this way or by another secret passage.

Her family had owned the building for generations, but few of them were members of the Sons of the Magi—a name she had once suggested this be changed to "Children of the Magi", only to get a snicker. Apparently ancient sexism wasn't to be removed from the society. Her mother had believed in all of it before her death, but her father didn't and hadn't been told about any of it. He had suggested selling the library more than once until Luna just bought it from him to put an end to that. Now the place was considered a cultural site. If only people knew what was in the hidden basement, and that generations of collected magic memorabilia were suddenly relevant and housed here.

Luna reached the hidden basement behind Andy, who took her hand. They came around the corner to hear the low voices of a dozen members, who had a tendency to speak quietly here even though the place had been soundproofed. There were no windows down here, and so the lighting was bright enough to reveal the ancient cracks in the grey stone walls—some repaired, others newer. The problem with a secret location was that you couldn't bring just anyone down here, so society members of varying skill levels did any maintenance. Andy was surprisingly handy with tools and had fixed a thing or two for her.

Their peers said hello as people began filing into the Sanctum, a room with an old, mahogany table long enough for twenty people on each side. At its head sat Oliver, his receding hairline cutting into his close-cropped brown hair as he leaned over a book while facing them. He had taken this business a little too seriously even before magic started happening, always dressing in black jeans and a black shirt, his round spectacles making him look like a scholar. And she supposed he was, for he had read every book in this place more than once, she was sure. Not the books upstairs for Londoners to peruse, but the spellbooks and scrolls collected in antiquity and ever since, all sitting one room over across the hall. Beside that was the treasure room, the walls filled with supposedly magic items. Other rooms had seen little use until recently. Now people were trying to get spells to work now in one of the three labs: one for potion work and the like, another for summonings, and a third for everything else. But none of them had worked so far.

Luna and Andy sat in two of the high-backed chairs closest to Oliver, who scrutinized a spellbook, his dragon-embossed goblet of red wine beside it. He always insisted the room be lit with only candles or torches, for effect, though that just made it harder to read anything. The walls weren't tall enough for tapestries, so they had settled for paintings of fantastic scenes depicting dragons, knights, fairies, and more. A few swords, maces, and suits of armor graced the walls or stood in corners. Everything had had the air of being pretend until recently—and it had all become very real for Luna this afternoon. As she mused, other members took positions at the table or along the walls. They had room for fifty and numbered twenty-eight, all but three in attendance. These were the heady days of the Sons of the Magi, and some had canceled vacations to get back to England for these meetings.

A young man they called the herald stood up once everyone was seated, and started the meeting. "This gathering of the Sons of the Magi is called to order, presided over by your Grand Master, Oliver Leiber."

He sat down as Oliver rose.

"Wizards," he began in a commanding voice, "we have called each other thus for a millennium, though none of us had the power flowing through us. None of us could wield the might of the gods. None of us could rule over others as wizards should. Until today. Today is a day we and our ancestors have long sought, for today, one of us has finally cast a spell."

Luna started, as a murmur went through the room. How did Oliver know she had cast one? She wouldn't put it past the bastard to have cameras in her place, but Andy was too observant not to notice even something carefully hidden. Sometimes he checked their flat for cameras or listening devices out of an abundance of caution, as he put it. Perhaps he hadn't been diligent enough. But Oliver's next word made her growing upset quiet.

"Rebecca Stinson, please come to me so we can show our brothers and sisters you are the chosen one, the first to lead us into this new world for which we have waited."

Luna frowned as a petite blonde rose to her feet and came to the head of the table across from them, a tight tan skirt and blouse combination revealing her ample curves. Why did it have to be her, of all people? That she and Oliver were having sex was no secret, though they acted like no one knew. It wasn't like they went on dates, but their amorous looks weren't fooling anyone. The looks Rebecca had sent Luna over the last year had suggested Rebecca thought she was the new #2 in the society just because she was screwing Oliver. Now Luna felt some jealousy about what spell she was going to do.

She didn't have long to wait. The lovers made a few more remarks about the importance of what everyone was going to see. Then Rebecca appeared to concentrate, holding out one hand as if cupping something invisible. For several moments, nothing happened. Then a ball of light the size of a tennis ball appeared, hovering over her hand, which she dropped, leaving the ball hanging in space. No one made a sound. With a slow flicking motion, Rebecca sent the light gliding down the table to the far end, then brought it back, though it sputtered and faded out before returning to her. Then the questions started.

"When did you first cast this spell?" someone asked.

"This morning," Rebecca replied.

"How many times?"

"This is now the third. It is easier each time, and I am able to control the ball more."

"Were you intentionally trying to do it? Or was it an accident, like so many of the stories we hear?"

"A little of both."

Luna stopped paying much attention to the chatter, as it was clear this wasn't as momentous as Oliver made it seem. Rebecca was nothing special, just another random person who had magic talent. She just happened to be one of them, and Luna agreed with Andy not to give in to a frequent idea of Oliver's—to recruit people who had shown magic talent from around the world. Oliver seemed to want to do it as if to gain control over all of them, promising them training or help in exchange for some sort of allegiance to the Sons of the Magi. But that wasn't what the group was for.

Their ancestors had formed the society after magic mysteriously stopped working a thousand years ago. They had wanted to preserve spells and magic items for the day when magic returned. Most had thought that wouldn't take long. The earliest books in their secret library included the diaries of those who had lost their powers, and their fading memories of how to cast anything as they neared old age and died. Like everywhere else in the world, magic had become a myth even to some of their descendants, who had never seen a spell done. Or a faerie, goblin, troll... the list went on.

How odd it was that today was the first time Luna had seen magic. And she'd seen it twice. Who among them might be next?

Oliver interrupted her thoughts with a veiled question. "Unless one of you is holding back, Rebecca is the first among us to perform magic."

Luna opened her mouth—and then a sharp pain struck her shin. "Ow! Andy!"

"Sorry," he said, looking sheepish before turning to Rebecca. "This is all great news. I think we need to come up with some sort of plan for your advancement."

Luna sat frowning as the others talked of ways to help Rebecca, even though none of them knew the first thing about wizard training. Somewhere in the middle of it, Andy took her hand and turned to her, giving a quick wink no one else saw. When he squeezed her hand, she squeezed back. He had stopped her from admitting she had cast a spell. Did he know? Of course he did. He could be so infuriating. He kept secrets so well, and somehow knew one of hers. She would've pulled her hand away in annoyance, but she wanted him to know she was cooperating and understood his message not to say anything. She just didn't understand why he wanted that. Or how the bloody hell he knew!

As she watched Rebecca bask in the glow of being the first to do magic, Luna was kind of glad she had said nothing. If she had wanted to be the center of attention like that, she would've accepted her rightful place as Grand Master. Oliver only had it because he was a man, for one thing, but also because he had pushed for it and Luna didn't care much. She owned the place, after all, and that brought its own power. Since magic had started working, she had wondered whether her decision was a mistake—but it was too late now.

Oliver rose at the head of the table. "In light of Rebecca's achievement," he said, "we must once again consider contacting the Stonehenge Four. You know my thoughts on this—that they seem to be central to the reawakening of magic on Earth—and therefore, we might be able to get answers about what is happening. Perhaps they know why. Perhaps they can help us regain the power of our ancestors. Perhaps they can help us gain control over what is happening in the world.

"But now it is even more important. We don't know how much control they have over their own abilities, and we've already discussed how Matt Sorenson looked surprised when he vanished in front of the TV cameras. But it is possible that he and the others have more control than we think—so they can teach Rebecca, and then others among us. And they may be very interested to hear about our treasure trove of items, and that we are descendants of wizards from long ago. We can position ourselves as partners with them, maybe ones even able to train them as much as they can help us. This is an alliance we should pursue—and, as Grand Master, I am making the decision to contact them."

"Hold on," said Luna, irritated. "You don't have that authority. Might I remind you this is a secret society and no one, not even a Grand Master, has the authority to just reveal us to the world?"

Oliver sneered at her. "You revealed us to the man sitting beside you and we welcomed him. He's not the only one who was brought into the Sons of the Magi instead of born into it. And we are not revealing ourselves to the world, as you put it, but to four people worthy of being included in our aspirations."

"You mean *your* aspirations?" she asked. "You've always talked of wizards resuming their rightful place as masters of the world, as if they ever were before. Just because some people have power like that doesn't mean they should have power over other people's lives."

He smirked. "Of course, it does. But I am not talking about bringing the world to its knees." He adopted a friendlier tone. "Listen, Luna, we've all heard reports of people being killed for their new powers. The healer in India who couldn't heal people on demand, so they decided she was holding back and tore her to pieces. The shaman in Africa who people decided was possessed by evil spirits, so they stabbed him to death. The wizard in the southern United States, who got burned alive when people decided he had made a pact with Satan. And we know that the police, the FBI, or whoever are hunting the Stonehenge Four. Will they hunt us if they know about us? Will they hunt Rebecca? Will they hunt you if you prove to have the talent and anyone finds out?"

Luna said nothing, frustrated that he was making sense. She didn't want him to. Something told her he could not be trusted with power of any kind. With any luck, he would have no talent for wizardry. They should've been thankful that it was Rebecca and not him that showed signs. It was just as well she hadn't revealed her own magic.

Andy said, "The problem with contacting the Stonehenge Four is that they have the most media attention on them. They seem to be in hiding, with good reasons, as you just mentioned. It might not be so easy to gain access to them."

Oliver looked down his nose at him. "This, coming from you? The man who has found so many magic items? Surely you can find a way—or do you not want to?"

Andy replied, "As you made clear to Luna before I was accepted here, we need to know more about new recruits before making them some sort of offer or arrangement."

"Then I suggest you get busy reaching out to them before I take matters into my own hands."

Andy frowned at him. "You haven't already?"

"No. I recognize your talents and delegate, so this is something you need to do before I delegate to someone less capable—someone more likely to screw it up and ruin our chances of forging a mutually beneficial arrangement."

Luna stifled a groan on hearing Oliver outmaneuver Andy. She'd never heard that before. Her boyfriend always seemed a step ahead of everyone. But he was also wilier than anyone had a right to be, and she half expected he would turn this to his advantage in some way. After all, Oliver had just ceded control to him.

"Fine," said Andy, and Luna knew he was thinking the same thing from the slightly forced sound of annoyance in his voice. She knew what he sounded like when genuinely annoyed, and this wasn't it.

"There is something else we should discuss," began Oliver. "Samhain is just days from now. As all of you know, Halloween is the night when the barriers between this world and Elfhame are thinnest. We have a better chance of seeing faeries now than ever before—perhaps even of greeting and welcoming them to Earth. This is the first Halloween since magic returned. There have been scattered reports around the globe of elves, pixies, and even a goblin appearing in the wilderness. Many people don't believe the tales, but I do, and so do some of you.

"I predict that at this year's All Hallows' Eve, there will be a great awakening and we will see many creatures, great and small. We should collectively go to some of the most prominent places rumored to be doorways between worlds, and there we should wait for their arrival. We can communicate with each other throughout the night, videotaping what happens and ensuring that mankind's reborn relationship with fae is beneficial to us and the world.

"This All Hallows' Eve will also be special for another reason, and I believe it is foreordained that the night will be magical in every sense of the word. The harvest moon, a full moon, fell on October 1st. When there is a second full moon in a month, it is called a Blue Moon, and we will be having one on All Hallows' Eve for the first time in seventy-six years. The first full moon after the harvest moon is also known as the hunter's moon. So we will have at once a hunter's moon, a full moon, and a Blue Moon, all on All Hallows' Eve, the very first Halloween to occur after the reawakening of magic."

Luna had known some of that, because the Sons of the Magi were aware of many legends of old—but she hadn't realized this conjunction of moons would occur. "What sort of opportunity do you think this provides? You think the fairies will truly walk among us?"

Having resumed her seat, Rebecca answered coolly, "Yes. We've been monitoring this for some time. And we know that there are many—in England and Ireland especially—who are preparing to ward off the evil spirits, the faeries, like people did in the days of old."

"If that's true," said Andy, "then people will protect themselves."

"Yes," said Oliver, "but many will not, and there will be nothing we can do for them. There will be too many people. I do anticipate many shocked people that night. It is possible that it will forever change the world."

Luna thought that that had already happened, and it wasn't for the better. Was there to be some sudden explosion of changes now? The world could hardly handle what was already happening. She asked, "But what does this have to do with *us*?"

Oliver turned to her. "I would like the Sons of the Magi to be more proactive—to be at some sites where fairies are believed to cross into this world."

"What for?" Andy asked, scowling. "I'm very familiar with these myths—and most of them say that the faeries are nothing like Disney movies make them out to be, but very sinister. If you're right, then we just set ourselves up to be attacked, or kidnapped to Elfhame, or something worse."

Oliver said, "You know there are ways to protect ourselves. Like iron. This is known to hurt the faeries so they won't touch us. And we can dress in—"

"Yes," interrupted Luna, "but they might think we mean to harm them with it. They could see iron as provocation. And we don't know if it's gonna work anyway. All of this is myth. What if real faeries aren't even fazed by iron? Is that really something you want to take a chance on?"

Oliver smiled and looked around them. "Perhaps we should take a vote and see who wants to be present and who does not. No one is forcing anyone to go, and no one will make people stay behind. I, for one, will be at Stonehenge that night. Rebecca, too. And I would like others to be at other locations we think are the most likely to have visitors. What does everyone say?"

Luna watched as some people nodded and others cocked their eyebrows. None of them knew what they might be getting themselves into, and those without caution were likely to come away from Halloween changed forever, and not in a good way. She had no intention of going anywhere near these supposed doorways and increasingly thought Halloween was an especially good night to stay indoors—maybe with the blood of a slaughtered animal over the threshold, like people used to use, to keep fairies out. She caught Andy's eye and felt certain he agreed.

As the meeting turned into a long planning discussion, Andy led her out and to the treasure room. That was the informal name for the place where all the supposedly magic items were kept. All four walls were lined with mismatched bookcases, floor to ceiling. Cabinets with glass doors formed two hallways between them, and there were a number of items atop cabinets on stands or in small cases. In the room's center stood a pedestal with a small skull reputed to belong to a faerie, and to let the holder control the fae. Security cameras were in two corners.

No one else was here, and Andy said, "I think we need to do something about security in here now. We never did it before, because none of the expensive stuff is here. But now we have to worry about inexpensive stuff having actual power."

"Yes, I know you like to call it the trinket room instead. I think there's a chance some of this stuff is real."

He looked about to say more when Oliver walked in. "Let's talk about it at home."

"There you are, Luna," said Oliver, sauntering over. He seemed even cockier now than usual. "What do you think about having Rebecca try her hand at some items in here? Maybe she can figure out which ones are real."

Andy responded before she could. "The only problem with that is that she might set something off. I think we should wait a bit and have a plan. And I'm not sure testing anything while we're in here is a good idea. One item could set off others, blow the building up, you never know."

Oliver chuckled without humor. "Well, you do make good points, as always. Let's think about this and get started with at least a few this week. I want to make progress. You never know when we might need to use something, if only we can find out how it works or what it really does." He looked around at the hundreds of items. "This could take a while, but yes, let's not blow ourselves up."

"Okay, Oliver," replied Luna. "We'll think of something."

The Grand Master left, and Andy turned to her. "Him using these is exactly what concerns me. No one is ready for any of this. There are things here that, if the description we have is right, could set in motion events we can't stop. This might be the most dangerous room on the planet."

Luna bit her lip. He was right. Suddenly it all seemed so foolish, this society of theirs. More security was needed, but not just something to know who came and went. This room needed to be locked up—and almost no one should have the key.

She trusted Andy, and a quarter of the items were his. But Oliver, as Grand Master, would insist on having a key. Did they care what he wanted? Luna owned the building and could just lock it all up. Andy could take his items back. She could remove hers. But what precedent would that set? Both of them probably had useless, non-magic items, very powerful ones, and more that were in between. That same mix could exist among the few items Oliver or the others had brought. Most of what lay here belonged to the society, and had been here hundreds of years. No one could lay claim to it. Somehow, Andy had the biggest trove. One day he really had to tell her how he was so good at acquiring supposedly magic items.

They spent an hour socializing with their peers before walking home. She had to wait until they got inside her flat before asking Andy how he knew she'd done a spell. The door had hardly shut when she asked, "So how did you know?"

"Know what?"

She smacked his arm. "Don't be coy. I know why you kicked me under the table. Tell me, or you'll sleep in the rain tonight."

He smiled as if not taking her seriously. "I didn't know you could be so draconian! But I saw the laptop and that was no battery issue. I don't know what you did, but it looked like some sort of energy struck the screen in several places, smashing it and burning holes. There were at least four impacts that I could see."

Luna turned away, hands on her forehead, heading for the kitchen and stopping to kick off her shoes. When she didn't respond, he followed.

"You didn't do it on purpose. And you don't know how it happened or how to repeat it."

"One of these days you're going to tell me how you figure everything out all the time."

"It wasn't that hard, partly because I know you. You haven't said one word about trying to do anything magical. What actually happened?"

She sighed. "I was mad at the computer because it was giving me this error I couldn't get past. I yelled at it and made an angry motion with both hands. Suddenly these fiery darts shot out of my hands and into the screen."

He thought about that and said, "That sounds like a spell in one of the books. I think we should get it and have you try it on purpose. Or maybe a cantrip, like what Rebecca did. The important thing here is that you have magic talent."

Luna let out a breath. "I'm not sure I want it. It's dangerous. I mean, look what I did."

"That's exactly why we need you to learn control. I'll help in any way I can." He opened his laptop and began looking through the folders, searching for a file. "I've taken photos or scanned so many of the spellbook pages over the years, and saved them with names the spells on them. We don't even need to grab a book from the library."

Suspecting that he knew the answer, she asked, "Why exactly didn't you want me to tell Oliver? Or the others?"

"I don't trust him. Neither do you. He's always talked about wizards being the rightful dominant force on Earth—and now that magic's working, I don't want him thinking he's going to get his hands on you and turn you into some sort of tool to help him in whatever stupid fantasies he has."

She agreed and wondered if Oliver was no longer all talk now that this fantasy was technically possible. "Do you think he'll do that with Rebecca?"

"Of course." He opened an image and she leaned over his shoulder to look at it, seeing a picture of a hand with multiple blazing darts emerging from it.

"What do you think he's going to do?" Luna asked.

"I don't know, and that's what bothers me. We need to secure that treasure room even if he gets upset about it, and we need to make sure no one can find the magic items we have elsewhere."

"Have you sensed any power in yourself?"

"No."

She noticed that he didn't think about that long, and seemed certain. But then she would've felt the same way up until this afternoon.

They spent a while looking at the spell, but she didn't want to try it. Not here, anyway. Maybe they needed to find a field somewhere. That led them to start talking about places like Stonehenge, other henges, stone circles, and long barrows in the countryside. Each was distinctive in design or purpose, but Andy was certain that all but the barrows were doorways to the fae world—though he couldn't explain why he thought this. There was nothing in legend about it, but that was why he had set up cameras at dozens of them. It had taken a while, given that most of them were at least ninety minutes from London, and he had to do it at night when no one would stop him. That he was that good at sneaking around, or that comfortable in the dark countryside at night, didn't really surprise her.

They finally stopped for the night and settled onto the couch for a little quiet time—or so she thought. Then he opened his mouth and surprised her.

"I have a confession of my own," Andy began, one arm around her shoulders as she leaned into his chest. "Do you remember how I've been looking for Merlin's pendant for so long? Well, I finally found it."

"You did? That's great."

"Not really."

Luna chuckled. "Why?"

"The woman from the Stonehenge Four was wearing, it on that news broadcast about their reappearance at Stonehenge two months ago."

Luna remembered the blonde woman from that broadcasts and others since, but not the necklace. And this was a long time ago for just to be saying something now—but she let that slide for now. "That seems like an amazing coincidence, for one of them to have it. You've never told me what the pendant supposedly does. Are you going to confess that, too?"

"That's because I wasn't sure it was true and, given the story about it, Oliver finding out might be trouble. The story goes back a long way, and I've never seen it written down in all the books we've collected here over the years. It's the whole reason I got into searching for magic items to begin with. Supposedly, Merlin's pendant made all the magic on Earth disappear into Elfhame—and all the creatures, too, because if they stayed here when the magic went away, they would die. That's because they were all partly magical in nature. Even Merlin was half-fae."

She turned to him. "Yeah, I remember that bit. But you're saying this is why magic disappeared? That's new to me. And why is it dangerous for Oliver to hear this?"

"There's more to it. The story says that if the pendant is ever returned to Stonehenge, it would reopen the doorways between this word and Elfhame. Magic would flow from the fae world back into Earth, and the creatures would be able to return, too."

Luna's mouth fell open. "What? Wait. That would explain pretty much everything that's happening now, except we haven't heard much about things like faeries appearing."

"I think it's just a matter of time. It's why I put the cameras up—and if Oliver and the others are serious about going to some doorways in person, watching from the safety of a video feed is a lot smarter."

She almost laughed at the understatement. "Yeah, you said they were doorways before. I just didn't understand why you thought they were open now. I mean, I thought it was just a general thing about the world changing." Something occurred to her. "So you think the Stonehenge Four have Merlin's pendant and took it there?"

"Yes. I doubt they knew what it was, but I think they did."

"Does that explain their disappearance? Did they go into Elfhame?"

He cocked an eyebrow. "Maybe, but I don't think so. It's supposedly hard to get from here to there, but easy for fae to come here. I don't think they could've gone by accident—and it wouldn't explain their other disappearances. But do you see why it's dangerous for Oliver to know this?"

She considered. "Actually, no."

"If he knew about this and it's true, he would be doing what I'm doing, except more aggressively. I have those cameras set up at the doorways between worlds for a reason, Luna. I am positive creatures are coming through. If Oliver knew, he would be trying to meet them and get help amassing power for himself. Maybe he'd offer to be their guide in this world. I think it would be dangerous for everyone else for Oliver to gain some any prominence among the fae folk that return, like he's some sort of chosen human ambassador for the rest of us. I'm sure he'd put himself in that position if he knew. This is what I've been thinking for a while, and he just proved me right tonight. I'm certain it's why he wants to be at Stonehenge."

Luna stifled a groan. "Bloody hell, you're right. So what do we do?"

"I want to make sure Oliver doesn't get ahead of himself. I think there are forces at work here that none of us really understand. His ambitions might lead him to do something before anyone is ready."

"Like playing with magic items."

"Yes. The spell Rebecca did wasn't much, but you know he's going to push her. We just need to keep an eye on that. And you need to push yourself to see what you can do, safely. But my big worry is that treasure room."

"What do you want to do?"

"Steal every last magic item in it."

CHAPTER THIRTEEN

THE DEVASTATOR

M att looked around the room at his friends and asked, "So what are we going to tell our hosts?"

Along with Lorian and Rognir, they had been in their meeting room discussing several things—the conversation with Jack that morning, the revelations about Eriana and Soliander, and Kori's appearance within the Palace of Andor. But so far, they had only agreed that the news would upset everyone.

Eric said, "I think it depends on what we decide about this rescue attempt. We need to be proactive. I don't want to walk in there and say Zoran the Devastator has her and we don't know where he is or what to do. We need to hash out what we know about Soliander's alter ego."

Matt nodded. "Let's have a solution, even if they disagree or suggest changes. I think this is our mission, not theirs."

Eric nodded and turned to Rognir and Lorian. "So what can you tell us about Zoran the Devastator?"

Lorian said, "Not much is known before two years ago—which makes sense, now that we know he is Soliander. He conquered the Kingdom of Esson on the planet Delonin. Esson is a military junta, run by warlords. They believe power comes to those who take it. Perhaps it is fitting that Zoran used wizardry to summon monsters, dragons, ogres, trolls, and dark elves into the halls of power and subdue those in charge. They were outmatched and unsuspecting."

"I remember!" said Matt, images having flashed through his head. "He let them live as they had before, except they could only make major attacks at his direction. If they obeyed, he would make their strength rise with his. Most of them agreed. He killed those who didn't. Any resistance ended when he used them to invade the nearby Kingdom of Marduna from Esson, and they grew rich on the spoils."

The elf said, "Can you tell why he invaded Esson, or Marduna?"

Matt's eyes widened and he stood up. "Yes! For Everon."

Eric scowled in confusion. "What's the connection?"

Matt pieced it together while they waited for him. "Long ago in Marduna, a wizard killed a dragon and cast a spell on its blood. Anyone drinking the blood daily gained the ability to control the dragons. Naturally, the wizard only let his family drink it. Together, they controlled enough dragons that they soon conquered Marduna, and the wizard became king.

The royal family ruled for generations, but the wizard king died without writing down the spell he'd cast on the dragon blood. It would not last forever, so they killed a new dragon annually, draining its blood into the Dragon Pool, which was a specially designed and heavily guarded place. The new blood, mixing with the enchanted blood there, would gain the same enchantment. This is how they stayed in power, using their control of the dragons to inspire obedience within Marduna and cooperation elsewhere.

"The Ellorian Champions were summoned to destroy the Dragon Pool and succeeded. The result was that the royal family lost their source of power. The inevitable happened. Most were killed, either by the dragons or the unhappy population. But one member of the royal family, the heir-apparent, wasn't there at the time and survived."

"Everon?" Eric guessed.

"Yes. Real name, Prince Alinor of Marduna."

Anna said, "So now we know why Everon hated the Champions. We can assume that he became Soliander's apprentice for revenge, which ended up meaning he altered the Quest Rings. Eventually, Soliander broke the Champions free of the quest cycle. And within a year, he conquered Esson as Zoran, then Marduna."

Rognir asked, "But why Marduna?"

Matt said, "Revenge by proxy."

Ryan frowned. "What do you mean?"

"He can't find Everon, but he knows who Everon really is. He doesn't think Everon really cares for his own people, because the royal family had a brutal regime, but he's conquered them anyway. He's destroyed cultural places. He's stolen most of the kingdom's riches—not because he cares, but just to take it. He's enslaved people. And he's let the warriors of Essos have their fun, doing what we would call war crimes on Earth. He did this to Marduna while becoming their new king. That's what first earned him the nickname of Zoran the Devastator."

Ryan asked, "He rules more than two kingdoms, so he is an emperor. Has he declared himself one?"

Matt said, "Yes. Emperor Zoran of Essos. He considers that Zoran's home base."

"That was two years ago?" Eric asked. "What's he been doing since?"

Lorian answered, "He has attacked other kingdoms on other worlds. Some established he leveled to ruins, reducing them to a state of lawless barbarism. In those kingdoms, he razed major cities and towns. In other kingdoms,

234 | RANDY ELLEFSON

he destroyed defenses, leaving people to suffer the consequences of being attacked by ogres and the like. In one
island nation, he destroyed all the ships, leaving them defenseless against seafaring enemies and destroying their
ability to work the sea for food. These campaigns have also
lived up to his nickname. Sometimes he makes himself
ruler, other times not."

Eric asked, "Matt, do you sense why he has done this?"

Matt found himself nodding slowly even before being
asked. "Wow. Yes. His anger is titanic. This is revenge. The
kingdoms he has obliterated all have one thing in common,
as far as I can tell." He looked at them with a gleam in his
eye. "The Champions did a quest there and interfered with
whoever was in power. Ended their conquest—or their
possession of land, or an item used for evil purposes.
Sometimes the Champions ended up killing the existing
ruler. At other times, they killed beasts that had allowed
the ruler to maintain power by threatening others, like the
dragons of Marduna. Many of these places had ruling families or others who the Champions made enemies of. And
that's where it gets interesting."

"How so?"

"Soliander suspected that some of these enemies later
worked with Everon to trap the Champions—that Everon
sought their aid in creating the network of Quest Rings.
Soliander thinks there's no way that Everon could have
traveled alone to so many worlds and created so many of
the rings unless he had help. Soliander investigated some
of these enemies—and in several cases, he learned that he
was right. This is why he leveled the kingdoms."

Anna asked, "What are you saying?"

"I'm saying that if Soliander confirmed that a kingdom
had worked with Everon to imprison them in the quest
cycle, he obliterated that kingdom as Zoran the Devastator.

Essos was the exception. He just used them to destroy Marduna and other places."

"Holy shit," said Ryan. "That is messed up. I mean, that's an awful lot of revenge."

Matt nodded. "Remember, Soliander thinks Everon—and anyone who helped him—not only destroyed Soliander's life, but also Korrin's, Eriana's, and Andier's. Like us, they couldn't just live their lives when they could be summoned at any moment. But then Soliander still feels guilty for apparently killing the others when he broke them free of the quests. He also feels guilty that it was his apprentice who betrayed them. He is mad as hell and he wants people to suffer. He also loved Eriana, likely still does, and felt like he got her killed. Of course, this week, he learned that she's alive."

"Wait a minute," said Ryan, looking alarmed. "These places he destroyed still exist. Even if a kingdom or whatever fell, the land's still there. The people still exist. Destroying a kingdom just means destroying a government, unless he did as you say and actually leveled major buildings. But what if the Quest Rings are also still there? People who loathe the Champions could summon us."

"Yes," said Lorian, "but the quest must be a valid one—not one designed to trap you, for example. So you probably don't need to worry about someone trying to get revenge on you and thinking you're the real Champions."

Eric said, "There's something else that suggests we shouldn't worry about it much. No one knows that Zoran is Soliander. They won't know that one of the Champions has destroyed their country. They won't try to summon us in revenge."

"Unless he told whoever he was destroying," observed Anna.

Eric conceded, "True. But he clearly hasn't. Maybe the reason he doesn't tell anyone he's still alive is so no one

236 | RANDY ELLEFSON

knows what he's done. An Ellorian Champion is destroying kingdoms. He doesn't know where the others are. He may think they're dead, but he probably hopes they're alive. What if they are and someone knows their location? And goes after them because of what Soliander is doing as Zoran? He could want to stop people taking more revenge on himself or them. I mean, Everon's revenge is what got them into this mess."

"And us," observed Anna.

Rognir remarked, "Revenge can be taken on families, too. By living as Zoran, Soliander may be protecting the familiar here with us. It allows him to do what he's doing with fewer repercussions."

Anna nodded. "So maybe there's a small chance he's not as bad a guy as his recent behavior suggests."

Matt shook his head, knowing Anna tried to find a bright spot in someone's awful behavior. "No. He's killed a lot of people, directly—or by letting it happen. He's changed. I've seen memories from throughout his life. The ones from the last few years, as far as I can tell anyway, are pretty dark. He's in a bad place. Has been since the Merlin quest."

Anna asked, "Do you think finding that Eriana's alive has changed him? It's only been days, but still. Maybe there's hope."

"No way to know, but I would assume so."

Rognir suggested, "Then perhaps he can be redeemed."

"To be honest," began Eric, "as long as he doesn't come after us or anyone we care about, it doesn't concern me now."

For the next hour, they discussed a plan to rescue Eriana. Matt revealed that Castle Oste was Soliander's true home base. It could only be reached by magic or flying—and, even then, it was invisible from the outside. No one but the Lords of Fear ever came and went, unless Soliander brought a prisoner. The staff were just enough to keep the place running, and they never left. Soliander wouldn't suspect a rescue, because he didn't know Matt had some of his memories of Castle Oste or its magic defenses. With the place mostly unmanned, they hoped for an easy mission because they could cast themselves right inside.

But they planned for Soliander and all four Lords of Fear to be there, even if that was unlikely. The lords were rarely present, and Soliander had many things to attend to. But they reasoned he had ditched any plans, if possible, to be with Eriana.

Partly for that reason, they agreed Taryn should come. Her presence might stop Soliander from attacking them, or at least compromise his aim. Matt knew the arch-wizard wouldn't hurt her. No one thought Taryn would side with her brother against them, especially after learning of his actions as Zoran, but they also felt certain she wouldn't attack Soliander either. She was compromised, as Eric put it, but they wouldn't be able to talk her out of going.

The plan was for the four Champions, Taryn, Lorian, and Rognir to go. But they needed help. Lorian was primarily a swordsman and archer who happened to have magic skills, making him a fair wizard. But he wasn't strong enough to cast *himself* anywhere, never mind eight people. The magic affinity test he'd once administered to Matt suggested Matt was more than strong enough—but between his inexperience, nerves, and pressure, Matt didn't want to do it for himself, not to mention so many others. He imagined arriving a thousand feet above the ground, or halfway inside a wall. No, someone else had to do it.

This was among the issues they discussed with their hosts, in another meeting with tightly controlled attendance. Only the king and queen, Prince Dari and Princess Cariss, Taryn, Eriana's brother, and the princess from Coreth were present. As expected, Taryn insisted on coming and met no objections. To their surprise, Dari insisted on joining the rescue party. Visibly startled, the king seemed pleased by his show of courage—while the queen only looked worried and tried to talk him out of it, to no avail.

Eric had confided in Matt about his talk with the prince, but he hadn't discussed it with the others. Eric and Matt were arguably closer, even though Matt had grown up next door to Anna. Eric had wanted someone else to know about the conversation. Anna sometimes disapproved of things like goading someone, even if they worked. They hadn't told Ryan either; Eric said he didn't want Ryan to think he was sneaking around too much and hiding things, even though he had! Matt was more understanding and didn't object. He also shared Eric's wariness of the prince.

Discussions revealed that Andor's wizards could open a temporary magic portal to Castle Oste, Allowing everyone to step through. This was safer for the travelers than being cast there, but it brought the risk that someone on the other side could step through to Andor, unless the wizards ended the spell. That meant doing it again for the return trip. Cariss suggested that her wizard friend Mandrellan help with this, but she admitted she hadn't seen him since their arrival and didn't know where he had gone. Eric said he didn't like it anyway, because they'd need to get back to the portal location with Eriana and that might not be possible. After looking over the spell with Lorian, Matt felt confident that the two of them could do it. This would allow them to leave from wherever they found Eriana.

Later that day, they tested it and successfully created a portal to Lorian's home on Honyn. The portal looked like a doorway—an inch off the floor and surrounded with golden light. It gave a view of Lorian's empty bedroom, which they had chosen so they wouldn't startle anyone and find themselves attacked. Matt saw elegantly carved furniture and bedding with a tree embroidered on it.

The elf stepped through to the other side—but when Matt tried to join him, he found he couldn't! He bounced off the portal like he'd walked into a closed glass door. It even hurt his head where he'd bumped it. He tried sticking his hand through but couldn't. A perplexed Lorian stepped back into Andor without trouble. First Eric, then Ryan, and finally Anna all tried to stick their hands through and couldn't, but Rognir could.

"Jesus," said Eric, shaking his head. "We're idiots. The quest has bound us, and we've always heard we can't leave. We forgot about it, maybe because we never tried before."

"Language, please," said Ryan. He was never one for taking the name of the Lord in vain, as religious as he was.

Anna looked dejected. "Great. What now?"

Matt was frowning. Something wasn't right. "But we've left a planet before. We left Honyn to go to Soclarin on that quest, so why can't we do it now?"

Eric observed, "Going to Soclarin wasn't really part of the quest, either. Maybe it was considered relevant. We left Honyn through the Dragon Gate to Soclarin. We were there to close the gate, which we could have done from the Soclarin side, not the Honyn side. Maybe that's why we were able to go through."

Matt conceded, "That makes sense."

"Doesn't help us here," said Ryan.

Matt saw that Eric was thinking hard. So was Lorian. He tried to work out a way around their problem, privately admitting Eriana's rescue might not include him and his friends. But his knowledge of Castle Oste was invaluable. He really needed to go.

Eric's head snapped up. "I have an idea. Wait here. Can you keep the portal open? I need ten minutes."

Matt looked at Lorian, who nodded, and Eric ran out of the room. Some spells drained his energy while they were active, but this one didn't. The portal would last only five minutes, but it could be shut off with a few words and extended with a few more. Lorian indicated that extending it was far less taxing than casting it again—so they waited, wondering what Eric was up to.

Fifteen minutes later, they heard Taryn's authoritative voice commanding someone to get out of the way. Not too many people were allowed in this wing, to minimize the number of witnesses to anything they said or did. She opened the doors wide and stepped aside as Eric came in carrying the dragon egg case. He stopped in front of the portal as Taryn closed the doors.

Matt arched an eyebrow. "What are you planning to do with *that*?"

Eric smiled. "Send it to Honyn." He didn't elaborate and the others exchanged glances. Sometimes he could be cryptic.

"What's the thought here?" Ryan asked.

"The egg goes through, and since it's on Honyn and we're supposed to get it, we can also go through."

Matt's eyes widened before he laughed. "That's brilliant."

Grinning, Eric said, "I thought so. Here goes."

He stepped up to the still-open portal and gently tried to push the case through before any part of his body. The end of the case did indeed pass through, but then it stopped. He tried again to no avail, then turned the case around, but the same thing happened at roughly the same point. Watching it, Matt knew why.

"The moment the egg itself touches the threshold, even inside the case, it stops."

"Shit," said Eric, stepping back. "I thought that would work."

Rognir stepped forward with one hand out for the case. "May I?"

Eric shrugged and handed it to him. The dwarf repeated the same test, but this time the case kept going. He stepped all the way through the portal with it to stand on Honyn. He turned back and gestured for someone to join him. Standing nearest, Matt extended his hand, expecting it to stop again, but it went through. Surprised, he then passed into the portal and out the other side to stand beside the dwarf. On a hunch, he suggested Rognir stick the case partly back through, and it worked. Matt then took it and tried, able to pass back to Andor with it. Rognir followed.

"So what just happened?" Ryan asked.

Matt answered. "We're not supposed to take the egg off the planet, so we can't. Rognir can. And then I could pursue him. I was able to bring it back because we're supposed to."

"Interesting," said Lorian. "The case is quite a large thing to take on the mission with us, but I know of a magic Bag of Desires that will reduce it to almost nothing inside. I used one for the soclarin ore."

"I remember," said Matt. "Maybe you should go get it now while the portal is open?"

The elf smiled and spoke a few magic words to extend the portal's life. Then he stepped through and into his bedroom and out of view.

Anna asked, "So we're going to take a delicate dragon egg on a potentially violent mission? If something happens to that egg and we never return it, the quest fails and we never go home."

"We can protect it," said Eric.

"How?"

He opened his mouth, then shut it. From the doorway, Taryn said. "The easy way would be to enter my brother's

242 | RANDY ELLEFSON

castle, then hand the egg back to someone here and continue without it."

Matt smiled at her. "Simple and obvious. Thank you."

"That I can live with," said Anna.

Lorian came back moments later, and they closed the portal. Their hosts had already agreed that they would be allowed to wear and use the Ellorian Champions' equipment, provided that no one let it be seen until they left. King Sarov wanted them to capture Soliander if possible. While they assured him they would try, they didn't think they had much of a chance—until the king gave them the Crown of Voids Taryn had used on Matt. If they could get it around Soliander's head, he'd be far easier to deal with, though no one believed they'd get near enough. They hoped to see no sign of him at all.

With the plan settled, they rested for two hours and then reconvened in their meeting room, the doors sealed. Behind a changing curtain, the four of them put on their respective outfits. Taryn, Lorian, Rognir, and Prince Dari were all present. So were a dozen of Taryn's Dark Blade warriors, whom she had sent for after the dragon egg quest trouble. A handful would come with them, just in case more trouble than expected broke out. The remaining Dark Blades would stay behind in this room in case trouble followed them back or reinforcements were needed. Eric had also suggested that two wizards remain to open the portal in case Matt or Lorian couldn't make one themselves. This would allow them to send the Dark Blades through if needed—and, if the group at Soliander's made it back to the portal location, it would mean they could also return that way.

After a final check to ensure everyone was prepared, Matt and Lorian cast the spell and the portal to a lower room in Soliander's hidden Oste Castle opened. They saw only darkness until one of the Dark Blades threw a burning torch through. It landed just a few feet inside on dark stone and cast dancing light around the storage room, filled with crates and barrels. It seemed obvious to Matt that no one was there—he'd chosen it for that reason—and so the warrior stepped through, picked up the torch, and made room for the others. Rognir went through with the dragon egg case, and the Earth friends all stepped through without issue. The dwarf then handed it back to someone on Elloria and the remaining party joined them.

Matt looked around, experiencing a kind of déjà vu from having been here as Soliander. The small room was damp, musty, and cold. Only one stairway ascended, and he noticed that Soliander's staff did not send a pulse up his arm, as it usually did when it detected magic, other than the portal. When he was the one casting a spell, it didn't pulse, presumably by design so that didn't distract him.

"Let's leave the portal open a minute," said Eric. "I want to check up these stairs first."

"No," Dari disagreed. "It leaves Andor exposed to a threat, and I cannot allow that."

Eric sighed. "There's no one here but us. It'll just be a minute."

"There won't be anything there," said Matt, "just a larger storeroom with stairs descending to rooms like this one. Whoever goes first, leave the light behind in case anyone's there."

"Right," Eric said. "I'll go first, Taryn and you behind. You're our guide, Matt, so I need you up front all the time."

"Yeah, I know. Let's go."

The three of them went up the stairs, being careful not to trip or scuff their feet and cause noise. They could see a dim light, and Matt knew that a single torch lit the big room above. He was right. No one was there. They could see an assortment of supplies, a table and chairs, and a lone torch burning next to an ascending stairway. They lis-

244 | RANDY ELLEFSON

tened, then crept over. For a moment, it seemed like all was quiet, but then they heard two voices speaking elven. That surprised Matt until he remembered that Soliander had dark elves working for him.

The voices came nearer. He, Taryn, and Eric hid behind a crate once they realized the elves were coming down. They reached the bottom of the stairway, one carrying a torch, and remained unaware of the intruders until Eric and Taryn approached from behind. They nearly reached the elves when the elves sensed them and turned. Eric punched one elf in the face, knocking him and the torch he held to the floor, while Taryn put a choke hold on the other. Then Eric jumped on the fallen one and put a hand over his mouth.

"Don't make a sound," he said in elven. "You're going to tell us where Eriana is. Do you understand?"

Matt was standing beside them by now, and saw only defiance in the dark elf's eyes. "They're not going to cooperate. They fear Zoran more than anything we can do to them. Just tie them up."

By now, the rest of the group had come up the stairs with Prince Dari in the lead. The dark elves were soon bound, gagged, and put into two different storage rooms so they couldn't help each other.

"What's up these stairs?" Dari asked, peering up.

"We're below a courtyard. This stair leads to a hallway within the exterior walls of the castle. We're getting close to the tower where Soliander does his work."

By now, they were all familiar with such buildings and terms. While 'the castle' meant the entire structure, it could also mean only the fortifications—like the walls, towers, courtyard, and a drawbridge if one existed. Then there was the keep, the building inside the castle.

Ryan asked, "Why is there a courtyard if no one can get here by foot?"

"Dragons need somewhere to land."

"Good answer."

A frowning Dari observed, "I thought we were trying to be under one of the other two towers, where we're likely to find Eriana."

Matt knew where Soliander's rooms were, and which tower Diara was in unless she had been moved. That meant Eriana was likely to be in one of the other two towers. She could still be anywhere, but he knew those towers had the best rooms and Soliander wasn't going to put her somewhere repugnant.

"We are, but this was a better place to arrive—and the upper rooms have magical wards on them, ones that would've interfered with the portal. Besides, I want to get into his rooms. There are very useful things in there."

Eric shook his head. "Stealing from Soliander wasn't part of the plan."

"This is an opportunity we can't miss. And there's a chance Eriana is there."

"There's an even better chance my brother is," Taryn said, "and I would very much like a reunion, even though that isn't smart."

"The king wants us to capture him," Matt reminded them. He glanced at the Crown of Voids attached to Taryn's belt. He hated that thing, but wouldn't think twice about putting it on Soliander.

Dari added, "I agree with the wizard."

Matt looked at Eric. "We could get some very helpful things, like the scroll on how to create the keystones for a Home Ring."

Seeing Eric's grudging acceptance, he flashed an apologetic smile. He hadn't been sure about mentioning it earlier, afraid they would disagree. Now he asked to borrow Lorian's magic Bag of Desires, which reduced items to such small sizes that the bag still looked empty. The elf handed it to him.

After discussing a plan, they crept up the stairway, finding a corridor straight ahead. To their left side stood the exterior castle wall. The other side was open to a courtyard. No one was there. The sun cast long shadows, suggesting that it was late afternoon. The main building, or keep, loomed overhead. Behind them to one side stood the wooden door to Soliander's hundred-foot-tall tower.

They made it inside without trouble, closed the door, and began to climb. They passed a handful of potentially occupied rooms, one on each story. Always quiet, Eric went first, with Taryn and Matt following. The others waited, to minimize noise.

As they ascended, Matt saw that the first- and third-floor doors were already open, with no one inside. The topmost room was for magic experiments. One floor down was Soliander's study, where Matt expected him to be. And one floor down from that was the Scribe Room, full of less important scrolls and books. It was from this floor that Eric came back down to him and Taryn quietly.

"There's an elf in there," he whispered, firelight from a wall sconce dancing over his intense features. "He's copying scrolls. From the way he's sitting, he'll see us."

"I don't leave enemies at my back anyway," said Taryn, fingering her sword.

"I think I will have to take care of it," said Matt. "Gotta be quiet in case Soliander's up one level."

"I might get him with a knife," Eric suggested.

"What if you miss? Anyone in there is likely to be a wizard. He might have magical protection, too, even if he doesn't expect anything here."

Matt had learned quite a few other spells—but he'd rarely had no chance to practice casting them on people, because it would hurt or they wouldn't like it. Now he could have no such scruples. He reached into one of his robe's pockets to get a piece of valerian root. Pulling the hood up and over his face, he left Soliander's staff with Taryn and confidently strode into the Scribe Room like he was Zoran the Devastator.

The dark elf looked up in surprise. "Master, I didn't realize you were—"

"Sleep," Matt commanded, and the elf's eyes closed, his head landing on the table before him with a thud. He started to slide off, but Eric came forward and caught him, then gently lowered him to the floor. "Darron," whispered Matt in recognition. "An apprentice."

As Taryn entered and gave Matt the staff, Eric asked, "Anything in here you want to take?"

Matt thought for a second, looking around the room, getting a sense of what was where, and what Soliander was unlikely to miss any time soon. The last thing he wanted was that guy coming after him. As a result, he didn't take many tempting items, but he did grab several spellbooks of rarer magic, and books on demonology, witchcraft, and necromancy. To cover the theft, he moved the books a little to disguise a gap.

"Okay," he began, "let's go."

They reached the next level together, seeing the closed mahogany door and its scenes of wizards, dragons, and knights battling. Soliander's staff sent a pulse up his arm. If the door had been open, that would've meant the archwizard was there. But the door being closed didn't tell them anything because it formed a perfect seal that let no light—or anything else—out. Eric held two knives as Taryn took the Crown of Voids in one hand and Matt thought over the word to magically unlock the door. Only Soliander and he knew it.

With a final nod, he whispered the word and threw open the door, eyes darting to the empty chair behind the huge black desk, and then around the room. He strode in, Taryn right behind. But Soliander wasn't here.

Eric entered. "Think he's above us?"

Matt listened for a few moments. "No. The stuff he does up there makes lots of noise. Let's check after I look around."

Eric turned to Taryn, "Why don't we check? He doesn't need us in here."

"Right."

They stepped out and disappeared up the stairs. Matt tried to sense from Soliander's memories where certain things were. The square room was familiar and yet new. A hulking fireplace to one side sat cold and dark, with no burning embers. Bookcases lined with jars, vials, and jugs filled two walls. Papers, books, and an assortment of loose items like quill pens lay on the desk.

In the corner stood a rosewood cabinet, the sight thrilling him. This was where Soliander kept the staff and robe he wore as an Ellorian Champion. Matt stepped toward the cabinet but stopped on feeling the strongest pulse he'd ever received from the staff. He couldn't remember what the spell was or how to get rid of it. Maybe it was just as well. Stealing those would be tempting but foolish. He imagined opening the cabinet and leaving a sarcastic note about not stealing them and suggesting the arch-wizard return the favor and let Matt keep the copies.

His eyes fell on a bookcase full of rings, headbands, wands, and more. He saw one orb under a black velvet cloth, then pulled that off to see a dark sphere. He had seen one like it before, right before smashing it into three pieces. With a quick glance at the door, he took it, the stand it was on, and the cloth, which was a bag for it. These disappeared into the magic bag, and he re-spaced the items on the shelf to disguise their absence. Right as he finished, Eric and Taryn returned.

"He's not here," revealed Taryn, sounding relieved and disappointed. "Are you done?"

"Almost." Matt moved behind the desk, trying to sense where the scrolls about creating keystones, Quest Rings, and Home Rings were. Then suddenly he knew. They were in the dreaded rosewood cabinet that he didn't...

...the spell came into his head, along with the knowledge of what guarded it. His eyes went to it immediately and Eric stepped toward it.

"Don't!" Matt cautioned.

Eric winced and clutched his stomach, doubling over and backing away as his breathing grew hard. But once he had backed up, the pained expression left and he straightened, questioning eyes on Matt.

"One spell will make you sick if you get close."

"And the second one?" Taryn asked.

"Nasty demon shows up long enough to take you somewhere you don't want to be."

She arched an eyebrow at him. "And you're getting in there?"

"Will the staff let you get to it?" Eric asked.

"No, because his copy of the staff is in there, so he can't use it to open it from the outside. There's a counter-spell."

The others moved away as Matt walked close to the cabinet but not near enough to trigger a reaction. He closed his eyes, focusing on the words Soliander used. This cabinet wasn't opened often, but the memory was vivid due to its importance. He began gathering energy and felt the familiar surge of power.

"From other worlds where you abide,
Do not come here and to my side,
A moment's rest to let me by,
After me, all others die."

The magic flowed into the space before the cabinet. Nothing had visibly changed, but he felt the sense of menace lift.

"The demon spell is suspended. I can eliminate the other one, but I can't put it back, and that would let him know we'd been in here sooner. Leaving a pile of vomit wouldn't help."

"I have an idea," said Eric, turning to Taryn. "Can you get Anna?" She left and Eric said, "I'm wondering if she can either heal one of us as we get closer or suppress the effect on us."

"We each have a Trinity Ring, too. One of its healing spells might help."

Eric looked at the silver ring. "Yeah. I already used one."

"There's another problem. The actual lock. Think you can pick it?"

"While I'm puking? Soliander is clever—I'll give him that."

Taryn returned with Anna and explained the situation. They knew by now that Anna tried to reach out to a god every time they arrived on another planet, so it came as no surprise when she said she had already made contact. Eriana and Soliander had created the Corethian Amulet to help with that, because they had often arrived somewhere with no knowledge of the gods, not to mention a relationship with one.

They let Anna commune with the god. Matt grew impatient to get out of there. Soliander could cast himself into the room at any moment. If Matt learned more control, he might be able to create portals on his own, but casting himself somewhere still unnerved him. Maybe he'd try it in a field sometime.

Anna soon surrounded them with a shield that muted the spell's effects. Eric pulled his lockpicking tools from a pocket and stepped toward the cabinet, feeling only a slight twinge of nausea. He knelt before the gold lock and fiddled with it until it clicked.

"Wait," said Matt, stepping closer. He pressed a secret handle on one side and the cabinet doors opened. "If you pull the actual handles, a poison needle pricks you. Puts you in a coma until he revives you for interrogation. I must admit, he knows how to protect something."

"No shit."

"Stand back. *Enumisar*." The word of power switched on the light atop Soliander's staff. An identical light, on the staff leaning against one corner inside the cabinet, also came on. Hanging beside it was the robe. Matt bit his lip, tempted. But he reached for the drawers to one side, finding the scrolls he wanted. It made sense that Soliander hid hidden them here. These were the original instructions, which someone else could alter—like Everon had—to imprison them in quests. He picked up the scrolls and stepped back.

Then he had an idea. "See if you can find two scrolls just like these for decoys. If he sees them, he may never look inside to realize they've been replaced."

Eric and Taryn scoured the room, but saw nothing, so they went down one level and returned with two scrolls. Matt put them in the drawer, dropped the real ones in his Bag of Desires, and cast a final glance at Soliander's staff, still glowing. He switched off the lights on both staffs, closed the cabinet—the lock clicked shut—and stepped away. The demon spell would resume in minutes. They tried to make sure the room didn't look disturbed before leaving, Matt remembering that the spell on the door would reactivate by itself.

They descended the stairs to find Ryan waiting by the room on the first floor. He nodded at the doorway beside him.

"We caught two more servants. They wouldn't tell us where Eriana is. They're tied up."

They continued to the bottom and regrouped. They were standing in the front corner of the rectangular castle, beside the courtyard. Each corner had a tower. Matt knew that Diara was in the tower diagonal to their position, at the back of the castle. They would only get her if Eriana wanted them to. There were two other towers, which gave them a 50-50 chance of guessing which one Eriana was in. He opted for the nearest one at the front, across the courtyard. They skirted the outside wall. The walkway on the second level would hide them from above if anyone was in the keep, which was several stories high.

Matt said the tower was the same as the one they'd just been in, and since they weren't expecting magic trouble, he did not go up with Taryn and Eric. The others waited impatiently, Matt feeling good about how things had gone so far. Sneaking around Soliander's home took some of the intimidation out of the arch-wizard.

Then he saw movement through the tower door, which they had neglected to close. Across the courtyard, a figure in dark leather sauntered toward Soliander's tower, but looked their way and stopped. She could almost certainly see Matt and probably Ryan.

Kori of Nysuun turned and sprinted toward the keep, screaming for Lord Voth.

CHAPTER FOURTEEN

A Lady of Hope

Anna heard the shouting and saw her friends' alarmed faces. Lorian sprinted up the tower. They had two options. If Eriana was above them, they could all just get her, cast the spell to open a portal, and disappear back to Andor. If she wasn't, they'd be fighting Kori, Lord Voth, and whoever else to reach her. Kori hadn't screamed Soliander's name, at least, suggesting that he wasn't there. Their third option was leaving without Eriana, but there was no way. Anna wasn't abandoning her. They only had one shot and it had just gone to hell.

Lorian reappeared, with Eric and Taryn right behind. No Eriana.

"Which way did Kori go?" Eric asked, eyes intense.

Ryan pointed at the tower diagonal to them. Was it the one with Diara? Matt hadn't said. Anna was about to ask when Eric said they had to run to evade an attack. They started into the courtyard toward the main building. Soliander's tower stood to the left, a rear tower rose to the right, and the other rear tower was across the courtyard and beyond the keep straight ahead. Halfway to the keep, dozens of undead raced from a door in it and from the left and right toward the rear towers. Some were skeletons with maces and hammers in their gloved hands, but most seemed like wights, with mummified flesh, soiled clothes,

253

white hair and eyes, and long nails like claws, their hands empty except for a few that wielded swords or a flail. Since many gods saw undead as an abomination, Anna felt this battle was hers more than anyone else's, and she reached for the Corethian Amulet.

Ryan took center position while Taryn and Eric flanked him. Lorian stood beside Eric, and the Dark Blade warriors completed the line on either side as the battle began. Prince Dari hung back with Anna, Matt, and Rognir. Was it cowardice, or did he mean to protect them from the swarm?

Behind the attackers stood Kori and Aeron, a short black man with a shaved head, curving welts covering his face and hands. Anna didn't understand where the necromancer had summoned the undead from. Was there a graveyard nearby? Lord Voth, the undead knight, strode through the keep's door and into the fray, wielding a black sword rimmed with frost. He turned toward Ryan, baleful eyes settling on Matt behind him. Lord Voth had a score to settle. Matt had burned away his flesh so that he wore gloves to control his sword. He seemed eager to cut his way through Ryan to reach him.

Anna urgently reached out to a god. She instantly felt the deity seeing through her eyes, then an indignation not her own. When she swung her arm, it felt like someone else controlled it. Four of the wights flew back. Three crashed hard into the stone keep, their bones audibly shattering. The fourth tumbled across the courtyard, landing on an area of broken cobblestones where bare earth could be seen. Weeds sprang up to entwine around its limbs, repeated tugs downward cracking its body as the weeds pulled it under to disappear.

"The name of the goddess, lass," said Rognir, "so I may help?"

Anna gripped the dwarf's shoulder, giving him an immediate connection. His hammer glowed white. He ran into the melee beside a Dark Blade warrior, whose sword had had little effect. One hit of Rognir's hammer shattered the wight's leg so that it fell, and another blow caved its head in. The dwarf then enchanted the warrior's sword.

Those with magic weapons were faring better. In Ryan's hands, Korrin's sword gouged huge chunks of mummified flesh from wights, but he barely kept pace with the onslaught of slashing hands, his armor deflecting blows that made it past his sword. Eric had bloody cuts to his hands, all of them turning black. Anna warned him she was behind him and healed him before stepping back.

She heard Matt yell, *"Kunia!"*

Anna looked over in alarm, knowing that anyone in the spell's path—friend or foe—would go flying. A half dozen undead flew backward, two striking Lord Voth, who stayed upright and went for Ryan. Anna focused her thoughts on everyone's weapons and made a rising gesture with her hands. Their swords began to glow, slicing through body parts more easily, severed limbs dropping but still crawling toward them on the ground.

Someone screamed, and Anna turned to see a Dark Blade warrior pulled into the wight throng by his sword arm. Two of the wights tore at him, then threw his body to Aeron's feet. With his palm over the corpse, the necromancer made circling motions. The body struggled to its feet, turned back to the fight, and only took two steps before the enchanted sword in its hand burst into flames that quickly consumed it.

A second wave of undead surged around Aeron and Kori and through the keep door. Anna thought they needed to flee to the right and other tower there, but then more undead ran from it around the line of defense toward Matt.

He conjured a huge fountain of flames to set them ablaze, but they kept coming.

Eric yelled, "Matt, which tower is Eriana in?"

But the wizard fell under the swarm. His screams were high-pitched, wild, and incoherent until he roared *"Enumisar!"* and a fireball rose upward, throwing burning undead into the air forty feet and shocking Anna with the heat. The still-burning undead landed with a snapping of limbs that didn't stop them from rising.

Anna went to heal the numerous gashes on Matt's hands and face but heard him say *"Minurarki"*, activating the least powerful healing spell in his Trinity Ring. She turned away and saw Kori looking back over her shoulder at the tower behind her, then at Eric. Kori nodded. Was she telling him which tower Eriana was in? It seemed improbable. It had to be a trick. They would need to cut through the undead to reach it. Eric seemed to agree. He turned toward the remaining tower on their right.

"That way!"

Anna watched Kori's face register alarm and disappointment. Then she flung aside more undead to clear a path as Prince Dari led them. She followed him, her eyes darting around to see who else she could help. Taryn and her men were retreating while fighting, but it seemed that Lord Voth would be the biggest challenge, because any spell to thrust him back wasn't working. Dari bashed open a door to the keep and they began retreating inside. Then Anna realized how to slow Lord Voth.

She yelled, "Everyone but Ryan and Eric, into the room right now! Trust me!" As they ran in, the undead surged forward and she again called out, "Ryan and Eric, now you!"

They obeyed and ran for the door, but Lord Voth slashed Eric across the back. He screamed in pain, but kept moving. The undead surged forward, Lord Voth right behind. In grim satisfaction at her plan's success, Anna swung her arm again and the undead flew back and into Lord Voth, toppling him. With the way clear, they slammed shut the door and barricaded it. Anna rushed to Eric and healed him, sudden fatigue making her weak. Rognir began healing others as needed. The barricade would not hold, and the doors leading outward beckoned. Two of the Dark Blade warriors tried to hold the barrier as repeated thumps against it came near to knocking it off its hinges.

Dari said, "We need to escape to Andor before the elf and wizard get too badly injured and cannot open a portal. You saw what just happened to Matt."

"No," said Taryn, her face gashed in two places. "We are not defeated yet."

Breathing hard, Eric said, "We have to keep moving and reach the other tower, the one behind Kori."

"No!" said Anna. "I saw the look she gave you. It's a trap."

"It's the right tower," said Matt. "Diara is in the one nearer to us."

Anna didn't know what to believe now. Why would Kori help them? A tryst with Eric couldn't end years of service to Soliander, or Zoran. Then she had no time to ponder it as a big crash at the door sent both Dark Blades tumbling. One stayed on his feet and backed away but the other fell and was immediately set upon by undead tearing at him. Fear and anger tore through Anna, and she once again made a throwing motion that hurled the undead from him. But she was too late. They had ripped his throat out. She nearly stumbled from fatigue.

Someone yanked her by the arm into a shambling run, and she turned to find Taryn pulling her away. Matt brought up the rear, stopping to engulf the undead in flames and set the room ablaze before he joined them. Allies standing in the way had constrained Matt before, but now he did horrible damage to what pursued them. Flames were engulfing the keep.

She stumbled into another room with a wide table, with maps, goblets, and plates of food spread on it. Dari, Ryan, and Lorian thrust it against the door and followed the rest of them into another room. They seemed to be going in the right direction, but once half their group had made it past a door on their left, it burst open. Undead flooded the room and separated the group. Rognir slammed his hammer through leg after leg as Anna hurled the undead up against the wall one more time. Everyone heard Matt yell *"Kunia!"* and ducked as he threw this onslaught back, too. Dari grabbed her arm and pulled Anna onward, stumbling. She was so tired. They couldn't keep this going.

By now they had reached a hallway leading to the tower, and they hurried to catch the others. Anna heard the clanging of swords ahead and came around the corner to see her friends battling Lord Voth, wights, and a half dozen spectral knights. The new and terrifying additions looked like ghosts in white, their silvery swords cleaving an arc of light through the torchlit darkness. Only those with enchanted blades could ward off the blows, and she saw with dismay her earlier enchantment had had worn off. She didn't have the strength to do it again—and so she watched as men's swords turned to frost, then shatter on the next parry. Several Dark Blade warriors went down screaming.

Matt yelled, "Down! *Kunia!*"

Everyone ahead of him had dropped to one knee, and now the wights flew backward, narrowly missing Kori and Aeron. Ryan rose with his sword up to block Lord Voth's blade, which had wounded his other arm, chest, and leg. He was being beaten backward and taking more damage. Fear surging, Anna focused her will and squeezed with one outstretched hand. Lord Voth was in mid-swing when his sword arm stopped. He seemed confused until his eyes blazed with hatred for Anna. Ryan stabbed him through the heart and pulled out the bloody sword, but the undead knight cocked his head as if amused—until Ryan chopped it off. The head didn't move, because Anna still held him, but then she pushed and the body and head tumbled away. She fell to one knee and Prince Dari helped her up.

Only now did she really see and hear the spectral knights howling in pain from a bright light consuming them. She saw the cause—Rognir chanting and swinging his hammer in a circle by its handle, the light fanning out from the whirling weapon. Taryn bashed open the tower door and they began filing through it, Rognir coming last and ending his assault. There was nothing to barricade the door with and they began climbing as fast as they dared, Dari and Lorian helping Anna until Ryan hoisted her over one shoulder despite having to climb so far. Using a spell, Matt blew open every door as they climbed. The one far below burst open, and she heard the scrambling of many feet. Whether or not Eriana was at the top, it was time to go.

"Eriana!" Taryn was shouting as they ascended. "It's Taryn of Aranor and the new Ellorian Champions! Are you here?"

Anna thought she heard a faint woman's voice answer, then hard banging on a wooden door. Ryan carried her over a landing, through a doorway, and into a room, where he set her down and she straightened, feeling woozy. The group slammed the door shut and tried barricading it as she turned and came face to face with the Lady Hope, Eriana of Coreth.

"My god," said Eriana, putting hands on her, "you're pale." She spoke a few words and sudden strength and energy filled Anna, who blinked in surprise. Then she laughed in relief at seeing the priestess, whose power they sorely needed. Despite the situation, she still noticed that

Eriana wore a yellow robe, which struck her because she'd only seen her in Earth clothing before. She looked well.

"We're here to rescue you," said Anna.

"Time to get the fuck out of here," said Eric. Loud bangs rocked the door. "Matt! Lorian!"

"On it," said Matt. "Clear a space."

With so many people in the small room, they had nowhere to create the portal without being bumped into. They grabbed the bed and shoved it up against the other furniture now by the door. Lorian and Matt moved to the place where it had been. Then glass shattered to one side. Anna saw a wight climbing in through the window, having scaled the tower's exterior. Another wight followed as Rognir clubbed the first one. A second window shattered, then a third, wights entering to separate the rescuers into small groups. The door finally splintered, more wights pushing in. Anna backed away, seeing them about to be overrun.

Suddenly, a concussive blast hit the room and smashed all of the wights to dust against the walls. It also shattered the mirror and any remaining glass. Anna turned in surprise to Eriana, seeing grim satisfaction.

"Wow," she said, "you *are* strong."

"You'll get there," said the priestess.

Anna doubted that, but wasn't going to argue. She saw that Matt and Lorian had the portal open. Through the shimmering doorway, she saw the meeting room in Andor and Taryn's Dark Blade warriors watching intently as if debating whether to come through.

"Time to go!" shouted Ryan.

Then suddenly everything was happening at once and Anna couldn't keep track. A spectral knight glided through the door. Another followed, more thuds knocking back the furniture before a huge bang shoved it away and Lord Voth, head reattached, stepped into the room. One of the

Dark Blades struck at him and was cut down. Dari was nearest and traded blows as he retreated. A wight clambered through the window behind him only to have Rognir bash it to pieces, but more of them were swarming in the other windows. A roar of flames from Matt's staff set three wights afire, one hitting the bed and setting it ablaze as smoke filled the room.

Lorian called out, "Eriana! Anna!" and they stepped toward the portal, the priestess hesitating.

"I have to help," Eriana said, thrusting her hand forward at the spectral knights. A blast of wind halted their attack. Lord Voth paused his swings at Dari long enough to pull out a knife, which he tossed at Eriana.

"No!" shouted Anna, jumping in front of it. The blade cut into her chest, a searing cold chilling her. She fell into Eriana, who pulled her back. And now the spectral knights pressed onward, more sliding through the walls and one rising through the floor.

"Into the portal!" Lorian shouted. He grabbed Anna and hauled her backward. Suddenly she passed through to Andor with him, her wide eyes watching the unfolding scene. Then a robed man was beside her, removing the knife, the pain causing her to look away from the portal until he healed her. By the time she looked again, another Dark Blade warrior had gone down and more wights were surging through the windows. They surrounded Dari as Rognir clubbed one down, trying to reach the prince. They were being overrun. Eric grabbed Ryan and pulled him back, eyes on Matt, who blasted more undead backward. Her three friends stood by the portal with Eriana.

Rognir, Dari, Taryn, and a few Dark Blades were struggling to retreat. And then one warrior was cut down. Rognir bashed the offending wight, trying to reach Dari, but one of the spectral knights traded two blows with the prince, shattering his sword. Then Lord Voth grabbed Dari by his wrist, which turned white. He screamed and tried to jerk free to no avail. Eriana made a gripping motion, and from across the room, seemed to snap off Voth's hand at the wrist.

"Go!" said Eric, shoving Ryan toward the portal. He clambered through reluctantly.

"I have to help my men!" Taryn shouted, moving forward.

"No!" Eric yelled. "It's too late. Look at him!"

Anna looked around Ryan's shoulder at the action, seeing Rognir dragging a grimacing Dari toward freedom. One of the remaining Dark Blades had hideous wounds to his torso and was already stumbling to one knee, about to be killed. Only a few of Taryn's men were left as more wights came through a window. Eric pulled a reluctant Taryn toward the portal and into it with him. Anna had to get out of their way and couldn't see anything more as Matt arrived, too.

She heard another scream of pain, a shout from Rognir and a kind of battle cry that sounded like Dari. Then Rognir stumbled through the portal dragging a protesting Eriana behind him. Two of the Dark Blades came through, one falling to the floor and being dragged away by the other. Over Eric's shoulder, Eriana saw two wights holding the prince by the arms and bearing him to the ground. Lord Voth and the spectral knights approached the portal. Behind them stood an impassive Aeron, his undead wreaking havoc. Eyes intense, Kori watched beside him.

"Close it!" Eric shouted to Matt and Lorian. "We can't save him. Close it or they'll come through!"

With a few frantic words from Lorian, the portal shut off, sudden silence filling the room. Anna turned Eric around by the shoulder.

"What happened?"

Eric shook his head, eyes clouded. "He saved Eriana. The wights came in and were charging her. She was looking elsewhere, so Dari charged them and knocked them all down." He looked at the priestess. "He saved her."

Anna opened her mouth, then closed it. "And then we left him."

"I know," Eric said, eyes troubled. "I know. We couldn't get to him."

Eriana put a hand on Anna. "He's right. There was no way to reach him without more of us getting hurt or killed. What he did was extremely brave."

Anna sighed, wondering how they were going to explain this to the king and queen. First Korrin had gone missing for three years, and now Dari had been captured by Soliander's Lords of Fear. That reminded her of the missing Lord.

"It's good Garian wasn't there. Or Soliander. Just one of them and we wouldn't have made it. Barely did as is. Is everyone okay?"

Virtually all of them had the black, festering injuries, while a few had frosty handprints on their armor or bodies. Those who could help began healing them. They had lost Dari and most of Taryn's warriors. But they had gained Eriana. Was her life worth theirs? Probably, as much as Anna might have once thought all lives were worth the same. That kind of thinking went out the window in circumstances like these.

Standing beside Matt, Taryn put her sword away and regretfully said, "I don't like leaving men behind, though they knew the risks." She reached up to wipe sweat from Matt's face, an act that surprised Anna. "You were impressive back there."

Eric asked him, "Any sense of whether Soliander will kill Dari?"

Matt pursed his lips. "I don't think he would. He's still loyal to the Champions. The real question is whether the Lords of Fear will know who Dari is and avoid killing him, or even whether they'll know Soliander wouldn't want it."

"Kori would know who he is, I'm sure," Eric said. "I doubt we can rescue him. They'd be expecting us now. Not sure how to frame this to his parents."

"They'll understand," said Taryn. "It's something Korrin would do. Honestly, the king might be happy to know Dari sacrificed himself like that. We'll just be honest."

No one said anything for a moment as they began to disperse, put away weapons, and decompress. In watching Eriana, Anna saw a look of resigned acceptance about the loss of life incurred to rescue her. It presumably muted her relief. Anna knew from her own experiences that death was part of the job, something they all had to get used to. It was harder for some, like her and Ryan, than others. Then Anna realized the priestess had no idea of where they were or everything that had just happened.

"It's okay," she began, smiling. "We're on Elloria, in Andor, at the castle. The king and queen agreed to let us rescue you when we found out Soliander had taken you from Jack's apartment. You are safe here and they know the truth about the rest of us, that we aren't the real Champions. Almost no one outside this room knows, though, which is why we need to change out of these outfits before we leave. You're fine in yours."

As Eriana absorbed that, a slow smile spread across her face. "You brought me home? This is really Elloria?" She strode to the nearest window. Would she recognize the city? Eriana threw open a partially closed curtain, sunlight streaming over her as she pushed the windowpane out. Warm air wafted in. A view of the port and ocean lay beyond the flags of Andor flying from various buildings and on the sails of ships.

Anna couldn't imagine being away from Earth and everything she'd known for twenty years and then suddenly getting back. It felt good, having done this. Their goal had been to rescue Eriana from Soliander, mostly because Jack had said she hadn't gone voluntarily. Until now, she hadn't really considered that a side effect would be getting Eriana home. Coreth was technically many miles to the southeast, but it wasn't worlds away anymore. When Eriana turned around, tears on her cheeks, Anna felt her own tears gathering.

Eriana walked up to her and wiped one from her face. "You look great in my robe. It suits you." She turned to the others. "It's the first time I've seen you in action. Very impressive—all of you. And I cannot thank you enough. Gratitude hardly begins to describe it."

"Many worlds owe you a debt," began a smiling Lorian as he approached, "so thanks are not needed, my lady."

"Lorian!" Eriana gave him a hug, which he awkwardly returned. While she had undoubtedly noticed the elf in the fighting, there had been no time for greetings. "Not elven custom, I know. I never thought I'd be so happy to see an elf! Or a dwarf!" She turned to the usually-taciturn Rognir.

"There must be some dust in my eye," said Rognir, wiping at it to muted laughter.

"Your brother is here," Anna revealed. "And Princess Alia of Coreth. We can take you to them."

Eriana put one hand to her mouth and fresh tears spilled down her cheeks as she nodded.

First, they changed out of the Champions' clothes once more. Anna offered her copy of Eriana's robe and Corethian Amulet to the priestess, who demurred, saying that they belonged to her now. Anna had never felt that was true, but the blessing changed that. She thought it would be nice for other people to see the Lady Hope, Eriana of Coreth, striding down the halls of Andor once again after having been missing for three years. But then maybe this had to be kept a secret a little longer. Questions would swirl, especially about her aging.

Taryn left to arrange a meeting with the king, queen, and others who had known about the mission. Anna sensed that the warrior and Matt were developing an interest in each other, however subtle. And then there was Kori and Eric. The assassin had told him with a look which tower Eriana was in. Anna didn't understand it.

As the group escorted Eriana to meet their hosts, she wore a cloak with the hood up to hide her face, but this couldn't last. It wasn't fair to her. She was finally home home after twenty years and had to pretend she was still missing.

Once the door to the secured throne room closed behind them, she pulled back the hood to a cry from her brother. He ran to her, Princess Alia following. With their laughing and crying, Anna gave into the tears. Ryan put an arm around her and smiled. To her surprise, his eyes were moist. Was this the first time he had felt like a hero, too?

The grinning king, queen, and Princess Cariss broke whatever protocol might have been in place and approached Eriana, the queen giving her a hug and chatting privately for a few minutes while Anna and her friends pretended not to listen. With the initial reunion over, talk turned to the mission with all of the survivors present.

"What of Dari?" Princess Cariss asked, worry dampening her smile. "Why is my brother not here?"

Eriana put one hand on her arm, her face sorrowful, and described what had happened. The king stood taller as if proud, the queen put one hand over her mouth but didn't cry, and Princess Cariss openly wept.

"He has finally earned the statue he so long desired," King Sarov remarked, "though he may never see it."

Anna tried not to look shocked at what struck her as a cold remark. Was that all he could think of, that it was a good death?

Ryan cleared his throat. "Your Majesty, there is still some chance we may be able to recover him."

But the king shook his head. "Soliander will not fall victim to this ploy a second time."

Anna knew that he was right. They had gotten lucky, too.

"I think we need to address Eriana's presence, Your Majesty," said Eric. "While she may be older, some people will recognize her anyway, and it's not fair to ask her to pretend she's not who she is. But we need to work out the repercussions of acknowledging she has been found. Questions will be asked about where she's been, and where the others are. And we might have to address the fact that we are not them."

The king turned to Eriana. "We may need you to pretend a while longer, my lady, for the sake of your replacements."

"I agree," said the priestess.

Feeling relieved, Anna said, "We might need the help of Eriana and the others, when we find them, to say that we've impersonated them with their blessing."

The king nodded. "We will also say that Andor approved of the charade, and that you rescued Eriana. I will formally declare you friends of the Empire of Andor." He turned to Princess Alia of Coreth. "While I cannot speak for your king, please encourage the same from him."

The princess smiled at them. "You will be friends of Coreth, certainly, and I will speak to His Majesty about an official declaration of friendship from the Kingdom of Roir."

For the first time, Anna felt excited about the truth becoming known. Coming to Andor was the best thing that had happened to them so far. The king announced a private celebration that evening.

But first they split up, Eriana going with her brother and Princess Alia to get reacquainted. The royal family left to deal with their grief over Prince Dari. And the four Earth friends freshened up before meeting with Lorian and Rognir, who would soon return to Honyn.

From their meeting room, they decided to send Lorian to Jack's apartment with a note about developments. Jack wasn't there, but had left a note beside his laptop for them. The elf seemed fascinated by the décor and a glimpse of cars moving past the windows. They almost had to yell at him to get him back.

With the portal closed, Ryan read Jack's note aloud:

Eric, Anna, Ryan, and Matt—

I'm leaving notes about what's happening in case you come back when I'm not here. More details are in the computer. Login information on the fridge. We found a suitable estate and are buying it. Daniel told his parents the truth about what's happening. The video of Soliander kidnapping Eriana convinced them it's all true. They are onboard, funding the estate. We'll tell Matt's and Anna's parents next. Your phones are here and charged up. Frozen food in the fridge.

—Jack

"Well," said Eric, sitting back in relief, "it sounds like he's got things under control."

Ryan sighed. "I'm not sure how I feel about my parents knowing."

"They were going to find out sooner or later," said Eric. "Maybe he did you a favor."

"I must admit," began Anna, "I love being able to communicate with someone back home."

"Hey," said Matt, looking excited, "I just realized we can send other stuff to Earth. We can't bring anything back ourselves, but why wait until we're returning? Open a portal and send things through."

They talked it over and agreed to send spellbooks and materials to Jack's apartment before completing the dragon egg quest and going home. Matt could finally practice magic and worry less about memorizing spells to bring back. Lorian could send more supplies from Honyn with help from friends. Matt could even go to the elf's home for training. If a quest happened, he would just be summoned from there.

Anna felt so much better about their situation. They could communicate with Earth. They could send someone else through. They could even go back, provided they carried something like that dragon egg first. They were also getting much-needed training. They had allies—and many more answers than before. This was nowhere near being over, but their situation had improved a lot. And then another possibility walked through the door when Eriana joined them, having freshened up.

They got each other caught up. The priestess admitted that she'd believed Soliander could be redeemed, but her faith took a hit on learning of his activities as Zoran the Devastator. And yet she understood that his actions were born of grief and revenge.

And she had a big revelation.

"It should be possible for you to create your own Home Rings," she began, "based on what he told me. I tried to get him to help with creating the keystones, but he's not there yet. You have the scrolls telling you how. Now you just need soclarin ore to do it."

Matt arched an eyebrow. "We gave a bunch to Lorian on the Dragon Gate quest."

The elf nodded. "I still have it."

"I haven't looked at the scrolls yet."

Eriana said, "You should before you do the quest here. There is one last thing you need. The keystones can only be created at Soli's old home in Aranor. I know where it is and can lead you there."

Matt perked up. "Yes, I see the room we need in my head now. It is guarded with spells." His eyes narrowed as he thought hard. "My copy of his staff will get me past most of them at his place. He's cleaned it out, though. There shouldn't be much there."

Eric observed, "I'm worried he's altered the spells since you interacted with him. He knows the staff can get you past them."

"Yes," said Ryan, "but he doesn't know we have so-clarin, or the scrolls, and maybe he won't realize Eriana's told us this. He wouldn't expect us to go there."

"Maybe," said Eric. "We need caution, and we should hurry before he figures anything out."

Anna sighed. He was right, but it had been a long day. "First thing in the morning? Matt needs to study the scrolls. Maybe Lorian, too, and we need the ore."

Eriana said, "Yes, tomorrow at the earliest. I need to look at the scrolls as well. My help was needed to add the healing to the original keystones, and I think I'll need to do it again. No offense, but I'm not sure you're strong enough."

"What about me?" Matt asked. "Do you think I'm strong enough to create these keystones?"

Erianna nodded. "I think so, yes. From what Soliander told me, Everon wasn't that strong a wizard and yet was able to create them. The reason more healing strength is needed is that it takes great energy to heal even one person, not to mention four at once—and unlike the wizard, I can't just use a spell. He has to use multiple spells, like the one to change our clothes, or to actually summon us, and the one to create the oracle that asks summoners questions. These are all different and must be done one at a time. If it was all one spell, I'm not sure even Soliander could cast something that complex."

That made sense to Anna. She hadn't considered that the magic came in pieces, like parts of a puzzle or machine. It did raise the question of what happened when one part of it failed. What if they arrived somewhere and hadn't been changed into their outfits? Or showed up nude? Or they stayed home but were suddenly in the Champions' attire? Was there a failsafe that would leave them all at home if one part of the magic failed? Everon could have tampered with all of this. But Soliander presumably had the original spells in the scrolls, not Everon's tampered versions. Anna wondered whether and how the keystones for a Quest Ring and for a Home Ring were different, but Matt wouldn't know until he looked at the scrolls. Now she wanted to see them, too.

That night, they had a private and muted celebration with their hosts—absent Princess Cariss, who was still grief-stricken over the loss of her brother. The queen was similarly muted, and Anna made a point of not seeming too jovial. She whispered to the others to be sensitive. Ryan took it a step further and approached the queen for a few private words that Anna didn't overhear, though she saw the queen take his hand and put her own hand on his shoulder. In all their adventures, Anna had almost forgotten how thoughtful Ryan could be. Shortly after the exchange, the queen left early.

The king seemed more jubilant and even gave a toast in Prince Dari's honor, beaming like a proud father. Had he waited until his wife and daughter weren't present? Did he consider being captured and possibly killed honorably better than staying behind, safe here at the castle while others went into danger? She suspected that this was so. She would never understand people who thought that way. The pride that Dari had done something noble and selfless she understood, but not the rest.

After dinner, they gathered once more as Matt, Eriana, and then Lorian went over the spells in Soliander's scrolls. The elf would cast some of them for Matt, who would do those requiring the most power. Everyone else departed to let them study in peace. Anna was the last to go, her eyes on Taryn sitting with Matt and offering encouragement she only heard some of. She wondered how many times Taryn had done the same thing with her brother. Had she helped Soliander become so strong? Had she guided his character? According to her, she was the big sister who had kept him in line. Sometimes Anna felt the same way about all the boys, but especially Matt, since they'd grown up next door to each other.

Anna didn't doubt Taryn had guided Soliander's development as a person. The woman was capable, commanding, rough, and able to physically take on men. Anna could only do the latter with words and logic. Taryn seemed like she could do that, too. Maybe she would be good for Matt, however brief their relationship was likely to be. He could use a strong woman—someone who understood his position. Taryn knew better than them the struggles Matt faced, maybe even the fear he felt on wielding such power. Matt hadn't said much about it to them, but Anna had seen him muted when doing some spells. In battle, he showed no sign of it. Was he somehow in his element there—not confused, not overthinking, just doing what he was capable of?

But now he faced his biggest challenge, with a lot riding on it. If they could create these keystones for their own

Home Rings, it would significantly impact their fortunes and feelings of safety on being sent home. He had to know that. With that in mind, she walked over to him, interrupted his talk with Taryn, and gave him a kiss on the forehead, smiling at the questioning look he gave her.

"For luck," she said. "I know you can do it. But we're all here to help."

He flashed the sweet smile she had so often seen when growing up together but had not seen much of lately. They had come a long way and she wanted him to know she was proud of him, so she told him so and then left them alone.

CHAPTER FIFTEEN

KIRA MORI

Special Agent Kira Mori preferred to work alone, but she couldn't say being assigned a partner had surprised her. The investigation into the disappearance of Erin Jennings had taken some unexpected turn—and the world seemed full of those lately. What started as a missing person's report had led her straight to the Stonehenge Four, FBI leadership praising her for the lead of the century, as they called it. She had to admit, it was big, and too important for just one agent to handle. It seemed like she had half the D.C. field office working on what she had uncovered in the hottest case in the country. She stood before them now, ready to brief the teams executing search warrants on a handful of properties as a result of her work.

Someone at the upper levels of government had decided these four friends from Maryland were able to magically disappear and reappear wherever they wanted. What was to stop any or all of them from dropping into the White House and killing the President? Nothing that she could see. But her investigation led her to believe they weren't that kind of a problem, if they were one at all. Logic suggested that the woman, Anna, had not purposely disappeared from her moving car on I-270 while driving it, hurting or killing her three friends. Or that she had intentionally reappeared in the middle of the same road and gotten herself struck by a car.

Kira sighed. Logic had little to do with any thinking in politics anymore, but that and the truth were her job. There was no room for bullshit. While she couldn't deny that there was a problem with the Stonehenge Four, and that they were somehow involved with the missing Erin Jennings, her impression was that they were caught up in something beyond their control—just like so many people involved in reports of sudden magic abilities hurting or killing people. She'd already investigated one of those and knew that everyone was, in effect, a victim of things they didn't understand. While she needed to find out what was going on, she wasn't of a mind to cause problems for people who already had them.

But she wasn't going to tell Jack Riley that when she arrested him.

First, she had to bring her new partner, Special Agent Wade Carter, up to speed—along with the rest of the agents. She brushed her long, black hair bob out of her face and stepped in front of the podium, rows of agents before her and a slideshow at the ready. Most were white, a few were Asians like her, a handful were black, and only three were women. After a quick introduction, she got started.

"This began as a missing person's report for Erin Jennings of Florida. Her husband indicated that she flew to Maryland to meet an unnamed person in Gaithersburg. She is a collector of antiquities that are rumored to have magical properties, and she has been doing this for over a decade. As we all know, reports are coming in around the world of magic happening, so in light of more recent discoveries in her case, we have confiscated all the items found in her home.

"One person of interest is a private investigator, Karl Parsons, also of Florida. She kept him on retainer to find these antiquities and arrange meetings with buyer, but he claims he had no knowledge of this particular transaction, and Mrs. Jennings had arranged it on her own.

"We were able to track the rental car she obtained near BWI airport in Baltimore, and we found it near an apartment complex in Gaithersburg. Witnesses said it had been there for several days without being moved. We impounded the car but found nothing of significance, including no signs of a struggle or blood.

"And now we get to the more interesting part.

"We found that Mrs. Jennings stayed at the Hilton hotel in Gaithersburg and then, without checking out, she got a room for a single night in a nearby Marriott. We checked the security footage and found nothing of interest at the Hilton, but the Marriott turned up something unexpected. Mrs. Jennings was seen in the company of Eric Foster, Ryan LaRue, and Matt Sorenson, three of the Stonehenge Four. At that time, the remaining one of them—Anna Sumner—was in Shady Grove hospital in Gaithersburg.

"In the video footage, it appeared that Mrs. Jennings acquired the room at the Marriott after walking across the street from another hotel, the Spring Hill Suites, which she exited with them. Further investigation revealed that none of them had a room at Spring Hill Suites. However, Quincy King, the LaRue family attorney, did have a room there—and yet he was not seen to enter or leave the property. It is believed that Mr. King acquired the room on behalf of Ryan LaRue and the other two men. This may have been to help them evade the considerable media attention on them, or for some other purpose. It also appears that the Stonehenge Four were the people that Mrs. Jennings had come to meet, but we don't know that for sure. Why they exited the Spring Hill Suites with her, and why she acquired another room at the Marriott across the street, is also unknown.

"There was another man with them at these hotels. He was seen using a car at the Spring Hill Suites, which is how we acquired his license plate and identity. His name is Jack Riley. He recently quit his job as a manager at Starbucks for unknown reasons, but possibly in anticipation of a ransom for Mrs. Jennings, who is wealthy. He has an apartment in Gaithersburg near where Mrs. Jennings' car was found. So near, in fact, that we believe she was last with Jack Riley before her disappearance.

"Despite all of this, Mr. Riley has remained in the area, and we have been monitoring his activities. He does not appear to be using his own credit cards for transactions, but rather cards associated with Mr. King, the attorney. Furthermore, he has been seen in the company of Daniel LaRue, the younger brother of Ryan, one of the Stonehenge Four. Mr. Riley and Mr. LaRue have been visiting estates for sale in Darnestown Maryland, with the intent to purchase one.

"I should also mention that Mr. King, the LaRue family attorney, is representing Anna Sumner in her legal troubles stemming from both car accidents in which she was involved on I-270. This strengthens the connections among the Stonehenge Four.

"We investigated footage of Ms. Sumner at Shady Grove Hospital. It was known that she was paralyzed and in a coma. And yet she vanished without a trace some days ago. There is no footage of her exiting the hospital, leading to speculation that, as has already been documented, she left by supernatural means. A thorough search of the hospital did not find her. Despite this, days later, she was not seen reentering the hospital, but she *was* seen leaving in the company of Mrs. Jennings. She was walking and appeared to be in perfect health. The pair got into Mrs. Jennings' rental car.

"At present, all of the Stonehenge Four are unaccounted for, as is Mrs. Jennings, who disappeared sometime after this after a final communication with her husband in Florida. He subsequently filed the missing person's report that opened this investigation. There is an arrest warrant out for each of the Stonehenge Four, and for Jack Riley, for potential involvement in the disappearance of Mrs. Jennings. There are also arrest warrants for Ms. Sumner and Mrs. Jennings, for assaulting a guard at Shady Grove Hospital during Ms. Sumner's escape. And we also have search warrants for the homes of the Stonehenge Four, their families, and Jack Riley.

"This is still primarily a missing person's case, and potentially a kidnapping one. However, due to the national security concerns regarding the Stonehenge Four, we will face a lot of scrutiny. For those of you unfamiliar with this, some people believe that they can appear where they want without warning, bypassing all traditional security measures. This means they are a potential threat to elected officials like the President. However, we have examined their social media and see no signs of domestic terrorism or interest in it. Out of an abundance of caution, we have sought them for questioning—but now that they are involved in a missing person's case, we have the justification for warrants that some agencies and individuals in government had previously sought and been denied by the courts.

"I do want to observe that none of the suspects has a history of violence, except Eric Foster, a trained martial artist and instructor. However, he has not used a weapon before. He was a juvenile delinquent in and out of the foster system. It seems he lived on the streets for a number of years, using petty theft and burglaries to sustain himself. We do not consider the suspects to be armed, or at least not with traditional weapons. Due to their apparent ability to use magic, they are still considered to be dangerous. It is imperative that we capture them alive due to the extraordinary nature of their apparent abilities and their potential role in magic events throughout the world."

Her partner, Special Agent Carter, spoke up. "Why do we think they have something to do with magic?"

Kira replied, "No one witnessed their original disappearance at Stonehenge, or their reappearance. However, it was around this time that magic seemingly began, based on the earliest reports of incidents around the world. They did not have a believable explanation for their absence of three weeks. It was only later when they disappeared again, this time on camera, that we realized that this might have been what happened at Stonehenge, minus the camera. We therefore suspect that the Stonehenge incidents were the first instances of magic happening on Earth. But this is conjecture. It is one of the many reasons why we must get answers from them."

She fielded a few more questions before the teams began to disperse. A number of simultaneous but hopefully peaceful raids were to be carried out in the next two hours. She and Special Agent Carter were soon knocking on the door of Jack's apartment, a dozen other agents and field technicians standing by to collect evidence. No one answered after repeated knocks and announcements that the FBI had a warrant, so she used the apartment manager's key to open the door. But no one was inside. It didn't take long to find Mrs. Jennings' purse on the kitchen counter—and that was all she needed to know that Jack was involved. No woman leaves her purse behind. She turned and saw login information on a note attached to the fridge, wondering whether it went with the laptop in the other room.

Kira was about to grab it when she heard a strained voice ask, "Hey, what's going on?"

She stepped out of the kitchen into the living room to see a tall, slender young man with short brown hair and a friendly demeanor. He wore jeans and a grey t-shirt under a light jacket for the fall weather. He held a bag of groceries in one hand, his keys in the other. His concerned eyes moved among the people helping themselves to his possessions, no doubt noticing the "FBI" emblazoned on their jackets.

"Good afternoon, Mr. Riley," Kira began, approaching him and pulling out her handcuffs. "I'm Special Agent Mori with the FBI. You are under arrest for the kidnapping of Erin Jennings."

Jack wasn't having a good day. The surprise of arriving at his apartment and seeing the FBI agents going through his things wasn't one he'd forget. He'd known at once that it related to his friends—or he'd thought so, anyway. The female agent telling him he was under arrest for kidnapping Eriana, aka Erin Jennings, was the new shock of his life—perhaps even more startling than the moment Eric and the others had reappeared in front of him months back. He'd known enough to keep his mouth shut. Now, it seemed especially smart that he and the others had already signed paperwork to retain Quincy as their attorneys.

Now he and the lawyer sat alone beside each other in a holding cell somewhere in Rockville, Maryland. In a few minutes, his questioning would begin, and aside from saying nothing at all, he didn't know what to do.

"Did they tell you anything?" he asked.

"Apparently. They found Eriana's purse in your apartment and her car nearby. And they have footage of you with her at a hotel. Her husband reported her missing.

282 | RANDY ELLEFSON

That's something we didn't see coming. That set all this in motion."

"Shit. So what do we do? Can you get me out of here?"

Quincy sighed. "Honestly, I'm not sure. She's gone and you're the prime suspect. They have reason to hold you and even have you arraigned. That will take a few days, and I can't get you out until then."

Jack went cold. "So I'm spending a few days in jail?"

"Listen, we both know what really happened, and you didn't kidnap Eriana."

"Yeah, but what am I supposed to tell them? That a wizard from another planet did it?" Then he realized something. "Well, I do actually have the footage of Soliander taking her. Not sure it's a good idea to let them see it."

Quincy's eyebrows had risen. "They've already got it. It's on your phone?"

"Yeah. And laptop. I didn't think of that. So if they've seen it, why not let me go?"

"They might not have seen it yet. But they probably will. I know they've got your stuff. The question is whether we want to tell them about it to get you out."

"They'll have a ton of questions. Do I have to tell them anything?"

"No. It's proof you didn't do anything to Eriana, and that's enough. You don't have to explain how you know her, or why she was at your place. Normally they would want your help in locating her, but that doesn't really apply here, given that a wizard took her, presumably off the planet."

"They're going to hear a bunch of things on that video that maybe Eric and the others don't want them to."

"No stopping that now. We'll just have to deal with it. This might be an opportunity, to be honest."

"How so?"

"The FBI have been wanting to talk to them about a lot of things, assuming them to be a problem or dangerous in some way, but they haven't had much to go on. The legal case against Anna for the accidents is the closest, but that didn't open itself up to FBI involvement. Eriana's disappearance did even though it had nothing to do with them. It led right to them and you. But that footage makes it clear someone was after them and they had good reason to be evasive."

"Are you thinking that instead of the FBI being a problem, they could help protect all of us?"

"Something like that. I don't think we can get far with it yet, but that tape is the first sign that they're victims and not perpetrators. I think we need to approach this from the standpoint of wanting to tell them more but thinking they won't believe us, and they can't make you say anything or hold you after they see that tape. Today we set the stage for them becoming allies, I think."

"Okay. So let's tell them about the video. Part of me feels like it's not my place to tell them what's going on with Eric and the others after they see it, so I don't want to say—"

"You're in jail for it," Quincy interrupted. "It just became your place to tell. You're a part of this if you weren't before. Time to act like it."

He got up and left the room to tell the agents they were ready to talk. When he returned shortly afterwards, Special Agent Mori was with him, her black, button-up collared shirt tucked into black pants. She cut an athletic figure and seemed sharp-eyed, like someone he'd rather have as an ally than after him and his friends. He sat up straighter, trying to look less intimidated. The agent slid a picture of Eriana across the table to him.

"Mr. Riley," she began, not wasting time, "do you know Erin Jennings?"

284 | RANDY ELLEFSON

Jack felt better handling this now that he and Quincy knew the FBI would see the video. No sense in lying about certain things. "Yes."

She slid another photo over, showing him with Eriana. It looked like a picture from a hotel security camera. "What was she doing at your apartment?"

"Visiting."

"Can you be more specific?"

"Do I need to be?"

"Were you having an affair with her?"

Jack's eyebrows shot up. He hadn't expected that. "No."

"We found her purse inside and her car nearby. Why would she have left without either?"

"The better question is, why would I be dumb enough to leave evidence like that if I *had* done something to her?"

Her gaze hardened but her tone remained neutral and cold. "Your intelligence is still being assessed, Mr. Riley, as is your honesty and forthrightness, all of which may affect what happens to you. You appear to be the last person to see her. When was the last time?"

He thought back. "Five days ago, in the morning."

"Have you had any contact with her since?"

"None."

"Don't you think that's odd that she would leave her purse and rental car behind, and not go to her hotel room for five days? Aren't you concerned?"

Jack knew how to answer that one. "Yes, I'm very worried about her, and you would be, too, if—"

Quincy waved him off.

Agent Mori asked, "If what, Mr. Riley?"

Jack frowned, and wondered how long they would play games here for. "What else did you want to know?"

Special Agent Mori placed a velvet cloth on the table, something hidden under it, between them. She pulled it back to reveal a golden amulet, which showed one figure kneeling beside another that was rising from a supine position. He recognized Eriana's Corethian Amulet, which Anna supposedly had a copy of while on her quests. This was the only known magic item on Earth, though he suspected there were others. That the FBI had it meant Eriana wasn't getting it back anytime soon, not unless Eriana returned to claim it. Even then, would the FBI hold onto it? Could they? If they knew it was magical, they might try, so he wasn't admitting shit.

"Do you know what this is?" she asked—and he realized from her eyes that she'd seen his look of recognition.

"An amulet," he said.

"We found it in Erin's hotel room. It doesn't seem like normal jewelry, does it?"

He shrugged. "I'm not familiar with women's fashions. Looks a little bulky."

"Did she get this from you?"

He failed to hide his surprise. "No. Why would you think that?"

"She came up here to meet someone to acquire antiquities she thinks are magic items. We were wondering if that someone was you."

Listening to Special Agent Mori piecing this together was interesting and disturbing at the same time. "No."

"Why don't you just tell me what you were doing with her? And, better yet, where she is now."

Jack looked at Quincy, thinking that there wasn't much left to do here.

The attorney spoke up. "You've confiscated his phone and laptop. There's a video on there that you might want to see."

She didn't look intrigued. "And what's on it?"

"We think it's better that you just watch it and come back to us."

Agent Mori leaned back. "Since you seem to be repping a lot of them, you probably know that we executed search warrants on the LaRue estate, Anna Sumner's condo, Eric Foster's apartment, and Matt Sorenson's home—so we have a lot of evidence to go through. I'm sure we'll get to yours eventually."

Quincy frowned. "Cut the crap. You didn't find anything at those locations because there's nothing to find, including any sign of Erin Jennings."

She leaned forward. "You seem awfully confident she's not at any of them. It's almost like you know where she is."

Quincy leaned forward, too. "I know where she's not, and so do you—because if you'd found her, we wouldn't still be sitting here having this conversation with the questions you asked about her whereabouts."

Jack watched the agent sit back, her expression suggesting Quincy had her on that one. Then she reached into a bag and pulled out four red iPhones, several wallets, some keychains, and Anna's purse. Jack's face fell. Since Eric, Ryan, Matt, and Anna had all been asleep in his apartment when summoned, all of this had been left behind instead of going with them. From what they had told him, if they had the stuff in their pockets, it went with them—but it stayed in some sort of buffer, to use Matt's computer analogy, while they were on a quest. When they returned to Earth, the spell gave back everything. This last time, that hadn't included the items on the table now because they'd been asleep, and who sleeps with a wallet, keys, or phone on them? Jack had put the items away, but now the FBI had them.

"So tell me," Special Agent Mori began, "why do you have the phones, keys, wallets, and purses of Anna Sumner, Eric Foster, Matt Sorenson, and Ryan LaRue? Did you kidnap them, too?"

"Of course n—"

Quincy held up a hand to quiet him. "Is that a crime?"

"Kidnapping? Of—"

"No, having the possessions of his friends."

"Who are all missing?"

"Who said they were missing?"

Jack tried to keep his face neutral. It was true that they had been gone almost a week, but no one knew that. More importantly, Daniel having told his parents the truth suddenly seemed like a stroke of genius. They hadn't reported Ryan missing. Since then, Jack, Quincy, Daniel, and Daniel's parents had talked with Matt's and Anna's parents. As a result, Matt and Anna had not been reported missing. They had so far left Eric's former foster parents out of it. While he kept in touch with them, they didn't talk that frequently, especially since all of this had started. Jack doubted someone had reported Eric missing either. He tried not to smile.

Special Agent Mori looked startled by the question, and Quincy asked, "Has a missing person's report been filed on any of them? Because I'm their attorney and I haven't seen one."

She hesitated. "No, there hasn't been."

"Then this is irrelevant. And you had no business taking these things. I'll be taking them with me when I leave here."

"It's evidence."

"Of what?

"They were found in the same place as Erin Jennings' items, and she *has* been reported missing."

"That doesn't mean they are related to her supposed disappearance."

Agent Mori rose to her feet, wrapping up the amulet to take it with her. "Until we find her, we're adding the Stonehenge Four to the suspect list. Since you don't seem to be in a cooperating mood, Mr. Riley, I'll give you time to think over your situation. We have a nice cell picked out for your overnight stay.".

CHAPTER SIXTEEN

A DEAL WITH A WIZARD

The one place Soliander felt the safest had been violated. He wasn't a man given to fear. Wielding as much power as he did, that wasn't the issue. His name inspired reverence, awe, and terror. No one defied him and lived to boast about it—not anymore. Everon and others had done it once, and look what had happened. Years of his pain, suffering, and forced servitude. Most of them he had tracked down and killed—or worse. Many were lying in the crypt below for Aeron to summon when needed. In the bowels of this castle suffered the worst offender, the priest who had lent his healing powers to Everon during the creation of the altered keystones. His torment would never end—not until Soliander's did, and he felt certain his never would.

Or he *had* felt certain until finding Eriana. He wasn't given to disbelief. That paralyzing reaction could get a man of his power killed—or worse, ensnared again. So no matter how fantastical something appeared, he could quickly accept its reality and counter any threat it posed. But Eriana was no threat, though she had briefly spelled him. He might have seen that coming but he hadn't expected it, his guard down. She had never spelled him before, but then he had never spelled her either. Was this to be the new normal or an aberration? He had lost her again now, but it

290 | RANDY ELLEFSON

wasn't the same. He would find her but not kidnap her like that. He had meant what he'd told her that he couldn't bear to leave the Earth without her.

He still grappled with the implications of her being alive, of all that had happened since those imposters first appeared, and of what he had learned. They had changed much, and it was too early to tell where all of this was headed. That Eriana lived mattered more than anything. He was curious about Andier and Korrin, but that was all. That planet Earth would be fascinating one to visit again. These imposters were intriguing, repeatedly proving themselves far more capable than he had expected. They certainly didn't seem to fear him or his Lords of Fear. Perhaps they were worthy replacements for the Ellorian Champions, but he couldn't let them keep using his name indefinitely. Regardless, their lack of fear seemingly matched his own, or appeared to. The fact that they had violated his home had made him uncomfortable, but not because of fear.

This was about power. For so many years, all control had been wrested from him—and he'd sworn it never would be again. He'd laid waste to kingdoms or conquered them, partly in the name of control. He'd seized the Orbs of Dominion, again for control. And he'd built an impregnable castle that no one was allowed to enter or leave except for him and those he brought. All for control. No one was to enter the castle without him personally making it happen. No one knew this place existed unless he wanted them to, and he now realized that this had made him lax in his preventative measures. His control here was absolute.

Or had been. How the imposters had known to enter Castle Oste, then subdue some of his servants, fight off the Lords of Fear and a host of undead, and rescue Eriana before leaving with her was a mystery Soliander would solve by any means necessary. On his initial examination, he had noticed two minor scrolls missing, but nothing else important—and of course they hadn't gotten into the rosewood case. He would double-check his tower later. But the fire had destroyed the keep and he wasn't sure it was worth rebuilding. As bold as they were, he doubted they had been looking for him and they must have been there for something more important than a few spells that weren't worth the trouble.

But first, he would deal with the prisoner.

Prince Dari of Andor sat before him, bound to a chair—not with ropes, but with magic, and unable to move anything but his head. His sword lay on the floor beside him, his own blood dripping to the floor beside it, several festering black wounds on his skin. One hand was still white and painful from the touch of Lord Voth. A look of strain marred what handsomeness he had, but somehow the sullen expression Soliander was used to remained.

It had been a long time since he had seen Korrin's brother, but nothing had changed. He was still a boy in a man's body—all insecurity, resentment, and fear. Soliander knew why, though not because Korrin had discussed it. The knight seemed a little oblivious to his younger brother's jealousy. No, he knew from rumors, observations, and Dari's own words, but this knowledge was no achievement. Dari lacked many things, and subtlety was among them. He would make a poor king, unable to hide his thoughts, and yet he considered himself worthy. He was alone in that regard, and that only seemed to make him whinier about being denied, by birth, a role he wasn't suited for anyway. Could he have been suited for it had Korrin never been born? Such questions weren't worth pondering. What mattered now was just what to do with the prisoner.

In a silence broken only by Dari's pained panting, Soliander watched him from behind his black desk and admitted, "I have no use for you."

Dari's tortured eyes met his and looked away, dancing between shelves of spellbooks, scrolls, glass vials, and other magic items. The prince asked, "What does that mean?"

"Maybe you can help me decide. If Korrin lives, he would not be pleased if I killed you. If he's dead, it doesn't matter."

"Then I hope he's alive."

An unsurprising answer. Or was it? "Do you? You've often seemed to wish he'd never been born. Wishing him dead was only a small step from that."

After hesitating, the prince said, "All men want to be king, but few are as close as I am and yet doomed to never be one. You are a king now and should understa—"

Soliander's gaze intensified and silenced the prince. Nearly everyone thought Soliander was missing and had never been a king. Zoran the Devastator, on the other hand, was. Several times over. But how did Prince Dari know this?

Coldly, he asked, "What makes you think I am king?" Dari looked unsure how to answer and Soliander said, *"Soranumirae."* The prince's eyes widened as he struggled to breath, eyes bulging and imploring the wizard to stop. Soliander let his victim's face start turning blue before releasing him. *"Earimunaros."*

The prince sucked in a huge breath and sat gasping for several seconds, starting to babble. "Jack. On Earth. He heard you tell Eriana you are Zoran the Devastator. When you took her."

Interesting, he thought. "But the imposters were already on Elloria when I did that, and have not returned to speak with Jack."

Dari shook his head. "They cast a spell and spoke with him. That's how we knew that you had taken her and who you are. There were also rumors that the Lords of Fear work for Zoran."

Soliander had made no secret of that. He hadn't known that Jack was there when he'd spoken to Eriana, or that he was going to kidnap her, or that the imposters would learn of it so soon. He frowned. This was exactly the kind of mistake that had him keen to plan things carefully. It was also why he had incinerated people like his apprentice Darron. Maybe he should be more forgiving. He hadn't done anything to Darron this time; the elf could hardly be blamed for not being prepared for the raid, given that Soliander hadn't been either. If only he had been here, instead of training Garian before their own next raid...

Dari seemed to have recovered and said, "You know what it is to have this power, this esteem."

"I had both before I became king. You have neither, and would likely remain that way even if you *became* king."

Petulantly, with defiance, Dari said, "You don't know that. Power changes a man."

"Usually for the worse."

"Not in my case. You know, I can tell, that I resent being overshadowed by my brother, that nothing I do is considered enough. With him and my parents gone, this changes. I will be free to be viewed on my own merits instead of as a lesser version of my damned brother or father."

"If you were man enough to take command of a kingdom, you would be man enough to take command of yourself."

"I have. That is what I am doing here. I did not wait for anyone else to rescue Eriana. I did not sit back. I am here."

"And you are captured."

"I let it happen so they could get away. You know that."

He had a point. The Lords of Fear had confirmed it. For once, Prince Dari had surprised him—not only by joining this mission, or fighting in it instead of cowering in a corner, but by giving himself up to the Lords of Fear of all people, so that those whose power Dari resented could escape to safety. Maybe Soliander had misjudged him. But he didn't think so. Dari had always had the potential, just not the will. He wondered what had changed.

"Why did you do it?" Soliander asked.

Dari breathed hard through his nose twice as if working up the nerve to say it. "I've had a taste of life without Korrin around for three years now. And it has been good." He paused as if to gather his thoughts. "I don't need everyone to respect me. I know I am not the Pride of Andor like Korrin. I just need them to stop making comparisons and acting like everything I do is shit. I can be my own man if they let me, but they wouldn't until he was gone. I had done things even before then, despite what you say—and no one cared. Just like you, they pretended I'd done nothing. That attitude is the problem, not mine. I didn't need anyone's praise, but to do good things and be sneered at for them? Just because they weren't as grand as Korrin's? Of course I resent that. You would feel the same."

Soliander agreed with that, but wasn't going to admit it. "What changed?"

"He was gone. That was it. That was all it took. It's almost laughable. I wasn't what changed, just the judgments thrown my way. No longer harsh, not even praise, just recognition. Simple. In time it was almost like Korrin had never existed. But as I became used to not having his shadow over me, not being denigrated, yes, I changed. I lost all the attitude I had about my damn brother."

"And now he might be back."

Dari snorted. "Yeah, now he might be back."

Soliander didn't have to think through the threat this likely posed to Dari's inner life. Korrin's return would be the worst thing that had ever happened to the prince. It made him wonder. "Have you become reckless now? Did you throw yourself into danger to prove your courage, or something else? Do you even care what becomes of you if Korrin is found alive?"

Dari laughed bitterly. "I have nothing left to lose."

"But you have lost nothing yet. Does the mere possibility of Korrin's return threaten you so much?"

"Yes. And I have already lost something. The chatter, the rumors about the famed Ellorian Champions returning, they have turned all eyes to Korrin already—and he hasn't even been found! Oh, I understand the fascination, you've all been missing all this time. I see it. The whispers had disappeared along with you, but now they are a roar of interest. If anything, the Ellorian Champions returning after three years will make you even more fascinating."

"Yes, it will." Soliander wasn't really interested in it, but he understood the fame nonetheless. Imagine how it would be if everyone knew what he'd been doing? He almost laughed at the tongue-wagging that would ensue.

"And I will become more invisible than ever. I've already heard some people joke that they wish I was the one who had disappeared."

Soliander saw the anger and defiance in the prince's eyes. Now he had some understanding of why the prince was here. "You seek glory."

"I seek respect."

Those could almost be the same thing. Almost. "Whose respect do you truly want?"

"First? Yours."

"And how do you plan to get it? You have nothing to offer me to earn this respect."

Dari shook his head. "You don't want the imposters meddling in your affairs any more than I want them meddling in mine, but we both interfere with them. In that sense, we are already allies."

Soliander had no allies and liked it that way. He preferred people who were beholden to him in some way—and very afraid of him. His ruthlessness, often demonstrated to witnesses very much on purpose, was a means to an end. A life without trust was a lonely one, but being at peace was more important to him than anything else. No one needed to know the extent of his plans or aspirations. His Lords of Fear knew some of the things he was doing; other subordinates knew different things. But no one knew everything. He carefully chose what to reveal, always anticipating betrayal and making it impossible. People could fail and disappoint him, but they could not betray effectively if they didn't even understand what they were being made to do. It was the closest he could come to feeling secure in his new life. And it was one of the reasons why the intrusion into his home unsettled him.

And Dari had helped make it happen.

The wizard said, "I don't see you meddling, but helping."

Dari nodded. "This time, yes, to gain their trust. But I have already caused problems for them." He lifted his head as if with pride. "You know of the quest to return the dragon egg, I assume? It was my father's doing. When I learned, about the egg and his plan, I made a plan of my own. I sent word to the trolls nearby and they attacked and stole the egg. If they hadn't been so slow to destroy and use it, these imposters would be trapped on Elloria even now, never going home. They would be out of your way."

Soliander watched him carefully. Dari was more dangerous than he had realized. The depths of his resentment came as no surprise, but he had thought better of the prince. Such feelings could turn many towards wickedness; he just hadn't thought Dari was one of them. How unlike Korrin he truly was. A darkness lay inside the prince, and Soliander knew what to do with such men. They were perhaps the easiest to manipulate, to bend to his will. However much Dari might've tried to hide what he felt—and he didn't try hard—it was plain to see. He would have to do better at that to be truly useful. Openly wearing one's heart on one's sleeve makes it easier for someone else to rip it out.

That Dari had wanted to trap the imposters on Elloria also surprised him. He and the real Champions had been acutely aware that failing to complete a quest meant they would remain in that world for good. The pressure had been intense, always lurking at the back of their minds—if not the front. Somehow, they had never failed. And neither had these imposters. He had to admit to intense curiosity about them and how they were managing to get by. Eriana said the presence of his staff in Matt's hands had much to do with it, and he'd considered taking it from Matt to see how they would fare without.

But it only occurred to him now that he might want these imposters not to fail. Or at least, only to fail when—and where—he wanted them to. Should he choose the land in which they became trapped? He normally only found out where they'd been summoned to once they were done, it difficult to interfere with them—or even help. Maybe he should take a cue from King Sarov and devise a quest for them on his own terms. The idea had merits, and Dari had given it to him. Perhaps the prince was useful after all.

Soliander asked, "What did you hope to gain from trapping them on Elloria? Surely you don't want them around in Andor forever? As places to be trapped go, it is ideal for them, and our families are sympathetic."

"You would have chosen somewhere else? I cannot disagree, but this was my only option at the time. Perhaps another chance will arise, if you let me rejoin them."

"But what is your reason? They have done nothing to you."

298 | RANDY ELLEFSON

Dari sneered. "Haven't they? They're the ones doing these quests, creating renewed interest in the famed Ellorian Champions. Even when they are unmasked before the worlds as imposters, that will only cause *more* interest."

Soliander almost smiled. Truly, there was no winning for the prince. "And you can either rise with them by helping as you did today, or destroy them." He felt grudging admiration for the prince's maneuvering.

"I would do both, with them none the wiser. If they do not know I work for you, then I will be a spy in their midst and learn many things I can pass—"

"I already have spies in Andor."

Dari smirked through his pain. "Then why didn't you know we were coming?"

Soliander arched an eyebrow. He couldn't very well argue with that. "Go on."

"They are keeping things a secret, and have done well with that—but it will not last. On other quests, they'll be discovered as imposters. Sooner or later, someone who knew you and the others will summon them and recognize the situation, even they don't understand it. The elf, Lorian, from Honyn, already knew. Now dozens in Andor know. Eriana has been found and is back on Elloria walking around, where she will be recognized. And we know you are alive. It is only a matter of time."

This was a problem Soliander would need to address. Only in the last few days, on since learning that the imposters were in Andor, had he begun to consider it. Eriana and the others also knew he was Zoran the Devastator. She wasn't bound to keep that a secret, and likely wouldn't, nor would others much longer, if at all. He felt no need to explain himself to anyone, but it might be better if he controlled the narrative. He ruled with ease as Zoran partly because his behavior was consistent and therefore not a mystery. But everyone would question why Soliander had pretended to be gone and lived under the name Zoran—and they'd be disturbed by the contrast between Zoran's destructive actions and Soliander's heroic quest work. That mystery could undermine faith in him as Zoran, people questioning whether he'd still be the ruthless Zoran or the noble Soliander.

The truth was a threat, and he cursed himself for not having seen it coming. He had assumed his friends were gone forever, and so he'd no contingency plan for their reappearance. He certainly hadn't foreseen these imposters. Something would have to be done. And he might have to decide who he wanted to be going forward—Zoran the Devastator, or Soliander the Majestic Magus? Maybe the best idea was to let everyone know the truth about the Ellorian Champions and what Everon had done to them. Sure, it would make people realize they hadn't wanted to do all those quests, but he no longer cared about their old reputation. Not really. People might even realize he wasn't as noble as he'd seemed and be less surprised by his behavior as Zoran. Would people blame him for his actions if they knew he was hunting down everyone and every kingdom involved in Everon's betrayal and destroying or conquering them? People might even sympathize—especially if they learned how he had broken free and thought the other three Champions, his friends, were dead, and that it was his fault.

Yes, it was sympathetic. Maybe he should just admit it all, his dirty secret, the one he'd worked hard to keep hidden, and begin to live openly. He would still be feared, maybe even more so. No one crossed Zoran—but to go against Soliander? And after what he had done to those who'd betrayed him? Maybe the truth was not a threat, but the greatest asset he had. The idea almost made him laugh.

Prince Dari interrupted his thoughts. "I am among those who know everything they are planning and doing right now."

"Only while they remain on Andor. Once they finish the quest, that will not be the case anymore."

"Not if I win their trust. They've discussed having some people go to Earth to help them set up there. I can be among them."

Soliander had to admit that he was learning much from the prince, and without even casting the *Mind Trust* spell on him. Sometimes an old-fashioned interrogation was more entertaining, if not so revealing. "And how do you plan to earn their trust?"

"This mission was one way. My sacrifice at the end was another. I can change their hearts about me and likely already have. I can show that I have changed, that I will risk my life for theirs."

Soliander nodded. The prince was more resourceful than he'd expected. "And after all of this? What happens when they have no more need of you?" The prince hesitated and Soliander frowned, then raised one hand, bluffing that he would suffocate Dari again.

"I want to be King of Andor," the prince quickly admitted.

That was not exactly unforeseen. "Your father is."

"He must die, of course."

This was getting interesting. "And you plan to let that happen naturally? Or were you hoping to accelerate it?"

"It won't matter to me if I am not to be king."

"And if you *are* to be king?"

"Do you need me to be king sooner or later?"

Soliander replied, "I don't *need* you to be king at all."

"Of course, but once you have time to think how I can be of use, with the forces of Andor at your disposal, you may realize I can help you sooner as king."

He had a point, but making him king based on some vague possibility of future usefulness was a lame offer that seemed in perfect keeping with Dari's lack of esteem. Soliander stifled a smile. What Prince Dari failed to realize was just how much betrayal upset him, though the prince was wisely dancing around killing his parents or asking Soliander to do it. If Dari thought Soliander would hand him the throne of Andor later for some cooperation now, but Soliander ultimately failed to live up to his part of the bargain... well, that would be the perfect fate for him. It was almost too easy. Certainly, if Korrin showed up and claimed the throne, Soliander would not back Dari over his old friend. But neither could he help Korrin's brother to murder their parents. The prince would have to do it on his own, but he would worry about that later.

"Your brother is heir-apparent," he said. "Have you given up hope that he still lives?"

"That doesn't matter. My parents have not given up hope and will not name me heir-apparent."

"And what if they do and die? What if you are king and Korrin still lives and returns to claim what is his?"

"It will be too late."

"By the laws of Andor, he would still be the rightful heir."

Dari shook his head. "Not if I change those laws once made king, before his return. And I will rule in allegiance to you. I understand you have a similar arrangement with Lord Voth in Aranor."

"King Voth has shown his allegiance. But you have not."

The prince held his gaze. "I can give you something to show you I can be of use to you as King of Andor. Aren't you wondering how we knew where this place was?"

Soliander's gaze intensified. "Tell me."

"The news is worthy of a kingdom."

"If you are correct, I will make you King of Andor, in servitude to me."

Dari's eyes blazed triumphantly. "The wizard, Matt. You attacked him with the *Mind Trust* spell. When he broke free, some of your memories—many of them it seems—became his. They are scattered... and it is hard for him to recall anything on purpose, or sometimes to understand what they mean. But that is how we knew about this place."

A feeling of vulnerability swept over Soliander like never before. No one had ever cast that spell on him—and he had long ago vowed that no one would survive doing so for long. But now his own use of the forbidden spell had backfired. Worst of all was that he hadn't realized for what, two months now? What did Matt know? It could be anything from his entire lifetime. Secrets he had never shared. Embarrassments carefully hidden. Plans yet to come to fruition. The reason why the spell was forbidden had never been so clear to him before, his every thought and feeling potentially laid bare.

But he couldn't stop using it, even if he resented the intrusion into his own privacy. No, he would have to persist. There was only one way to find out what Matt knew—to repeat the spell on him, this time with better precautions.

Soliander eyed Dari. If he had known this sooner, things would not have stood as they now did. The prince could indeed be very useful, and he was right. This one piece of information was of extraordinary value, surely worthy of a kingdom—for it might allow Soliander to evade many problems and set many traps, provided no one found out Dari had told him. He decided to make use of the prince for now and let things play out. A spy this close to the imposters could gather even better intelligence. Now it was time to see if Dari could think of his own solutions to problems. Soliander had already made up his mind what to do next, but decided to test his captive.

"How do you propose to return to Andor?" he asked. "You are no wizard, so you can't send yourself. They will not try to retrieve you—either because they do not value you, or because they know we would be expecting them."

The prince appeared to consider this. "You would have to send me."

"But they will wonder why I would do so."

"You said it yourself. You have no use for me. Why not just return me as a sign of good faith?"

"But I could just kill you. Will they not wonder why I have not? And why would I show good faith?"

Dari shook his head. "They don't know whether you're good or evil, and they're not sure what you're capable of. Letting me go would confuse them; surely that would be beneficial. Besides, killing Korrin's brother would send a clear message about what to expect from you, and that would not be tactically sound. Keeping them guessing is better."

Soliander nodded. It wasn't a bad answer, but it wasn't quite good enough. He hadn't expected Dari to suggest the rest that he had in mind—but few men would, even Korrin. "I should also demonstrate that I am still someone to fear, should I not?"

"Absolutely."

"I'm so glad you agree." Soliander rose and walked over the prince. "Are you right-handed or left-handed?"

"Why?"

Soliander picked up Dari's sword.

CHAPTER SEVENTEEN

THE KEYSTONES

The one thing Ryan would never get tired of was riding a dragon. He rode a glistening silver dragon with Anna strapped in behind him. Eric and Eriana rode a red one, while Matt sat behind Taryn on her black dragon. Lorian and Rognir followed on another while four of Taryn's Dark Blade warriors rode two more. They weren't expecting much of a fight because Matt was certain the place was abandoned and only magical traps awaited them.

They had flown instead of using another magic portal, to save both his strength and Lorian's for what was to come. Creating one keystone would take a lot of energy, even from Eriana. Making four had inspired Matt to ask Anna if she could heal or rejuvenate them in some way, and she was fairly certain she could. It would take much of the day, but they were hoping to fly back before nightfall and had left before dawn. Taryn warned that the skies near the Towering Peaks were more apt to fill with unsavory creatures at night, though she refused to describe them when Ryan asked. She didn't say no when he said 'griffon' or 'wyvern'. Now part of him wanted to see them. Surely, they wouldn't take on this many dragons, would they?

Though their destination had been due east of Andor, they had flown northeast past Allowyn and over the low mountain range, the Hills of Andor. The aptly named Towering Peaks farther west caused this detour. At nearly thirty-thousand feet tall, they posed a challenge for their mounts. He had always though dragons were incredibly powerful—and there was no denying it while riding upon one's back—but the thinner air coupled with swirling winds made it harder for them to fly over the mountains. The dragons that called the tallest areas of the Towering Peaks their home were often much smaller, their habitat inhibiting their growth.

Since their rides weren't from those mountains, they skirted them east toward Ogreton before swinging south into Aranor. The mountains formed the western edge of the kingdom, foothills stretching eastward into a desert Ryan saw in the distance. Only from maps did he know that the Dorman Ocean lay farther off. The only signs of water he saw were lakes and one river rushing out of the Towering Peaks.

But now they were descending in tightening circles that were still a safe distance from Soliander's rectangular, four-story keep of grey stone and a taller, lone tower. A two-story wall and moat surrounded them until it ended in the sheer cliff mountain face behind the keep. As they descended, the dragons veered off toward the structure's front, scouting for any trouble on the ground.

Ryan's eyes skimmed over the tall grassy areas. He saw a trampled path indicating recent passage. At least something was down there, he knew. Enough groups of trees were present to hide a few people, but there was clearly no significant force here—not that he expected one. He just wasn't sure what people would do on learning that the most powerful wizard anyone had heard of had been missing for three years. Taryn had told him all about rumors of

Soliander having fantastic magic items or creatures here. Long before he vanished, foolish people had tried to steal things from him and regretted it. But with the wizard gone, had they become emboldened?

The dragons landed on a grass-covered hilltop and settled low so the riders could disembark. They would be coming inside for added protection, which made Ryan feel significantly safer. No one in their right mind would fight a dragon, and yet he was supposed to be Lord Korrin, the Dragon Slayer. Part of him wondered if the real Korrin was nuts. Sure, Ryan had killed one on Honyn, and helped Matt kill another, but that had been out of necessity. Korrin had apparently sought out problematic dragons to stop them. The man had to be crazy. He couldn't really blame Prince Dari for not following in his older brother's footsteps, could he?

The dragons morphed into their human form. The black and red dragons had dark skin, but the others were light-skinned yet tanned. Their hair color revealed which was which. Their huge saddles would be left unattended because no one could steal one easily, but they would bring any valuable contents.

Eric interrupted his thoughts by saying, "Matt, Taryn, I think you're up. We'll stay right behind."

The group set off, one of the dragons trailing farther behind after listening intently in one direction and apparently being satisfied. They stepped onto the dirt road winding through the trees and foothills. It sometimes blocked sight of the keep and its tower, which didn't look like they had been damaged in a siege or attack. If anyone had come here for the contents of the castle, it hadn't been an army. He saw no footprints or even horseshoe tracks, and wondered if people kept to the path or just didn't come at all.

"Is this road safe or booby-trapped?" he asked Matt.

"Pretty sure it's safe for now. But that will change as we get closer."

Taryn said, "You cannot rely on the scattered memories of my brother. You may not understand them as much as you think. But in this case, I am familiar with Soli's approach to safeguarding what it is. A wizard once captured me to gain that knowledge."

Ryan noticed she didn't say what had happened. "Something tells me you took care of him with a sword."

"Dagger, technically," she replied, smiling. "I know some of what may lie before us."

Eriana said, "I am also familiar with this place, but mostly the inside. He preferred just leaving the spells outside alone and casting others directly inside."

They stepped around a final group of trees to see a cleared area a hundred square yards to the moat. But it wasn't empty. Two figures appeared to be standing on the path not far from the drawbridge, but neither were moving. Ryan stepped to one side to get a better look. The skeletons of several horses lay together not far from them, with more piled closer to the raised drawbridge. There seemed to be other piles of something Ryan couldn't identify, but he saw a shield against one pile and a sword sticking up from another.

"The staff just warned me something is here," said Matt.

"No surprise," muttered Eric. "Can you tell—"

A roar from beyond the wall interrupted him and a blue dragon climbed from within the courtyard and over the wall to stand before their destination. It roared again and bolts of lightning crackled from its mouth to strike the ground near them.

"It's an illusion," said Matt, watching it.

Ryan snorted. "Could've fooled me."

"Not me," said the black dragon with them. "Very good spell, but no dragon would believe that."

"So we just ignore it?" Ryan asked. That wasn't going to be easy.

"Basically, yeah," said Matt.

"What about those two men standing out there?" Anna asked. The fake dragon roared again.

After a moment, Matt said, "Pretty sure that's a time delay spell. I've seen it in his books. Anyone who steps within its radius will move about one inch a day but have no idea that it's happening."

Ryan looked over at the men again. "I don't suppose we can tell how long they've been in it?"

"When we get closer," said Matt. "The staff can help me tell where it starts. Based on that, do the math. They might have actually been caught in it long before the Champions disappeared."

"They're on the path," Ryan observed, "so I assume we don't want to be."

They waited as Matt surveyed the area, the dragon roaring again. He finally sighed. "The only things I know for certain are that it's like a minefield, with different spells set to do different things in different places. And the staff will warn me when I get close to one."

Rognir smacked him on the back. "Lead the way, my friend!"

Even some of the dragons smiled at this. The group set off, letting Matt go first, with Taryn, Eriana, and two of the dragons next. One dragon said they would be prepared with a magic shield if something dangerous started. And it did, more than once. A cloud of poisonous green gas surrounded them at one point until dissipating. A volley of energy darts struck at them just after they continued; Ryan wondered whether Soliander had planned for the gas to make someone run forward only to be struck by the darts.

It might have worked, too. They soon came across the first skeleton, its armor full of round holes, each charred and with no sign of a projectile remaining. As they neared the dragon illusion, one of the real dragons flicked a wrist at it and the spell vanished. Matt detected any other spells and guided them safely around until they stood at the moat.

"How do we get the drawbridge down?" Ryan asked, eyeing two stone pillars that would flank the bridge once lowered.

"Here," Taryn said, stepping forward. She rubbed her black boot across the dirt to reveal a square metal plate. In the center was a hole with several notches in it.

"Made of soclarin," Ryan said.

Matt flipped Soliander's staff upside down and inserted the crystal at the top into the hole, where it clicked. The stone drawbridge creaked as it lowered. Ryan looked down into the dark moat, unable to see if anything lived in it. They walked across without incident. Matt explained that because the staff had opened it, any spells that might have been there were deactivated.

"I assume any spell we undo remains that way, so he'd have to come back and re-cast it?"

"Yes. So if he ever comes here, he'll know someone was inside."

Taryn observed, "He'll know it was you, but that's his problem. Honestly, I believe he should be helping you create these keystones for your Home Rings and if he has a problem with us doing this, he can talk to me about it."

Ryan smiled. "We can be nice and close the drawbridge before we leave."

"Yeah," started Eric, "let's not piss him off any more than necessary. We broke into two of his homes in two days."

Matt made them wait. A spell to detect someone's presence was active until one dragon dispelled it to save his strength. Ryan wondered if they could help Matt and Lorian with the magic needed for the keystones, so he asked.

The black dragon replied, "We need to see the spells. Let us get there first."

They crossed the courtyard to the keep, where the room they sought lay in the basement. When they reached the iron door before them, Taryn stopped them.

"I know this one."

"So do I," said Eriana. "It's a physical trap."

Eric asked, "How do you get—"

Taryn ignored the door handle and shoved inward three times, the door swinging freely on the third push. "It's not actually locked, but if you grab the handle, you'll get a surprise. Never told me what it was."

"Poison," said Eriana, frowning, and Ryan sensed she disapproved. "It's part of the door handle and kills in seconds. He said the poison will never run out."

Ryan remarked, "Then no one has made it this far. No body."

They stepped inside a dark entryway, Matt lighting his staff to reveal cobwebs in one archway and a stone stairway rising into the dark. To either side were passages leading away. They followed one of these passages around corners and through doors to the back of the keep, disarming a few traps both physical and magical. Taryn knew about some of them, Eriana about others, and Matt about the rest. They soon found a stairwell curling down into blackness.

Taryn flipped up a lever on the wall twice. "Don't go down the stairs without doing that. There's another at the bottom, but you pull down twice."

"I'm starting to think he doesn't want anyone to come in here," joked Eric.

On reaching the bottom, they found three doors. Taryn indicated the right one. Matt stopped at the door to Soliander's laboratory, and hesitated.

"Everything okay?" Eric asked.

The wizard didn't answer at first. Then he did so slowly, pausing between sentences, and Ryan could tell he was trying to recall things from Soliander's memories. "There's more to this than having the staff. There are spells. Physical traps. We have to disarm them all to get in. He made them to stop Everon from ever using this room again, from ever creating more keystones and Quest Rings. Now it's our problem. This might be the single most secure place of Soliander's. He doesn't come here anymore. I may not be able to disarm it all, and even if I can, I might not have the strength afterward to create the keystones."

Ryan sighed. "Great. I bet that was part of his plan."

The black dragon offered, "We should be able to help."

Everyone but the dragons and Matt stepped back. After a few minutes, they cleared one spell, then another. Matt guided Eric on how to disarm a physical trap. With that done, a panel in the wall opened for Matt to insert Soliander's staff, a seemingly failsafe way to protect the room. Two more magic traps and one physical one remained, but then the door finally opened, the dragons having done most of the dispelling.

As Ryan stepped through with the others, he saw a large room with empty shelving, bookcases, racks, and tables, some askew as if ransacked. At the room's rear, a furnace made of soclarin ore waited for Rognir and the soclarin ore he dumped from Lorian's Bag of Desires. The dwarf suggested breaking shelves to start the fire, but a dragon breathed flames to start it instead. Ryan hadn't known they could do that while in human form.

Ryan watched as Rognir, Matt, and the dragons set about creating the physical component of the keystones.

First, Rognir bashed the ore with his hammer until it became a fine sand, into which he mixed charcoal Matt found in a nearby bin. Rognir added the soclarin ore and charcoal mixture to the furnace. Molten soclarin soon fell from the bottom, where the dwarf collected it for the dragons to reheat, and then he hammered it into a long, flat bar on an anvil. The dragons melted it until it oozed into four keystone molds, each with a center hole into which Soliander's staff would fit. The four new Champions each added a piece of their hair to their own six-by-six inch keystone.

With this done, a tired Rognir flopped onto a stool. During the hours needed for the molten keystones to cool, the supernatural component had to be added. Matt and the dragons had been studying the scroll, and they began their work with Eriana. Eric suggested that the rest of them leave. Ryan knew it was a good idea, though he'd wanted to watch. Everyone was afraid to wander around Soliander's home, so they just sat outside the door and on the stairs for hours, chatting. Finally, the door opened.

Rognir said, "It is done."

Ryan got to his feet. "It worked?"

"Yes. You have four keystones. And an exhausted wizard."

They filed back inside to see Matt slumped in a chair. Anna knelt beside him and put her hands on his chest, where a soft glow preceded the wizard sitting up a little more. But it seemed that no amount of healing would take the fatigue away. Eriana seemed exhausted, too.

Ryan walked with Eric over to the keystones. They were wet and steaming from having been dipped into an old vat of water. Each was of a bluish metal. They didn't seem as important as he knew them to be, but then magic items seldom gave off signs of what they could do. He hefted one in excitement, seeing Lorian turn to him with the magic Bag of Desires, into which Ryan placed them one by one.

"We should get out of here now," Ryan said. He realized they were fortunate to be able to create keystones on a planet other than Earth, where the supernatural was only just awakening. Maybe Eriana and Matt would not have been able to harness enough power there.

"Wait," said Anna, her white robe stained by the charcoal, ore, and dirty room. "I know we've seen Korrin's Home Ring and what happened to it. This might be our only chance to see Soliander's."

Ryan frowned, "You're right, but I think it's too dangerous here."

Matt spoke up, his voice weak. "It's a little melted. I remember now. There's really nothing to see. The top and bottom are melted, but the keystone is intact. Not sure it would work, but it doesn't matter."

"Good enough for me," said Eric.

Ryan couldn't disagree. Seeing Lorian lend his support to Eriana, who leaned on him, he went to Matt and put an arm around him, half carrying him from Soliander's laboratory. They wasted no time climbing the stairs, going across the courtyard, and passing over the drawbridge. Eric placed Soliander's staff into the hole to close the bridge, and they carefully picked their way back through the field to where they had landed before. It didn't seem like anyone or anything had disturbed their saddles. Before long, the group had mounted and took to the sky with just enough sunlight to avoid worrying much about skirting the dangerous areas of the Towering Peaks. Night had fallen by the time they reached Andor, Matt sleeping most of the way.

The wizard recovered some energy by the time they changed and ate a late dinner with their hosts, who surprised them. Prince Dari had returned, but he wasn't present. Soliander had let him go with a message—that he was not coming after Eriana or the imposters, as he called them. The arch-wizard understood that he would have done the same thing to rescue Eriana, had their positions been reversed. But he warned them not to get in his way again. He also claimed that if he encountered any sign of Korrin or Andier, he might take them away for a time to talk with them, too, though he would ultimately let them go. As a sign of his good faith, he had returned the prince—but as a sign that he would still be a menace should they confront him again, he had removed one of Dari's hands at the wrist.

"What do we think of this?" Ryan asked as the four friends sat alone in Anna's room that night.

Eric shook his head as he sat beside her. "I don't trust Soliander."

"What about Dari?" Matt asked. "Not sure what to make of him since the mission."

"Me either," said Eric, "but we may have misjudged him. We'll be going home tomorrow, and probably won't see him again anytime soon."

"Part of me wishes we could stay longer," said Anna. "We're safe. No one can summon us. And I could use the rest. We all could."

Eric squeezed her hand. "Yeah, it's a nice thought, but we have to protect Jack and our families by setting up the estate."

"You know what I'd like?" Matt began, yawning. "Lorian wants to visit Earth. He can stay and help Jack. Hide his ears and he's set. Maybe someone else from here, like Taryn, can come. That way, we aren't the only ones able to deal with a Soliander."

Ryan laughed. "I'm not sure we can deal with him, but point taken. Taryn is an especially good idea in case he shows up."

Eric nodded. "I'm not sure we can ask her. She has a life here."

"I'll do it," said Matt. "I think she'll say yes."

Eric smirked at him. "I think she has a soft spot for you."

"It's strictly professional," Matt deadpanned.

———— ● · ● ————

As Matt left the others behind, he sought out Taryn because he felt like it was his last chance to see her alone. He didn't really know what he wanted to say, just that he hoped she would come to Earth and see them. Well, no—to see *him*. Should he make it personal? Or make it sound like it was just business? He frowned.

He had often acted like a chicken shit, as he thought of it, doing things like making an excuse to stop by and see a woman. He knew that that was driven by insecurity. It was as if he somehow felt his company wasn't enough reason for someone to talk to him and he needed another justification. He had been dimly aware of this for a long time and tried to make himself stop it, but he hadn't quite gotten the hang of it.

But he felt certain Taryn would respect him more if he just admitted that he wanted to talk with her. No explanations—no excuses. He would enjoy her company and offer only his. If she turned him away, that would suck, but at least he'd have tried. With the mortal danger he faced seemingly every day, this wishy-washy thing didn't suit him—not that it ever had. But he had grown into himself, escaping Soliander, killing a dragon in midair, and facing down undead. Surely women couldn't still strike fear into him, could they? He laughed and felt renewed confidence. Maybe he would even kiss her when she opened the door. If she looked at his lips even once, he was doing it.

As he had often done in Andor, he had taken a less crowded route to his destination, not that many people were around once after dark. It wasn't like on Earth, where it could be so bright at night that many people didn't care the sun had gone down. This particular hall looked empty until he rounded a corner and found a tall man in a blue robe approaching him. The hood was pulled up and partially hid his face. Matt glanced at him, lost in thought, his mind drifting to Soliander and his days working with soclarin ore to fashion the keystones.

By now he had come within paces of the hall's other occupant, and he looked at him to nod a greeting. The man lifted his head, dark eyes unfriendly and staring at him. Suddenly another image flashed into Matt's head, one familiar but not his own. He recoiled, a defensive spell struggling to form in his panic.

"Kunia!" the man snarled. Matt slammed into the wall, cracked his head, and fell unconscious to the floor.

CHAPTER EIGHTEEN

THE CRIME SCENE

Eric was looking forward to going home. However much they got used to living in a medieval or Renaissance era—and he wasn't sure of the difference, but he missed taking a shower. And coffee. And watching videos, whether YouTube, TV, or cable. But he had to admit that things were quieter without those modern amenities. Last night he'd fallen asleep reading a book

As he thought about it while dressing in the morning, he wondered if the Home Rings should be built for mobility. What if someone like Soliander or the FBI showed up at the estate and they couldn't return? Putting the rings on wheeled platforms would mean they could roll them into a truck, if the measurements were done right. He didn't know if the Home Rings had to be a set size. The Quest Rings were pretty much never the same as each other, being built from local material. The one element common to all was a keystone.

He soon knocked on Matt's door, but got no answer and decided to let him sleep in. There was still no sign of the wizard as Eric enjoyed a quiet breakfast of boiled eggs, omelets, pastries, fresh bread, and fruits with Ryan and Anna. He finished eating first and finally went to wake

Matt again but got no answer, no matter how much he banged on the door. Anna and Ryan joined him, looking amused. Two of the guards heard the banging and approached, unlocking the door at his request. He threw open the doors to see a made bed. It was obvious that he hadn't slept here.

Turning to the others, he asked, "You don't think he spent the night with Taryn, do you?"

Anna nodded. "He might have."

"Good for him," said Ryan.

"Good for who?" asked a female voice, and Eric turned to find Taryn walking up to them, dressed in her leather armor to escort them.

"Uh, nothing. Matt's not with you?"

"No. I came to bring all of you to the king. He'd like a final farewell."

Eric exchanged a look with the others, growing concerned. "Matt's not here, and he didn't spend the night in his room."

Taryn scowled and strode into Matt's room, quickly assessing it before addressing Eric as she turned to question the guards. "Check for the staff and robe."

"Right." He didn't see why Matt would take Soliander's items, but their presence or absence might tell him something. On opening the cabinet in the meeting room, he found everything there, so he closed it again and they caught up with Taryn.

"Who was on duty last night?" she asked a guard, getting a name before turning to the three friends. "He didn't leave this morning. Not this way. We need to check with last night's guards."

Eric agreed and they set off in search of Matt. None of them had ever gone missing. Maybe there was an innocent explanation, but he doubted it. When the previous night's guards revealed that they hadn't seen Matt, the grim determination on Taryn's face matched what Eric felt—and the worry from Ryan and Anna.

While Taryn didn't have official authority, she derived influence from her commanding presence, being Soliander's sister, and having the ear of the king. She made the captain of the King's Guard start a room-by-room search of the palace and lock it down. Word went out for others to meet in the great hall, where the king and queen, Eriana, Lorian, Rognir, Solun, Princess Alia, Prince Dari and Princess Cariss all straggled in. A tense hour passed before they learned that they had found the body of a nobleman in an unused room.

"How did he die?" Eric asked, wanting to confirm if this was murder.

The guard replied, "A spell that burned holes in his flesh. Each wound had a black mark around it, like fired caused it."

"I know that spell," said Lorian, scowling. "A simple attack one."

Eric turned to Eriana. "Do you think it was Soliander? He's the most likely suspect after the raid we did."

She nodded. "He would do whatever got the job done. But you said his staff and robe are still here?"

"Yes. So it wasn't him?"

Ryan asked, "Do we think he'd want Matt more than his stuff? Wouldn't he get it all?"

Eriana shook her head. "No, Matt's not more important to him. Not unless he knows Matt has some of his memories, but he doesn't. And I don't know what he *would* do on finding out. It's not like he can remove the memories without..."

Eric grew cold. "Killing him."

"Or messing up Matt's mind in some way," she said. "In my talks with him, I told him how important the staff is to your continued success. He wouldn't agree to let Matt keep it, but I don't see him taking Matt and not the staff at least."

"Who else would take Matt?" Anna asked. "Almost no one knows we're here and who we really are."

Eric saw that Prince Cariss seemed lost in thought, her brow furrowed. He asked, "How many wizards are in the castle?"

The guard looked unsure, and the king ordered all of them politely rounded up, so someone went to do it.

"Can you tell exactly when he died?" Anna asked.

"Last night, my lady."

Taryn asked, "Where was the body found?"

The guard answered and Eric swore. "Matt tended toward less crowded ways to get around. Can we see this location? The body?"

Before these quests started, he had never seen a dead body. Now it sometimes felt like hardly a day passed without a corpse. That it could one day be him or his friends had never felt more real. He wouldn't tolerate any chatter about this being a coincidence. The world so often seemed to revolve around them once they were summoned, and it pretty much did. This had everything to do with them. He was certain.

The king agreed to let them see the scene, Prince Dari and Princess Cariss joining them. Eric hadn't seen the prince since his return, and had been eyeing him for how he seemed to fare. Losing a hand wasn't the change that concerned him. Rather, Dari had been moody and upset with them right up to the raid on Soliander's Castle Oste. He had fought well there, as if he'd grown up during the fight. But what about now? The missing hand had to bother him. He had asked Eriana about it because Aeron, the necromancer, had grown back Kori's hand, so why not Dari's? The answer was that Lord Voth's grip on Dari's wrist had damaged it in such a way as to prevent that.

The change concerning Eric was the prince's inner life. Dari seemed somehow more sure of himself. King Sarov was certainly proud of him. Was that it? Had he finally earned the esteem he craved? Was the missing hand even a sign of his valor? It kind of was—but no one except their small group knew why it had happened. This suggested that Dari might want to tell people the truth.

When they reached the small room with the body, Eric stepped inside with Taryn, Eriana, and Lorian. The thin, middle-aged, balding man still had his eyes open and looking in different directions until Eriana closed them. The elf and priestess examined the body, confirming that the wounds were from spells. What caught Eric's attention was the body's position.

"Look at the way he's lying," he said. "It's like he was thrown in here. Unceremonious. Whoever did this was in a hurry."

"Yes," said Lorian. He straightened to examine the walls. "Either that person has excellent aim, or this is not where he died. I do not see any damage to the walls from a stray missile."

Eric exchanged a look with Taryn. They stepped into the hall to examine the walls. Eric saw it first—a hole about the size of a quarter had burned the wall next to the lantern. The hole was above his head, and yet the victim's wounds had been at chest level. As Taryn stopped beside him, he delivered his conclusion.

"The wizard was down on the floor when he cast the spell upward. It's the only thing that makes sense."

"I agree," she said. Taryn pointed to a red smudge a few feet away. "This is blood with a bit of brown hair in it, but that man is bald. So he was attacked with magic in one place—but someone with brown hair like Matt was attacked here, and left the blood mark."

Lorian stepped out of the room with a blue cloth and a blood-covered dagger. "I did not see blood on the victim. The energy wounds don't bleed but they were in places that would take a minute or two for him to die from. This means he was alive when he was put in this room. I turned the body over and found a dagger with blood on it and a piece of torn cloth on the blade. Neither the blood nor the cloth is from him. I believe he stabbed the wizard who killed him."

Eric mulled that over and finally said, "I'm speculating, but what if something the wizard did to Matt made him strike the wall with his head and leave that blood mark? Then maybe the wizard was bent over him when the other guy came around the corner and caught him, so he did the spell that killed him. But maybe he wasn't quite dead when the wizard put him in the room there, and the guy managed to get out a dagger and stab him."

They considered that and Taryn said, "Plausible. Right now, I think we have to assume someone has Matt. We need to round up the wizards and their clothing. Whoever it was would have changed and maybe healed themselves with a potion or device, or with someone else's help, in which case there's a witness."

Standing a bit removed from the group, Princess Cariss had put one hand to her mouth and stood scowling, lost in thought, her eyes troubled. Eric remembered that she had a wizard friend she'd mentioned a few times. He approached her.

"My lady, do you know of anyone?"

She looked up, startled, then met his eyes and looked away before nodding. "Mandrellan."

Eric remembered the name. "You said you hadn't seen him in a while, is that right? Since our arrival? Is it still true? Was he here recently?"

Her eyes widened. "Yes. Yesterday. But, I, uh—"

Dari stepped forward and gripped her arm. "You are always gossiping with him! I saw how excited you looked when you left the throne room the day these four arrived. You didn't tell Mandrellan who they are, did you?"

She looked guilty and unsure how to respond. "I, I did, yes. I'm sorry. I didn't think... he's always been so loyal. He has tried to find our brother so many times."

Dari frowned at the others. "He wears blue robes most days. We may have found our man."

Eric asked, "Would he have a reason to want Matt? What does he know, Your Highness? Can you remember what you told him?"

"Yes. Yes, I first teased him that we had successfully summoned the Champions, and—"

Eric interrupted. "I'm sorry, how did he react to that?"

"Well, with concern, really. But I think it was because I hadn't told him we were trying it and he felt I didn't trust him enough to tell him."

Eric wasn't sure what to make of that and asked, "Was he relieved to learn it wasn't true?"

"No. It excited him to learn that we had seen Eriana and Soliander."

"Happy excited?" Eric turned to Eriana. "Ever hear of Mandrellan?"

"No," she said. "I do not know him. He could've been excited for many reasons."

"It wasn't that kind of excitement," said Princess Cariss. "He seemed concerned, especially about Soliander. Oh, and when I said Matt had some of Soliander's memories, he grew quite agitated and left shortly after."

Eric's eyes narrowed. "I've heard enough. Taryn, I—"

"Let's go," she said, and they began walking. "Princess, where would he be?"

Princess Cariss explained that Mandrellan had a house a few blocks from the palace. It didn't take long for them to settle on a plan of action—the palace guards and King's Guard would be questioned to learn if Mandrellan had been seen leaving. No one could say that he had, and so their search of the palace intensified in case he was on the grounds. The princess wasn't sure how strong a wizard Mandrellan was, or whether he would be able to open a portal or cast himself from the palace to the house.

As the palace search continued, Taryn led Eric, Anna, Ryan, Lorian, and Eriana to Mandrellan's two-story house, but he wasn't home. The servants claimed that Mandrellan had come and gone several times during the week without saying where he was going, often not returning for a day or two. In their opinion, this meant he had gone to his home planet, as that was the usual reason he gave for overnight absences. He had last been there the day before. They assumed that he had left Elloria once more.

Eric cursed. The last thing they needed was to have to chase the wizard to another planet, assuming he had gone. Taryn said that the World Gate was the most likely way he would have left if so. It was in the Hall of Worlds, a name in frequent use among planets that had such gates, which the kingdom operated for its citizens or those who could pay to travel between planets. The heavily-guarded building lay on the opposite side of town from the castle. Before long they were mounted and cantering or trotting through town as fast as they dared, a horseman ahead blowing a trumpet to signal people to clear the road. To Eric's surprise, that actually worked, and they reached the plaza before the Hall of Worlds in a few minutes. The building stood three stories tall in white marble, with wide double doors and a row of statues out front—including those of the Ellorian Champions. Eric glanced at Eriana, who smiled sheepishly.

Once inside, Taryn led them left toward the departure gate, which was on the opposite side to the arrival gate.

Scores of people were here, but it was nothing like an airport terminal back home. Most of those able to travel between worlds were wealthy or on state business. Eric hoped this meant it would be easy for someone to remember seeing Mandrellan come through here—but they might once again have to round up everyone who worked here, just like in the palace. It could get time-consuming.

The chainmail and tunic-guards who were present saw them approaching with a handful of the King's Guards and snapped to attention. Taryn ordered that the area be cleared of witnesses to their conversation, so Eric waited impatiently with the others. He saw the concern on Anna's face, and the grimness on Ryan's. They could not let Matt down. The thought heightened his determination and he turned to one of the guards at the gate.

"Do you know a wizard named Mandrellan?" he asked. "Have you seen him pass this way and through the gate in the last day?"

The balding guard perked up. "Yes. He said he would be back tomorrow. Just going home for some rest."

The first part of that calmed Eric. Now they knew something, at least. "Was he alone?"

"Yes. Just a small bag with him, nothing more."

Eric turned to Lorian. "That magic Bag of Desires you guys use. You can't put someone in it, can you?"

The elf said, "Actually you can, but they'll die."

"How quickly?"

"Seconds. They suffocate because their lungs collapse."

Taryn said, "We'll need to go after Mandrellan, but we should get a better idea of where he went after stepping through the gate."

The guard perked up again. "He said he would be back tomorrow. Just going home for some rest."

Eric cocked an eyebrow. Those were almost the same words, and his demeanor had been the same, too. He looked sideways at Taryn, who met his gaze and turned to the man.

"Did Mandrellan go through the gate?" she asked.

The guard perked up. "Yes. He said he would be back tomorrow. Just going home for some rest."

Taryn swore and banged a fist on her leather-clad thigh. "He's been spelled. Lorian? Eriana?"

"Got it," said the priestess, stepping forward. She put her hands on the man's temple and spoke a few words, upon which he blinked rapidly and seemed surprised to see her standing so close.

"Have you seen Mandrellan pass this way?" she asked.

"Yes, my lady, several hours ago."

She asked, "Was he with anyone else?"

"No."

That Mandrellan had put a spell on the guard spoke volumes about his evil intent to Eric, who asked, "Did he have anything with him?"

"A large chest."

"Large enough for a body?"

The guard's eyebrows shot up. "Uh, well yes, technically. But he couldn't get it through the gate. It wasn't for lack of trying. I mean, it was small enough to fit, but every time he tried, the end of it would go through and then stop when he pushed it more. I helped him, but we couldn't get it to budge. Then he seemed to realize something and cursed."

So did Eric on realizing what this meant. "That motherfucker has him. I'm gonna kill him."

"I don't understand," said Eriana, scowling. "How do you know that?"

Eric felt surprised he had to explain to her of all people standing there. "We can't leave this planet because the quest bound us here. He tried to take Matt through and couldn't."

Eriana nodded, then scowled again. "How did you get me from Soliander's?"

"Someone stepped through with the dragon egg, and then we could follow. Then we put it back and continued the quest while it was still here, safe. Presumably, Mandrellan doesn't have the egg." He looked alarmed and turned to Taryn, who wheeled away and barked orders at the guards. Several took off toward their horses at a run, sent to ride back to the palace and protect the dragon egg.

"Okay," said Eriana, "I get it. It's been a long time since a quest bound me. And I hadn't stopped to think about how you achieved that before. Very clever, by the way. We never tried that."

Ryan asked the guard, "Where did Mandrellan go when he realized he couldn't get the chest through? Did he still go through without it? Or is he still on Elloria?"

"He walked away with it and went through there." The guard pointed at a doorway to one side.

"Answers that question," said Rognir, hefting his hammer. "Let's go get him."

⸻ ❖ ⸻

Matt was dreaming about Soliander again. First came images of the wizard issuing orders to a dark elf in a room with black walls. Then came memories of his staff, the one Matt had a copy of, in a cabinet along with the robes he had always worn as one of the Ellorian Champions. The same robes Matt had. The room had jars along shelves, and rows of spellbooks and scrolls. Matt had been there, but these didn't seem like his memories. He saw an image of a dark castle among mountain peaks. It was on the planet Cygnus.

The dark elf appeared in another scene, speaking of someone he had succeeded in locating at Soliander's be-

330 | RANDY ELLEFSON

hest. Names of a planet and city flashed through his mind before images of Soliander leveling a city block in pursuit of someone. The devastation was horrifying, though Matt experienced it as rage, satisfaction, and pleasure. But it turned to disappointment when the one he sought was not among the many bodies found in the rubble.

Someone cursed and Matt stirred. A pain in the back of his head made him moan. For a moment he straddled two worlds, both being asleep and awake, before he left one for the other. But something was wrong. He felt groggy, certainly, but not from sleep or fatigue, just a haze of confusion. And yet his mind still raced through dreams. No, memories. These were Soliander's memories, in his mind. Someone held his forehead gently. A cloth was over his mouth. A gag. He tried to pull away but couldn't, his eyes slowly opening as the visions continued so that he saw one thing in his mind and another in front of him. A man in a blue robe stood before him in a room so dark Matt could see nothing else.

And suddenly Matt knew what was happening. He had experienced it once before, when another wizard had violated his mind this way. Like Soliander before him, the man had cast the forbidden *Mind Trust* spell on Matt and was sifting through his memories. Like a sedative, the spell made him feel compliant, but he knew it didn't always work. He reached out to feel magic power and gather it within him to unleash on this wizard, but he felt nothing. Just like on Earth, there seemed to be no magic to touch and control. The only other time he'd experienced that was...

"Yes," said the man, his voice commanding, "you're wearing the Crown of Voids. I keep one on hand. Terrible device. As a wizard, I object to it on moral grounds if for no other reason—but that's solely when someone intends to use it on me, of course. They're really quite useful. I offer yourself as a case in point. You'll cast no more magic, Matt Sorenson of Earth. Because when I am through with you, you will die."

Matt tried to talk but couldn't, not that he needed to. The man could read his every thought. As he'd done with Soliander, Matt resisted the sifting through his mind. Instantly, the images shifted away from Soliander's memories to his own—personal memories of him nude in the mirror, or lying on his bed touching himself. He felt heat in his face, a sheen of sweat soaking his clothes.

"That won't be very impressive to the ladies," the man said, laughing. Humiliation tore through Matt. "The spell works whether you're conscious or not. You just can't be dead. I can see whatever I want. Should I keep going until you succumb and stop fighting me? Maybe then I'll leave your most embarrassing memories alone."

Anger filled Matt like never before. He tried to pull his hands forward but found them bound behind him as he sat on a chair, to which his ankles were also tied. At his resistance, the man dove straight into detailed memories of sexual encounters, thoughts, and fantasies, porn Matt had viewed, bathroom troubles, encounters with girls he had poorly flirted with, and more. And all the while he kept up a commentary on what he saw—laughing, mocking, disapproving. Matt flushed with a shame that grew deeper by the moment, sweat dripping down his back, his heart pounding. He fought again only to have the invasion of privacy worsen. Matt moaned at the complete command the man had over him, his helplessness making him cry out for him to stop. But the man dove deeper still and Matt trembled.

Finally, the invasion stopped for a few moments. Matt blinked in confusion—relief, even gratitude overwhelming him. But that caused a new shame, to feel thankfulness toward someone humiliating him. He sobbed on realizing he just wanted to cooperate, to let the man see what he wanted so that he would be satisfied and maybe not see it all, leaving Matt at least something private.

The man accepted his surrender, then asked Matt to voluntarily show him something embarrassing as proof of compliance. He felt a tear roll down his face and did as he was told, more tears falling once it was done. Then the man helped himself to whatever he wanted to know, which was everything. About Soliander. Eriana. The quest to Earth. The Earth itself. The quests they had done. When his attention turned to Matt's families and friends, their homes and personalities, Matt realized he posed a threat to everyone he knew and loved. What if this man captured them and did this to them? He begged the man to stop, to leave them out of it. But he kept going. With a scream, Matt fought back again.

A bolt of lightning lit the room as it struck him, causing a shock of pain beyond anything he'd ever felt. It knocked the breath from him. And then he couldn't breathe, another spell stopping all air from filling or leaving his lungs. His body convulsed as he suffocated for what seemed like forever. When it finally stopped, his lungs heaved for air that was suddenly burning as a fire engulfed his legs. He screamed uncontrollably and didn't even notice when it stopped.

"Shall I keep going?" the man asked, before grabbing his jaw and pouring a liquid down his throat over the gag. Too senseless to resist, Matt swallowed. The physical pain faded and was soon gone altogether so that he sat dazed, grateful, and bizarrely calm. Had he been drugged? He no longer cared. Avoiding pain of any kind was all that mattered. He knew that the man was training him to submit and that doing so was shameful, but he didn't care anymore. Tremors came and went through his body—as if a cold deep inside him, one that no fire could ever warm, had taken hold. The man gripped his forehead and began the *Mind Trust* spell again. Matt stared up at him blankly, compliant, terrified, and unresisting. Two words filled his mind over and over, first directed at his friends, and then at his master before him.

"I'm sorry."

———— ● ● ● ————

Anna let Eric and Ryan lead the way, Taryn right behind them. Lorian and Rognir brought up the rear, though the elf was their only wizard right now and perhaps he should've been up front. Only now did she realize how much she had come to rely on Matt. He was a novice but a powerful one, and he always got the job done. Lorian was more swordsman and archer with a dose of magic. Would it be enough to counter whoever this wizard was? Maybe she would have to do something personally. She needed to spend more time talking with Rognir about defense options, like putting up a shield as Matt had done. As she walked, she put one hand to her amulet and began communing with a god to get a sense of what help she could hope for.

They had stopped at the door leading from the Hall of Worlds into whatever lay beyond, Eric turning to Taryn. "Do you know where this leads to?"

"Let's find out," she said, pushing past him.

The rest of them followed her into a stairwell that went up and down. They descended, Anna wondering why they'd chosen that direction, but there was no time to ask. They exited into a long hallway on the first level down, servants moving supplies of one kind or another. This floor seemed to act like a warehouse, and they searched rooms one by one without finding Matt. They descended from a staircase in the middle to the final floor, which had only two lanterns on the wall.

Eric and Taryn motioned for everyone to be quiet as they started toward one side, listening and trying the door handles. Some were locked. Eric suggested they return to those. Then a door farther away opened, and a blue-robed man stepped into the hall. He turned in apparent surprise, and then ran for the stairs at the end as everyone chased after him. Eric was fastest, Lorian right behind, but Taryn stopped at the door the man had exited and tried the handle. It was locked. She bashed at it with her shoulder until Eriana put a hand to the door and spoke a few words. It glowed briefly, but a spell kept it closed.

They dashed after the others, hearing the commotion up the stairs as a boom of thunder sounded and someone screamed. On reaching the main level, Anna heard a huge rumble as the ground shook, an awful cracking sound following through the door to the World Gate room where her friends had gone. Stones loudly thudded on stones. More screams and yells split the air, and a cloud of dust washed over her. Fearing that the building had collapsed, Anna waved her hand in a futile effort to clear the dust and stepped through the door.

At first, it was hard to tell what had happened with the dust kicked up, but the stream of sunlight through the broken ceiling left no doubt about a cave-in. Eriana brushed past her to a man with a bloody gash on his head, healing him before moving on to another person. Men were shouting for help, either for themselves or others, and as Anna moved farther into the room, she could see why. Huge stone blocks had crushed several people, either killing them or smashing their limbs. People were trying to lift the blocks off, but got nowhere until wizards magically lifted them away. Eriana moved between the wounded, her healing touch bringing quick relief. Anna wanted to do the same—but first she frantically looked for her friends. She finally saw Eric crouched beside Ryan, who had a smaller slab pinning one leg. Just as she arrived, Eric and another man managed to move it, Ryan gritting his teeth. His leg was broken.

Anna knelt beside him and put a hand on the leg, reaching out to the goddess Drakonon and finding the healing touch easy due to their repeated connections. The power flowed through her and into Ryan, who stopped gasping as his leg mended.

"What about you?" Anna asked Eric.

"I got out of the way faster."

That didn't surprise her, as agile as the martial artist was. As she moved to help another victim, she asked "Where is the wizard?"

"He made it through the gate after pulling the ceiling down on us."

Anna stifled a curse, thinking that they needed to head back to that closed room immediately. But first she and Eriana finished healing the wounded. She peeked at the priestess to see if there was anything noticeable about her technique to pick up on, but it didn't seem so. When she straightened, she saw Taryn forcibly arguing with an intimidated-looking wizard, whom she grabbed by the wrist and began dragging toward the stairs.

She followed ahead of her friends, catching up with Taryn and the wizard just as he broke the spell on the door the blue-robed man had exited. Then Taryn bashed it with her shoulder twice and it splintered enough to stick an arm through and unlock from the inside. Taryn and Anna entered, taking different paths around a chest-high wall of crates before them. More crates lined the walls of the twenty-square-foot room, a long torch burning by the door. Once they'd navigated the crates in the way, Anna saw Matt tied to a chair in the room's center, his head hanging down as if unconscious. Relief washed over her as she and Taryn reached him together.

Anna got down on one knee before Matt. "Are you alright?" She pulled the gag from his mouth, but he still didn't respond except to move his head a little. She wondered if he was only partially conscious and gently lifted his chin to see his face, which bore a haunted expression, jaw slack and eyes half-open. He didn't seem to recognize her.

"Matt, it's Anna. We're all here. You're safe now."

At that, a lewd smile ran across his features and he began to laugh, the sound turning a little wild. She checked him for physical wounds but saw none. Taryn began untying him as the others gathered around.

"What did he do to you, that wizard?" Anna asked. "He's gone now, okay? He's not even on this planet anymore."

Matt began to rock against the chair like a toddler trying to comfort himself. With the ropes no longer holding him to it, he almost fell off into her and would have if Taryn had not grasped him by the shoulders. Anna finally breathed a prayer to grant Matt peace and watched hopefully as he stopped rocking and slumped more, leaning back in the chair. He blinked several times as if clearing his sight or mind. Some clarity appeared in his eyes, which turned to look at her. This time recognition appeared—but no other reaction. Not relief. Not happiness. Not anything. He just stared blankly at her.

Anna asked, "Who did this to you?"

When he didn't answer after several seconds, Taryn came around to his front and knelt, one hand taking his. "Was it my brother?"

Matt's head turned toward her. Then he smiled broadly, beginning to laugh silently as he shook his head, like a schoolboy with a funny secret he wouldn't tell.

"Who?"

"He knows *everything*," Matt finally said, his voice cracking.

"Who? Who did this to you?" Taryn asked. "Mandrellan?"

He leaned toward her, unsteady, and whispered the answer. "Everon."

———— ✦•✦ ————

It had been a long day and Eric lay down on his bed, tired and unsure of what to do. He was sick of talking, guesswork, and machinations. His life had been full of those since that fateful day at Stonehenge, when they were first substituted for the Ellorian Champions. At least on Elloria, they didn't have to pretend, but everything felt different now. They had been physically wounded before, supernatural healing sparing them weeks or months of recovery. But now Matt had wounds of the mind and spirit. And no spell was going to fix that. Anna had done something to calm him, but it wasn't enough. When Taryn helped Matt to his feet, he had wobbled as if mental imbalance had led to a physical one. Even once he was on a horse, with Taryn behind him and controlling it at a walk to the palace, Matt's face had been oddly blank—like a mask, his eyes down. And he wouldn't meet anyone's gaze.

Hours had passed since then, with Matt in his room and only Taryn beside him. Eric wasn't sure what to make of that. He had noticed Taryn's determination to find Matt and concern at his condition. Was she taking care of Matt like she'd taken care if Soliander when they were kids? Was that a reason why she seemed drawn to him? Matt hadn't said much beyond admitting to Everon's use of the *Mind Trust* spell.

"He's afraid," Matt had said. "Soliander is hunting him. He's very afraid."

And he had better be, because now Eric wanted Everon dead and would happily turn him over to Soliander in a bargain for peace.

They let Matt rest but didn't want to leave him alone, and the wizard chose Taryn to keep him company. Eric didn't disagree, but found trust harder to come by. Still, of all the people they had met on Elloria, Taryn was the most trustworthy—and so he, Anna, and Ryan regrouped with Lorian, Rognir, Eriana and their hosts.

Talk turned to raiding the places belonging to Everon as Mandrellan, on Elloria or any other planet. But Matt was in no condition for it. Lorian stepped up, taking Rognir and a force of men, including some Dark Blade warriors with Taryn's approval. Eriana went with the expedition, which returned hours later. They hadn't found Everon, just Mandrellan's house. After investigating, Lorian surmised that Everon had killed the real Mandrellan years earlier and taken his place, moving to a new city and giving himself a plausible origin story. Then he'd come to Elloria and introduced himself to Princess Cariss by saving her life in a scene they believed he had concocted to gain her trust. The princess was furious, guilt-ridden, and embarrassed that the man who had betrayed her brother had been here all along. They surmised that Everon had placed himself where he would be among the first to hear if the Champions returned.

They knew he'd kidnapped Matt because he had some of Soliander's memories, which could include how close to catching Everon Soliander was. Now he knew of Soliander's hideouts and where Diara was. Would he be foolish enough to attack Castle Oste to recover Diara? Soliander wouldn't be expecting him, but had undoubtedly fortified the place. Everon wasn't a fool, and maybe a bigger threat to them, but Matt had likely been a means to an end. Maybe they didn't have to worry about Everon, another enemy.

They decided to stay another night for Matt's sake—and theirs. Once home, they could be summoned once more. Matt needed a break even more than the rest of them, but one day wouldn't be enough. In the meantime, Eriana and Rognir decided to visit Earth with the keystones. The dwarf could fashion the Home Rings, while Eriana could keep Rognir out of trouble on the unfamiliar planet. He wasn't an elf and could pass for a little person, but he didn't know the world and might be too much for Jack to handle. It would likely take them days to create the rings, and speed mattered.

Eriana expressed mixed feelings about returning the place that had been her home for half her life. She had only just been reunited with her brother. But the king and queen pledged to bring her to Elloria whenever she wanted. They granted Solun a permanent room in the palace beside one set aside for Eriana, not the guest quarters they had been using. Eriana would split her time between worlds as needed and eventually make it to Coreth. She admitted that she felt obligated to help the four Earth friends, find Andier and Korrin, and discover how to convince Soliander either to help or to stay out of their way. Eric gave her a bigger hug than he meant to before she disappeared through a portal with Rognir to Jack's apartment.

Thinking of Matt with Taryn still in his rooms, Eric lay on his bed, remembering his own time alone with a woman. Part of him wanted Kori to show up now, partly so he could tell her about Everon being here so she could tell Soliander. The information wouldn't just be a peace offering, but a fresh lead for the arch-wizard to get revenge. It could solve two problems at once—keeping both Soliander and Everon busy.

One in pursuit. The other fleeing.

CHAPTER NINETEEN

SHARDS

Taryn asked minutes after his friends left, "What do you want to do?"

Matt wasn't sure how to answer and lay staring up for a long time on the bed, still fully dressed. She lay next to him, facing him, one hand on his chest. The feeling of being exposed would not leave him, he felt, until the person to whom he had been so exposed was dead. And now he knew the answer to her question. "I want to kill Everon."

"I will help you," she said at once.

He turned his head to her, their noses nearly touching. He saw clear-eyed resolution, and a strength he had admired since laying eyes on her. This admiration had grown. He felt drawn to her in a different way now—beyond attraction to her beauty, to her sharp mind, to her personal power and command. Now she offered a kind of safety, like a rock to steady him. Something about that steel gaze calmed him. He wanted more. Needed....

Matt kissed her and met no resistance. Instead, a firm, confident response drew him in. He gladly lost himself in it, feeling like he found himself in doing so. Always awkward with a woman, he somehow felt sure now when nothing else seemed certain. She made love to him the first time, and he to her the second. And, through it all, there were no thoughts of anything outside their shared bed.

When it was over, they napped—and he wondered if a nightmare would tear him from sleep, but it never came. He fancied nightmares to be afraid of Taryn, if not himself. When they finally woke, her growling stomach brought attention to his own hunger. She called a servant for some food and hot water for a bath. They spent more hours just being quiet together. Somewhere in all of it, Matt felt remarkably restored, wondering if it was an illusion. He wasn't dealing with what had happened, he knew, just escaping it. Perhaps that was all he needed today, but he also had some thinking to do.

Taryn sat sharpening her sword as he read through his spellbooks, not saying what he was looking into for. Something about making preparations while she sat there tending to her weapons pleased him. They could be fearsome together, and likely would be. But first he had something to do without her. There would be no going after Everon today or anytime soon. Matt wanted to be stronger, but he also wanted to feel safer. Taryn couldn't be with him all the time. She had already said she wanted to come to Earth, but even so, Matt would just get summoned, and she wouldn't be there on the next quest.

She could still come with him on the one he was about to attempt—but he wasn't sure if she would approve, and he felt too vulnerable ever to truly be at peace unless he did what he was planning. He could protect himself, all of his friends, and the woman he was falling in love with. Everon would never do to them what he had done to Matt. The idea threatened his self-control, only just restored, and so he pushed it from his mind.

He looked into the spells he needed, sometimes sending for a guard to get him the ingredients. Taryn eyed him curiously but without judgement, and he knew what she was thinking. If his next act was to return to Earth, and he couldn't take anything with him, why was he gathering spell materials? The fact she didn't ask was a sign of respect, maybe even trust, which made him feel guilty that one of the spells he was going to cast would be on her. He thought about it every few minutes, part of him wondering if he was repeating the explanation to himself to silence the doubts in his head. He told himself it was a simple spell, a small one, and it would only accentuate what was about to happen anyway. And that excuse would have to suffice.

He also looked into a spell to make people forget that he had passed by. The invisibility spell would've been better, but it seemed a little advanced. He really needed to practice these things, and he reminded Taryn to send spellbooks to Earth for him when she got a chance. That was a good explanation for his gathering of materials, but he didn't say it. She was easily smart enough to conclude that that was what he was doing, even though it wasn't. Another pang struck him. But at least he wasn't telling her a lie.

By late afternoon, Matt decided to put on a show of feeling better, so they left his rooms and met up with Eric, Anna, and Ryan. His friends seemed both concerned and relieved that he appeared to be feeling better. And he was, partly from Taryn, and partly from resolve. He learned that Eriana and Rognir had left for Earth, and agreed that this was sound. They ate dinner together and resolved that they would return to Earth the next day, arriving in the middle of the night. Jack should've been expecting them soon. Eriana had been told of the time differences to remind Jack that the friends would be appearing in the middle of the night. He should probably sleep on the floor of his bedroom unless he wanted to find Anna beside him. Ryan joked about wanting a woman to magically appear in

344 | RANDY ELLEFSON

his bed, prompting laughter Matt imitated but didn't really feel. Maybe he could be okay again after all of this was over—but he wasn't sure whether he meant this quest or all of them. Or murdering Everon. He had changed and left parts of himself behind. He wasn't sure he was ever going to feel whole again.

He and Taryn retired to bed early for another round of intimacy. It once again filled him with peace that surprised him after the day's events. He waited for her to drift off, then slipped from bed to review the sleeping spell, casting it on her moments later. He couldn't risk her waking and wondering where he had disappeared to again.

Matt took some gold from her coin pouch, wondering how to make it up to her. He put on undergarments and a robe, but carried his boots as he snuck out. He wasn't supposed to use Soliander's attire or staff, but he would need it all where he was going.

Taking a cloak with him, he padded quietly in long socks to the meeting room, knowing Eric was a light sleeper and just a door down. He probably wasn't even asleep yet. The meeting room had not been guarded so much as their wing of the palace, and he slipped inside. It didn't take long to outfit himself, a feeling of comfort filling him once he had Soliander's staff in one hand. He needed to stop thinking of it that way. This was Matt Sorenson's staff. Fuck Soliander.

He threw the cloak over himself and left. On reaching the doors of their wing, he opened them to find the two guards turning to him. One began to ask if he needed anything, but Matt wasn't in the mood for a conversation the men would never remember anyway. He immediately cast the spell to make them forget having seen him, and walked away.

Knowing where the dragon egg was kept, he wasted no time in getting there, again casting a spell on the guards.

On reaching the case, he deposited it into the Bag of Desires and headed for a palace exit. Then he left the grounds and entered the city streets, making every guard he passed forget his passage. It was fortunate that the spell wasn't taxing because he had to cast it so much.

Walking the dark streets of Andor alone would have given him pause just a day earlier, but not now. Something had taken all the fear from him. He felt aggressive and dangerous. Just let anyone try to stop him and he would incinerate them if needed. That might get him in trouble with their hosts—and they seemed like good people, so he wasn't interested in doing that to anyone—but he still didn't feel concerned for his safety. He didn't feel safe so much as like he had nothing left to lose. It gave him a kind of abandon, a willingness to take risks. He felt free, as awful as the source of that freedom was. Something about Everon violating him so utterly had made him cease to give a damn about his physical safety. There were worse things that could be taken from a man.

He had previously seen beggars on the street. Now he offered one a gold coin to assist him, so the young man eagerly followed. No one molested him on his walk to the Hall of Worlds, where lanterns and torches lit the exterior, the gusts of ocean air making them cast dancing shadows. He had been here before, apparently, while unconscious in a box, the thought of which hardened his glare.

Entering the large main room with his beggar in tow, Matt wasn't surprised to see few people present. The gate would likely have been turned off if all planets were on the same time frame. He approached a guard, explaining his need to visit the planet Rovell and offering more than enough gold coins. The guard agreed to change the gate's location via the wizards who were controlling it. With that done, Matt cast the *Forget* spell, which would work for another two minutes. He made sure to capture everyone in its radius, including his beggar. Then he pulled the Bag of Desires from a pocket, gave it to the beggar, and unceremoniously shoved him through the World Gate.

Matt followed, seeing the Hall of Worlds in Ortham once again. Nothing had changed in the weeks since he'd been here except the presence of more guards, many of whom recognized him as Soliander. He waved them off, gave the beggar another coin, took the Bag of Desires with the blue dragon egg in it, and shoved him back through to Elloria. World Gates were technically bidirectional like most portals, but to control traffic, many places would not allow them to be. Matt didn't care, since he was going to make everyone in Ortham forget him anyway. He cast the spell and left. So far, so good.

Putting the cloak and its hood back on to evade recognition, he left the Hall of Worlds. It was mid-morning here, and this suited him. Part of him didn't care who saw the dragon, but he wanted no question and no trouble. He asked for the nearest stables and bought a horse, food and drink, and left Ortham to go north. He ignored anyone he passed on the road.

An hour later, he left the road for the wilderness, unafraid of wild animals or even worse dangers. But nothing came, and he got off the horse and set about summoning an old dragon friend. Another hour passed before the huge red dragon flew toward him and he removed his cloak. Jolian soon landed and morphed into a human in red, form-fitting leather. She looked as sleek and powerful as ever as she sauntered over, wavy crimson hair to her mid-back.

"It is good to see you, Soliander," she said, smiling.

"And you as well. I'm afraid I have an urgent need, or I would not have asked you to come."

"Whatever I can do for you, I will. What of the other Ellorians?"

"There was no time to get them. I need you to take me to the dwarves of Morcanon Kingdom immediately. Can you do that?"

"Of course. Is this about the Orb of Dominion shard you left with them?"

He wasn't sure whether he should admit it, but said, "Yes. I have reason to believe someone knows where each of the pieces are and has the means to get them. We must prevent that."

Her eyes intensified. She knew just how dangerous the shards were because Soliander had used the master Orb of Dominion to enslave her brother through the slave Orb— she just didn't know it was the real Soliander who'd done it. Matt had the master now, so there was no danger to someone having the slave, but he wanted both in his control. It was only by good fortune that he had stored the Bag of Desires with Soliander's items. If he'd had it with him when Everon captured him, the bastard would have the master orb even now. There was nothing stopping him from getting the slave shards, now that he knew where they were. Matt had to get there first.

Jolian morphed back into dragon form and Matt climbed up her wing to sit upon her back, where she would hold him on using magic. He knew a spell to do that himself, but hadn't learned it. He needed to not be dependent on anyone anymore. As she lifted into the sky, he realized he felt comfortable without a saddle now, his bravery seeming both familiar and new at once.

They soared away from Matt's horse, which he had tied to a tree branch. Hopefully it would be there when he returned, but if not, so be it. They flew past Ortham, its towers and castle far below, then south over the green treetops of the Artem Woods. To the east rose the snow-capped Galla Mountains, which they flew parallel to for many miles. They finally turned toward them into the morning sun, arcing between the peaks, the streaming rays of sun casting shadows they flew in and out of as they descended.

The dwarves had seen dragons before, including this one—but, even so, the sight of one unexpectantly trying to land in the cleared space outside their mountain fortress at Hamarven caused a brief panic. Jolian settled onto the stony ground, and kept still and unthreatening as Matt climbed down. Then she morphed into human form beside him. Only now did the dwarves calm, some of them recognizing him as Soliander. He used that name to good effect, asserting that an emergency required him to see the Queen of Morcanon at once. He chafed their delay in arranging a meeting but knew that this delay would be the longest.

It didn't take long to convince her that he needed the slave orb shard he had left with them. It wasn't theirs anyway. With apologies for his haste, he had it tucked into his Bag of Desires beside the master orb and was airborne on Jolian within twenty minutes. They flew halfway before veering east into the mountains again, past the town of Valegis to the nearby Kirii Cave. The almost man-sized, batlike kirii were likely to attack them inside, but the injured leviathan that Jolian had almost killed in the underground lake within was potentially worse. This was another task that Matt would previously have avoided—but he felt no fear as they descended through a tunnel with Jolian striding beside him, his staff lighting the way.

On reaching the dark shores of the lake, he didn't bother hiding their presence, instead blasting the cavern roof with fire and setting enough kirii ablaze that they would likely avoid him. They screeched and screamed, scattering to other areas farther away. The waters surged as the leviathan moved, but at Matt's suggestion, Jolian morphed back into a dragon and spat fire at the surface. The speed with which the leviathan moved away told Matt that Jolian would keep it at bay.

Matt stripped naked, no longer shy. Then he cast a wa-ter-breathing spell and another spell to help him see. He waded into the icy lake, not complaining like he would have before, and dove in headfirst. The water appeared bright to his magicked eyes, schools of various fish spread throughout. He looked in the direction of the leviathan and saw huge eyes watching him in the distance, tentacles swirling, a mouth of teeth as big as him opening and clos-ing. The sight gave him pause, but he turned away and swam into the depths.

Spires of rock rose from the bottom. It was a hundred feet below him in deeper areas, but less so between here and the small islands before him. That was where they had thrown the shard. Ryan had done it, and Matt was glad he'd seen where the splash was. He had never been skinny-dipping and now felt freer than ever as he continued down, occasionally glancing at the leviathan, which hadn't moved. Soon he was between the spires and other for-mations at the bottom, forty feet deep, fish moving out of his way. He didn't know much about them but had attack spells at the ready, and the Trinity Ring on one finger to heal himself if something hurt him. He spent ten minutes searching in vain, wishing he knew a locator spell. Then he saw the shard, further right than expected, the curved part of it facing up. His fingers closed around it and he began ascending.

Halfway up, he looked toward the leviathan and saw that it was gone. Head whipping around, he saw nothing and struck out for the surface. There were still another ten feet left when he saw it coming like a torpedo, ghastly burn marks and wounds from Jolian's claws on across its head and body. Jolian's huge feet splashed into the water, too far away to help. Matt stopped swimming and faced the beast, ready with the force blast spell he so often used. With a simple change, he could use it on himself rather than a target, but he wasn't sure that would work. Failure meant death. He turned his back to the surface, and just before the gaping jaws reached him, invoked the spell.

"Kunia!"

Matt felt himself hurled backward, up and out of the water and into the air, flailing wildly as he turned to see his trajectory. He heard thrashing water where the leviathan swarmed below him. The stalactites above were nearing fast, kirii clinging to the ceiling. Jolian moved toward him—but so did the leviathan, even as he began to fall. The dragon and leviathan were converging on his apparent landing spot in the water. Jolian spat another torrent of fire into the lake below Matt, the heat washing over him. He splashed into the water and could see nothing for the bubbles.

Suddenly, a huge mouth closed over him and he panicked as it pulled him through the water. He broke the surface, water gushing from the mouth and over him—a huge, rough tongue against his bare backside and enormous teeth all around him like a cage, except behind him where the blackness of a throat waited. A spell on his lips, he suddenly noticed that the teeth were shaped differently from the leviathan's. And they weren't closing to crush him. Water dripped from his hair into his eyes until he wiped it away to see past the teeth and out into the cavern, its walls rushing by until the stone floor hurtled toward him—and then stopped. The jaws slowly opened. He climbed down, past the teeth, and out of Jolian's huge mouth to turn back to her, a mix of fear and gratitude rising up in him. His heart had never pounded so hard. And he had never felt so alive.

"You are unhurt?" she asked, still in dragon form, her voice booming off the cavern. Matt turned and saw the leviathan lurking—not too far away, but keeping its distance.

"I think so," he said, still amazed. He held up the shard, a little surprised he hadn't dropped it in the madness. He glanced around again. They were on the shore near where they'd entered, his robes piled to one side. He walked over and put them on, stuffing the shard into the Bag of Desires. Then he came to the surface again.

"Get that fucking thing out of here," he said, referring to the leviathan. Jolian roared another spout of flames and the beast disappeared under the waves.

But it wasn't yet time to go. He had to acquire a second item, one that was almost as important for protecting his mind from ever being intruded upon again. The *Mind Shield* spell countered the *Mind Trust* spell and required the eyes of blind fish to cast. He pulled out a vial with oil in it and spilled two drops into the waters, then spoke the spell.

> *Into the waters, seek and find*
> *All the creatures, make them mine*
> *Bring them here, all of one mind,*
> *Caught like a fish on hook and line*

The water trembled as sea life from within it sprang toward him. He only cared about the blind, silver sparis fish among the smaller red ones and the larger black fish. He began scooping them into a second bag, aware that putting anything living in the magic one would kill it. He was going to kill them anyway for their eyes, but he needed to avoid damaging them.

He had brought multiple jars to fill because they'd be less conspicuous to carry back than a big, heavy bag of wiggling fish. Matt had always been squeamish about anything slimy or slippery—but after filling the bag with as much as he could, and throwing a bunch of other fish ashore, he sat down and started cutting eyes from heads quickly and efficiently. Jolian offered to help, and they quickly had the jars full and stowed. He rinsed his hands of the smell as best he could for now, and soon they were on their way.

This time, they flew northeast toward the ruin of Ashing on the plains beyond the Galla Mountains. Matt had been here with Jolian (and Eric) once before, and she knew where to land on the yellow grass outside the shattered town walls. She morphed into human form again and walked beside him as he led the way to the empty square. They had probably been the last people here, but he and Eric had made her stay away from where they'd hidden the piece. One less person to know. Now it didn't matter, but he asked her to wait as they reached the empty square, a low, broken wall surrounding it. In the center stood a broken statue that seemed like the obvious place to hide something, which was why Eric had suggested using the wall instead. Matt knew the piece was still there before he even saw it, because the two pieces he already had begun to vibrate from the bag. This was why he had left Jolian behind—to prevent her from knowing what he was about to do.

He placed the first two pieces on the ground where she couldn't see. Then he pulled the final piece from inside the broken wall, placing it next to the others. They moved toward each other before lifting up and reassembling into a dark sphere. As the cracked pieces merged, a soft white light emanated from them and then vanished. The slave Orb of Dominion had recreated itself. He took one last look at it, dark and silent, wondering how soon he would cross a line that, once crossed, offered no hope of redemption. He felt dimly aware that this was an early step into evil, and that awful men had likely justified their actions the same way he was justifying his.

For a moment he almost gave in to tears, his desperation was so strong, his conscience still intact. Would any goodness in him end when he used the orbs? Was it immediate, or a slow descent into evil? He never thought he would stand on the precipice of moral wrongs, but here he was. Would he look back on this one day and regret it, or be glad of the protections he had wrought despite the consequences to others? Better them than him. He sighed. His decision had been made and he would question it no further. He could get what he wanted by more honorable means, but that required trust, and he wasn't feeling trusting. He wasn't sure he would trust anything ever again.

For a moment, he pulled out the master Orb of Dominion to compare them, seeing that it was also dormant, dark and silent, as expected. One could almost be forgiven for not realizing the awful power it held, to control the minds of others forever once they had looked into the slave orb. But as a wizard, he felt it calling to him, compelling him to use it. The two spheres were otherwise identical when turned off. With an effort, he ignored it.

His mission accomplished, Matt put them away, rejoined Jolian, and flew back toward Ortham and his horse. By now, it was mid-afternoon and he needed to finish this. He let Jolian leave after giving his thanks and a farewell, and galloped back to Ortham. He encountered no problems, gave the horse away, and reentered the Hall of Worlds. Using his identity as Soliander, he convinced the gate operators to change the destination to Elloria. Then he cast the *Forget* spell and stepped through.

Upon arriving in Andor, he spelled the guards there, too, feeling fatigued from all that he'd performed. This was the most magic he'd ever done in a row—and now he had pulled an all-nighter, too. He knew that he and his friends would be sent home within a few hours, the Quest Ring rejuvenating him. He just had to last until then. He'd run out of what he needed for that spell, too, so he'd have to do his best to look like he'd just gone for a walk when he returned to the palace. He left the Hall of Worlds behind and stepped outside, seeing the dark sky beginning to lighten. Then a smooth elven voice spoke to him from behind.

"Matt?"

He turned to see Lorian coming out of the hall as well, brow furrowed. *Shit. What is he doing here?.* He decided to ask.

Always polite, the elf answered, "I just returned from Honyn. I was asking my queen permission to join you on Earth for a time, perhaps in the company of other elves. I would need assistance with that level of travel, as you do not have a World Gate there for me to step through."

"Of course."

"Where are you from? I thought I saw you walking away from a gate. Aren't the others with you?"

Matt continued toward the palace with him, wondering what answer to give. "No. There was something I needed to take care of."

"Where?" When Matt didn't answer at once, Lorian mused, "I assume not to Honyn? There are only so many World Gates, and you weren't at the one I used. I would have seen you. Did you go to Rovell?"

Matt stifled a frown, aware that Lorian knew of the Orbs of Dominion quest. "Yes. I went to ask the dragons if they would come to Earth to help us."

The elf said, "Did you check on the shards from the orb? You said Everon knew everything, and I assume that he'd learned their location."

While Matt normally loved smart people, this one was becoming a problem. "I did retrieve the shards, yes. That was my other reason for going."

"Why didn't you bring the others?"

"I only realized late last night, and felt I needed to go immediately." Matt sensed from the troubled look in Lorian's eyes that he wasn't convinced. Worse, he was going to say something to the others.

"Is it reassembled?"

Thinking fast, Matt answered, "No. If we go to your room, I can show you." He suddenly felt nervous about what he was thinking. There was an obvious way to prevent Lorian from saying anything, but the idea sickened him. Did the moral precipice have to loom so soon after falling over it became possible?

The elf said, "Maybe I should hold onto a piece, or take it to Honyn."

"Let's talk about it in your room."

Lorian nodded, and they walked to the elf's suite in silence, passing the palace guards without issue. They soon stopped by a room near Matt's wing of the palace, Lorian leading him inside and pouring himself a drink. Matt discreetly put his hand into the Bag of Desires and rearranged the two orbs. The master was inside a velvet bag designed for it; the slave was not. He could only tell because the slave orb felt slightly repulsive to his hand while the master seemed comforting, as if willing him to hold and use it. He reversed them and then pulled out the velvet bag, now holding the slave orb, and placed it on a table.

"Will you be able to bring other people with you to Earth?" Matt asked. He felt nervous. A little sick to his stomach. But he had to do it.

"Yes. And I am looking forward to learning more about your world and how I may help you there, especially when you are gone."

"Thank you. You have always been a good friend to us." Matt walked toward the bedroom as if just stretching his legs, the knot in his stomach growing. "I guess you haven't seen the orb before, have you?" he asked, turning back to see the elf gazing at the bag. "It's off, so I don't think it's dangerous now. Not much to see, really."

He slipped his hand into the magic bag and grasped the master Orb of Dominion as Lorian stepped over to the bag, fingers gently touching the velvet as if unsure whether he should open it. The elf glanced at him and Matt smiled as if to mock Lorian's concern, even as he drew magic power to himself and felt the master orb in his hand grow warmer from turning on. Lorian looked at the Bag of Desires, then tentatively pulled it open for a quick peek. Matt yanked out the master orb and saw with grim satisfaction that Lorian's visage appeared in it via the slave orb. "Obey and serve," he said into the master, which now had a golden sheen to it. "My will be yours."

Lorian's face grew relaxed. "My will is yours."

Matt looked at the elf, who hadn't moved. The knot in Matt's stomach had gone. He felt calm. Regretful, but safer. He wouldn't make Lorian do anything unsavory, certainly. He just needed help right now, and Lorian was the one who could provide it. In time, he would use the orbs as needed to protect himself and those he loved. And a task he had for Lorian would set this protection in motion.

First, he had to test the bond.

"Come to me, my friend," he said, and the elf walked toward him obediently, stopping before him. Their eyes met. Matt searched them for reproach, or fear. Hatred. But he saw nothing like that. Just calmness, a kind of trust and willingness that caused embarrassment to fill him. He had betrayed that trust, and yet Lorian only trusted him more! Was he just as evil as Everon now? He wouldn't do the same *things* with the power, just protect himself—but then was that all Everon felt he was doing? He frowned. Soliander had cast that *Mind Trust* spell on Matt, too. He wasn't sure whether he was going down the right or wrong path now, but it didn't matter. Protecting himself mattered.

What good was all this power if he couldn't even do that? He sighed.

"I'm sorry, Lorian, but I must do this. I want you to act normally toward me in all ways, except that when I tell you to do something, you do it. Do you understand?"

The look of obedience disappeared from the elf's face, and yet he answered, "Yes."

"I want you to come to Earth like you were planning to do. But you will bring these orbs with you, and you will give them to me when we are alone. No one can know that you have them. Do you understand?"

"I understand what you want, just not why."

"I am not going to tell you."

"This does not surprise me."

Matt scrutinized him. He had to know how much of the elf was still there. How he felt. How he judged what Matt had done. He wanted the elf's respect and felt certain he would never have it again if he undid this spell, and the thought filled him with remorse. "Do you know what I have done to you?"

"You have used the Orbs of Dominion to make me obey you."

Hearing Lorian admit it made a pang of guilt strike him. "How do you feel about that?"

Lorian seemed to consider before answering. "I want to help you. I do not mind this. I do sense that my desire to help you has risen considerably."

"Are you offended?"

Lorian raised an eyebrow, then smiled. "If you undid the spell, I sense I would be greatly offended and never forgive you without a great explanation. As it is, I am content. And I trust you."

Matt sighed and turned away. "I still want you to think for yourself. Can you do that?"

"Yes. I have not become a thoughtless servant, if that is what you are thinking."

"I kind of was, yeah. It's not what I want. I just need you to sometimes do something for me without arguing, and while keeping it a secret."

"I am otherwise free to act as before?"

"Yes. Please believe me that I don't want any more control over you than necessary."

"Thank you." The elf looked at the master orb. "I will need a way to carry these to Earth. The Bag of Desires?"

"Yes."

"Say no more. I will take care of it." He turned to go as Matt watched in resignation. He suddenly realized he had to make sure Ryan never cracked the slave orb—which had a silver sheen to it now that it was on—like he'd once done, to make it stop working. Lorian would be one potentially angry person confronting him. He didn't know how many more there would be, but he intended only to use it on enemies. And yet he had just established precedent.

Matt had another task for Lorian. Now that no longer had the materials for the *Forget* spell, he couldn't take the dragon egg back to where it belonged without arousing suspicion. At his direction, Lorian left with the dragon egg case in the magic bag and the slave orb in the other, inside the velvet pouch. Every time Lorian encountered resistance from guards, he pulled out the orb, which the men looked into. And Matt ensnared their minds from the safety of Lorian's room. He didn't have to make the guards forget. He just had to stop them saying anything about it. The elf put the egg case back and then repeated this stunt with the guards standing outside Matt's wing of the palace before returning to Matt. The wizard left both orbs with the elf in the magic Bag of Desires before returning to his rooms. The guards let him by without comment, and he ordered them not to speak of it. They agreed, having no choice.

With all the evidence of his actions elsewhere, Matt crept down the hall to the meeting room, where he changed out of Soliander's clothes and put the staff back. Then he returned to his own room. Taryn was still asleep. He gently climbed in beside her, exhaustion and relief filling him. Wondering if the Trinity Ring would restore some energy to him, he still let himself drift off. But his dreams offered no comfort, alternating between visions of Everon probing his mind at will and Matt doing the same thing to Lorian, or Taryn, or his friends. He wasn't really the same, was he? He vowed not to become a monster, but he had an awful feeling it was already too late.

⸺ ✦ ✦ ✦ ⸺

Ryan had mixed feelings about going home, but it was too late for them to change their minds. Hours earlier, they had returned the dragon egg to the blue dragons of Novell. Unlike when they first recovered it, the delivery was as uneventful as they had hoped. The dragons were suitably appreciative—which made Ryan feel guilty, even though King Sarov was the one who had arranged for the theft, not them. That secret was closely-guarded so as not to make enemies of the blue dragons or the Kingdom of Novell that worshipped them. He had felt chagrined during the celebratory banquet thrown in their honor in the island kingdom, but at least it had been quick and that kept the size down.

Earlier that day, they had made their farewells to their hosts in Andor. With Prince Dari returned, minus a hand, the king and queen had been in better spirits. Dari himself seemed a changed man, no longer hostile towards them, but Ryan wasn't sure why. Had he accepted that they were victims in this whole situation and hadn't done something to his brother? The mission to Soliander's current castle had seemingly cured his attitude problem, which was fine with Ryan. The last thing they needed was more crap to deal with.

Princess Cariss was now the one who seemed haunted, but Ryan knew it was because she'd befriended the man responsible for betraying Korrin and the others. Her guilt had been plain to see, and several people—Anna, Eriana, and himself—had tried to convince her no harm had come of it. But she wasn't ready to let it go. To make amends, she had pledged to help them, though she admitted she didn't know how she could. She saw Everon's treatment of Matt as her fault and couldn't meet Matt's eyes. Ryan wished he could do something more to ease her mind, but had run out of time to think of anything.

Taryn and some of her Dark Blade warriors had flown with them on dragon-back from Andor to Novell, she and Matt sharing a ride. She seemed to be a good influence on him and Ryan resisted the urge to tease his friend. It didn't seem right—not because of what Matt had been through, whatever it was, but because Matt suddenly seemed like a man instead of an awkward boy in a man's body. That was another thing he didn't really understand. But if Taryn made him feel that way, then Ryan considered her a friend. She seemed trustworthy, and their relationship was certainly better than whatever had happened between Eric and Kori. *That* was something to tease someone about.

Now they stood inside the Quest Ring on the hill where they had first arrived. So much had changed since then. This had been their most consequential quest yet—he doubted that another would rival it. They now had friends, help, and keystones, plus a way to communicate with Jack or anyone else back home while they were gone. He felt so much better about their situation—and once they had created the Home Rings, a major problem would be resolved. Now that they had turned in the dragon egg, they could be summoned at any moment, but he was hoping to get home first.

Matt was still outside the Quest Ring, getting a last kiss from Taryn and not being shy about it. His friends shared an amused glance.

"Why don't *we* get a kiss?" Ryan joked, holding his lance and glad he hadn't needed it.

Eric smirked at him. "Come here, big fella."

"I didn't mean from you!"

Anna laughed. "I don't think I need to see this."

They were still laughing when Matt joined them, cocking his eyebrow at their amusement. In the past, the wizard would've looked like he assumed he was being made fun of, but now he seemed indifferent. Once again, Ryan thought he seemed more confident and that the change suited him.

One of Andor's wizards cast the spell to turn on the Quest Ring. Ryan watched as the words of blue fire swirled up the pillars around them and Elloria vanished. The familiar roaring sound and buffeting wind struck him as he faced Matt, whose black robes had vanished to leave him nude. Ryan knew the same thing had just happened to him, and covered his crotch with one hand. Eric never bothered—and, to Ryan's surprise, Matt didn't either this time. He always kept his eyes straight ahead at Matt, unless he glanced at Eric—which he'd done enough times to know that Eric was always staring straight ahead at a point above Anna's head as she stood across from him.

Then each of them were dressed in their Earth clothes, but since they'd all been sleeping, this wasn't much. Ryan and Eric only wore shorts, while Matt also had a t-shirt on and Anna stood in a shirt and pink panties. Jack's apartment materialized around them, Matt lying on the couch, both Ryan and Eric on the floor. Ryan quickly got up and stuck his head into Jack's bedroom, where Anna had been, and saw her sitting up in bed. It was early afternoon and Jack wasn't there.

But there was a note from him on the table next to the laptop, urging caution.

CHAPTER TWENTY

THE DRAGON LORD KING

Vianden, the Dragon Lord King of Elfhame, felt certain he could smell Earth all the way from his throne of human skulls. That was how much he longed for it. A thousand years had passed without that scent, and while it was familiar, something was off. There was a mustiness, a dirtiness, a toxicity, all sapping some of his enjoyment of it otherwise nostalgic aroma. The Land of Fae had its own delights, but he wanted to go home.

Dragons were of the Earth, not Elfhame. He didn't belong here any more than the rogue humans who had sometimes wandered in. But unlike them, he remained uncorrupted—a dragon is not so easy to pervert. And yet it had happened in a good way long ago. As the magic of the fae world first crept into the Earth, the oldest of its creatures, the dragons, had merged with it so that it became part of their nature. As such, they could not survive without it.

And so they were here—many of them, anyway. That wretched human, Merlin, had drained all the magic from the Earth, leaving the dragons with a choice to flee into

Elfhame or die. Some had chosen to remain, though he never found out what happened to them. They had refused to believe, flying above the forested fields even as Merlin's spell ended. But he'd heard that others intended to bury themselves deep within the earth, below the mountains, slumbering until such time as magic returned and they awoke. He hadn't been among those who believed they would survive, and he was curious to find out if they had. The dragons of Elfhame numbered in the hundreds, and that was enough for the revenge he sought. Humanity was to pay for what Merlin had done, because saving them was the reason he had done it.

The doorway stood open. They all did, but then the smaller ones had always cracked ajar at times, as if they hadn't quite been sealed all the way. This let the magic flow for a few yards, and sometimes a faerie or two stepped onto the Earth for just a minute. Some had died that way, like fish flopping on land and unable to breathe unless yanked back to safety in time. And occasionally a human had come through and been seized upon. Since no one had watched the doorways for hundreds of years, these wayward adventurers sometimes traveled quite far into Elfhame before being discovered. And they told such interesting tales of the world beyond! But Vianden hadn't believed any of that nonsense, thinking them mad.

Now, though—with all the doors, big and small, wide open—he wondered at the truth of it. It was the stench that gave it away, that Earth had changed in the last thousand years. And something told him he wouldn't like what he saw any more than he enjoyed what he smelled. What had they done to Earth to make it stink like that? His long pent-up desire for revenge had fostered in the weeks since the open doorways had first been noticed.

And it was partly his force of will keeping the fae from rushing into Earth en masse. But they also knew that the magic had to flow through the gates and far enough, and that this would take time. He could feel the potency of it falling in Elfhame, his own strength fading from what he had become accustomed to. A millennium ago, when first arriving here, he had been stunned by the burst of power in him—all that magic concentrated here and filling him. It had helped him conquer this land into which he was never supposed to come. Other dragons and even the fae had been slower to adapt to the surging magic, unsure what it meant, unable to accept what had happened. Their indecisiveness had kept them passive and led to his rule over them. Fortune favored the aggressive. And he would retain his power here when he left for Earth. Why rule one land when he could rule two?

He had sent a dwarf through to Earth, but it hadn't returned—and when he'd sent others after it, its decapitated body had been found and brought back. This seemed like a declaration of war to Vianden, who already had an appetite for destruction. If the Earth had been poisoned in some way, as a creature of nature, he was not going to be pleased. Nor would the other fae. There was already chatter among them that something was amiss, concern muting their pleasure at finally returning. This played right into his hands, for he intended to conquer the Earth and needed his fae army to do it. The humans might have sealed their fate.

What they called Stonehenge, a shrine to their relationship with the fae, was the most powerful of the doorways—but so many more existed all over the planet. Perhaps it had been a mistake to send the dwarf through the Stonehenge one. Was it under watch? Could the humans even tell that magic had returned and that the fae were not far behind? Were people expecting them? He had heard of damage to the monument, another rumor that sowed discontent among the fae. Were the humans so disrespectful as to not honor this relationship, long severed, in hopes that they would return? The fae had always been capricious. Moody. Vengeful. And while they blamed Merlin for their banishment to Elfhame, they weren't above blaming humans. Their wave of anger was growing into a tsunami.

He suspected Earth would be easy to conquer. The fae had had the last thousand years to continue practicing magic; the humans had nothing. Had they forgotten it altogether? They didn't live long enough for anyone who'd used it before still to be alive. His advantage seemed so clear that he felt no particular rush to visit, given the risk that magic had not spread far enough. Step farther into Earth than the magic had gone, and fae would fall over dead. But he felt confident that the time had come. Samhain was coming, the night when the barrier between worlds was thinnest, the magic ready to surge forth and complete its rebalancing between Elfhame and Earth.

Merlin had long since died when his spell was finished—whether he had remained on Earth and perished, or that awful explosion of magical energy had killed him. It had destroyed a wide swath of Elfhame before it regrew, the fields burnt, the ponds poisoned, the air burning with toxic fumes. And many had died. So many that even those in the Seelie Court were angry and pliable with thoughts of revenge, like Vianden had been putting into their heads for centuries. His own heart burned with hatred—for the blast had kicked up faerie dust in a storm of nearly molten, liquid debris that had seared itself into his chest, a silver crest on his otherwise black scales. The scar was a permanent reminder. But with Merlin gone, there was no one specific to take revenge upon.

The Ellorian Champions were long gone, too, since humans don't live a thousand years—though some people who had been brought here had been made to suffer nearly that long, the effects of Elfhame on humans the stuff of legend. He knew the Ellorians' names and faces as surely as they would have remembered his. He had stood beside Morgana when she summoned them to Earth. He had heard them promise to stop Merlin's spell. He had learned that they intended to betray Morgana and work with Merlin. There had been nothing he could do to stop it, having spent all his magical strength to help Morgana summon them. And so he had left Earth for Elfhame—and now he would leave Elfhame for Earth.

He rose from his throne of skulls and strode down the steps in the obsidian hall of the Unseelie Court he had conquered, the glistening glass reflecting all who walked upon it or between its shining walls. A few elves and dwarves watched in silence, as did another dragon in human form. A satyr shifted on its hooved feet, its bare-chested torso the closest thing to a human form Vianden regularly saw. Each of those in attendance commanded a host of others and would lead his forces to Earth. But it would take time to conquer all that he desired. Only days remained before their invasion began. The fae would return en masse to Earth and take back a world they were meant to rule all along. The humans had had a thousand years. The fae would take forever as punishment.

And Vianden, the Dragon Lord King of Elfhame, would rule over it all.

<hr />

"This gathering of the Sons of the Magi is called to order," Luna announced, standing at the head of the table in the Gilded Library's secret basement, twenty of their nearly thirty members sitting at the high-backed chairs. She hadn't waited for the usual guy to say it or for their Grand Master, Oliver, to arrive, because she really didn't care and would've preferred this talk to happen without him. But no sooner did she say the words than the man himself strode in with his pet, Rebecca, following. Both wore tight-fitting black clothes, as if they were signaling their alliance with attire.

"You have no authority to call this meeting, Luna," said Oliver, coming toward her.

"And yet you showed up. You had no authority to remove magic items from the treasure room, especially ones that didn't belong to you, and yet you did it, anyway." A murmur of disapproval spread through the room.

She and Andy had discussed his idea of stealing every magic item from the treasury but concluded that this would've been overkill. They were justified in taking back the ones they owned until further notice. Storing the inexpensive ones here hadn't mattered before magic worked, and now that it did, they could be dangerous. Most were supposedly not that powerful or important. And so they had decided to take all of theirs and install a dual locking mechanism whereby Luna and Andy would have one key, and Oliver could have the other, both being needed to get into the room. It seemed the only fair way to prevent Oliver, or themselves, from taking anything without the other party knowing.

But when they had arrived the night before to collect their share, they had discovered dozens of items missing. This included all the ones they considered important, and several that belonged to either Andy or Luna. They knew Oliver had done it—though when they checked the security footage the found that the cameras had gone dark and remained that way, leaving them only able to see the last time the items had been there.

Before leaving, they had helped themselves to their own items. They didn't install the new lock. Andy thought he knew where Oliver would've put the pilfered pieces, admitting that he had followed their Grand Master more than once due to distrust. The result was them driving to an office Oliver rented and Andy breaking in.

But they hadn't found the items. They next tried Rebecca's place, and on seeing that she wasn't home, Andy again succeeded in breaking in with skills Luna found surprising. Once more, they found nothing. Where they were hiding them, they couldn't tell, but Andy suspected Oliver kept them close at hand—either at home, in a locker somewhere, or maybe in his car. He ducked all of Luna's questions about how he knew different ways of breaking into places. The ones with only physical security were one thing, but he seemed able to bypass computer measures and PINs easily, sometimes pulling out a little computer to help. Her suspicions that he was a hacker seemed too real, and she stopped herself from asking for fear of the answer. Maybe later.

They weren't sure what might happen if they told the society of Oliver's theft. But putting pressure on him to reveal the items or the reason why he'd taken them was what Andy called a "discovery" ploy, getting him to reveal information that might help to recover them. And so here they were.

Oliver asked, "What makes you think I was the one who re—"

Seated beside Luna's empty chair—as she still stood at the table's head beside Oliver—Andy interrupted. "Because you and Rebecca are the only ones who didn't act surprised just now."

Smirking unconvincingly, Oliver asked, "Did you check the security cameras?"

"They were disabled."

Another murmur of disapproval and, from the looks of those in the room, they seemed to sense that Oliver already knew all of this and was being coy. And that Andy's and Luna's accusation was correct. His next words revealed that he sensed the mood, as he dropped the act.

"As Grand Master, I have the authority to protect them, to ensure their safekeeping."

Frowning, Luna said, "That's not your job. And to protect them from whom? This is a secret society, remember? No one but us knows they're here."

"Perhaps not everyone here can be trusted."

Andy replied, "Says the man who stole property from just about every person in this room. You need to return all of it immediately."

"I need to do no such thing. What are you going to do, call the police? MI6? They are confiscating all items believed to be magical, so even if they found the items for you, you'd never see them again."

Not wanting to be so close to him, Luna took her seat and said, "Better with them than in your hands."

Oliver stood alone at the table's head, his eyes boldly moving from one member to the next as if to scare them out of questioning him with Andy and Luna. "That's ridiculous. I have shown no signs of magic talent, and might be unable to use *any* of the devices for all you know."

"Then you won't mind returning them."

"I'm not going to do that. And you can't compel me."

Andy rose, dark eyes glittering. "How about if I bash your head in?"

Luna put a hand on his belly to restrain him and stifled a smile. Everyone knew he was a trained martial artist and had an element of danger to him, so it came as no surprise when the smirk fell from Oliver's face. But Oliver looked at Rebecca in such a way that Luna wondered if she'd learned an offensive spell instead of just that ball of light trick.

She said, "I would like the Sons of the Magi to vote on whether it is appropriate for the Grand Master to take these items that belong to individuals here, and yet are on loan to the society, and hoard them for his own purposes."

"I second the motion," said Andy.

And soon others agreed to the vote. It didn't go in Oliver's favor, though several people known to be his friends sided with him. Luna wasn't surprised but felt satisfied, especially with Andy's next words.

"I further propose that Oliver has by sundown tomorrow to return the items or be removed as Grand Master, with Luna taking his place."

This caused another murmur that quickly turned into agreement. Some wanted Oliver removed immediately, and Luna saw the tide turning in her favor. If Oliver kept acting as he had, he would soon be out. She wondered if that would make him more of a problem and not less.

"The next order of business," Luna began, "is tomorrow night, Samhain. Some of you have decided to be present at places we believe to be magical doorways between Elf-hame and Earth. In the event fae *do* come through, I want to remind you to be cautious. The fae can be dangerous. If you have any charms or offerings to prepare, I suggest doing so. And remember that iron hurts them, so having it may be viewed as an act of aggression instead of self-defense. There is no telling how they will react. I think it is best if none of you go."

"Yes," Oliver sneered, "we already know of your fears. No reason to repeat them."

"Then you and Rebecca are still going to Stonehenge?"

"Of course."

"Perhaps we will see you there."

Rebecca said, "Not if we see you first."

Very mature, thought Luna, refusing to show irritation. The meeting didn't last much longer, but they did bring up the dual lock mechanism and it met with near-unanimous agreement—so Andy installed it and kept one key, Oliver taking the other.

The next day, October 31, saw Luna and Andy making plans for that night. Some of it was the ordinary stuff, like turning off all the lights so no one thought they would answer the door for trick-or-treating. The rest related to their impending visit to Stonehenge. Andy insisted they not bring any supposedly magic items because they didn't know what they did and couldn't control them, whereas a faerie *might* know and turn the items on the humans. They had confirmed that Oliver hadn't returned the items by the deadline, meaning Luna was now Grand Master. This was a less important result than the return of the items, but they would go after Oliver soon enough. They spent time reading about the monument again, and about legends of the fae and Samhain. They didn't know what time the fae might arrive but suspected midnight, so they packed a cooler of drinks and snacks and got dressed.

Luna wasn't wearing anything special. Thinking it better to not draw attention to herself, she had on jeans, jogging shoes, and a sweater over a t-shirt. To her surprise, Andy emerged from the bedroom wearing what could only be described as tight-fitting black leather armor, a sword at one hip. He wore a belt that seemed to be made of black rope. She had seen him in the outfit once or twice on previous Halloweens but never with the sword—and what he had previously said were knife holders had always been empty, but were now filled with blades. He also sported well-worn, matching boots and wore a silver ring she'd seen on one hand. A different unfamiliar ring was on the other hand.

"Where did you get that?" she asked, eyeing the weapon.

Smiling, he did a slow turn as if to give her a good look at the outfit, which seemed more like real armor to her than a costume. "I've had it for a long time, but never took it before. Police frown on real weapons being worn for Halloween."

"Can't imagine why," she deadpanned, coming closer and putting one hand on the hilt. "Do you think we'll need that?"

"Yes," he said, and she met his gaze, seeing he was serious.

"Is it magical? Is there anything about fae only being hurt by magical weapons?"

"I guess we'll see. You have everything else? Then let's go." Andy led her out of the flat and down the elevator to the basement parking garage, where they headed for his black Jeep.

"Why don't we take my car?" Luna asked. "It's more comfortable." It was also far nicer. She had never understood why he kept the fifteen-year-old Jeep, though he maintained it well. He could afford better and had a second vehicle, a BMW, too.

Andy shook his head. "We may need to turn off the daytime running lights to approach Stonehenge the way I intend to, without anyone seeing us."

"Can't we do that in mine?" she asked as she opened the door.

"No. All newer cars in the UK have the lights. You've always asked me why I keep this old Jeep. Now you know."

As she got in the passenger side, she said, "Just how long have you been riding around in the countryside without any lights on?"

He flashed a smile as he started the vehicle. "A long time. I told you that I've always thought Stonehenge was a portal between worlds and I might one day see something there. I used to go out there all the time without the lights running."

"You don't go anymore?"

"You would've noticed if I went, since it's a three-hour round trip. I'd given up seeing anything by then, anyway. Or at least, up until the Stonehenge Four arrived."

"I wish you'd had a camera there then."

"So do I."

The traffic diminished as they drove further west into the countryside, away from London. Using Andy's phone camera feed, Luna repeatedly checked the various cameras. Most locations were considerably less famous than Stonehenge; there, either no one had gathered, or there were just a few people who she sometimes identified as Sons of the Magi. The night vision cameras gave a good view of people who had no idea they were being watched.

Soon, though, things began to happen.

"Hey," she said, "there's something going on at one of them. It looks like a ball of light, maybe two. Yeah, it's definitely two of them, circling around the three people gathered there."

"A Will-o'-the-wisp?" Andy asked as he drove.

"Maybe. It doesn't seem like it's fake in any way."

"How are people reacting?"

"They're just watching them. They don't seem afraid."

Andy sighed. "You know a Will-o'-the-wisp is supposed to lead people away to harm. Let me know if they follow it."

"Okay. I want to check the other cameras." Most of them didn't show much, if anything, and she finally turned to Stonehenge. "We're going to have company there."

"More than Oliver and Rebecca?"

"Yeah. A lot more. I don't see them, but there are maybe two dozen people right now."

"Anything happening?"

"Doesn't seem like it."

"I have a bad feeling about this."

Luna didn't disagree and wasn't sure what to say. Nothing else changed on the cameras as they neared Stonehenge, which stood in the middle of open fields with no bushes or trees to hide behind. Andy had set up the hidden camera in a ditch where the landscapers allowed grass to grow long for wildflowers. The distance wouldn't provide much detail, but he hoped faeries would give off light and be easily visible. The full moon shone brightly across the dark sky. Only a few clouds cast deep shadows on the ground. The Jeep would be visible even after Andy turned off the lights.

As they approached on the A303 road, the monument appeared in the distance. It looked creepy in the moonlight, like something out of a painting. They saw no lights on or near it, except flashing blue police lights that gave them pause. They drove past it on the right, then bypassed a narrow access road they could've used if they were unconcerned with being seen. Instead, they continued to a traffic circle and then north. Seeing no other cars on the road now, Andy turned off the vehicle lights, but it was still easy to see where they were going. A minute later, they reached another circle and turned right again, going past the visitor center, its lights off. The access road was the main route to Stonehenge.

"How close do we go?" Luna asked. "I'm wondering where others parked."

"They're probably at the bus drop-off point, really close, and less concerned with being seen. There's a stand of trees up there, halfway to it, with a little dirt road inside—and a gate, but the lock is easy to pick. It's a bit of a hike from there but I want to keep out of sight, including from the police."

He slowed the Jeep and rolled down the windows, cool air coming in. Luna reported that the camera showed no changes—nothing supernatural. Yet. Andy inched the car along before turning left into the trees toward a steel gate. He got out and picked the lock with a speed that surprised her before returning to drive further in and park. They exited, taking a final swig of water, Andy strapping the sword to his waist.

"Are you sure that's a good idea?" Luna asked. "I mean, if the police see it, they might object."

"They'll assume it's part of a costume and not real. If what I think is about to happen *does*, the cops are the least of our problems."

Luna eyed him. "You're starting to worry me."

Andy held her gaze. "I'm sorry, but I think a host of fa-eries are about to come through Stonehenge to this world, and the results are going to be awful. I'm leaving the car unlocked, the keys inside. If something happens and I can't stay with you, I want you to run for the car, get in, and drive away. Even if you have to go without me. Do you understand? Can you do that?"

Luna felt a coldness creeping over her with every word. "I...I think so."

"You will be fine. I'm not trying to scare you."

"Okay. Okay. Let's just go and see what's happening."

Andy led her away from the Jeep and they jogged on the paved road—passing the crossing street they had ig-nored earlier, then the visitor drop-off point, which buses from the visitor center used. Most of the vehicles, includ-ing the police cars, were well past that toward the road's end, where they shouldn't be. Stonehenge lay farther still across the mostly flat, low cut green grass, away from the pollution of the roads. Reaching the first of several parked cars, they recognized Oliver's black BMW and slowed to a walk. Now Luna realized that the one van she'd seen be-longed to a TV station. No one else was here, just at the monument, where the police didn't seem to be bothering anyone—making Luna wonder if they'd just arrived.

At the street's end, a walkway veered right to pass near Stonehenge. Straight ahead, another path went toward the Heel Stone, a fifteen-foot-high rock over two hundred feet outside the stone circle. She and Andy had visited before to stand in the center of Stonehenge and gaze at the Heel Stone, which marked the place where sunrise appeared on the horizon at the summer solstice. But people could also stand at the Heel Stone at sundown and watch the sun fall through and behind Stonehenge. Two people stood at the Heel Stone now as midnight approached.

Luna couldn't yet identify a reporter or cameraman within the monument. They definitely didn't want to be on camera. She saw that someone had brought a goat. People in the past had sometimes sacrificed animals on Samhain. Surely they wouldn't, would they? Andy led her toward a point between the Heel Stone and Stonehenge, but they hadn't quite made it there when a commotion started at the monument.

"Down!" whispered Andy, and they dropped to their bellies on the cold grass inside the actual henge, or ditch, surrounding the place.

Luna watched as a soft light began to glow within the monuments. The outer circle of stones had once held stone slabs atop them, running all the way around. But many had collapsed or gone missing stones, except around the area that was considered the entrance—the side facing the Heel Stone. Inside the circle should have been five trilithons arranged in a horseshoe shape. Each trilithon was made up of two pillars with a slab across the top. The two on one side were intact, but only one on the other side was, be- cause one trilithon had fallen, the top slab and one sup- porting stone toppled. The same thing had happened to the lone trilithon at the top of the horseshoe; its stone had fallen inward to lie next to an altar stone that had been knocked out of position. The bottom of the horseshoe shape lay open in the direction of the mostly intact entrance and the Heel Stone in the distance.

Now, across the bottom of the horseshoe, a shimmering wall of blue and golden light began to glow, starting from the ground and rising to the height of the stones. It grew in brightness as if becoming more substantial, the onlookers nearby backing away in all directions. The new light made it easier to see that most attendees were in costumes with masks depicting skeletons and undead, though one seven-year-old girl was dressed as a fairy.

Andy admitted, "I've seen things on the video feed before and haven't told you, because I wasn't entirely sure they weren't human."

Luna looked at him in annoyance, trying to let that go. "Seen what?"

"A few floating balls of light, short figures moving, and once a man in a black robe walking around, not necessarily in that order. But I haven't seen a portal like that open."

Luna wasn't sure what to say about that—but if there was any doubt that a portal to another world had opened now, it ended when a small ball of white light emerged to fly above the onlookers, who gasped and murmured. A second ball joined it, then a third. All three whizzed around the stones, weaving in and out and above in widening circles.

"Will-o'-the-wisps?" Luna asked, trying to piece together fairy stories she had heard. She could make out the cameraman now, and the reporter near him. The police were standing around dumbfounded.

"I think so, yes. They are supposed to be bad luck and to lead people to their deaths."

Luna pointed at the Heel Stone. "Look!"

Andy followed her gaze. Two people stood by the stone, one of them with a ball of light before her. "Rebecca," he said. "She cast that cantrip again."

"And Oliver beside her." The ball of light made the pair easier to see, but it quickly moved away from them and toward Stonehenge, passing very near to where Luna and Andy lay in the ditch. It flew over the entrance and near the Will-o'-the-wisps that it resembled. They began to swirl around and follow the ball, which started moving back toward the Heel Stone. Intent on their pursuit, they didn't seem to notice Andy and Luna as they passed by.

"I hope she knows what she's doing," Luna whispered.

"They are fools."

Another commotion came from the portal. Something larger passed through this time, a bare-chested man with curled horns amid his long brown hair. He carried a quiver of arrows around his shoulders and a bow in one hand. From the waist down, he was a goat.

"A satyr!" whispered Luna in disbelief, as people began backing away again in fear.

"Two more coming through."

But there were more than that, some of them jumping onto the fallen sarsen stones and looking around, sniffing at the air. One began playing a merry tune on a pan flute and gesturing at the humans around them, as if to encourage them to dance and relax. At first, no one moved, but then the girl in the fairy costume broke away from her parents. She was the first to start dancing with a satyr. After a minute, the mood shifted. The girl's mother reached into a bag she held and pulled out a cupcake. They couldn't hear her words, but she clearly offered it to a satyr, who bowed and took it, eating it in one bite. Other satyrs then crowded around seeking more, which she gave, a celebratory mood evident as the satyrs hooted and howled with pleasure, causing laughter. The officers had their hands on their Tasers but hadn't drawn them, and the reporter was making the cameraman film it all after backing away for a wider shot.

A satyr pulled a treat from a pouch and offered it to one of the men. He sniffed at it and then took a small bite, as if to be polite. Seeing that nothing happened to him, a woman accepted an offered treat and ate it all in two quick bites, to the delight of the satyrs, like they were breaking bread together. Luna had heard stories of such food making all Earth fare taste like ash so that people could only consume the faerie food or die. But those present were unwary and soon half a dozen had shared the treats. Even some of the police took part.

Now the men and women began dancing in greater numbers—some by themselves, others with each other or with the satyrs, who moved everyone away from the portal and toward the altar. The reporter joined in as her cameraman backed away even further to frame the shot. More figures emerged from the doorway—short figures, with long beards and hammers on their waists or in their hands. The dwarves ignored the merrymaking and instead began to lament the state of Stonehenge, with its missing pieces and fallen stones, their gestures and body language revealing their upset. Nearly twenty came through, all inspecting the damage and gesturing like they were wondering how to fix it.

More figures arrived, this time people who looked like humans but taller, slenderer, and carrying bows and long swords. Their skin was dark, and they moved with a lithe grace that made Luna wonder if they were elves. But she was too far away to see any pointed ears or slanted eyes. She assumed that they were dark elves because nothing else matched the stories she'd read. They took up positions leaning against the stones, watching but not participating in the dancing, which was becoming increasingly frenzied.

A woman cried out that she needed to rest, but somehow she couldn't. And as Luna watched, the woman began to transform—her shoes falling off, horns appearing on her head, and a satyr ripping off her blouse and bra from her to bare her upper body to the night sky. The woman laughed, but it was the sound of madness as she helplessly danced while turning into a satyr, the faerie food she had consumed transforming her. Others began to transform as well, sometimes ripping their own shirts off, their pants and shoes splitting to accommodate the goat legs and hooves. The little girl broke free of the dancing and hid behind a standing sarsen stone, but her smile showed that she seemed to think this was a game.

"We should help," Luna said, though she had no idea how and felt too afraid to go over there.

Andy shook his head. "I don't think there's anything we can do, and I'm certain worse is going to come through. It's better to see what that is first before exposing ourselves. I don't want you doing anything but leaving anyway."

Over at the Heel Stone, Rebecca had ended her spell. The three Will-o'-the-wisps were hovering around her and Oliver without much movement.

Andy said, "I'm dying to know what's going on over there."

Luna saw the phone in Andy's hand light up, so she covered it with one hand. Then she looked at it, seeing a notification from one of the cameras. Andy unlocked it and kept an eye on their surroundings as Luna pulled up the camera feed. And there she saw at Silbury Hill that a black, yellow-eyed horse had someone on its back as it bucked, trotted, and jumped around the mound, another portal open atop the hill. The rider was a terrified-looking man who appeared to be trying to jump off but was unable, his arms flailing wildly instead of hanging on. Then the horse turned toward the hill, charged up it, and leapt back through the portal, carrying the man to Elfhame.

"My God," said Luna, watching the other people on the camera feed running away, "it took him."

"Damn Oliver," said Andy, scowling. "I knew this kind of shit might happen."

Watching the camera feed, Luna gasped again as the horse reappeared on Earth without the man and cantered down after one of the fleeing attendees. Andy turned off the phone.

"They're all dead already. And we have our own problems."

Luna shivered. These weren't Disney fairies—they were more like the those from the old stories. She kept her eyes on Stonehenge, where two satyrs suddenly leapt upon the goat someone had brought and tore into it with their teeth. The animal bleated in terror right up until they ripped its throat out. Other satyrs, including some of the transformed humans, set upon it and gorged themselves before lifting blood-covered mouths to the sky and singing. One offered something to the little girl, and Luna had the horrible impression it was the goat's heart. The girl came forward timidly, but, on seeing it, screamed.

And the scream changed everything. Several faeries flew through the portal into Stonehenge and immediately turned to the little girl in her fairy costume. She continued screaming as they whirled around her so fast that blurs of light were all that could be seen. Suddenly the girl began to lift into the air from the force of the wind they'd whipped up. Above the monument she rose, kicking and shrieking as the faeries carried her away. The spell of merriment broken, her mother yelled at them to stop and a satyr grabbed her, viciously kissing her. One of the officers pulled out a Taser and could be heard shouting orders. Others shouted back at him, likely not to fire for fear of hitting the girl. Up, up and away she rose, hundreds of feet—and then the whirling faeries around her separated and flew away. Luna gasped as the faint sight of a bundle fell from the sky, shrieking all the way down until it struck the ground with a sickening crack. The screaming ended abruptly.

One of the officers who was still human opened fire at the faeries—but missed the fleeting targets, who encircled him as he fired his Taser at them. It struck one of the elves, who fell back against a stone. As the officer began to rise into the air, another policeman pulled out a Taser and an elf leapt at him, sword swinging. It chopped off his hand as he screamed. Luna couldn't watch as the faeries dropped the other officer from a great height. He crashed onto the altar stone and didn't move again.

The cameraman began scampering toward the cars, but an elf fired an arrow that struck him through the neck. He fell twitching to the ground, his camera bouncing across the grass to lie facing the monument. Four of the dwarves ran over to him and hefted their axes high in the moonlit sky, chopping him to pieces and brandishing his limbs and head in the sky as they returned to Stonehenge.

The commotion had stopped Luna from noticing another new arrival. This one stood tall in dark leather that matched his skin, a silver crest on his chest. Short, spikey black hair topped an angular face and a jaw that seemed harsh. Several of those present snapped to attention on seeing him, creating the impression of authority.

"Oh my God," said Andy, eyes wide. "I know him."

That startled Luna. "You do? From where? I mean, what legend or drawing?"

He shook his head. "No. No, we've met before."

She didn't quite believe him. Magic had only awakened a few months earlier. "Where? When?"

Andy didn't answer at first, his face mostly blank save for a mild scowl as he stared. "A long time ago, right here."

"You're not making any sense. How is that possible?"

He looked at her sideways, then pursed his lips as if resigning himself to something. "I'm afraid I'm not who you think I am."

Her heart lurched. All those times she had wondered if she really knew him, and if he was hiding something, roared to the surface. She opened her mouth to say something when the new arrival spoke in a voice so loud they heard him clearly, even though they had been unable to make out anyone else's words.

"Greetings, one and all," he said, the voice commanding and smooth—and the elves dropped to one knee, the dwarves bowing. The satyrs grabbed everyone else and made them lie face down. "I am Vianden, Dragon Lord King of Faeburn in Elfhame, Lord of the Fae. I am pleased to see you gathered here to welcome us, for we have waited a thousand years to be reunited. But I must say that I am already disappointed. You have let this shrine to the doorway between our worlds suffer so mightily that I could easily think you never wished to see us return. And so few of you have come. Do you not respect us? Do you not love us? Do you not fear us? Perhaps I should summon my friends to rectify all this." He turned to the portal behind him and spoke words that sent a chill down Luna's spine.

"As darkness falls, so may you rise,
To see this world with burning eyes.
Hooves of flame and breath of fire,
Ride again through fen and mire.
Innocent or evil be,
Spy the chosen as you please!
Come forth my friends and be set free;
Hunt for souls to fill our need."

The sound of horses galloping thundered into being as Vianden stepped aside. A giant black horse jumped from within the portal, bearing a huge man with a helmet made of a deer skull, enormous antlers wicked in the bright moonlight. The horse's flaming yellow eyes glowed in the night—and, as it jumped over the fallen altar, flaming footprints were left behind. The rider carried a huge club with metal spikes on the end. He stopped at the top of the broken trilithon horseshoe and pulled out a great horn of bone and gold.

As he blew a tremendous blast of sound that shook the ground, nightmare horse after hideous steed leaped from within the portal to tread upon the Earth—each bearing a rider with translucent wings, or a ghostly apparition, or a humanoid creature shifting every moment from monster to human and back. Hundreds of them jumped and galloped past the leader of the pack and into the fields, leaving a trail of burning hoofprints as they wheeled in two different directions. They began to encircle the monument from a distance as if waiting for something. And then it came through the doorway—scores of huge black dogs with flaming eyes. They charged in the directions of the four compass , and the horses broke ranks to follow.

"The Wild Hunt," said Andy.

Luna nodded. Sure, she had heard of the legend, but seeing the actual creatures in the flesh was an entirely different thing. She was about to ask him about getting out of there when the reporter screamed, slugged the satyr holding her down, and started to run. But she didn't get far. As she headed for the vehicles, a rider broke from the pack and chased after her. For a moment, Luna thought the horse would trample her—but the rider never slowed as he neared and leaned over, grabbing the woman by the hair and hauling her before him, stomach down on the horse, as if she weighed nothing. The horse wheeled back toward the portal, leaping over a fallen sarsen stone before disappearing from the Earth, the reporter's shrieking ending abruptly. They were gone.

As Luna watched Vianden, the three Will-o'-the-wisps from the Heel Stone flew past her position on the ground to encircle Vianden's head, where they slowed to a hover. Luna looked back at the Heel Stone to see Oliver and Rebecca still there. Vianden looked toward the Heel Stone and began marching that way after the Will-o'-the-wisps. One of the elves followed as the others returned to lounging idly. The satyrs struck up their tune again, making people dance, and the dwarves resumed inspecting the broken monument.

But Luna no longer had eyes for them as the dragon lord came nearer, the Will-o'-the-wisps ahead of it, an elf trailing. She slunk down further in the ditch beside Andy and held her breath as the procession passed not twenty feet from them on its way to the Heel Stone. They stepped over a raised walkway and then off it to reach their destination. Rebecca curtsied, and Oliver bowed before straightening and holding aloft a small item.

Andy cursed. "I think that's the Faerie Skull from the treasure room."

Luna turned to him in alarm. "You mean the one that's supposed to control fae?"

"Stay here," whispered Andy, starting to rise.

"What?" she asked in disbelief.

"I can't let him use that."

"But Andy..."

He had already risen and started across the ground, not trying to hide his presence as he strode with one hand on his sword. Luna watched him go, unable to decide whether to stay or follow. What Andy thought he was going to do she didn't know. He was no match for the forces at work. She finally decided she had to see and hear what was happening, if nothing else. She began moving across the cold grass in a low crouch, keeping a distance from Andy and trying to move off to one side so that when anyone saw him, she might remain unseen if she stayed low enough.

"Lord Vianden," Oliver said loudly enough for her to hear, "welcome to Earth. I have here an item rumored to control your kind. In a show of good faith, I am returning it to you for destruction."

Andy stopped on hearing these words, but Rebecca saw him and pointed. "Look!"

Luna dropped to her belly. Vianden and the elf turned as the Will-o'-the-wisps suddenly swarmed Andy, who pulled out his short sword as if to threaten them. They began to shriek in pain and fly back and away, toward Luna.

"It burns. It burns!"

The elf put a hand on its sword hilt and advanced on Andy, who stood twenty feet away. That was when Vianden ordered him to stop. He himself approached Andy with growing intensity on his moonlit features, as if delighted.

"How can it be?" Vianden asked rhetorically. "How can you be here, Andier of Roir? It has been a thousand years, and yet you have hardly aged ten."

Luna gaped at the comment, especially when Andy didn't dispute it.

"Why don't you go back where you came from?" Andy replied. "This world is no place for you."

The dragon lord smiled. "But I *am* where I came from, Andier. In fact, it is you who do not belong here, Ellorian Champion. Where are you companions? All I see is a terrified girl on the grass."

Luna started as the dragon lord looked at her. The Will-o'-the-wisps descended on her as she rose to run away, but they began to swirl around her and she felt her feet leave the ground. She screamed, knowing they would drop her to her death. When she next looked at Andy, she saw him make a throwing motion. Something silver flew toward her left side, where a shriek of pain hurt her ear and she fell a few feet to the ground, the other Will-o'-the-wisps moving away from her. She landed hard and twisted one ankle, falling to her side. Not a yard away lay the Will-o'-the-wisp, which she now saw was a faerie like the ones of Disney fame—a three-inch female in a tight green outfit, large wings spread out on the ground, with one broken. The light shining from her midsection was dimming because Andy's throwing knife had pierced her through. Moments later, the faerie died. A puff of green smoke rose from her and headed for the portal, into which it disappeared.

"So you care for this one," Vianden said, amused. "She won't get far. Why don't you come join us? I believe two of your kind were about to pledge their loyalty."

Andy said, "Oliver speaks for no one on this world."

Vianden turned and began approaching the Heel Stone again. "Perhaps I shall change that."

Andy glanced over at Luna and seemed to mouth a question as to whether she was alright. She nodded despite the ankle. Part of her wanted to crawl away after the implied threat against her. Instead, she took the nearby knife. Iron could hurt fairies, the legends said. If that was true—and it seemed to be, from the way they had reacted a couple of times—she needed to get to the car. She had no idea how much iron was in a car, but there had to be enough in the frame to keep a faerie out. She'd never manage to crawl so far, but at least she was armed.

While the dragon lord returned to Oliver and Rebecca at the Heel Stone, the elf did not, blocking the way so that Andy could not bypass him. Luna wondered why Andy just didn't go around him, but he apparently intended to go through him.

"Step aside, dark elf," said Andy.

In response, the elf drew a sword. Vianden turned at the sound and said with humor in his voice, "Kill him."

So quickly she hardly saw it, Andy threw a knife underhanded with his left hand—and was drawing his sword and charging before the blade struck the elf's shoulder. The elf grunted and pulled it out, inexpertly flinging it back. Andy caught it on his own blade and knocked it aside. Then their swords clanged in the night air. At the sound, the satyrs, elves, and dwarves began to close in. They would soon be upon her, but there was no escaping them now. She turned back to see Andy expertly parrying aside the elf's blows. She only knew his own strikes were landing because the elf grunted at each one. Then Andy plunged his sword through the elf's belly. Luna lay gaping at his display of sword-mastery as he pushed back the dead elf. It fell to the ground and lay unmoving. Only then did Andy fall, too, and Luna realized he was wounded.

"Somehow I knew you would triumph, Andier," said the dragon lord, amused. He turned back to Oliver and Rebecca. "You I shall make King of England if you swear fealty to me. And she will be your queen."

Oliver bowed his head. "Thank you, Your Majesty."

"But you must earn it first. We have much to discuss, but tonight is for celebration. Give me your arm."

Oliver hesitated but then extended his right hand. Vianden grabbed his bicep and spoke words Luna didn't hear. A burst of light appeared, and Oliver gasped in pain. Vianden let go of him and turned to Rebecca, who timidly extended her own arm. While this was happening, Luna saw a soft glow briefly appear around Andy, who began to rise.

"You will bear the Mark of the Dragon Lord," said Vianden, casting the spell on Rebecca, too. "No fae will hurt you."

Rebecca nervously asked, "Are you really a dragon?"

Luna didn't hear his answer because the approaching elves, dwarves, and satyrs had reached her. Holding what looked like a cupcake in one hand, a satyr painfully grabbed her arm and yanked her to her feet. She tried to keep weight off her injured ankle as she swung the knife in her other hand. There was no way this beast would force her to eat that food and turn her into one of them. The knife struck home, buried in its bare chest, blood already dripping from the wound. A sound somewhere between a human moan and a goat's bleat came from the satyr before it let go of her and fell dead, taking the knife with it. Luna fell to one knee and heard another grunt of pain above her. Then an elf dropped dead beside her, a knife sticking from its chest. Luna looked over to Andy and saw him throwing another even as an elf closer to her also collapsed. The blade Andy had just thrown struck a satyr in the leg and it stumbled away.

Suddenly a huge figure appeared behind Andy... and Luna realized Viaden had transformed into an enormous black dragon with a silver crest, wings outstretched to cast shadows on the Heel Stone, Oliver, and Rebecca. She stared in awe, wondering if he was going to breathe fire all over them or devour Andy—who turned and threw a knife, not at the dragon, but at Oliver. The blade hit his hand, which he yanked back with a yell, dropping something.

The Fairie Skull, Luna realized. If Andy could get it and it worked, he could control the fae.

"Take them to Elfhame." The dragon's booming voice startled Luna. Vianden launched himself into the air with powerful thrusts that made Luna shield her eyes until someone yanked her to her feet again and began pulling her toward the portal.

"No!" yelled Andy, starting toward her—but then he whirled around and ran toward Oliver, his bloody sword in one hand. For all his cockiness, Oliver was no match for this onslaught and swiftly backed away with Rebecca, nearly falling over in his haste. Luna struggled to see what was happening as an elf pulled at her. She purposely went limp so they'd have to drag her—but then someone picked up her legs as she kicked at them, trying to slow this down, her ankle badly hurting from the motion. She heard Andy's voice ring out.

"Fae of Elfhame," he yelled, holding something aloft, "I command you to stop."

But the ones carrying Luna didn't obey. Those closer to Andy, mostly elves and dwarves, had stopped. He ordered them to stop the others and began sprinting closer, likely hoping the Faerie Skull would get close enough to control the fae carrying Luna. But then a gunshot rang out. Two more, and Andy fell to the ground as Luna screamed. She heard a soft humming sound as the gold and blue light grew brighter. She looked up in horror as the portal to Elfhame loomed before her.

"Welcome home," sneered one of the elves. Then they passed through it and left the Earth behind.

———— • • • ————

At the same moment he saw Luna disappear through the portal, Andier felt the power of the Trinity Ring wash over him, the bullet wound in his leg healing completely. He had avoided using the ring for the past ten years he'd been trapped on Earth without magic, because Eriana wasn't around to replenish the healing spells in it. Now two of the three spells were gone. To one side stood Oliver, brandishing the gun that had shot him and advancing. He apparently wasn't that good a shot, having taken three bullets to hit Andier only once, and in the leg. The Faerie Skull lay on the ground several strides away, having bounced across the low grass when Andier had dropped it. Could he still control the fae nearby if he wasn't holding it?

"Stop him," he commanded, pointing toward Oliver.

The elves, dwarves, and two satyrs obeyed, striding toward a startled Oliver, who pointed the gun at them.

"You are not to harm me!" Oliver shouted, raising up his sleeve to show the Mark of the Dragon Lord. But the fae didn't stop. Andier knew that stopping his advancement and hurting him weren't the same thing. And Oliver didn't have enough bullets to kill them all. And would Vianden be pleased?

Andier rose and stepped toward the Faerie Skull. Then an arrow whizzed past his head, and two more struck the earth near the skull. He looked toward Stonehenge and saw a dozen satyrs and a few elves advancing on him. More arrows flew and he barely dodged them. The skull was so close, but they knew what he wanted and were already aiming at it. Cursing, Andier backed away, scanning the scene. Without the skull, he stood no chance. In the distance, in the opposite direction to his Jeep, he saw Vianden's huge body in the bright, moonlit sky, flying away. Below him, the Wild Hunt was returning, their fiery eyes and burning hoof prints lighting up the night. Andier had already decided to run for his Jeep when two more arrows flew at him and he rolled to the ground and onto his feet again. More gunshots rang out, and he took off at a sprint. He would have to rescue Luna another day.

He had a head start on those fae he didn't control. And he knew they'd been commanded to capture him alive, which would give him an advantage if he had to fight, since he could kill and they wouldn't. But the moment they caught him, more would surround him and it would be over. The Jeep was his only chance, especially if the iron in it kept them at bay.

He regretfully sprinted past police cars and the TV truck, since he didn't have the keys. Hotwiring a car was one of the many skills he'd picked up since arriving in the English countryside a decade earlier, but many newer vehicles were impossible to hotwire if they had a key fob and he wasn't prepared with an RFID booster. The one safe bet was his Jeep, if he could reach it. The way seemed impossibly long, but everyone was on foot and he was a fast runner who kept himself in excellent shape.

He ran past the cars belonging to Oliver and the other civilians, seldom looking back because it would only slow him down. But the dwarves were easily left behind—and the satyrs were struggling, too, their gait as unnatural as their bodies and inhibiting their speed. Only the dark elves kept up with him, but they weren't gaining.

Andier reached the tree grove and leapt over the steel gate he hadn't locked before. Another arrow whizzed past him, and then he was safe beyond the trees. He leaped into the driver's side, tossed the sword on the passenger side, and slammed his hand on the lock. He pressed a button and the Jeep revved. Something banged the back of the car and then he heard screams behind him.

"It burns!" the elves shrieked. "What evil wagon is this?"

Andier smiled in grim satisfaction. Then he put the car in reverse. They probably bad no idea what he was about to do as he stomped on the gas.

"Welcome to modern Earth, motherfuckers," he yelled as he ran over them. The Jeep bounced over their bodies as they screamed, either from being crushed or the iron underside—he didn't care which. The fae were quick studies—others jumped out of the way until he swerved to hit more of them and bashed open the steel gate onto the road. He threw the car in gear and stomped on the gas, peeling out onto the asphalt and charging toward Stonehenge. The stragglers hadn't seen him run over the others and he plowed through a couple of satyrs, windshield smashing from the impact as he purposely left the road to hit more of them. Then he was clear, careening across the grass toward the stone circle. More fae fired arrows at the Jeep, and he finally decided to turn on the headlights and roof's light bar to blind them. They put up their hands to shield their eyes, and he plowed through the elves and dwarves he had previously controlled with the Faerie Skull.

He heard more gunshots as Oliver fired at him, and decided it was time to go. The thought of driving through the portal flashed into his mind, but he'd never get the Jeep through and around the remaining stones to do it, and there was no telling what lay on the other side other than a bunch of fae.

Andier drove back onto the road to London, still scanning the area. And that's how he saw the leader of the Wild Hunt coming after him as the rest of the pack returned to Stonehenge. They began leaping back through the portal, each rider with one or more humans thrown across the saddle before them. Then Andier went over a hill and lost sight of them. In his rearview mirror, the leader charged after him, keeping pace on its supernatural hooves even as Andier reached higher and higher speeds.

A chaos of other cars filled the roads. Whether due to the passage of the Wild Hunt or the sight of Vianden, who was now breathing fire on whole streets of homes and setting them ablaze in the moonlight, the light traffic was in disarray. Some cars had stopped on the highway in haphazard positions. One had turned over on the grass. Two had crashed headfirst, with one of them still burning. Some cars were intact and had pulled over. Arrivals that Andier figured were more recent were pointing at Vianden and taking cellphone videos. Other people were running across the fields in panic. Andier expertly weaved his Jeep through the obstacles, narrowly missing vehicles as he swerved around them into oncoming traffic and then back into his lane. All the while, the Wild Hunt leader came on behind him.

Andier put his sword on his lap as the obstacles cleared. No cars would come from behind, and he'd been gaining on the taillights of those ahead in his lane. Now he slowed, giving himself room and knowing he would not outrun the beast coming for him. It gained rapidly now, coming up the left side—the wrong side, the side where he wasn't. He was about to slam the side of the car into it when it had the same idea, the horse colliding with him and whinnying as if in pain. The car jolted right and he struggled to bring it back in line, purposely slamming it into the horse again as he did so. It ran into the field and then returned, its rider swinging a huge, spiked club that smashed into the roof and crushed it down.

To do what he was thinking, he'd have to get them on the other side of the Jeep. He pressed the button to roll down the windows before the car took too much damage for them to work. The left one only went down halfway, but it was enough. He pulled a knife from within his armor as the rider smashed the other side of the windshield. Andier threw the knife out the window and struck the horse, which moved away, bucking wildly as if trying to dislodge it before the rider regained control.

Now they were behind the car and approaching the driver's side. Andier lifted his sword with his right hand, putting the blade on top of the door. The back window smashed in a shower of glass as the galloping horse came nearer, its rider swinging again at the roof and plunging downward. Andier knew that the same blow over his head would have connected with his skull. Then the horse's chest was right beside the window and Andier rammed the

sword outward as hard as he could. The blade sliced clean-
ly into the horse's chest and it squealed in pain. Then the
sword was torn from Andier's hand as the beast plunged
headfirst into the ground, throwing the rider through the
air, where he tumbled, the antlers on his skull helmet
breaking as he rolled. Andier slammed on the breaks and
skidded to a stop, then threw the Jeep into reverse and
roared up beside the rider, hardly stopping the car before
leaping out.

With a knife in each hand, he ran up to the fallen
horseman and stopped. One of the broken antlers had
punctured his chest and he lay panting, blood gushing out
of his nose and mouth. He wasn't long for this world, a
world in which he didn't belong. Andier felt no sympathy.
He had battled too many monsters, stopped too many evil
men, and fended off too many that wanted him dead or
worse. Death came with the territory. When someone innocent, like that little girl back at Stonehenge, was killed,
then he felt sorrow. But even then, he felt it later, not in
the heat of battle, where sentiments got men killed. Whatever this rider was, the hate-filled glare in his dying eyes
told Andier what he needed to know—that the world was
better off without him. He wasn't one to leave a soon-to-
be-dead enemy behind. Something could always heal them.
The closest thing to mercy he had was cutting the rider's
throat to end his suffering, and watching him bleed out.

Then Andier took the helmet of deer antlers and gathered up some of the broken bits, tossing them in the Jeep.
He also took the great horn of bone and gold. The rider
himself didn't seem special, but he took the huge club, too.
Then he returned to the dead horse and pulled the sword
from its chest, finding the knife still lodged in its side.
With Soliander's magical sword of soclarin ore, he hacked
at each hoof until it came off. He carried the hooves back
to the Jeep and threw them inside, then grabbed a plastic

bag and returned to gouge out the horse's eyes. He also cut the heart from the beast and dropped it in the cooler with the eyes. He didn't know if any of these things might be useful as magic items or for spells, but being prepared had its advantages.

Satisfied with his handiwork, Andier went back to his Jeep. He'd need another vehicle to avoid suspicion, so he turned around and drove back to the area where all the damaged cars were. People were still milling around, so he kept going until he found an intact one that was abandoned and undamaged. A quick look inside showed that the key fob was there. He unloaded everything from his Jeep, then removed the license plates. There wasn't much he could do about the VIN number, but he would be disappearing anyway. He had no friends except from the Sons of the Magi, and no family. Only Luna, and she was gone. No one would be filing a missing person's report or looking for him except Oliver.

Andier of Roir drove off into the night for London, intending to break into the treasure room and clean it out in its entirety.

And the time to contact the Stonehenge Four had come.

CHAPTER TWENTY-ONE

A NEW HOME

Special Agent Kira Mori stared at the video as it played for the fifth time, her partner Special Agent Wade Carter beside her. This was the kind of footage that took a while to digest because it showed so much of great importance. And all of it was beyond the ordinary. It wasn't the actions, though the scene did end with an overt spell. Still, she had seen those recently. Everyone had. No, the conversation was the stunner.

At Jack's apartment, she had seen the laptop and the login info on the fridge, but she'd left it to the techs because Jack had walked in. And now the techs had seen the contents Jack and his lawyer had told her about. There was a log of Jack's activities and what had happened at the apartment, when "Soliander" kidnapped "Eriana" while Jack was there. Security footage showed the man take her wrist, speak a word, and begin to vanish as Jack ran into the room and dived at them, yelling for them to stop. The video ended shortly afterward. It also revealed that Eriana and Erin Jennings were the same person.

"Well," Kira began, mystified, "we know Jack isn't the one who kidnapped her."

"Yeah, no shit. Need to get this Soliander's face on every news channel. This guy sounds dangerous, probably a lunatic. He was talking about laying waste to kingdoms and cities. He mentioned Merlin."

That was definitely odd. The name Merlin had come up often lately, only because he was the only supposed wizard from Earth's past. And with magic turning up, people talked about new Merlins appearing any day. Apparently, one already had. But in the video, they talked of Merlin like he was real.

Kira said, "And the Ellorian Champions were mentioned, and something about imposters. My impression is that the Stonehenge Four are the imposters, whatever that means."

"I wrote down those other names. Korrin and Andier. Lorian, Zoran. Everon. She said something about this guy Soliander attacking Lorian and Matt before. And something about a Dragon Gate in Honyn."

Kira shook her head. "No, *on* Honyn, not in. He said something about a thousand worlds, and leaving this planet without her a second time—that he can't do it, so he took her with him in this video. Honyn is another planet. This is bizarre."

"Yeah, but these days anything seems possible. Certainly, we won't find her if she's not on Earth." He shook his head. "I can't believe that sentence just came out of my mouth."

"The other big thing is that this Soliander guy was after the Stonehenge Four. Jennings asked whether he would have killed or immobilized them if he'd found them here. And it makes you wonder how he was able to track them. Jack doesn't seem to be one of the people he was after, but it's hard to tell."

Carter said, "That would explain why we can't find them. They might be hiding from this guy. Here we thought they were perpetrators of something—but it's starting to look like they're victims, or intended victims. Kill or immobilize. There's a choice you don't hear every day. She obviously knew this guy."

Kira nodded, having recognized that the two in the video appeared to love each other. Or had. "Maybe all of this is why Jack quit his job, to be harder to find."

"It could also explain why they've been looking at real estate. Do you think they're trying to find somewhere to hide? Somewhere that isn't a hotel room?"

"Yes. To hide from the media. Maybe us. From this Soliander. And it's also probably why he's not telling us anything." She looked at her partner soberly. "I think they might need our help."

A knock on the door interrupted them, and she turned to see her superior wearing an expression she couldn't read. "You're not gonna believe this. Erin Jennings just walked in the front door."

———— ••• ————

When the portal to Jack's apartment disappeared, leaving Eriana standing beside Rognir, she couldn't help thinking Soliander had kidnapped her the last time she'd been here. But she brushed that aside and went looking for Jack, eager to see him. She'd last seen him charging into the room and diving at Soliander. That was brave. Foolish, but brave. The least she could do was reassure him that she was alright. But he wasn't there.

In fact, the place seemed "off" somehow. She had been here several times, and her memory tipped her off. A lamp had been moved a few inches, another turned a different way. The couch pillows were uncharacteristically organized. iPhone cables had been neatly coiled. They had put two similar pictures of the Washington Nationals back on the walls, but each in the other's place. It was as if the place had been disturbed and then someone other than Jack had attempted to restore order. Either that, or he'd changed his mind about a bunch of little things.

"What do you think that means?" Rognir asked, when she said something about it.

Opening more and more cabinets, she said, "I don't know. My purse was here and I'm not seeing it. Help me look."

They searched the kitchen, living room, hall bath, Jack's bathroom, and the master bath. There was no sign of it. The dwarf kept stopping to gawk out the window, prompting her to explain things like cars and phones, but she avoided turning on a TV, despite his curiosity. Her missing purse meant no car keys, no money or credit cards, and no smartphone. Jack's laptop also appeared to be gone. She had no way to contact him and belatedly realized she needed to memorize his phone number.

"So what do we do?" Rognir asked, sitting on the couch. "This furniture is wonderful."

Eriana smiled as he examined it. "I'm thinking. If we leave the apartment, we should lock it, but then we can't get back in. Your clothes are more conspicuous than my robe, which I can pass off as a dress if I can borrow a belt from Jack. Take off the tunic. The undershirt is not the style here, but it'll do. Your leather pants and boots might pass. No carrying around the sack of armor or weapons. And we need to protect those keystones, after all the trouble we went through to create them."

"Agree. But not even a knife?"

"Not even a knife. No one here is armed that way, and you'll just get shot by overzealous police."

"Crossbows or longbows?"

She opened her mouth, then shut it. Explaining guns could come later. "I need to call Quincy, Ryan's attorney, but I'll have to find a phone and a computer to look him up. Can you stay here? Then I can leave but not lock up. If I'm unsuccessful, we can stay the night and have food. I know you probably want to play around with stuff." She looked at the TV and sighed. "Okay, look, I'm going to turn this on and put on a news channel so you can see what's going on in the world. Just let it play, absorb what you can, but otherwise don't touch it."

"Sure, lass."

She set him up with something to watch and got herself ready, then stepped outside. It took an hour to walk to the nearest library after asking multiple people where it was. She didn't have a library card or PIN to access a computer, but she asked a teenage girl to look up Quincy's number for her. Then she found a phone and called him, learning that Jack was in jail for kidnapping her. She sighed, not blaming her husband for reporting her missing. If she'd thought of that, she might've had Jack email or text him from her phone. After talking it over with Quincy, they agreed on a plan.

An hour later, after updating Rognir and leaving him glued to the TV, the two of them walked into the building where Jack was being held. Eriana had already called her husband to put him at ease during a tough conversation for all the dancing around the truth she'd had to do. She would have to be honest with him soon, but first she had other issues to deal with. Something about her old life intruding on her new had pushed thoughts of him from her mind. Now she felt a clash of worlds and felt certain that relationship might not survive the truth.

After talking to her husband, she'd called her private investigator, asking him to catch a flight to Maryland immediately because she needed him. Telling him the truth was another conversation she wasn't looking forward to having, but he would adapt better than her husband, she thought. She wasn't really prepared for either conversation, having long since stopped thinking it would ever be needed. Even now, she didn't have time to worry about it.

Now it was time to free Jack, but Quincy had warned her about the video of Soliander taking her and that they might need to answer some hard questions. If she had learned anything from Andier, it was to play a situation by ear—so they soon met Special Agent Mori and her partner Carter in a meeting room with Quincy beside her in a suit. The mahogany table was bare except for two sealed water bottles for her and the lawyer, and a notepad for each agent. A TV hung on one wall.

As she sat, Special Agent Mori said in greeting, "Mrs. Jennings. Or should I call you Eriana?"

Not reacting to the revelation, she replied, "Erin, please."

"Has your attorney told you we have a warrant for your arrest?"

Eriana was expecting this and was prepared. "Yes, but for what? You claimed a security guard said I did something to him."

"He says you knocked him unconscious by touching his arm."

Smiling, Eriana asked, "Sounds hard to believe, doesn't it?"

"Lots of things don't sound that hard to believe any more, Mrs. Jennings."

"Is there proof? A witness? Any history of me doing this?"

Special Agent Mori frowned, and when she dodged the questions, Eriana knew this wouldn't go far. "You were seen walking out with Anna Sumner, who was under arrest."

"How was I supposed to know that? She wasn't wearing handcuffs or anything that would've tipped me off."

"Her arrest was all over the news."

Quincy spoke up. "You can't prove she knew that."

Folding her arms, Special Agent Mori added, "Maybe you weren't aware because you were spending all your time at the hospital. Footage shows you waiting around day after day. You knew she would go back there after disappearing days earlier."

"Everybody knew that from the news she'd disappeared and reappeared on the highway before that."

Special Agent Mori changed subjects and Eriana knew another angle had closed. "What is your relationship with her?"

"Personal."

Arching an eyebrow, Special Agent Mori asked, "Care to be more specific?"

"No."

"Okay. Okay. Let's try something else. When you arrived today, you said Mr. Riley had nothing to do with your recent disappearance. I just want to be clear. Are you claiming no one kidnapped you or held you against your will?"

"Jack didn't."

Special Agent Mori sighed. "Why don't we both cut the crap?" She turned on a TV and played the entire video of Soliander abducting her. "Who is this abducting you?"

Seeing the video again saddened Eriana, and she hoped the authorities weren't planning to release it. They would probably *do* it in order to find Soliander, but it would make her famous. Or infamous. "An old friend of mine. And as you can see, I am free."

"But you didn't want to go with him."

"You cannot tell that from the video. I said nothing about refusing."

"Where is this Soliander now?"

"I don't know."

"Where did he take you?"

Although they had talked about other planets on the video, Eriana wasn't going to admit it and gave a half-truth. "I'm not entirely sure."

"How did you get back?"

"The same way I left, a spell."

Special Agent Mori held her gaze. "Are you a wizard? A witch?"

"I am not."

"How do I know you didn't just cast yourself back from wherever you were?"

"If I could do that, I would have appeared in Jack's cell, then disappeared with him. Instead, I'm sitting here talking to you. I would've done the same with Anna at the hospital, and yet I walked out the door. As that video shows, Jack was not involved. He is a friend, and I would like to see him released immediately."

Quincy added, "You have no case, and you know that you don't."

Special Agent Mori said, "Oh, don't worry, Jack will be free to go. We're processing him now. But there are bigger concerns here, so I'm hoping you'll cooperate. We are not your enemy, Mrs. Jennings, or Mr. Riley's. If anything, based on the conversation on that video, the Stonehenge Four—and I assume you know who I mean—have an enemy in this friend of yours, Soliander. And it seems that you and they might be in need of our assistance."

That surprised Eriana. But she wasn't interested in training the FBI anytime soon. There were things far bigger than them going on, and they wouldn't understand or accept any of those anytime soon. Keeping them from snooping might stop things getting out of hand more than they already were. But the idea of them not bothering the new Champions held great appeal, so maybe there was a path forward.

Eriana said, "Well, if you're offering help, you can start by getting the media off their backs."

"Freedom of the Press. There's nothing we can do about that."

"Fair enough, but bullets aren't going to stop a wizard like Soliander—so, while I appreciate the offer, I don't see how there's anything you can do. Actually, no. You can return all the items you seized from my home in Florida. You know the ones I mean."

Special Agent Mori shook her head. "We have a mandate to confiscate all magical items."

Then it was good she didn't know about the keystones Rognir had with him at Jack's. "You know they are magical? Just because I collect items rumored to be magical doesn't mean any of them *are*."

The agent smiled. "After what I saw on that video, we're assuming they are. You know a wizard and apparently have for some time. That's enough for us to hold onto them. That goes for the amulet we found in your room, too."

Eriana frowned. "You have no reason to believe that is magical. I have other jewelry, a purse, a phone. Are you claiming every last thing I own is magical?"

"No, but that one was in a special case and wrapped the same way the artifacts of yours are, and so we assume it is the same."

Eriana stifled annoyance. That was a good point she couldn't counter. But she wouldn't really need the Corethian Amulet anytime soon. She'd already reached the god of Earth.

"Well, then I don't think we have anything more to discuss. Quincy."

They rose to go, and Special Agent Mori said, "Okay for now. But we'll be in touch. We have a lot of questions for you, Mrs. Jennings. You're planning to stay in the area?"

"You can reach me through my attorney."

It took a few minutes to get her things, minus the amulet, which Eriana wondered how to get back from the FBI. Some of her powers had returned—enough to knock out a handful of people—but that approach would just heighten scrutiny on her and the others. She would have to find another way. Maybe when Matt returned, or if Lorian arrived, they could use magic to reacquire the amulet or the magic items the FBI had confiscated. She wasn't sure what to make of Special Agent Mori except that having a friend in the FBI was better than an enemy. They would discuss what to tell the FBI once they were all together. Certainly, the new Champions needed fewer problems. Now it was time to assume her role as a matriarch to them, keeping both herself and everyone else out of trouble, even if she had to use her fast-returning powers to do it.

Jack felt uneasy as he drove Eric, Anna, Ryan, and Matt from his apartment to the new Briardale estate. If someone summoned them on a quest, all four of them would return to this stretch of Route 28. The trip was only fifteen minutes long, and once they were there, this danger would end. Rognir would soon make progress on the Home Rings, so maybe they would even be free to travel soon.

Less than a day had passed since Eriana and Quincy had freed him from the FBI. Being fingerprinted was one of many experiences he never expected, the black ink hard to remove with this weird, sandy-feeling cleaner goo they'd given him. His cell had at least been clean and empty of others. For the first time, he had questioned his role in everything, his life upended and in peril in various ways. He still wanted to help but now questioned the cost. Once they got the estate set up with the Home Rings, would he really still be needed? Their parents now knew, and so di Quincy, Daniel, and Eriana.

But he could never walk away. Not after what he'd seen. Curiosity about what was going on next would drive him crazy, though yet hanging around to find out might cost him dearly. He stifled his misgivings and continued bringing them up to speed on what had happened with the FBI and the estate, which the LaRue family had now purchased. The main house had five bedrooms, with another three in the guest house, and there was a room above the stables. Some furniture had been ordered, with a few temporary furnishings already set up. Except for Eric, their parents had packed up a lot of their belongings for them and would come to the house for a kind of reunion. Jack had done the same for Eric. There was a lot to do, but things were moving forward.

"What about the Home Rings?" Eric asked. "How are they coming along?"

Jack slowed down and turned off the road into a wide driveway, two black steel gates barring the entrance. As he rolled down the window and punched in the security code, he said, "We're trying to get the stone Rognir wants for it—but, like a lot of things, we can't just go get it the same day. We've ordered it, though. I forget the delivery date, but it's coming. We were thinking of putting them in the stables, each one inside a stall. They can be on platforms like you wanted, so we can easily roll them out and up into a truck. We can also store your gear in the stalls."

Ryan said, "Gotta keep the Rings away from the horses though, so we don't scare them when we return."

"The barn is L-shaped, so we can reserve one area at the end for that."

"I'm excited," said Anna, looking out the front window.

"We paid more money to get the estate immediately. Technically it will take another week or two, but the previous owners moved out long ago and they've agreed to let us rent it for a month while we finalized the paperwork."

Jack gave a running commentary as they drove down the driveway between two wide fields sparsely dotted with trees. One field, to the right, had a pond with a nearby gazebo and a walkway to the main house—which was two stories high and painted yellow with white trim. A covered porch ran around it, a flower garden with manicured bushes hugging it. To the left stood the blue and white house, which Jack called a guest house—but it was the original home, nearly a hundred years old, built long before the newer one two decades ago. It stood a bit closer to the road and had a two garage spaces to the main house's three. The driveway ran between the houses to and around the stables, which had a handful of parking spots.

The stables were a red, two story, building with a silver roof. They had left most of the upper floor empty for storage, and just to air it out. To the left of them stood a matching indoor riding ring, a covered archway running between the buildings for protection from bad weather. Further to the left were the outdoor riding rings, one of which already had several jumps set up. Typical horse enclosures could be seen in the numerous fields.

Aside from catching up with Eriana and Rognir, the new Champions made plans, including arguing over who was taking which room. They offered Anna and then Eriana the master suite, but the two women decided to take the guest house together. Eriana insisted on giving her protégé its master bedroom. With Jack as the estate's caretaker, everyone agreed he should take the main house's master suite, which flattered him. Eric and Ryan took two bedrooms on the upper floor, but Matt wanted to use a basement room because it was next to a room he would use for studying. While Eriana and Rognir had brought a few supplies to Earth with them, the fun for Matt began in earnest when new arrivals appeared in Jack's apartment and he drove them over.

Everyone expected Lorian and Taryn, who had changed into the Earth clothes bought for them. But neither Prince Dari nor the dragon Jolian, in human form, had been anticipated. Borrowed jackets had hidden their conspicuous attire long enough to get them from the apartment to the van. Once they reached the house, the sight of an elf in jeans and a t-shirt was almost as odd to everyone as that of a dwarf in shorts and flip-flops, Rognir having made himself at home. Now it was Lorian's turn to start gawking at items like the TV or microwave when someone warmed up water for his tea. Taryn did little more than cock an eyebrow, while Jolian frowned as if she disapproved. Sensing that no one was in the mood for serious talk, they enjoyed a night of just hanging out together.

Jack wouldn't accept that Jolian was really a dragon until darkness had fallen and they'd all stepped outside. They'd talked about the dangers of Jolian flying around during the day and ruled it out unless absolutely necessary. Even at night, she might be seen or, worse yet, have an encounter with planes, helicopters, or even drones—all items she needed to understand before flying. With that in mind, she morphed into a dragon now behind the stables. They hadn't brought a saddle, so when she suggested taking Jack for a quick look around the area, he declined, not ready for that. Instead, she took Ryan, and they were gone long enough that everyone went back inside.

Despite being present, Prince Dari did not join in the camaraderie, choosing to spend his time watching the TV beside Lorian. His offered explanation for coming was that the Kingdom of Andor was prepared to lend considerable aid if needed and he would act as liaison. Jack had heard only a little about the man and sensed tension between him and everyone else, like Dari was the odd one out. Jack tried to befriend him by helping the one-handed man do things like open a bottle of beer, and he seemed to lighten up a little.

To Jack's surprise, Matt looked uncomfortable, his eyes on Jolian after she returned with Ryan. He didn't know what to make of it as Matt followed Lorian into the kitchen, then excused himself downstairs. Minutes later, Lorian whispered something to Jolian, who went after Matt. Curious, Jack was tempted to sneak down to see what the wizard and dragon were up to, but he decided that being the newly appointed caretaker of Briardale still didn't entitle him to know *everything* going on. He settled back into his chair and waited for them to return.

Matt waited nervously for Jolian. Doing this to Lorian had been one thing, but a powerful red dragon, with her own magic, was far more formidable. He knew it would work on her because Soliander had enslaved her brother before—an enslavement that only ended when Ryan smashed his sword, made of soclarin ore, over the slave orb and broke it into three pieces. Those were the same three pieces Matt had just retrieved with Jolian's help. She would know at once what this was, so he had thought hard about how to get her to look into the slave orb. He wasn't sure what failure would mean. It wasn't like she would kill him, but he'd have a lot of explaining to do.

When asked why she was on Earth, Lorian explained that it was his idea. A dragon might be very beneficial on Earth, and with all the Honyn dragons banished and unfriendly anyway, the obvious choice had been one with whom they were on good terms. So he had gone to Rovell to ask Jolian, who was the first of potentially quite a few who would come if needed. He hadn't asked the dragons of

Elloria because he didn't really know them and Taryn, who did, had been here. Lorian had learned about Matt's recent mission with her right before Matt used the Orbs of Dominion on him.

But Matt worried that Jolian would accidentally reveal their mission to get the slave orb shards. Almost as bad was her ignorance that they weren't the real Ellorian Champions. Since Jolian had been used to hearing them use their real names, she'd hadn't reacted to that here on Earth, but he had seen her questioning looks grow in frequency and intensity as the group talked in such as a way that made it clear what their identities really were. Her friends seemed to have forgotten that she didn't know. So he had decided to kill two birds with one stone. He would tell her the truth about that to put her at ease. And he would make her keep quiet about their mission. If handled right, she wouldn't be an issue.

Now he stood in his bare study, a built-in, oak bookcase with doors on the bottom the only furnishing. Reaching into the Bag of Desires Lorian had given him, he felt the cold slave orb first. Retrieving it, he placed it on its stand inside one cabinet. Next, he took out the warmer master orb in its velvet bag and laid it on the bookshelf in plain sight, still inside the bag. He put his hand in long enough to turn it on, the dark glass glowing with a golden sheen before he covered it with the bag again. He looked at the slave orb to confirm that it was also on, a slight silver sheen on it. Then he closed the cabinet to hide it.

He heard soft footsteps descending the carpet runner atop the wooden stairs, so he stepped out of the lit room to see Jolian reaching the bottom. Her eyes glanced at the shields, bows, and other items in the otherwise empty rec room. Then she saw him and came over.

He smiled. "Jolian, I am glad to see you here on Earth, though I was not expecting it."

"This world is fascinating."

"It will take some getting used to." Matt turned back into the office, and she followed. "I wanted to remind you of your promise not to tell the others of our mission to collect the Orb of Dominion shards. I haven't had a chance to tell them and would rather they hear it from me."

"I remember. Lorian reminded me as well. Is this it?" She indicated the velvet bag.

"Yes. I'm afraid that it reformed while in Lorian's possession. I will have to ask him how, as the pieces should have remained wrapped and separate."

Jolian nodded, eyes on the bag. "So, this is what enslaved my brother."

"Yes. I need to put it away, still in the bag. There's a stand in that cabinet, to one side of you, behind the doors. Would you grab it for me?"

She turned without a word and as she knelt, her hands reaching for the knobs, Matt discreetly slipped the velvet bag back from the master Orb of Dominion beside him. When she opened the cabinet, he looked into the master, seeing her face reflected in it, now that her eyes were on the slave orb.

"Obey and serve," he said. "My will be yours."

Jolian's alarmed expression relaxed. "My will is yours."

Matt breathed a sigh of relief, but noticed that he felt depressed and hollow, his victory feeling like defeat. He tried to shake it off but knew that wouldn't work. He still felt guilt every time he looked at Lorian; the dragon would be no better.

"Please close the door," he said, "and stand up. I'm sorry for doing this but, I need to be sure you won't say anything. You are free to act as you normally will, but if I want you to do something, you will agree to, though I still want you to voice any objections."

Jolian was looking at him with a sadness in her eyes. "I understand and will do as you ask." After hesitating, she remarked in disappointment, "I had thought better of you, Matt Sorenson."

He flushed and looked down. "So had I. If anyone asks what we were talking about, it was your help training me in magic."

"And is this something you want?"

"If you're able to."

"I am."

"Thank you. Please go upstairs. I'll be right there."

After she left, Matt quickly put the items back in the magic bag because it was the easiest way to hide them. He just had to keep Taryn from going through his clothes. A little tired of this new life of his and wanting her comfort, he called her to come down to him. They were soon together on the inflatable queen mattress in his new bedroom. It wasn't the sturdiest thing to have sex on, so they just held each other, Matt's growing guilt making him sleep restlessly. At least everyone thought he had an excuse for disturbed sleep after what Everon had done. No one asked him anymore how he was doing, though he sometimes still saw concern in their eyes. But it was fading, like he wanted. He didn't enjoy being hovered over, though he appreciated that it meant they cared.

The next several days were a flurry of activities as they made significant progress at Briardale. Furniture was delivered, more was ordered, and the estate started taking shape. They set the archery targets up outside and both Lorian and Taryn began instructing for all four Champions in both the longbow and crossbow. Both trainers thought the swords they had needed improvement, but they resumed training with those as well. Prince Dari offered to return to Andor and bring back a supply of suitable weapons.

Ryan and Eric worked with Lorian on building rolling platforms for the Home Rings, while Rognir chiseled away at the marble stone that had finally arrived. The dwarf had already carved a symbol into each Home Ring—a glowing hand for Anna, a shield for Ryan, a staff for Matt, and a dagger for Eric. Working tirelessly, he was able to complete one a day, starting with Anna's. Matt used a cantrip to identify which keystone had which DNA. Each time the dwarf placed a keystone into the slot he'd reserved for it, Matt cast a spell on it so it would merge with the marble and complete the ring. This was one of the first spells he'd been able to do on Earth, and he noticed that the magic came somewhat easily now. A pulse of light would indicate that the keystone was ready, but the only way to test the Rings would be to be summoned on their next quest and returned home. Even without that confirmation of success, they relaxed.

The first horse, the one Ryan already owned, was soon in the stables, which they began stocking with things for the horses and with their personal arsenal. Ryan's mother was a skilled rider and took the lead on finding more horses for the others. Jack had been looking after Anna's cats, and now relocated them as he cleaned out her condo. They also acquired two trained guard dogs, mostly to alert them to trespassers. Matt had wondered what their reaction to Jolian might be even in human form. The cats clearly loved her, climbing into her lap—but the dogs were intimidated and meek, keeping their distance, as if recognizing a predator who far outclassed them. She had to make overtures of friendliness to get them to relax, and then they seemed to view her as the dominant one whose approval they sought.

Since it took both Matt and Lorian to open a portal to another world, and Matt could vanish at any time, they agreed that Lorian and Prince Dari would return to their respective planets to make various arrangements. They would procure supplies unavailable on Earth, like appropriate weapons or wizarding items. Once a week, someone from either Honyn or Elloria would communicate with Jack at the least and, if necessary, open a portal to Briardale to help. Since Matt could cast the spell to communicate across worlds himself, he would always be able to tell Jack where they had gone, and the others might be able to come and help. But once those arrangements were made, Dari and Lorian returned to Earth, partly out of fascination with life there.

Just when everything seemed to be going well, the FBI paid a visit. They had no search warrant, and Special Agent Mori and her partner Carter professed just to be checking up on their wellbeing. The group agreed to humor them and let them in while restricting them to the main house. Anyone from another planet was discreetly asked to sequester themselves in the stables out of sight. Each had an accent that would prompt questions about their origins, and they belatedly realized they needed some hats to cover Lorian's ears.

The four Champions, Eriana, and Jack entertained them for an hour, mostly dodging questions about their disappearances unless the honest answer might get them left alone. And so they admitted that they didn't vanish on purpose, having no control over it—and could not appear somewhere at will either. The agents accurately figured out that they returned to the same place, so they didn't bother denying it—or that this was one reason they now had the estate and were not planning to leave.

Where his friends saw potential trouble and interference in the conversation, Matt saw opportunity. The agents seemed to believe he and the others were victims of something beyond their control, and were even sympathetic, but he wanted more power over the threat they posed. And he had the means to achieve it. Being in danger on a quest was something they couldn't do much about, though his quickly-growing skill now that he could practice on Earth was helping. But being in danger while at home was unnecessary. With this home established, and hopefully with the Home Rings working, they could have so much less to fear. And now these two agents were right here in their oasis from danger.

Matt repeatedly caught the eye of Special Agent Mori, trying to suggest with a look that he wanted to tell her things alone. He finally excused himself and went to his study downstairs, where he retrieved both Orbs of Dominion from the Bag of Desires and laid them on the counter. Footsteps began to sound on the steps, and he double-checked it was her and not someone else before relaxing. She gazed around at the room, but there was little to see here now except martial arts materials like gym mats. All of the weapons, like swords and bows, had been moved to the indoor riding ring.

"Well, Mr. Sorenson, I got the impression you wanted to talk to me about something."

"You are astute," he replied, stepping into his trap. She followed, her eyes quickly going to the only items on the bookcases, two Orbs of Dominion side-by-side. "They may be my friends, but we don't always agree on things."

"You've been through a lot together—more than you're telling me, I'm sure."

"What you don't know is that I will soon tell you everything so you can best help us, but all in good time. I understand that you are interested in acquiring magic items, so I wanted to give you one without them knowing. I feel that it's dangerous."

He touched the master orb and both orbs turned on. She kept some distance, but continued looking at the slave orb Matt had put closer to her on purpose. That was all he needed. She asked, "What does it do?"

"Obey and serve," he said. "My will be yours."

A look of peace came over Special Agent Mori's face. "My will is yours."

This time, Matt felt no guilt about it. He could control someone threatening him. And this was exactly why he'd acquired the orbs. Feeling excited about what came next, he remarked, "I understand that you have a trove of magic items taken from Erin Jennings' home."

"Yes, they are being examined."

"You will find a way to bring all of them to us here. This is not to be done in secret. You will convince the FBI to let them go because it has been determined that none of them are magical, even though quite a few likely are."

"I do not understand how I will do that."

"I do. You will also get Eriana's Corethian Amulet and return it."

"I understand."

Matt pointed at the slave orb. "I would like you to take this with you to the FBI field office, the one that arranged for the raids on all our properties. Do whatever you have to, but make sure you call a meeting with as many agents and superiors as possible. Make sure that no one can see in and that the door is closed. You will tell me when this is done, leaving me on speakerphone. You will then unveil the slave orb and I will do the rest."

"I understand."

"I knew that you would. Now, would you send for your partner?"

———— • : • ————

Each of the new Champions, except Eric, had been reunited with their parents at the estate. They could finally reveal what was going on, and so it was another burden gone. Some of their parents had still found it difficult to believe—but after witnessing Anna's healing power, a cantrip from Matt, and Jolian briefly morphing into a dragon at night, there were no more doubts. All of this took place at a big dinner on Halloween night with Anna, Matt, Ryan, and their parents, Eric, Daniel, Jack, Eriana and her investigator, Lorian, Rognir, Taryn, Prince Dari, Jolian, and Quincy.

With the house not nearly big enough, they filled the indoor riding ring with tables for twenty and had a pizza party. There was continued amusement about the reactions to foods, drink, and everything else by the "outlanders," as Jack collectively thought of those not from Earth. Most had complained about the air quality, especially the elf Lorian, and Rognir had already commented that the food was making him fat. Some of it didn't agree with them either, and they were increasingly taking to eating salads. They also craved unprocessed meat. This prompted serious discussion of turning the estate into more than a horse farm, with its own garden and livestock devoid of the chemicals people in the United States were used to.

They had gathered at around 6 PM, and as dinner continued, the new Champions told stories of their quests, trying to focus on the lighter moments by silent agreement. No one needed to hear how much danger they were really in so often, but it came up anyway. They needed to warn their parents about Soliander in case he or someone acting on his behalf appeared. It served as a reminder that however much control they had gained over their situation, uncertainty still abounded. All of it prompted their parents' heartfelt thanks to the outlanders who had befriended their children and would continue to support them.

But when the clock hit 7 PM, Eric suddenly got up and turned on the big, wall-mounted TV the previous owners had left installed on one side of the indoor ring.

"I think there's something we need to see," he said, turning the channel to BBC News. "I have a Google alert set up on my phone for Stonehenge and there's supposedly a live camera crew capturing something there, something about fairies."

The television came on and immediately showed a big, shimmering wall of blue and white light across part of the monument, figures emerging from it. The satyrs caught their attention because they were so different from the elves and dwarves that came next. No one watching the TV spoke as the scene unfolded, though Eriana groaned, "No, don't eat it," when the fae presented the humans with treats.

The watchers gasped as people turned into satyrs. And someone screamed when the little girl was dropped to her death, and an elf swung a sword at an officer and cut off his gun-wielding hand. Then the camera began bouncing wildly as the cameraman fled toward the flashing lights of a police car in the distance. The view became chaotic for several moments until it went still, the camera still filming on its side—and showing the cameraman in the foreground, an arrow through his neck. Dwarves came running and chopped him to pieces as some of the parents watching reacted out loud. The camera was close enough to capture a figure in black leather appearing through the portal and announcing himself as the Dragon Lord King of Elfhame.

Eriana rose. "Vianden! I know him. He's a dragon. He was with Morgana."

No one said anything more as they listened to the spell to call forth the Wild Hunt. After this, the scene became calmer, with less to hear. But with the camera angled just enough to show the Heel Stone, they saw what happened next. A man in black leather rose from the grass. Then white lights surrounded a woman near him and lifted her into the sky, before he threw something toward her and she fell to the ground. A sword fight between him and another figure was hard to follow, the camera tilted as it was, but it ended swiftly with him victorious until he collapsed. Then a white glow surrounded him, and he rose to confront those who had left Stonehenge to approach him and the woman. Moments later, Vianden turned into a black dragon and spoke so loudly that the camera picked it up.

"Take them to Elfhame."

The woman began screaming and fighting off those grabbing her, the man in leather throwing several knives that felled them one by one. But others picked up the woman and carried her toward Stonehenge. As this was happening, Eriana walked up to the TV.

"Those clothes," she said. "The movements. Can it be?"

"What?" asked Eric, stepping up beside her, but she just shook her head. It wasn't until the man in black leather ran closer to the camera that she gasped.

"Andier! He's alive!"

A murmur of surprise went through the room. They watched as gunshots rang out and Andier fell as if struck. Then he used an apparent Trinity Ring to heal himself and rise. The woman he was chasing disappeared through the portal to Elfhame, arrows flew at him, and he turned and ran out of view with fae chasing after him. For several minutes, not much else happened. Then a Jeep careened into view, running over a few people before more gunshots rang out and the Jeep disappeared. Moments later, a dwarf with a hammer approached and the camera feed suddenly cut off. Eric muted the TV as it went back to showing a news anchor, who looked horrified.

"I recognize the outfit," he admitted, looking at Eriana. "You're certain?"

She nodded, eyes looking excited but worried. "Yes, it's him. We've found him. No one throws a knife like he does, or moves so efficiently. I must get to him."

"What the hell is happening?" asked Matt's deaf mother, her words intelligible but with that different clarity the deaf often speak with. Her son began doing sign language for her.

"You'll have to go without us," said Eric. "We can't travel yet, not until we know these Home Rings work."

They began making plans but didn't get far. If anyone had lingering doubts about it all, they were soon dispelled. Eric was still standing, but Matt, Anna, and Ryan were sitting in different places at the table when a soft glow began to surround each of them, their alarmed parents leaning back. The Champions' faces registered surprise, then resignation. Anna had time to say she'd be back soon. Eric laid his phone on the table, then nodded farewell. Ryan tossed back the rest of his beer, and Matt turned to Taryn, planting a kiss on her lips. Most of those present looked resigned as they watched the four friends until they no longer could.

They were gone.

———— • •• • ————

Continue the adventure in *The Dragon Slayer* via the QR code:

ABOUT THE AUTHOR

Having written fantasy fiction since his teens, Randy Ellefson is an avid world builder whose work the Writer's of the Future contest has recognized three times. In addition to his popular world building books, he's the founder and lead instructor at World Building University, and hosts a related, popular podcast.

He has a Bachelor of Music in classical guitar but has always been more of a rocker, having released several albums and earned endorsements from music companies. A multi-instrumentalist who builds his own guitars, he's also band leader/manager, guitarist, and primary composer/lyricist for the metal band Black Halo.

A software development manager, he ran a successful consulting company for a decade before deciding to work for a comic book distributor.

Rand lives in Maryland with his son, daughter, and two cats.

Connect with him online

http://www.RandyEllefson.com
http://facebook.com/RandyEllefsonAuthor
https://linktr.ee/randyellefson

Buy books, music, and merch online at my store or others:
https://www.randyellefson.com/mywork

Randy Ellefson Books

Talon Stormbringer

Talon is a sword-wielding adventurer who has been a thief, pirate, knight, king, and more in his far-ranging life.

The Ever Fiend
The Screaming Moragul

www.fiction.randyellefson.com/talonstormbringer

The Dragon Gate Series

Four unqualified Earth friends are magically summoned to complete quests on other worlds, unless they break the cycle – or die trying.

Volume 1: *The Dragon Gate*
Volume 2: *The Light Bringer*
Volume 3: *The Silver-Tongued Rogue*
Volume 4: *The Dragon Slayer*
Volume 5: *The Majestic Magus*

www.fiction.randyellefson.com/dragon-gate-series

Ascension Quest

When Max awakens in a world unknown, he doesn't know how he got there or why he can't leave. And a mysterious

Life Counter that no one else has is steadily descending to zero.

Death Singer

www.fiction.randyellefson.com/ascension-quest-litrpg-series

THE ART OF WORLD BUILDING

This is a multi-volume guide for authors, screenwriters, gamers, and hobbyists to build more immersive, believable worlds fans will love.

Creating Life
Creating Places
Cultures and Beyond
185 Tips on World Building
3000 World Building Prompts
The Complete Art of World Building
The Art of the World Building Workbook: Fantasy Edition
The Art of the World Building Workbook: Sci-Fi Edition
Creating Life: The Podcast Transcripts
Creating Places: The Podcast Transcripts
Cultures and Beyond: The Podcast Transcripts
The Art of World Building Podcast Transcripts Omnibus

Visit www.artofworldbuilding.com for details.

Randy Ellefson Music

Instrumental Guitar

Randy has released three albums of hard rock/metal instrumentals, one classical guitar album, and an all-acoustic album. Visit http://www.music.randyellefson.com for more information, streaming media, videos, and free mp3s.

2004: The Firebard
2007: Some Things Are Better Left Unsaid
2010: Serenade of Strings
2010: The Lost Art
2013: Now Weaponized!
2014: The Firebard (re-release)

Black Halo

Where classic Iron Maiden meets Metallica stands Black Halo, Randy's traditional metal band, where he is guitarist, primary songwriter, and band leader. For more, visit https://blackhalo.randyellefson.com

2024: Utopia